MIND FUCK

Manna Francis

CASPERIAN
BOOKS

MIND FUCK. Copyright © 2007 by Manna Francis. All rights reserved. Printed in the United States of America. No part of this book may be used or reproduced in any manner whatsoever without written permission except in the case of brief quotations embodied in critical articles or reviews. For information, address Casperian Books, PO Box 161026, Sacramento, CA 95816-1026.

www.casperianbooks.com

Cover illustration by Orit "Shin" Heifets
Front cover image by Ceredwyn Ealanta (www.gothbunny.net)

ISBN-10: 1-934081-08-6
ISBN-13: 978-1-934081-08-2

I'd like to thank my husband, for his super-human patience and encouragement; and my editor, without whom the Administration would never have come into existence, for her endless dedication and firm hand with commas.

Chapter One

❖

The interrogation room was brightly lit and relentlessly white, and had a disinfectant smell that Toreth no longer even noticed. The guards had already delivered the prisoner by the time he arrived; the man sat at the small square table, on a plain metal chair screwed securely to the floor.

"Good afternoon." Toreth liked the little irony, although it wasn't often appreciated.

The prisoner looked up from his contemplation of the tabletop. He looked very much as he had at their brief meeting earlier, which was to say sullen, angry, and frightened. Toreth stood, impassive, letting his height and the breadth of his shoulders kick off the process of intimidation. Toreth's investigators had reported that the prisoner had put up a good front during his arrest that morning, but to Toreth's practiced eye he now looked not far from panic. The incidental tour of the Investigation and Interrogation Division's facilities that prisoners enjoyed during processing tended to do that. Like most of the idealist traitors who passed through Toreth's hands, the prisoner had apparently never imagined capture. Idiots, in Toreth's opinion, although it only made them easier to deal with.

This one was an interrogation virgin—never even been arrested before.

It didn't take long before the prisoner looked away again. Toreth brushed a few errant afternoon-coffeetime crumbs from his black uniform and sat down across the table from him. A little way away stood a more substantial chair fitted with restraints, and beside it a gurney surrounded by an impressive array of medical equipment. Shelves held racks of bottles and vials, and the narrow bench below them had an equally precise layout of instruments.

However, for now they both sat at the table, a spurious equality that did nothing to disguise the dynamics of the relationship between them. That was how Toreth preferred to start things out, although he held a minority opinion on that score. He felt that a chance for the prisoner to view the paraphernalia of interrogation neatly laid out was always salutary. Toreth liked to make it clear that a pro-

5

gression to unpleasantness was quite optional at this stage. Many prisoners couldn't bring themselves to make the denials that would send them that short distance across the room to the other chair.

Toreth laid a hand screen on the table between them. "My name is Toreth. Senior Para-investigator Val Toreth, in fact, although I don't particularly care what you call me. I've heard it all before, anyway." He noted a flinch as the prisoner quickly understood the implication. Good. It was always easier to work with someone who possessed an imagination.

"Now, we already have a quantity of information about your crime." Toreth paged through the documents on the screen, for effect rather than because he needed to read them. "You passed on restricted information from the Department of External Security regarding operations to detain wanted resisters attempting to leave Administration territory. We have dates, files, when and how much you were paid. Your partner was most informative, although I'm afraid we will still need to hear everything he told us over again from you."

"Go to hell." Unimaginative, and paper-thin bravado.

"As it is, there is more than enough information here to see you tried and convicted. And, I may add, executed. However, the Administration prefers things to be tidy. All I wish you to do is confirm what we have already learned. If you cooperate, execution will become re-education." Not, Toreth had always thought, much of an improvement. However, it got a reaction, a tilt of the head as the prisoner considered the proposal. "I can give you a guarantee of that in writing. I can have it authorized and in the hands of your Department of Justice representative within the hour. Well?"

The prisoner shook his head, and Toreth knew it was because he didn't trust his own voice.

"Ah, well. A pity." As usual, he meant it. A quick and easy capitulation with no damage to the prisoner always looked good. As Toreth stood up, he made a small bet with himself. "In that case—" He gestured towards the chair with the restraints. And because Toreth was very good at his job, he, as usual, won his bet. The prisoner looked towards the chair, and then towards the door, where the two guards stood mutely watching. Then he crumpled in the chair, the remains of his façade of composure dropping away before Toreth's eyes.

"What—where do you want me to start?"

After the guards took the prisoner away, Toreth paged through the draft of the transcript on his screen and smiled. Even Tillotson would have to call this a success. Everything matched up beautifully. Investigation closed. There was still another prisoner from the case to interrogate, if Tillotson was willing to authorize the time, but Toreth knew she wouldn't have any extra information. One of his team could handle it if necessary.

Checking his watch improved his mood even further; it was only midafternoon. Once he'd told Sara to start processing the transcript for submission to the Justice Department, he could begin the formal case report, and still get to the gym for an hour before he went home. Better yet, now that the case was closed, he'd be able to finish everything off tomorrow morning and leave work at lunchtime to spend a couple of hours at an almost-relevant seminar he'd spotted. Then he could take the rest of the day off without booking the holiday time.

Sweet, sweet success.

He left the interrogation room whistling, cheerfully and persistently half a tone flat, and headed for the lift up to his office, nine floors above.

Chapter Two

❖

The next morning, mist still skulked in shaded hollows and below the trees as Toreth walked to work. Early October, and here and there the leaves were beginning to turn and fall. However, the blue of the sky deepened steadily as the sun climbed, and the day looked set to be beautiful.

Before his secondment to the Mars colony, Toreth hadn't truly appreciated how good his life had been. To begin with, despite the fact that someone had felt the need to create a senior para-investigator post there, Mars base had no crime to speak of, certainly not the political crimes that interested I&I. Six months of investigating petty anti-Administration comments, on a strictly dry base, amid perpetual safety drills and in the company of the dullest people he had ever met, had taught him to appreciate Earth.

When his return shuttle had touched down and the doors opened to let in warm, humid air with a tang of shuttle fuel—rather than sterile, recycled dome air—he had vowed never to complain about anything again. Now that he'd been back for nearly two months, the shine had rubbed off a little, but he still enjoyed the walk in.

The Investigation and Interrogation Division Headquarters occupied part of a massive collection of buildings on the outskirts of New London. The Administration had built the entire complex ten years earlier, during the great reorganization, when they had moved various divisions under the umbrella of the new Department of Internal Security. With modern facilities and pleasantly landscaped areas between the buildings, Int-Sec New London was noted as a plum posting within the European Administration. Vast as the complex looked, the visible portion was only a part of the whole, which extended below ground, beneath and between the white stone buildings. If you could find your way through the disorienting windowless corridors—and if you had the security clearance—it was allegedly possible to reach any part of the complex without venturing above ground.

The most convenient access to I&I on Toreth's route in happened also to be the main entrance, where a large statue of Blindfold Justice kept watch over a pleasant grassy expanse. There was an early-morning busyness to reception as he worked his way over to the employee lifts and paused briefly for the security scan. Then the noise faded as the lift's door closed and it descended smoothly to the detention facility.

Down in detention, the walls were a cool light gray, the hard plastic floor a darker gray. Doors opened and closed by remote control until he reached the vast control room for his habitual morning visit. He could've checked up on his prisoners from his office, but he liked to talk to the security officers on watch. There were always little things that never made it as far as the official logs, and attention to detail frequently paid dividends.

Today there was nothing particularly unusual to hear. Six prisoners, relating to three cases, although none were scheduled for interrogation today. He checked the live cell feed on the monitor. His prisoner from yesterday lay curled up on the narrow bed, clearly awake. The records showed he hadn't slept at all well during the night. Probably regretting the deal he had made.

Experimentally, Toreth thumbed the door control, letting the door open a few centimeters before he closed it again. On the monitor, the prisoner jerked upright and pressed his back against the wall, fighting for composure.

"Are you interrogating again today, Para?" the officer beside him asked. "You don't have a room booked."

"No, just passing through. He's all done. Put him on the midmorning transport back to Justice."

When the lift up from the detention level stopped, Toreth almost stepped out before he registered the lemon yellow walls. Only the third floor above ground level, with no one waiting to get in—someone pressing all the buttons and taking another lift, no doubt. He stabbed impatiently at the control panel until the lift finally resumed its journey. He should have taken the stairs, except that meant dealing with security doors that were even more irritating. When the lift doors opened again, they revealed a pale blue lobby area with wall screens giving directions to the various sections on the fifth-floor level. The new potted plants that Toreth had noticed on Friday were already beginning to droop sadly beneath the artificial light. More plants had been installed in the long corridor over to the General Criminal section. Predictably enough, several of the more attractive ones had gone missing already. No doubt there'd be a memo.

Toreth's admin, Sara, shared a central open-plan area with the admins of the other seniors whose offices opened off it, and for once she was there before him. Seeing him arrive, she waved cheerfully. When he reached her desk, he said, "Morning."

"And a good one." Sara spread her arms. "What do you think?"

Trick question, because she was wearing the standard admin uniform of dark gray, with the I&I logo on the shoulder. He scanned her, letting his professional eye for detail pull out an answer. New hairstyle was a good first guess, but her black, glossy hair—from the same part-Southeast Asian genes that supplied her dark eyes and the golden cast to her skin—was cut in a shoulder-length bob. No change from the last few weeks. That left one other usual thing to try, so he checked her hands. The new ring stood out at once among the collection that adorned her slim hands. The three diamonds were large enough to classify it as an offensive weapon. Third finger of her left hand, too.

"You're engaged again?"

Her face darkened. "I wish you wouldn't say *again* like that."

"Why not? We both know that finger's just a jumping-off point for one of the others. Have I met this new contributor to the pension plan?"

"No, I don't think so. He's ... " Rings sparkling, she sketched a vague suggestion of height. "It was a bit of a surprise, really. I've not known him that long. And the stones are synthetic. But it's a nice one, don't you think?"

"Yeah, lovely." Toreth gave him a month, at the most. "Anything for me?"

"Your lucky morning, too—not a thing."

She was right; in his office, Toreth found no messages, no irate notes, and no compulsory summonses to pointless meetings. Not even anything from his boss, who had an almost psychic ability to ruin his day with a well-targeted memo. It was unusual enough that he checked with Sara. She set to work on the comm, performing her mysterious admin magic. The unofficial administrative assistant network promptly reported Tillotson as unexpectedly called away from the office for the day. After half an hour, he found his good mood evaporating anyway. When Toreth was out in the field, supervising active investigations, he longed for the regular hours and mod cons of the I&I building. Then, when the cases reached the interrogation stage, he missed the excitement and activity of the hunt. However, on balance, he had decided long ago that both phases generated equal amounts of boring paperwork.

Fishing in a drawer, he found a packet of slightly furry sugar-free mints. He sucked one slowly as he flipped through the pages on the screen. They contained the verbatim reports of the interrogation. Toreth sighed around the mint. He'd forgotten how boring checking transcripts could be. Normally he didn't bother double-checking the transcripts Sara authorized for transmission to Justice. It wasn't that he didn't trust Sara to do this one right—quite the reverse—but it was very important that the investigation went well. It had been his first big case since his return to headquarters and he wanted to make sure he'd missed nothing. Still uninspiring stuff, though. Toreth decided he'd do the first half of the record, and then reward himself with an extra biscuit with his coffee.

Half an hour passed before someone knocked on the door and opened it without giving him a chance to reply. It proved to be Chevril—wearing his jacket indoors, Toreth noted. Probably still showing off the senior's badge now on his shoulder.

"Morning, Chev."

"Busy?" Chevril asked.

"Yes." Toreth frowned, and then smoothed the expression away. He wasn't actually averse to the interruption, but he'd left instructions with Sara that he wasn't to be disturbed.

The diminutive senior strode across the office, brandishing a paper copy of the *Journal of the Association of Para-Investigators* like a passport. Chevril tended to stride—it was the only way he could keep up with most people. "I brought this back. Thanks." He dropped the journal on the desk. "I'm afraid I spilled a bit of coffee on it."

All his coffee, by the look of it. "No jobs you fancy?"

"Absolutely damn-all interesting. Fits the rest of my life. How are you?"

"Fine, actually." Toreth grinned. "Case cracked and on the way back to Justice. Still got a backup prisoner if I need any more details later." Maybe overt cheerfulness would encourage Chevril to go away. However, he didn't seem inclined to leave. Instead, Chevril wandered over to the window, and peered into the enclosed courtyard five floors below.

"Palm trees," he said, sounding surprised.

"They put them in on Friday. Didn't you notice all the plants up here, too?"

"Huh. Sprucing the place up for Secretary Turnbull's visit. I bet they take 'em away again the minute she's gone."

"Very probably. If there's a leaf left in the building by then."

"Are they walking already?" Chevril snorted. "Bunch of bloody thieves there are in this place."

There was a brief silence.

"Nothing to do?" Toreth asked. He made a note on the interrogation transcript as a halfhearted suggestion that he himself had plenty to do.

Chevril, typically, ignored the hint. "Not really. I'm still waiting to get a full team assigned. What's the point of finally getting promoted to senior if I'm stuck doing the same crap as the bloody juniors? I bet you didn't have to wait for your team, did you? If you can remember that far back."

Chevril's promotion had happened shortly after Toreth's return from Mars, and the saga of the team assignment had been in progress since. Despite the generous sprinkling of silver in Chevril's dark hair, he was only a month or two older than Toreth—they'd joined the Interrogation Division in the same year and later trained together as paras. The disparity between Toreth's notably early promotion and Chevril's much delayed one was yet another of Chevril's regular complaints, and not one that Toreth felt like going over again today. He looked for a diversion. "So what are you doing?"

"Filling out request forms for an m-f. The prisoner isn't even here yet, so I don't know why I'm bothering."

"Or not bothering, as the case might be."

"Too bloody right." Chevril pulled a hand screen from his back pocket, expanded the screen and laid it flat on Toreth's desk. He paged disconsolately through the half-completed form. "I mean, just look at this. 'Estimated Value of Information Expected.' I don't bloody know, do I? If I knew what information she had, I wouldn't need to interrogate her, would I?"

Toreth sighed. "Look, put down 'high strategic value.' Works for me."

"I've tried that. Mindfuck bounced the last one as insufficiently detailed."

"Well, maybe you should call them Psychoprogramming—it puts them in a better mood. Anyway, don't worry. It's a new quarter now, remember? They're always more relaxed at the start of a budget."

"They'll bounce it anyway. They're just looking for excuses. They're booked solid with fast-track re-education for resisters, or at least that's what Ange claimed when I asked her. Even Tillotson's favorite blond, blue-eyed boy didn't get a place for his star turn, did he?"

Toreth tried to recall the disciplinary penalty for punching a fellow senior para. He didn't know who'd started the rumor that he fucked Tillotson in order to get the best cases, but he'd given up bothering with denials. Like all the best rumors, the truth—that Tillotson was chronically heterosexual—had done nothing to dispel it.

"I was ordered not to apply," Toreth said. "They wanted him on his feet and making sense for the trial. When the m-f screws up, it screws up big time." Toreth unwrapped another mint. "They aren't the answer to everything, you know. They won't be putting Interrogation out of work for a long while yet."

Stoic philosophy clearly wasn't what Chevril was looking for. "How can they expect us to do a decent job if they won't make the resources available?" he demanded.

"M-fs are expensive bits of equipment, especially the new ones." Ostensible reasonableness would be sure to annoy Chevril even further. "And they need trained operators."

"So they should train 'em. Instead of wasting their money on designing yet another bloody interdivision request form with yet another set of bloody boxes to fill in."

"Write that down and put it in the suggestions file," Toreth said, adding a malicious smile.

Chevril rolled his eyes. "Oh, good idea. And then there'd be a machine free tomorrow and I'd be getting *my* mind fucked. No, thanks. I'd rather have the bloody paperwork. Just about." He snapped the screen closed and left, stealing a mint from Toreth's desk on the way.

Toreth picked up the coffee-stained journal and flicked through it, delaying getting back to work. He was one of the few paras who paid the extra subscription for a paper copy of the *JAPI*, although he didn't usually read it. The technical articles weren't up to much, and he wasn't interested in the job adverts. Despite this, the adverts were the reason he subscribed. There were always discontented paras looking for a way out of I&I who didn't fancy laying their extradivisional interest open to management scrutiny by reading the *JAPI* on the system. The paper copy was anonymous, unless you were actually caught with it. As everyone knew that Toreth was there for life, it didn't matter if he had it around.

Every week, as soon as the magazine arrived in his office, it was immediately borrowed and circulated until everyone who wanted to see it had done so. The more recent copies made an unread pile near his desk before they migrated to an unread pile by the window and were finally filed by Sara into the recycling system. So he knew, in a general way, which paras were happy and which were looking for something new. Which ones, like Chevril, were long-term whingers who were no more likely to leave than he was himself, and which had developed a new interest in life outside I&I. He had a word with people when they picked up the journal and another word when they brought it back, keeping his finger on the pulse of the division. Very occasionally, he even found things out before they reached Sara via the admin gossip network. In addition, a selection of paras from various sections owed him a low-grade favor, which was always useful.

He ran his eye down the coffee-stained pages: I&I postings at sections across Europe, other branches of Int-Sec offering openings for retraining, an assortment of corporate positions of various kinds. Chevril went on endlessly about the joys of corporate contracts, although Toreth had never liked the idea. Nothing, in fact, appealed to him more than where he was right now, boring paperwork or not. Unable to delay any longer, he pushed the journal to one side and dutifully returned his attention to his screen. At least he had the afternoon off to look forward to.

Chapter Three

❖

Toreth leaned back in his chair and listened to the lecture with half-closed eyes. From his seat three-quarters of the way back in the spacious auditorium, he couldn't make out much detail of the speaker, a Dr. Keir Warrick, beyond dark hair and a smart dark suit. However, he could see most of the rest of the audience: computer scientists, games manufacturers, stock market speculators, and God knew what others, but certainly including—he had no doubt—people in his line of work. A cross section of the Administration's New London elite: corporate, research, government, and military service representatives. Of course, Warrick was one of the leading authorities on the breaking new techniques of fully immersive computer simulations; SimTech was a small corporation, but it was considered the best in the field.

The technology was causing excitement in parts of Int-Sec—Toreth had heard about the seminar from a colleague with an acquaintance in Psychoprogramming. Something to do with machines that might, among other things, end up putting the personnel in Interrogation out of business altogether. Toreth doubted it. Machines could never replace humans in some fields, not even highly sophisticated machines with full-sensorium, interactive sim programs that could convince even the most skeptical and paranoid prisoner of their reality. They'd still need people to run them—the personal touch, one could call it. Plus, on a more practical level, he couldn't imagine the department coughing up the money for what would clearly be, for some time to come, staggeringly expensive technology.

He had to admit, though, it was interesting. Fascinating, even. He found he was a little sorry when the talk ended and Warrick began fielding questions from the audience about the practical applications of the new sim technology. Good voice, Toreth thought. Overarticulates. Sign of a control freak. He smiled. He enjoyed control freaks—it gave him something to take away.

Currently the man was evading a question from one of the more expensively dressed audience members about the potential applications of sim machines in

Administration leisure centers. The man had rephrased his question twice in the face of Warrick's polite references to confidentiality agreements with corporate partners in the leisure industry. Toreth checked the clock on the wall and wondered if the after-lecture buffet would be as terrible as they usually were.

A new voice attracted Toreth's attention. "Are you aware of the recent review in the *Journal of Re-education Research* which discusses the potential applications of simulation in the field of psychoprogramming?"

Toreth's eyes narrowed. Mentioning a restricted-circulation journal in public wasn't a clever move. He looked around for the speaker. There. A university type, earnest and obviously dangerously idealistic. The man continued, with the delightful addition of the academic's touch of distancing himself from a dangerous opinion. "I have heard it described as potentially the most effective tool of oppression since memory blocking." Toreth upgraded his assessment from "idealism" to "death wish." He had far better things to do than report the man, but even in the sheltered university environment there were doubtless others with both the time and the inclination.

Keir Warrick paused to take a sip of water from the glass on the lectern. "I am afraid that I have no helpful answer to give." He sounded disapproving, although Toreth couldn't tell whether of the question or the questioner. "I am aware of the paper referred to. All I can say is that it is not an area SimTech plans to exploit, but I have no more power over how the technology may be used in the more distant future than I do over the opinions of the questioner's acquaintances."

Toreth could well imagine that Dr. Warrick had been over these arguments a hundred times before and was sick of them. The Administration had the power to compel the licensing of new developments to the appropriate departments—the balancing factor was that the corporates as a block had the political clout to ensure that the Administration provided substantial compensation. In this case, Toreth could think of half a dozen highly useful applications without even trying; the interdepartmental fighting over budgets would be spectacular.

"Do you not consider that there are ethical obligations inherent in the development of new technology?" the idealist asked. Persistent, if not bright.

"Certainly," Warrick said evenly. "That is the reason that the university has provided us with the invaluable guidance of their ethics committee." That drew a scattered laugh from the academics present. "However, obligations cannot change commercial realities, as I'm sure you already know. And now," he moved his attention from the man's face, effectively silencing him, "I'm afraid I must bring the questions to a close. Thank you all for your attention today."

Appreciative applause followed the lecturer off the stage.

The food was unexpectedly good—excellent, in fact—suggesting it had been provided by SimTech, aiming to impress its guests. Toreth had just completed a sweep of the buffet table when a group beside him walked off and he caught sight of Dr. Warrick, standing only a few meters away and holding a glass of something colorless with ice in it, but no plate of food. Attendees ebbed and flowed around them, but for the moment the corporate had no one monopolizing his attention.

Toreth hadn't had any particular plans to approach the man, but curiosity drew him over. "Excellent lecture, Doctor," Toreth said.

The man turned his head. Impassive dark eyes looked at him out of a face dominated by high cheekbones, too much nose, and the most beautiful mouth Toreth had ever seen on a man. Warrick smiled just a little. "Thank you. And you are?"

Toreth hadn't worn the official nametag supplied, so he felt free to lie; the I&I name could be a handicap in casual conversation. "Marcus Toth. Pleased to meet you."

"You have an interest in computer sim technology, then. What business are you in?"

"Not business, Doctor. Government." Toreth gave the man a smile of his own.

"Ah. Are you hoping to license from us, Mr. Toth? If you are, I'm afraid you'll have to make an official approach to SimTech. Or are you simply a civil servant out on a career development activity during his lunch hour?"

"I'm neither. Just interested in the topic, that's all."

"People are generally interested for a reason."

"Of course. It has a bearing on what I do for a living. I fuck minds," Toreth said pleasantly.

"I see." Warrick took a sip of his drink, his expression calculating. "Neurosurgeon? No," he answered himself. "You didn't introduce yourself as Dr. Toth. Socioanalyst, perhaps, if you were more..." He thought for a moment, his fascinating smile flickering and dying again. "Arrogant," he said finally.

Toreth's smile grew. Lack of arrogance wasn't something he'd been accused of before.

Warrick looked Toreth up and down, obviously appraising him with care. "Para-investigator, maybe," Warrick said.

Toreth laughed, delighted. "Not even close. I study brain biochemistry, at the Pharmacology Division of the Department of Medicine. I saw the announcement of your lecture and decided to attend." Toreth leaned closer, glad he'd put in a little research before he came to the seminar. "I read your paper on preliminary computer sim in *Neuromanipulation* some years ago. Groundbreaking work, Doctor."

Warrick tilted his head a fraction, considering. "That journal was not circulated to the general public."

"No," said Toreth, giving him a just-enough-teeth smile. "It wasn't."

"I see. You fuck minds," Warrick said evenly. He put his glass down on the buffet.

Seeing the man with his eyes cast down, his hand stretched out to place the glass on the table, dark hair showing on his forearm where the cuff rode up, the impulse that had led Toreth to initiate the conversation crystallized into something sharper.

"Dr. Warrick?"

Toreth recognized the man who had introduced Warrick in the lecture—a dark-skinned man with a deeply lined face and a dated suit which screamed academic, in dismal contrast to Warrick's corporate smartness. As the two of them talked, Toreth took a step away and fitted his comm in his ear. "Sara," he said.

She answered with her usual speed. "Yes, Toreth?"

"Find me a room for tonight. Somewhere Marcus Toth would take a corporate." Toreth spoke under his breath—the comm's throat microphone was sensitive enough to pick up subvocalized speech from the movement of muscles without any sound being generated. With Toreth turned away from him, even if Warrick looked over he'd have no idea of the conversation happening a couple of meters away.

"How about the Renaissance Center?" Sara asked.

"Yeah, that's good."

The hotel was one of his favorite fuck venues—somewhere expensive enough to make a suitable impression on a minor corporate type, but not so expensive that Accounts would reject the expenses claim out of hand. The tone of the place was indicated by the real live receptionist he could faintly hear talking to Sara. "They have rooms available," Sara relayed, with the ease of a woman used to handling multiple comm conversations. "And they're discounting, so I can squeeze one of their mid-price rooms through expenses. Shall I book it?"

"I'll tell you in a minute."

"You will excuse me, I'm sure," Warrick was saying to the academic as Toreth looked back. The man nodded and withdrew into the crowd.

As Warrick started to turn away, Toreth stepped closer and gripped his arm. Through the sleeve of the man's expensive suit, Toreth felt the muscles tense underneath his fingers, and he saw the flicker of surprise in his eyes. Toreth changed his smile to something more appropriately suggestive. "One moment, please." Releasing the doctor's arm, he produced a matte white card from his pocket, wrote the hotel name on it, and held it out. "I'd be interested in continuing our conversation later."

Warrick's dark eyes didn't leave Toreth's nor did his face change as he took the card between the first and second fingers of his right hand. A couple of seconds' hesitation, and the card went into his pocket. Then a small nod and Warrick moved off into the milling crowd behind them.

"Target acquired," Toreth said, lips barely moving.

Sara laughed. "Room 212, west wing. Pick up the card at the desk as usual."

Toreth smiled, still watching Warrick's retreating back. "You're a star."

Toreth had planned a lazy afternoon. However, outside the university building, he summoned a taxi and in half an hour was back at his desk at I&I. He switched on his computer screen, ran the search on the Data Division security files, and glanced at the summary page. Thirty-three years old. Parents Leo Warrick (deceased) and Kailynna Avens. One younger sister and an older half brother, Dillian and Tarin—clearly one or other of his parents, presumably his mother, had had a taste for unusual names. An Oxford graduate, who had gone from his first job with the Data Division, to the Department of Medicine's Human Sciences Research Center, and from there to found SimTech. He'd divorced from his wife Melissa seven years ago, with no officially registered relationship since.

Toreth called through to Sara for a coffee, and then sat back to read Keir Warrick's security file.

Turning the card over in his hand, Warrick stared at the crisply written numerals on the back. It was indeed the number of the Renaissance Center hotel; a quick call placed earlier in the afternoon had confirmed that a guest by the name of Marcus Toth was registered there. Warrick leaned back and rubbed his eyes. It was late; he'd had a long day, and he was tired. He had much better things to think about than strangers, however attractive. But his mind would not leave it alone. He knew the man had lied to him, though exactly what about he was not certain. Yet, his mind added. One corner of his mouth lifted briefly at the implication.

Warrick felt sure that Toth was attracted to him—that smooth line about fucking minds was a challenge and the card an obvious come-on. He didn't put much faith in instinct, but in this case every warning bell had been set ringing after only a couple of minutes of conversation. The man might as well have worn a screen from neck to ankles flashing *Danger!* Whatever he was, he wasn't a researcher at the Department of Medicine. Warrick smiled at the idea. If more researchers looked like that, or more particularly moved like that, the university wouldn't have so much trouble recruiting—

Cutting that line of thought dead, he turned his attention to his computer screen and accessed the Administration's civilian files with practiced ease. Illegal, of course, but he'd done it often enough to feel safe. He entered "Marcus Toth," along with a guess for his age, and waited.

The computer threw up a complete background check for the man. Warrick scanned through it. Physical description, date and place of birth, parents' names and birth dates, schools attended, degrees earned, employment history, credit report—all the expected information kept on every citizen by the Administration. He noted that Toth was thirty-one years old, had a good though not outstanding academic record, a solid work history, and no current credit violations.

Bland, Warrick thought. Much too ordinary. So probably his previous guess had been right. If he had a ready-to-access false identity at his disposal, Toth was indeed likely to be a para-investigator, or some other Int-Sec denizen. The bastard had laughed when Warrick guessed his real occupation. He'd been *pleased.* A game. Well, he wasn't the only one who could play games...

Warrick leaned back in the chair and tried for precisely one minute to persuade himself to let it go. It had been a five-minute encounter with an ethically challenged Administration minion who had nothing better to do with his afternoon than sniff out new ways of hurting people. And hand out his hotel number to strangers. Absently, he rubbed the place on his arm where Toth had held him. There was no point in doing anything about it. This was a dangerous kind of game to get involved in, particularly right now, when he had so much else to worry about.

I want to see him again.

He thought that thought exactly once, then put it firmly out of his mind. And then he picked the card up again and contacted the number.

Chapter Four

When Toreth checked for messages at hotel reception in the morning, he wasn't surprised to find one from Warrick. The content threw him slightly. "Come and experience the future of mind fucking for yourself." Then the address of a building at the university, and a time—after lunch. Interesting approach. Toreth caught sight of the receptionist blushing, and imagined the cool voice dictating the message down the comm. Probably spelled out "fucking" to her, just to make sure it didn't get lost in the transcribing.

Toreth considered whether to go in to work. He had only two cases left now, both marked "interrogation pending." What that meant in practice was that the prisoners involved occupied valuable cell space while he waited for their Justice reps to pull their fingers out and process the damage waivers. If he went in to I&I, he'd have nothing to do but chase the waivers up through a maze of people who didn't give a damn. Sara could do that without him. This morning promised too much pleasurable anticipation to waste in a futile attempt to speed up the grinding wheels of the Department of Justice.

He called Sara to tell her he would be out for the next day or two, but she should call him in if a paperwork miracle occurred or any of the prisoners decided to talk anyway. The latter happened considerably more often than the former; the para-investigators weren't the only ones who suffered under the pressure of bureaucratic delays.

❖ ❖ ❖

Toreth spent the morning in the gym. Then he had a light lunch and reached the campus in plenty of time. The SimTech offices and laboratories occupied most of the Artificial Environments Research Center, a brand-new building set a little apart from the Computing Sciences Department. Toreth looked at the clean, elegant design and the abstract sculptures in the granite-paved area outside, and read corporate money and Administration interest. Plenty of both, if he were any judge.

The glass-fronted atrium proved to be as expensively decorated inside as he'd expected from the exterior. He sat in a chair comfortably upholstered in the SimTech gray and blue, while the receptionist called through to Warrick and authorized a security badge. With the potential of the sim technology outlined at the talk, the affluence was hardly surprising. I&I would be taking its place in a very long queue and having a contact here certainly wouldn't hurt. Or at least, if Tillotson queried the expenses, that would make an adequate excuse for spending division money running down a reluctant one-night stand. And the man had been reluctant... but not entirely so. Toreth smiled.

"Mr. Toth? Excuse me, Mr. Toth." The receptionist looked annoyed at having to repeat herself.

"I'm so sorry." Reflexively, he melted her irritation with a smile. "Miles away."

"Dr. Warrick is waiting for you. Security will show you up to the lab."

Security proved to be large, professional, and uncommunicative. The two of them rode in the lift up to the fifth floor in silence. When the doors opened, Warrick stood waiting. "Nice to see you, Toth." He shook hands, dismissed the guard with a peremptory wave, and escorted Toreth along the corridor.

The tour of the labs wasn't the perfunctory formality Toreth had thought it might be, and also proved rather enjoyable. One-to-one, Warrick was an even more engaging speaker than he had been at the lecture, adept at spotting which parts of the tour his guest found interesting and which to gloss over. It was purely business, though—either Toreth had completely misjudged his target, or the man was too deeply in love with the sim to mix work and pleasure. He suspected the latter.

Finally Warrick showed him through a heavy door, with card-controlled access and an iris scanner, into a room containing the sim machines. The room held four chairs, or, more accurately, padded couches. There were indentations for body and limbs, presumably to position them appropriately for the sensors and nerve stimulators within. The rest of the room looked like a stereotypical laboratory, with yards of tangled cables and slot-in components lying on the benches. "I'm afraid I have something to do elsewhere," Warrick said. "It won't take long, and there are a few things for you to get through first here. I hope you won't find it too tedious." Then, with a smile, he left Toreth in the hands of a technician.

The preparation took much longer than he expected. The technician explained what he was doing as they went along—a body scan to create an accurate physical representation for the sim, neurological baseline measurements, and other personal calibrations. Toreth nodded, made interested noises at intervals, and otherwise didn't pay much attention.

Eventually Warrick reappeared. "All done?" he asked the technician, who nodded and then left the room. "Excellent. Take a chair, please."

Toreth picked one at random and sat down.

"Settle your arms in. Get them comfortable."

Toreth did so, and Warrick pulled padded restraints from the sides of the arm-rests and began to strap his arms down. He didn't pull them anywhere near as tight as Toreth would have done, but then he was dealing with a volunteer, something outside Toreth's expertise. "Why does it need the restraints?" Toreth asked.

"I thought I explained all that at the seminar."

"Explain it again."

"The sim is a kind of dream, to put it very crudely. It feeds sensation in through normal sensory channels via the peripheral nervous system, and also by direct stimulation of the CNS, at the same time masking real-world inputs. Then, under the guidance of the computer, the brain interprets those signals as if they were real." Warrick moved down and began tightening straps across Toreth's legs. "The system should induce sleep paralysis for the duration of the sim, but that part, I'm afraid, still requires fine tuning. Sometimes the body mirrors the movements in the sim and it's possible to cause damage to oneself."

"Or to the very expensive machine?"

Warrick smiled. "Quite."

"Why not just use a muscle relaxant?"

Warrick paused, both hands resting lightly on Toreth's thigh. This time the smile was an odd half curve of the lips, which didn't bring any warmth to his eyes. "System flexibility. We don't have the luxury of assuming potential users will be drugged." He stood and walked around behind Toreth. "Get your head comfortable."

Leaning back into the padded headrest, Toreth moved his neck until he could relax. "All right."

Warrick fitted a restraining strap across his forehead. "You aren't at all claustrophobic, are you?" he inquired, and before he even finished the question he lowered the visor.

Toreth wasn't claustrophobic, but for a few seconds he seriously considered it as an option. The visor was totally opaque, with heavy padding over his ears. His eyelashes barely brushed against some kind of components right in front of his eyes. The mask stretched down over his entire face, curving around to rest against his throat; he swallowed, feeling the padded edge against his larynx. There was a long moment of silence, then a humming in his ears as sounds returned.

"Say 'yes' if you can hear me," Warrick instructed.

The sound quality was so good Toreth could hardly believe it was coming over speakers. Then he realized it wasn't—it had to be direct nerve induction. "Yes, I hear you," he said. He also heard a door open and close, and then footsteps as someone else entered the room.

"Good," Warrick said. "Now, you're about ready so I'll get myself set up. Once we're in the sim you don't need to talk—just subvocalize as if you were using any other throat microphone. If you speak out loud, you'll get a slightly strange echo effect in the sim. I'm sure you'll get the hang of it." Warrick's voice had grown softer, and then came back loudly again. The person Toreth had heard enter must have been strapping Warrick into one of the other chairs.

"While we're waiting," Warrick said, "I'd like you to choose a word and say it out loud. Some people don't react well to the sim. If you start to feel dizzy, or sick, or if you want out for any reason at all, say the word and the computer will disconnect you automatically and immediately. I suggest you make it something you won't say accidentally."

"Chevril," Toreth said clearly.

"That was fine. If you do disconnect, you'll find it's possible to slip out of the straps without waiting for the technician to come back. Now, we'll be able to do about half an hour. Longer is perfectly safe, but a first time can have some disorienting side effects, so it's best to stick to thirty minutes or so. Are you ready?"

"Yes."

There was a long pause.

"You have to open your eyes," Warrick said, a touch impatiently.

Toreth did so. Then he blinked and a few seconds later realized his mouth was hanging open. Warrick looked thoroughly delighted by his reaction. The other man stood a few feet away from him, and Toreth simply couldn't believe he wasn't real. That everything around them wasn't real. He'd seen the pictures at Warrick's lecture but dismissed them at the time as creative exaggeration.

Toreth was sitting in a low chair, in much the same attitude as the sim couch he had been in only moments before. Tentatively, he rose to his feet, the movement so natural that he felt convinced there had to be a trick involved. This couldn't be the sim. He looked around the small room: white walls and floor, no carpet, a few chairs scattered around a square table, a desk underneath a window. Through the window he could see the university campus, autumn sun shining. He'd expected something slightly disconnected, something obviously computer generated, but this was nothing like that. Wonderingly, he reached out and touched the back of a chair. Cool metal felt slick under his fingertips. "Fucking *hell*," he said.

Warrick grinned. "Not bad, is it? This is a simple test room—a copy of a real room on this floor, in fact." He opened the door, revealing a familiar corridor. "If you went out there, you could walk back to the sim suite. But you've seen that already."

He walked over to a console set into the desktop and pressed a few buttons. The scene around them blurred and then sharpened into a larger room, something like an old-fashioned private club room, with dark red walls and large comfortable-looking armchairs. Shelves of leather-bound books filled one wall, and there were carpets Toreth could scuff with his shoe, tables with glowing reading lamps, and an old library smell. Warrick stood by the controls, now set into a panel on the wall.

Still reeling from the impossible reality of the sim, Toreth tried to think of something to say which sounded even vaguely intelligent. "Is that always there?" he asked, pointing at the control panel.

"In a way, yes. But it doesn't have to be visible if it spoils the look of the thing." Warrick waved his hand over the panel and it faded away into the red wallpaper. He snapped his fingers and it returned.

Spotting a mirror on the wall, Toreth went over. Half expecting some strange effect, he saw only himself, imperfectly reflected in the antique mottled glass: short blond hair waved back from his forehead, well-defined cheekbones, blue eyes he'd always thought of as one of his best features—currently appearing rather wide—narrowish chin, and lips he'd prefer to be a little fuller. The usual slight shock of realizing that despite studious use of moisturizer, he was thirty-two, not nineteen.

He frowned at the reflection, trying to look a little less overawed by the sim.

Warrick appeared behind him in the mirror.

"It's just like me," Toreth said, then thought how stupid it sounded.

Warrick, however, nodded seriously. "Indeed it is. I had them take a detailed scan. Of course, it's possible to look like anyone in the sim. And be mistaken for them, if one is a good enough mimic." His voice dipped, darkening. "I spend a good deal of time in other people's bodies." Then, as Toreth looked around, he smiled. "Please, take a seat."

Toreth sat down carefully, feeling the springs give slightly beneath his weight, and ran his hands over the fabric of the arms. "I can't believe it," he said, almost involuntarily.

Judging by the widening smile, his reaction was clearly everything Warrick could have wished. Obviously showing off, Warrick clapped his hands, and a tray holding two glasses of something clear and fizzy appeared in the air beside him. He took the tray and set it down on a table. "Here, have a drink." He proffered a glass.

Toreth took it, pausing to brush a finger down the side. Beaded condensation ran at his touch and he watched a drip splash onto his leg. Except, of course, it didn't. The sim had fed the tiny impact and small, spreading chill directly into the nerves. He touched the spot, acutely aware of the separate sensations making up the simple gesture.

"Go on," Warrick said.

When Toreth took a sip, he discovered it was gin and tonic—the flavor was wonderfully real. He felt the cold liquid in his mouth and all the way down his throat. "That's amazing." Toreth was beginning to get annoyed with himself for sounding so overwhelmed, but it *was* pretty fantastic. He took another mouthful, licking the drops from his lips, marveling at the fizz on his tongue. Worth a trip here, even if the demo was all he got out of it, but judging by the meditative way

24

Warrick was watching him drink, it wouldn't be.

Warrick took a taste from his own glass. "Won't get you drunk, either, which is good or bad depending on how you look at it. I want to put in a controlled ethanol release eventually, but unfortunately all the pharmaceutical add-ons are still in testing. Stand up."

"Why?"

"Because I'm going to shift the scene and it makes some people queasy if they start out seated and end up standing. It's an inner ear problem." Toreth stood and waited as Warrick returned to the controls. "Now, this one we're very proud of. Not my personal work, but . . . "

The glasses vanished from their hands as the walls dissolved away completely to reveal a vast expanse of water meadow. They stood at the foot of a long, gentle slope leading up to a distant tree-topped ridge, dark against the vivid blue sky that arched over them. Elsewhere, the flat meadow stretched away until it finally shimmered into a summer heat haze.

"Jesus fucking Christ," Toreth said, giving up any attempt at intelligent comment.

Warrick laughed. "Beautiful, isn't it?"

"Is there anything you *can't* do?"

"Not a great deal, although there is plenty we haven't done yet. This is one of our more ambitious rooms. Come on." They started to stroll through the meadow, following a faint path. "We have relatively few outdoor scenes so far. This, a beach I'm afraid I won't have time to show you, a few places around the city—mostly on the campus because it's easy to take the measurements to create them. There is an experimental live shadowing program which covers a small area outside the AERC—what you see there should be exactly what happens in the real world. Then there is a good deal of the inside of the AERC; we're working on techniques for generating basic suites quickly from plans and photographs. And we have a number of more characterful indoor rooms, to keep the sponsors happy."

Listening with half an ear to Warrick's dark, rich voice, Toreth took a deep breath, savoring the air. It was warm and heavy with the scent of sun-drenched flowers. Bees hummed lazily past them and a soft lapping of water sounded from the riverbank a few yards away. The illusion was perfect, and he said so.

"Not quite. This room reaches the limits of the hardware; it exists primarily to test techniques for pushing the boundaries without impairing the user experience." Warrick pointed up the slope. "Notice how the rippling of the grass blurs with distance? Over there, as it were, we're modeling sections of grass, not individual blades. Also, the trees at the top ought to move more irregularly. And the clouds just drift; they don't break up and reform. Tricks like that allow us to dedicate more processing power to making the physical interaction point look and feel real." Warrick knelt down and stroked a clump of sedge, as if it were a particularly beloved pet. "See? Alive and a little damp; authentic dampness is really quite difficult."

Toreth knelt beside him and buried his hands in a thick, soft tangle of grass and flowers. Petals crumpled in his fist, then slowly uncreased themselves after he let go. Telling himself that they were purely an artifact of clever electronics made them feel not one whit less actual. He imagined taking prisoners into something this real. Everything that happened to them could be an illusion and they would never know. There was nothing he wouldn't be able to do to them, over and over again.

When he tuned in again, Warrick was still involved in his technical explanation. "And beyond that, the interactive tactile simulation is highly accurate. That's even more processor intensive, since it requires the computer to translate actions between objects it doesn't control. Let me show you." Warrick reached over and ran his virtual hand lightly down Toreth's back. "Didn't that feel real?"

Toreth nodded. "And what about pain?" he asked.

Warrick held his gaze for a moment, then stood up and turned back to the control panel, here hanging disconcertingly in midair. "Not in this program."

"But it can be done?"

"Yes, of course. Don't worry, you can report back that it would all be extremely useful for your purposes, if they could afford it."

"My purposes?"

"Interrogation." Flat voice, eyes intent on the console.

"I'm a—"

"Para-investigator. That's what you told me."

"No, I didn't."

"Not quite in so many words, no. But you told me you rape minds."

"I said, 'I fuck minds,' I think you'll find."

Warrick shrugged. "It's all in the inflection, really."

"So what do you think about my inflection?"

The strange half smile again, this time in flattering profile. "I think you probably can't tell the difference any more."

He knew before he invited me here, Toreth thought. He's known all along and he's disgusted by the idea of what I do, but he's still interested. The realization brought a sharp stab of excitement. He loved to see people wanting to do things they thought they shouldn't. He was about to speak when the meadow began to blur around him.

"I think you might like this next one," Warrick said. "It's a special favorite of mine."

The change from kneeling to standing without conscious movement did make him dizzy for a moment, but it passed before he felt any need to use the escape word. Toreth looked around the new room, noting how his vision adjusted instantly

26

from the dazzling meadow to the now dim light. It was a historical curiosity, a bed-room from centuries back, with dark wood-paneled walls and heavy wooden fur-niture. Uneven floorboards creaked a little under foot when he shifted his weight. Dominating the room was a vast four-poster bed, with tied-back curtains matching the rugs and tapestries. It was probably the largest bed Toreth had ever seen in his life.

Very subtle.

He examined the details of the room. Smoke-darkened pictures hung on the walls between the tapestries. On one wall, mullioned windows leaded with small, thick diamonds of glass showed only blackness beyond—nighttime, or perhaps simply nothingness, and he wondered briefly what the edge of the sim world would be like.

An ornate golden clock over the fireplace struck Toreth as a little anachronis-tic, given the rest of the décor. The low, crackling fire filled the air with the scent of wood smoke. There was another odd, almost sweet tang in the air, which prob-ably came from the candles burning in various metal holders. Candelabras, he re-called from somewhere. He wondered if the smell was authentic, and if so, how the hell he smelled it, since to the best of his knowledge he'd never experienced any-thing like it. He asked Warrick.

"Ah, you noticed? Observant of you. Yes, I can't guarantee the smell is pre-cisely as you would personally perceive beeswax candles. But it's averaged from a number of real-life perceptions. We hope to improve the technique, but for the moment the system feeds it directly into your brain. We have to do that for all the more exotic experiences."

There was a definite edge to that last comment, which Toreth chose to ignore for the moment. "So the sim affects brain function directly, not just through sensory input?"

"Didn't I say so in the lecture? Perhaps I was a little overtechnical. It's so hard to judge how to pitch an open talk." The control panel still hung in midspace. Warrick returned to it and started a more complicated piece of programming. "The brain can be controlled extensively, and quite safely. If you give me a moment, I'll show you. There. Lift your hand."

Toreth struggled to do so and found he couldn't even move his fingers, never mind raise his arm. The rest of his body was equally immobile. All he could do was breathe, blink, and speak. "What the hell?"

"That's a simple disconnect between input and output. Rather coarse, although the control can be finer."

Suddenly Toreth could move his head again, although his body below the neck remained frozen.

"The senses are open to fine control, too, of course."

More work on the controls, and the left hemisphere of Toreth's vision simply blanked out. A few seconds later his remaining vision switched into monochrome, inverted, and then the world returned to normal. If Warrick thought he was going to scare him into using the code word to get out of the sim, he was sadly mistaken. "Very impressive," Toreth said levelly.

"Why, thank you." Warrick left the controls, which slowly faded away, and went to lean against the post at the foot of the bed. Toreth had to look around to follow him, because he was still rooted to the spot. Warrick had apparently decided to forget this, and Toreth was damned if he'd remind him. "In fact," Warrick continued, "a lot of the truly impressive work is done by the brain. Integrating the signals, smoothing out the imperfections. It's a remarkably flexible organ. And it works both ways. With practice it's possible to train the brain to maximally exploit the sim environment."

"Yeah?"

"Very much so. For example—" As far as he could see, the man didn't move a centimeter. But suddenly Toreth felt a hand trace a path down his chest from his collarbone to his navel, the smooth palm brushing distinctly against naked skin. He looked down sharply, but he was still fully clothed.

"How the hell did you do that?"

"I imagined doing it." The hand returned and retraced the same path, more slowly. "The convention of moving the physical representation within the sim is purely that—a convention. With practice, intent alone is sufficient. Practice, and a little creative programming."

Warrick's voice never wavered from his lecturing tones. A second hand now joined the first, stroking gently up the backs of Toreth's thighs. The experience was utterly real and bizarre beyond belief. The hands kept moving and once or twice he caught Warrick's own hands twitching in unison with their invisible representatives. Warrick's eyes were hot and intent, watching his face for every reaction. Toreth felt himself starting to shake, even though the tremors didn't affect his paralyzed body. He looked away, trying to gain control of himself. This wasn't at all how things were supposed to happen. A third hand briefly cupped his face, turning his head back. Warrick was squinting slightly with concentration, and then the extra hand vanished.

"Damn. I can never keep that going for long. An internal visualization problem, I suspect." Warrick was overarticulating beautifully. "More hands would be so useful, don't you think?"

Both remaining hands were now concentrating their attentions on his thighs and groin, making it very difficult to shape any kind of answer at all. "I think—" What felt distinctly like a tongue ran teasingly down the joint between leg and body. He tried for humor. "I think you'll need them to fight off interested corporates. Not to mention the Administration."

"Mm." Warrick's face darkened and the sensations vanished. Quite without meaning to Toreth made a small sound of protest and Warrick's scowl slid back into the half smile, which was more a mask than an expression of emotion. "Sorry. Lost the thread. Where was I?"

Now he could feel illusory lips passing right through his equally illusory clothes. The mouth ghosted across his chest, drawing an involuntary gasp as a tongue lapped gently at his nipple. How the hell was it possible for the man to imagine doing something like that vividly enough to make it so real? Lots of practice, he'd said, and wasn't that a nice job?

Hazily, he tried to send a thought in return, something to even up the score in the game between them, but if he could have managed it under normal conditions, he was defeated now. The mouth was everywhere, biting, kissing, and licking all over, everywhere except where he really wanted it. He had the feeling—no, he was certain—that Warrick wanted him to ask for it. His mind flashed back to the lecture and he thought: Control freak. Oh, yes. However, Toreth wasn't going to give him the satisfaction. He gritted his teeth against the need and looked down at himself, trying to make it feel less real by showing his mind that there was no one there, that he was completely clothed, that there was nothing—

A hand he couldn't see slid around his body and took hold of the base of his cock, which in some weird reality was erect and accessible. The endless, tormenting touch of the lips had stopped. He swallowed, waiting for what had to happen next, unable to hold back the moan when the mouth closed around him. The mouth and hand began a slow rhythm. He didn't look at Warrick, he didn't try to struggle against the paralysis, he didn't—couldn't—do anything except stand where he was and accept what was being done to him. Fuck it, Toreth decided. Hadn't he come to the lab expecting sex of some kind? Enjoy what was happening.

Time passed in slowly building ecstasy. He found himself panting, reaching for the orgasm, wanting it and yet not wanting it, and . . . then the mouth was gone. No feeling of withdrawal—the exquisite sensations simply vanished.

"Ah, no, don't stop, don't—" He bit off the words, drew in a ragged breath. Warrick's mocking smile was still locked in place. For the past few minutes, Toreth had managed to forget that he was immobilized. Now he felt helpless again—helpless and humiliated because he'd lost even the pretense of self-control. Then Warrick's mouth twitched slightly and the tongue came back, licking, teasing. He closed his eyes, gave up resisting. "Yes. Yes, please . . ."

That was enough, because the mouth and hand returned in earnest, working quickly now. Invisible fingers gripped one hip tightly, which was pointless since he couldn't move, couldn't twist away, couldn't thrust, couldn't do anything except gasp out further humiliating pleas. After a minute, he opened his eyes again and saw Warrick still unmoving, still watching him with burning intensity. Fucking control freak indeed, but Toreth was far past caring. Their eyes locked and Warrick swallowed once, twice, and Toreth came—really came—into the virtual mouth.

29

When his vision cleared, Warrick still hadn't shifted from his station against the bedpost. Toreth didn't want to ask, but he had to because Warrick looked like he was willing to wait until the end of the world. "Would you, ah, please..."

Warrick snapped his fingers and the console appeared again, this time molding itself neatly onto the table beside the bed. He sat down on the edge of the mattress and made a few passes over the controls. Without warning, Toreth's body was back under his control—mostly. He made it to the bed before his legs gave out. He flopped down flat on his back and distantly admired the realistic drape of the curtains above as they swayed and settled back. Endorphin high, he thought, annoyed by how good it felt.

"You've got no fucking room to talk," he said after a moment.

"About what?"

"Not being able to tell the difference between rape and fucking."

Warrick was still busy over the console. "Oh, no, *I* know the difference. That was fucking. If you thought otherwise you should have stopped it."

"Stopped it? I couldn't move!"

Warrick looked around, the smile reaching his eyes this time. "All you had to do was say the word." Toreth realized what he meant even before Warrick elaborated. "The code word."

The code word. He'd completely forgotten—and yet he hadn't forgotten, not really, not for a minute. Game, set, and fucking match. He lay there, unable, for one of the few times in his life, to think of anything to say. Then the clock on the mantelpiece began a soft, complicated chime.

"Ah." Warrick stood. "Time's up."

Warrick escorted him out of the building; apparently security was required only for the way in. The first part of the walk passed in silence, but as the lift descended, Toreth began to feel a slow burn of anger building. No one did that to him. No one.

"Thank you for the demo," Toreth said as the lift door opened onto reception. He kept his voice light, casual.

"My pleasure. Are you quite sure you wouldn't like to get a drink in the cafeteria? The coffee is tolerable."

Toreth shook his head. "I need to get back to the hotel...and change, among other things."

Warrick laughed. "Of course. Well, it was a most enjoyable afternoon and a welcome distraction from the mounds of paperwork in my office." They reached the outer door. "Goodbye."

That had a very final ring to it. Toreth made it a rule to never do the chasing—

or at least for it never to look as if he were—but he couldn't let this go. He'd comprehensively lost this round, and they both knew it. "I think I got rather more out of the experience than you did."

"Not at all," Warrick demurred. "It provided some useful data."

Data? He was not fucking data. "Let me buy you dinner. The Renaissance Center, eight o'clock this evening?" Toreth saw him starting to form the refusal. "I'd like to pay you back," he added, and the edge in his voice wasn't entirely deliberate.

Warrick stopped, his hand on the door, his lips still parted on the beginning of a no. Got him, Toreth thought. Can't resist an open challenge.

The sardonic mouth curved into a smile. "Why not?"

Chapter Five

❖

Toreth took a long, hot shower, and then sat in his room wearing just a towel, bumping up his next expenses claim with the contents of the minibar. He poured a drink, noting absently how very convincing the gin in the sim had been. He could still be inside, and he would have no way of knowing. After a few minutes of trying to come up with a definitive test for reality, he decided to abandon incipient paranoia and work on more immediate problems.

Dinner tonight—all arranged and settled and already he was tempted to send a message canceling the whole thing. Dinner had seemed like such a good idea at the time, when Warrick walked him to the door of the AERC, relishing his victory with every step and bland word. In fact, it had been tempting simply to punch him in the face right there and walk off. However, that would have been cheap and easy. Worse, it would only have increased the score in Warrick's favor. Revenge required more than that, and dinner was the first step to getting it. He would see Warrick again, and he would come up with some way of demonstrating to him exactly how experienced professionals played mind games. Something to wipe that smile off his face and teach the bastard a lesson he'd take to his grave. The only problem was that his experienced professional mind was drawing a complete blank on how.

On the way back to the hotel, he had run through a very satisfying scenario involving drugs from work, a set of handcuffs, and a prolonged and nasty rape. Or, given the mood he was in by the time he'd finished polishing the details, short and nasty. He'd elaborated upon it in the shower, then discarded the fantasy to concentrate on finding something practical. Warrick had the kind of prestigious position that made him an impossibly dangerous victim for anything overt. Apart from some fairly outrageous expenses claims (a semiofficial perk for senior paras), Toreth didn't, by and large, do anything illegal. He saw the consequences every day at work. A bruised ego was hardly sufficient reason to risk prison or worse. In a way, it was also too unimaginative, almost pedestrian, after the experience in the sim. Worst of all, Warrick would win again. However much he screamed (and he would scream—the part of Toreth's mind still enjoying the fantasy added a gag to the list of props required), it wouldn't change that basic fact. Toreth would have resorted to force to get what Warrick had managed to enjoy without.

So. What exactly had Warrick done? He'd humiliated Toreth completely. He'd made him lose every shred of self-control. He'd made him beg, and then keep begging for more after that. He'd stood at a safe distance and watched every detail on Toreth's face while it happened. For God's sake, he'd even told him what he planned to do in the message he'd left at the hotel.

And he'd made sure Toreth had a way out for the entire time.

Every second in the sim, a single word would have dropped him back into the real world. Two easy syllables, and Toreth hadn't said them, even though nothing had prevented him from doing it. As far as he could remember, he'd never been unable to speak; in fact, thinking back, Warrick had never even touched his mouth. Not with fingers or lips. Which meant, of course, that Toreth had gone along with it. He'd wanted it. That wasn't like him at all. He didn't play that kind of game. All his preferred positions were on top, in charge and in control. He didn't get off at all on the idea of being tied up. Except that Warrick had done far worse than just tie him up, and he had enjoyed it. He had to admit that to himself, much as it didn't mesh with his cherished self-image.

Absentmindedly, he topped up his glass, caught a spill that ran down the neck of the bottle and licked his thumb. Would sucking a disembodied finger feel real? Probably. Everything else had been very real. Kissing disembodied lips would be extremely peculiar, although it would solve the problem of noses getting in the way. Warrick's well-shaped mouth had been one of the first things Toreth had noticed about him, back at the buffet after the lecture. That and his extraordinary dark voice...

Toreth realized that he had wandered rather a long way from the subject in hand. Specifically, revenge. He reviewed his options. Part of his mind still stood by the drug-him-and-rape-him fantasy plan, impossible as it was. Another part suggested canceling the meal and forgetting about the whole experience as quickly as possible. And a treacherous but insistent little voice advocated turning on the charm over some expense-account wine, persuading Warrick to come up to his room, and then the two of them fucking like amphetamine-crazed mink until they both passed out cold. Of the three options, the last one sounded like by far the most fun, and that with a man who had as good as said that he despised him. He sighed and opened a second miniature bottle of spirits. His self-image was having a wonderful day.

Then the answer hit him. There was a simple, safe, and logical response. Warrick had screwed with his self-image, so he would screw with Warrick's. If Warrick despised him now, so much the better. He would go to dinner and find out something about Warrick he could use. Something the man wanted without even knowing it, without daring to acknowledge it. Something dark and dirty. And then give it to him, gift-wrapped, for him to enjoy.

Half an hour after he had escorted his guest from the premises, Warrick lay at full stretch in the white marble bath. Blowing scraps of bubblebath foam into the air from his hand, he admired the rainbow play of light as they floated back down. Another tricky simulation problem beautifully cracked.

Set flush with the floor, the round bath—almost a pool—was large and deep, with a submerged ledge for sitting on all around the circumference. Warrick preferred to float, held in place and supported by invisible cushions. The rest of the expansive bathroom was silvery gray marble, with fluted columns and niches holding oil lamps. Peaceful and good for thinking in, it was one of his favorite sim rooms.

He heard a noise from a small cabinet by the side of the bath. Feeling too lazy to move, he concentrated on the catch, his fingers twitching slightly. The cabinet opened, and a dozen yellow plastic ducks in assorted sizes spilled out over the floor. The largest of them sprouted stubby legs and wings, righted itself, and waddled over to plop into the bath. It paddled busily through the foam, bumping into the smooth marble sides, and Warrick watched it with a slight frown. Someone had been at the artificial life programming suite again. Not that he minded—in fact, he encouraged it—but it had been careless to leave this installed. Corporate sponsors on a surprise visit might not be impressed by the abuse of their very expensive facilities.

He caught the duck and turned it over. It quacked in protest, and then stopped when he stroked its smooth belly. Nice touch. The legs were rather good as well. Letting the duck go, he watched as it disappeared under a mound of bubbles. He must find out who'd created it, and apply a little carrot and stick. Not too much stick, though. That would require a fair dose of hypocrisy, considering that he had canceled a fluid dynamics test this very afternoon in order to mind-fuck a stranger whose name he didn't even know. A scandalous waste of sim time and he would have been furious to catch any of the others doing it. Still, the fuck, mental or not, had worked out well. Not surprising, since the deck had been unfairly stacked in his favor, but that was the way he preferred to play any game. Especially with dangerous opponents.

Accepting the invitation to dinner had been a silly mistake, but one easily corrected by a message left at the hotel. Time to call a halt while he had a decisive victory to his credit.

The duck bumped into the edge of the bath, corrected its course, and circled for a while. Its collisions with the edges were now far less frequent, he noted. Not a bad little learning algorithm.

He pushed a wave of water towards the duck, setting it spinning, and laughed. Hypocrisy aside, he'd had a good afternoon. To start with, he loved showing people around his sim. (*His* sim. In a formal sense, Warrick acknowledged the large team behind the project. But in his heart, it was his alone.) God, he loved to see visitors' faces when they first looked around the meadow or the coral reef, and Toth had appreciated it. At least, he amended, Toth had appreciated it to begin with. Then he'd turned a coldly professional eye on it. Just a particularly unsavory example from an endless procession of Administration vultures, picking over his creation for their sordid little purposes. Warrick fully intended to resist as long as possible, and to make them pay dearly. However, in the long term, they would no doubt take it away and cut corners, rip out features, and cripple it until all its beauty was gone and it became a cheap, mass-produced tool. A tool of oppression, as that suicidal idiot had said in the lecture.

Warrick didn't object to the idea of the sim generating profit—he hoped to profit extensively himself—but he intensely disliked the idea of the uses the sim would be put to in somewhere like the Investigation and Interrogation Division. If Toth's reaction hadn't been so obvious, Warrick might not have gone through with his little scene in the bedroom.

On reflection, he'd never done anything quite like that before. Oh, he'd shown personal guests around various sims, and he'd even abused the expensive facilities from time to time. Nothing, however, so deliberate and, well, cruel. Not, Warrick told himself, that he'd done anything wrong. Toth could have stopped the sim any time he wanted to. He hadn't, so he'd enjoyed it. But had he been frightened, too? Perhaps a little. A little afraid and a lot out of control.

That was something in the sim reality Warrick couldn't duplicate for himself. He knew intimately how very safe it was. He'd designed it that way, and that was how he'd always liked it. Still, he felt an unexpected touch of envy at the unattainable experience. How had it felt to be so controlled? Held there, so absolutely in another's power. Old fantasies stirred, unexpectedly revived. It must have been...

He stretched out in the warm water and thought about what he'd done, how he'd constructed the encounter. He'd enjoyed doing it, which was perhaps a little disconcerting. At the time he'd been concentrating too hard to appreciate it fully, but now, replaying the scene in his mind, it brought a flush of arousal—the man's face had been so responsive. It would be good to see that again, to watch his eyes while he came. Maybe he wouldn't cancel dinner after all.

The thought startled him. What he had done in the sim was one thing; it had been under his control and, above all, perfectly safe. It would be stark raving insanity even to consider doing anything with Toth in the real world. The man, whoever he was, tortured people to death for a living. But he had to admit that it had been a long time since he'd felt this intrigued by the idea of having someone outside the sim. Inside the sim, everything was so perfect, so pleasant, that he had lost interest in that aspect of the world outside.

Why should now be different? Maybe it was an excess of financial concerns; at the moment, SimTech was a little less like fun and rather more like work. Maybe it was Toth himself, whom he'd had plenty of time to study—nicely built, with a swimmer's broad shoulders and narrow waist. Or maybe it was the open challenge in the invitation, and the spice of danger, although any danger in the meeting suddenly seemed rather insubstantial. No more real, in fact, than the virtual duck, which at that moment broke his reverie by nudging his shoulder. That is to say, absolutely real and quite unreal at the same time.

Perhaps he'd been spending too much time in the sim. Normally it didn't affect him, although once or twice in the past, he'd caught himself trying sim-world things in the real world. Then he had simply avoided going in until the overlap went away. Other people had had problems; it had badly affected one of the graduate students. SimTech's corporate psychologist had labeled it "excessive immersion." They'd reassigned the girl to the more theoretical aspects of the work and that had resolved the issue.

Not that he was suffering from excessive immersion now. No, that was simply a flimsy excuse for why he wanted to ignore his misgivings and see Toth again. To repeat the experience from this afternoon, only this time with more direct participation. Warrick imagined stripping Toth in a place where clothes didn't just vanish when dropped, imagined feeling real muscles slide under his fingers. It would be very good, despite the imperfections of the world outside, to taste real skin again.

However, he needed to be careful. There was danger and it was of his own making. He had set Toth up, and the man hadn't made the invitation to dinner out of gratitude for that. Everything depended on what Toth planned to do, and that was what he would have to find out this evening. Before he ended up in real-world trouble—the kind he couldn't escape with a code word.

Yes. He'd keep the appointment. But only if he could find out one small thing first.

Chapter Six

❖

Toreth had been five minutes late, but he still waited in the restaurant's bar for nearly half an hour before Warrick arrived. It was one of the more expensive restaurants in the Renaissance Center and surprisingly busy for midweek. Toreth passed the time in assessing the other drinkers—for the most part corporates dining with colleagues or illicit lovers—until he finally saw Warrick standing by the door, also examining the room. He caught sight of Toreth and strolled over. "Sorry I'm late," he murmured as he took off his jacket. "Delayed at work. I rushed over as soon as I could get away."

He didn't sound the slightest bit sorry, or look as if he had broken into anything more energetic than an amble in the last hour. Toreth merely took it as the signal that the game was on again, and noted that he had showered and changed recently. Toreth almost fell into the classic trap of claiming he too had only just arrived, but then remembered the empty glass in front of him. He settled for a shrug. "No problem. Do you want a drink?"

Warrick considered for a moment. "No, I think I'll wait until we eat. I missed lunch and I don't want to drink on an empty stomach."

And with the meal we'll have wine, which will come in a sealed bottle and be that much harder for me to tamper with, Toreth thought. Well, that established the base level of trust for the evening. He liked it. Warrick was justifiably cautious—maybe even a little apprehensive—but he was here anyway. He could work with that.

Just then, a waiter sidled over to announce that their table was ready. They took their seats and examined the ornately inscribed menus. Words like "naturally grown" and "outdoor produced" were scattered liberally around, and the steep prices made Toreth wince inwardly. If he didn't get this past Accounts, Warrick would be the most expensive fuck he'd had for some time.

"What shall we have to start with?" Toreth asked, as a silence filler.

Warrick turned the page back and studied the selection. "Well, to start with, you can tell me your real name."

Toreth blinked. Damn it, just when he thought he had a handle on the situation the man managed something else unsettling. "I beg your pardon?" he asked.

Warrick's gaze flicked up long enough to catch his flustered expression, and then returned to the menu. "I think now that this has extended to dinner, a real name is only polite, since you know mine. Usually I ask *before* letting someone come in my mouth, but I think, under the circumstances, that didn't really count."

Someone at the next table dropped a fork onto a plate with a loud clatter, but Toreth barely noticed. *Letting? Didn't count?*

He's baiting you, a calm part of his mind said firmly. Come on, you can do better than this.

Before Toreth could produce a response, Warrick looked up again. "Very well, if you insist. I shall guess." He laid the menu down and steepled his fingers. "Mm, let me see. Something like Toth, I imagine, because that makes it easier to respond to naturally. And you don't look like a Marcus, so let us discount that completely. Something like... Valantin Toreth, perhaps?"

At this rate, speechlessness looked set to become a permanent condition. After a moment he managed to say, "It's Val Toreth. And I always go by Toreth."

Warrick smiled briefly and picked up the menu again. "This does look very good. I think I shall have chicken livers—or perhaps scallops. Did you know that, traditionally, there is a rule that fresh shellfish should only be eaten in a month with an R in it? Or is that only oysters? I forget. In any case, October should be safe enough."

Toreth wasn't going to ask. He wasn't going to ask. He wasn't... then the question escaped through gritted teeth. "How did you find out? The files are supposed to be secure."

That got a 24-carat smile, to which, to his intense irritation, Toreth found himself responding. "The files are *always* supposed to be secure." Then Warrick shook his head. "However, I assure you that no illegal activity took place. I merely called the Investigation and Interrogation Division and asked to speak to a para-investigator called Toth—or something like Toth. The very pleasant receptionist asked me if I meant the tall, blond, handsome one, which I agreed was an acceptable description. Then she gave me your name and transferred me to another, equally delightful admin who said you were out of the building for the day, which clinched the identification."

Toreth was disgusted to discover that he actually felt flattered. Mentally, he glared at the feeling until it slunk away. "So why did you bother asking?" he said without thinking, and then cursed himself. He was making hash of this. Why? There was a simple answer: because he wanted too badly to win. So it was time to pay attention and start playing seriously.

Warrick turned the page of the menu, taking his time replying. "I was curious to see if you would be honest enough to tell me," he said without any particular edge to his voice. "I suspected not, but I don't like to make assumptions without evidence."

The reappearance of the waiter saved Toreth from having to respond. Warrick had made his mind up, and so Toreth ordered more or less at random and chose two half bottles of wine that would complement both meals. No point in drinking too much.

A platter of tiny but ridiculously elaborate hors d'oeuvres arrived. Warrick took one and began dismantling it, eating each component separately. A long silence developed, with which he seemed quite comfortable. Toreth watched him, still wondering exactly why he was here. The up-front revelation that he knew Toreth's name was a clear signal saying, "I know who you are, and you can be damn sure that someone else knows I'm here." Then he had dropped in the little barbed compliment and dismissed the whole deception.

Toreth picked up one of the little biscuits, topped with a fish and herb roulade arrangement, and disposed of it in two bites as Warrick began another delicate deconstruction.

The signals were intriguing—wariness and definite interest. Some people had a thing for interrogators and, by extension, for para-investigators. They were usually people who had no firsthand experience of the profession. Toreth couldn't understand it. There was nothing sexually exciting about interrogation—it was a skilled, technically demanding, and occasionally boring job. On the other hand, despite the general distaste with which I&I staff regarded "interrogator junkies," Toreth had no moral objection to taking full advantage of the kink when the opportunity arose. He had wondered before if Warrick fell into this category, but he'd decided not. For one thing, the man had too much imagination not to realize what the job entailed. For another, the contempt he had shown in the sim had been real, even if the setting hadn't.

Yet here he was. Interesting. Suggestive, maybe, that Warrick had some deeply hidden fascination in there after all. That would be a nice little piece of self-knowledge to give him. However, it wasn't worth pursuing quite yet; he'd wait until another glass or so of wine had gone down.

The appetizers arrived. Toreth's fish terrine turned out to be a close cousin to the roulade, and it was excellent. Warrick had settled on chicken livers. Toreth thought they were revolting, but Warrick clearly appreciated them. After a few non-remarks about the food, Warrick said, "Now that you've had a few hours to consider it, what do you think about the sim?"

"I think it's absolutely incredible." Toreth didn't even need to exaggerate, because it had been an amazing experience. All of it. Warrick seemed to expect elaboration, so he obliged. "I had no idea it would be like that. So real. The meadow was one of the most beautiful places I've seen in my life." He searched for the right word, one that Warrick would want to hear. "Magical."

No trace of the sardonic on Warrick's face now. "Yes. Yes, it is." Then his smile turned a little bitter. "Although your fellow civil servants generally have no difficulty in seeing past it."

Toreth shook his head. "You can't blame the Administration for appreciating the technology." Time to throw out an opening. "Or the potential applications."

"Applications." Warrick grimaced. "No, I suppose not." He took a sip of wine and that seemed to mark the topic as closed.

They ate in silence for a while, until Warrick laid down his knife and fork. He had finished the chicken livers, but the pastry shell that had held them he left discarded on the side of the plate.

"No good?"

"I'm not very fond of puff pastry."

"Then why order it?"

"I liked the rest." He wiped a sliver of bread around the plate to capture the last of the creamy sauce. "And it's too much trouble to ask them to make it without. Why? Does the waste bother you?"

"No. I was just curious."

"Ah. Curiosity." Warrick set his knife and fork precisely in the center of the plate. "That's a professionally useful trait."

Toreth shrugged. "I don't usually have any personal interest in the questions I'm asking."

"Mm. I meant as a researcher."

He clearly hadn't, but it was a cover for a question he had wanted to ask without asking. "Curious about my job?" Toreth inquired.

Warrick leaned back, increasing the distance between them. "A little, perhaps, yes."

"What do you want to know?" Make him work for it.

"Why do you enjoy it?"

Not, Toreth noted, *Do you enjoy it?* "The money's decent," he said. "The hours aren't bad. There's a lot of variety." Warrick watched him, silently assessing the reasons as he offered them. "I like the people I work with, and even some of the people I work for. It has an excellent career structure. And I'm good at it."

"Ah," Warrick said.

"Ah, what?"

"You make it sound like any other job."

"It *is* like any other job."

Warrick fell silent.

"Anything else you want to ask?"

"No, I don't think so."

The waiter arrived to clear their plates. Between courses, Warrick excused himself to go to the toilet. When he returned, he glanced at his nearly empty glass, and then knocked it onto the thickly carpeted floor with a casually accidental gesture. The waiter brought a clean glass and shared out the last remnant of the first bottle. Toreth smiled. This was pointed mistrust as performance art.

The main course arrived. The second bottle of wine was opened and poured. Between mouthfuls of his own meal, Toreth watched Warrick eat. He decided that his technique—and technique was the right word—exemplified everything about the man that he longed to strip away: calm, self-control, concentration, precision. He went through the contents of his plate methodically, dealing with each part in turn. The intricate bird's nest of potato slivers went first, then the tiny portions of vegetables, one kind at a time. He saved the steak until last. He divided the thick slice exactly in half and cut a forkful out of the middle. Blood oozed slowly onto the plate. Toreth didn't like overcooked steak himself, but this one looked as if it might still get some benefit from emergency resuscitation.

When Warrick took the first mouthful of meat, he closed his eyes, chewing carefully and thoroughly before swallowing. Opening his eyes, he saw Toreth watching him. He smiled, unperturbed to find himself observed.

"It is good?" Toreth asked.

"Quite excellent. Would you like to try some?" Without waiting for a reply, he cut off a thin slice, picked it up with his fingers, dipped it into the Bearnaise sauce and offered it across the table. Toreth hesitated for a fraction of a second, considering mouth versus fingers, then took it into his mouth. Slick fingers brushed his lips and he caught a fingertip with his tongue before the brief contact withdrew. Warrick licked his finger and thumb, and then wiped them on the napkin. Toreth just about remembered to chew. The virtually raw flesh tasted sweet and salty.

"It is good?" Warrick asked, exactly matching Toreth's earlier tone.

"Yes, ah, excellent."

Warrick nodded, and returned his attention to his plate.

That certainly settled Toreth's lingering doubts about what Warrick wanted, in general terms. All he had to do now was convince him that he would be safe.

Warrick decided against dessert, and Toreth didn't like sweet things, anyway. They settled for after-dinner drinks and coffees. As the waiter delivered the drinks, Warrick's napkin slipped from his lap. There was a tiny confusion as he bent down, and the waiter did the same. That was all it took for Toreth to reach across the table and drip a single drop from a vial into Warrick's glass. It was nothing very exotic—something to combine with the alcohol, which was a drug in any case, and spread a little happiness. An extra cushion of relaxation and acceptance. It was cheating, as Toreth readily acknowledged, but then Warrick himself had hardly played fair in the sim.

The bill came to a respectable total. Accounts would give him hell about this. Toreth gave his room number and the waiter withdrew. Time to go for the question they had been hedging around all evening. "Would you like to come up to my room?" Toreth asked.

41

Warrick laughed incredulously. "Excuse me for asking a rather obvious question, but do you think I'm insane?"

Slightly taken aback by the directness of the answer, Toreth shook his head.

"Ah, stupid, then. Neither of which, I'm afraid, is true." Warrick eyed him assessingly. "You are, what, half a head taller than me? And a good few kilos heavier, all of which is muscle." Toreth recognized the flattery slipped so casually into the conversation again, but, buoyed by half a bottle of wine plus extras, he enjoyed it anyway.

"So insanity or stupidity would be required for me to place myself in a situation alone with you." Warrick took another sip of his drink, savored the flavor for a moment. "And in any case, I don't sleep with torturers, Administration-approved or not."

Toreth blinked. Pretty fucking comprehensive putdown.

Warrick tipped his head back and drained the last drops from his glass. "At least, I try not to make a habit of it."

Or not so comprehensive. Testing his reactions again, probably. Toreth said evenly, "I wasn't planning to hurt you."

That got a sharp glance and Toreth had a sudden impulse to add, "Unless you'd like me to." However, that would have been too much. Instead, he spread his hands. "It would be stupid of me to even think about it, wouldn't it? You know who I am."

A meditative pause, pretending to come up with an idea he must have had long before. "I'll tell you what," Warrick said slowly. "If you do something for me, I shall reconsider the proposal."

Reconsider, not agree to. "What?"

"Tell me what you felt in the sim."

"I already did."

"You know what I mean."

Toreth thought about it. What would Warrick want to hear? What would make him agree? What would he know to be a lie? He looked around the restaurant. "Here?"

"We could adjourn to the bar, if you would prefer. There are some quiet corners."

They strolled to the bar, Warrick keeping a clear distance between them, and settled into an alcove, taking separate armchairs rather than one of the small sofas. Warrick crossed his legs, and rested his elbows on the arms of the chair. "Well?"

"I enjoyed it." Start with honesty, but not too much. See where this was going. Somewhere interesting, he was sure—Warrick had clearly put a lot of thought into the question.

"And?"

"And I enjoyed it. That's it. What else do you want to hear? A minute-by-minute account?"

"Maybe. But you're lying, anyway. If that was all there was to it, you wouldn't have wanted to call it rape, or felt there was a need—and I quote—'to pay me back.'" Warrick checked his watch. "Well, it's been a nice evening, but..."

He started to stand up. Toreth knew this wasn't a bluff. "All right."

Warrick scrutinized him, then sank back into the deep leather chair.

Toreth kept his words low. "You know what I felt. Code word or not, you trapped me and you humiliated me." He shied away from the vivid memory of his own pleading voice from the sim. "You took away my control and you made me beg you to fuck me."

Warrick's eyes were locked with his, flickering heat, and his lips had parted a fraction. That's what he wants, Toreth realized triumphantly. He wants what he did to me, or something very close to that. Now, how could he make Warrick ask for it? "You did exactly what you meant to," he continued. "It was the whole point of inviting me—you said as much in the message. You know it worked. Why ask?"

Warrick ignored the question and pulled himself back together. "So why invite me here?"

"Because, like you said, I was angry enough to want some kind of payback for it."

"And now?"

It was like talking his way through a minefield. "Now I'm not so sure."

"Mm. Not sure." Warrick shook his head. "That doesn't strike me as a sound basis for spending time alone with you."

"All right. I'll tell you how you can help me make up my mind."

"Well?" Warrick was all attention now.

He wants it, Toreth thought. Really wants it. All Toreth needed to do was ease the way to surrender, and give Warrick an illusion of safety he could believe in. "Apologize to me," Toreth said.

Warrick stared at him, licked his lips once. "What?"

"Apologize to me. It's not that difficult, is it?"

Warrick shook his head, but apparently it was. "I'm sorry," he said at length. Toreth started to speak but Warrick held his hand up. "I am sorry. 'Familiarity breeds contempt,' I think the saying is. Sometimes we forget that just because the sim is physically safe, it doesn't mean that it can't hurt. I went too far. If I distressed you, I apologize."

Toreth thought it was the most beautifully unapologetic apology he had ever heard. "Apology accepted. Now..." he said, pulling the pause out, "what can I do in return?"

Silence, and Toreth smiled. His catch was hooked, and only barely still resisting the pull to the net. "Very well, in that case let me guess. Something like the sim, but not quite. Changing places. Losing control for a little while. And some danger—just enough to give it an edge." His smile slipped into something almost predatory. "A different kind of game."

Warrick stared at him as if hypnotized, then nodded slowly. "That's ... a good guess."

"I read people for a living," Toreth said casually, and relished the delightful contradiction of the grimace of distaste on Warrick's mouth and the sharpening of desire in his eyes.

God, he loved being right.

Hypnotized was how Warrick felt, walking through the hotel corridors past people who had no idea of where they were going or what they were about to do. Not surprising, since neither did he, and for some reason that didn't make him as wary as he knew it ought. A feeling of unreality smothered the apprehension. Toreth walked beside him, humming out of key, not looking at him. They reached room 212 and stopped outside. Toreth swiped the keycard and held the door open, waiting for Warrick to go through first. Dimmed lights came up automatically as he stepped inside and the door closed behind them with a decisive click.

An ordinary hotel room with the usual layout and fittings, details he didn't seem to be able to focus on. He still felt caught in a dream, senses dulled except for a sharp awareness of scents. He caught the smell of shampoo and aftershave, reinforced as Toreth walked past him to lean on the back of an armchair. Warrick waited, seconds passing in building anticipation.

"Strip," Toreth ordered.

Warrick did so, silently, shivering in the warm air.

Toreth watched, making no move to undress. "Mmm." He walked around behind Warrick and pressed up against him. Warrick felt fabric touching him from shoulder to ankle, and he wanted it to be skin. Toreth bent down and Warrick felt his lips right against his ear. "Pick a word," he murmured.

Warrick blanked completely for a moment, and then said, "Plastic duck."

Toreth laughed, and he felt it all down the length of his body. "All right. 'Plastic duck' it is."

Toreth moved back, walking around to stand in front of Warrick. "Close your eyes."

"Why?"

Too fast for Warrick to react, Toreth slapped him across the face, rocking his head back, and the heat in his cheek set off an echoing flash of warmth in his stomach. "Close your eyes," Toreth repeated calmly.

Warrick obeyed. The handprint still glowed on his skin, each finger distinct. He felt himself hardening, the telltale response out of his control.

"You liked that?" Toreth started to move around him again, touching, rough and gentle, pain and pleasure, oddly impersonal and intensely arousing. "What else do you like, I wonder? Do you want me to fuck you? Not that I care whether you want it—I'm going to do it anyway. You were right to think twice about coming up here with me. Still think you made the right choice?"

Every so often, the touching stopped, and Warrick heard him undressing. It never stopped for long, though, and the words not at all. By the time Toreth stepped away, Warrick had lost all sense of place or time. There was only himself, in the dark, breathing fast and shallow as his heart raced to keep up.

"Give me your hands." Instant obedience this time, and Toreth took Warrick's wrists in his hands, squeezing tightly to complete the circle. "You can open your eyes."

When he did so, the first things he saw were his own hands, trapped by Toreth's, and he found he couldn't look away. The single point of contact between them captured his whole attention; everything else seemed distant and insubstantial. His pulse tripped against Toreth's fingers, blood humming with alcohol and desire and—something else? Had Toreth slipped something into his drink after all? Did it matter now?

Then Toreth spoke and the thought was lost. "No handcuffs, I'm afraid," he said. "If you'd let me know what you liked, I'd have brought something from work."

Warrick felt a fleeting rush of the real apprehension he'd experienced earlier in the evening. Then Toreth smiled. "But I don't need chains, anyway. Not for you." With that, Toreth pulled him forwards and wrestled him down onto the bed.

Warrick fought back, for real at first because of the surprise. However, Toreth had professional experience of restraining the unwilling, so Warrick's resistance posed him no problem at all. They finished with Warrick pinned face up underneath, struggles limited to fruitless writhing which felt so good it quickly began to take the edge off the fantasy of force.

"I don't need chains," Toreth repeated, "because you'll do what you're told anyway, won't you?" Warrick nodded, too breathless to speak. "Good."

Then Toreth kissed him full on the mouth, not kindly, and in fact hard enough to bruise. Real bruises, Warrick thought distractedly. Something people would see at SimTech tomorrow. The idea of tomorrow, of sitting in his office with this as a memory to relive, was almost as exciting as the hard body on top of him.

Toreth knelt up, straddling Warrick's thighs. "Turn over, then keep still." He lifted his hand again when Warrick hesitated. "Do it."

The threat was thrill enough and Warrick turned obediently, shivering at the rubbing of skin against skin where their thighs touched. Toreth planted his knee firmly in the small of Warrick's back. It pressed him down into the bed as Toreth leaned over, knocking things over on the bedside table and swearing under his breath. Warrick felt a fleeting hint of annoyance at the brief interruption. In the sim, he could think anything he wanted directly to hand. In fact, in the sim, they wouldn't need lubricant at all. This was why the real world had lost—

The shock of the cold gel made him squirm away, even though he didn't want to. Toreth lay down again, half on him and half on the bed but still pinning him tight. His fingers tangled in Warrick's hair, pulled his head around. "Keep still, or I'll break your fucking neck," Toreth whispered right in his ear.

Warrick did, clenching his hands on the sheet because, depending on how caught up in the fantasy Toreth had become, this might hurt. In fact, it was just a finger, and a not ungentle finger at that. That might have broken the spell except for the low stream of words hot against his ear, whispered threats and promises that squirmed down his spine. Two fingers, working into him harder, a little uncomfortable because he was out of practice at this in the real world—years out of practice.

It was the discomfort, undeniably actual, that tore away the last of the cocooning sense of unreality, twisting his nerves to a higher pitch of arousal. He was really here, really alone with this dangerous, desirable man who knew how to hurt, how to kill, how to take whatever he wanted without hesitation or compassion. Now he was wriggling, wanting more, forgetting to fight.

Then the fingers were gone and the rough voice said, "I want to hear you ask for it."

Oh, God, yes. Warrick shook his head, as best he could. The hand in his hair tightened and he shivered. Toreth's other hand gripped his right wrist, strong fingers digging into his tendons. "Ask for it."

"Bastard. Ah!"

Toreth twisted his arm up behind his back, sending a flare of pain through him, shockingly arousing. He'd never thought—

"*Ask.*"

He wanted to keep it going longer, but he couldn't. It was too real. Too perfectly real to bear. "Yes. Please, yes."

"Please yes, what? I want to hear it."

"Fuck me."

"Again."

Barely forcing the words past the excitement threatening to choke him, Warrick gasped, "F—fuck me."

The weight shifted, pinning him more completely to the bed. Toreth untangled his fingers from his hair and slipped his hand around to cover his mouth. "Don't want you screaming," he murmured in a voice that made it clear that was exactly the opposite of what he did want. Warrick closed his eyes tightly, dizzied with desire and anticipation. Toreth's other hand held his hip as he pushed slowly, slowly into him. "Does it hurt?"

Warrick shook his head emphatically. "Yes," he whimpered into the fingers pressed against his lips.

"Good."

He started to struggle again until Toreth took his hand away from his mouth and caught both his wrists, pinning them above his head.

It was perfect, as perfect as anything in the sim—and yet it wasn't, and the imperfections only made it better. His arms stretched out harder than he would have thought he wanted; a too-hard bite on his shoulder; the two of them moving perfectly together, then losing the rhythm for a few seconds, and the sweet relief as they caught it again. All the distant details the sim would never have generated or would have smoothed away: footsteps in the corridor, vehicles passing outside.

In the sim, his mind controlled the world around him; here, even his self-control was slipping helplessly away. Too much detail, too much sensation, leaving him shuddering with the intensity. For a weird, disconnected moment, a still-lucid part of his mind began to shape the idea into a project proposal. "Imperfections in the sensory modalities as a technique for enhancing the experience of fucking …being fucked…being *fucked*—"

Then Toreth thrust into him hard and froze, his fingers digging in painfully. Warrick gasped, half from pain, half from need. "Don't stop!"

Toreth laughed thickly. "Very—" He cleared his throat and started again. "Very good. But I want something else."

He began to rock his hips slowly, and Warrick couldn't stop a moan escaping. "What?" he managed. "Anything. Please."

Toreth released his wrists, twining his fingers in his hair again. "Touch yourself. I want to watch you make yourself come."

Warrick didn't move, not because he didn't want to, but because for a moment he simply couldn't make his shaking body obey him. Toreth grabbed his hand, forced it down, and then briefly halted to rearrange their bodies. In the sim, they wouldn't need to, but before Warrick could begin to shape the thought, Toreth's hand closed over his, wrapping his fingers around his cock and making him gasp at his own touch. "Do it. Yes, that's right. I want to watch you." He forced Warrick's head around for another kiss. "I want to see your eyes."

Toreth's fingers interleaved with his, urging him to make his strokes tighter and faster. As he did so, Toreth started to thrust into him again, deliciously hard and deep and everything was too good, too imperfectly perfect, to last any longer.

At the last moment he closed his eyes and turned his head away, screaming into the mattress as he came.

When he felt like paying attention to the world again, he found Toreth sitting cross-legged on the bed beside him. Warrick rolled over onto his back and looked up at him.

Toreth smiled. "What do you think about my inflection now?"

Warrick stared at him until his mind finally dredged up the reference. "Perfect. Absolutely fucking perfect. Emphasis on the fucking."

"Good." He got up and went off to the bathroom, whistling.

Warrick watched him walk across the room, muscles sharply defined under smooth skin. First thing tomorrow, he thought, I'm finding the gym at the university and signing up. Having an office job was clearly no excuse. Then the implications of the thought sickened him. Just like any other job. Except Toreth's job left him adept at knowing how far to push, how much pain to use and how to read the response to it. And, God, he'd loved it. Loved every minute of it, knowing who and what he was. What those hands did for a living. It's just a fantasy, he told himself. And it was just once. Just this once. Never again. Never, never again.

Toreth stood under the hot shower and decided it had gone remarkably well. He'd count it as a draw. Warrick was still probably ahead on points, but in this kind of game the score degraded quickly, and the last round was the one that really counted. Right about now Warrick would be thinking about what he had done, and who he had done it with. How much he'd liked it.

Very enjoyable it had been, too. A little overcautious in places, but that was only to be expected with an obvious amateur. Unusually, he found he wouldn't mind doing it again. Eventually. Sometime in the future when Warrick had had plenty of time to think about wanting it. He'd wait until Warrick contacted him. Watching the water run over his hands, he wondered if Warrick would be able to get them any more time in the sim. Toreth turned his face up to the spray and pondered the potential applications.

Once back in the bedroom, he listened to the splashing water as Warrick showered, and tried to decide whether to pack up and go home or spend the night at the hotel. In the end, he decided to stay. Since he was paying for it—or at least they were his euros until Accounts reimbursed them—he might as well enjoy it, even if the sheets were a bit of a mess. He could get a swim in before work and he loved hotel breakfasts.

Warrick had taken his clothes into the bathroom and emerged fully dressed, if a little tousled. Toreth thought he was going to walk straight out—which would have been fine with him—but he stopped by the door.

"Well, that was fun," Warrick said, his half-smile mask in place.

Toreth matched the smile, decided to test out his victory. "Yes. See you again?"

Warrick considered for a moment too long before he turned away without reply. The door closed behind him, and Toreth laughed.

Chapter Seven

Next morning, Sara was once more already at her screen when he arrived. Toreth stopped on the way into his office and sat on the edge of her desk. "In bright and early, I see."

She nodded, absolutely serious. "It's because I love my job so much."

"Incidentally, aren't the annual performance appraisals the week after next?"

Sara grinned. "I'd completely forgotten. I'll get the forms ready for you." They both knew she had nothing to worry about. Although she had a somewhat idiosyncratic approach to timekeeping, she was a damn good admin and his main problem was fighting off attempts by other paras to poach her.

Sara looked him up and down. "Good day off?"

"Not bad."

"Do anything fun?" she inquired, in a tone which effortlessly translated the question into "anyone fun?"

He grinned. "Weird and wonderful. I'll tell you all about it later. Have I got any messages?"

"Just one important one. Tillotson wants to see you as soon as you're in. He didn't say what about but he didn't sound happy that you'd taken the time off without him seeing a holiday request."

Toreth made a rude noise and opened his office door wide enough to throw his jacket onto his desk. "Get me a coffee, will you, Sara? With luck, I won't be too long."

He hoped the summons wasn't just over his taking holiday without approval; unfortunately, his immediate superior was exactly the kind of bureaucratic obsessive who would kick up a fuss over something so petty.

❖ ❖ ❖

When he arrived, Tillotson's door was wide open, and he could see the ginger-haired head of section watching the reception area. When he saw Toreth, he beck-

49

oned him in at once. Toreth waited to see how the opening of the meeting would go. When Tillotson decided to elicit confessions of illegitimate time off or expense account fiddling, he tended to go in for heavy-handed hints and verbal traps. A direct question meant his mind was on a different track.

"You were supposed to be at a seminar the day before yesterday," Tillotson asked, after waving him irritably to take a seat. "Did you go?"

A promising start. "Yes. Computer sim technology. Psychoprogramming is very keen on it, so I thought I'd take a look, see what the fuss is about."

"Who was the speaker?"

"A Dr. Keir Warrick."

Tillotson nodded. "Did you understand the seminar?"

"Some of it," he admitted cautiously. "It was very interesting." That clearly pleased Tillotson, so he added, "I got myself a guided tour of the lab yesterday."

"Good. Excellent, in fact. You've got a new case."

Toreth relaxed. Tillotson obviously hadn't found out anything about the last couple of days. "I have prisoners—"

"Your team interrogators can deal with them. There was a death last night at this Dr. Warrick's corporation. Here." He held out a hand screen, and Toreth took it, as the seconds in which he should have declared a personal involvement came and went. He wanted to hear about the case and anyway, as far as he was concerned, two fucks—one of which wasn't even real—didn't constitute an involvement.

Skimming the file, he went straight to the important part: the victim's political status. The girl had been a graduate student working in the AERC laboratories. No valuable discoveries to her credit, no history of involvement with dissidents, nothing at all to merit I&I attention. Last of all, he looked at the name and biographical details. Kelly Jarvis, which rang no bells. No important family connections, either. "Why are we interested?" Toreth asked.

"Because of the other file on there."

Toreth skipped to the next document, checking the name first this time. He whistled softly. Jon Teffera, co-owner of LiveCorp and its many subsidiaries. No need to look in the file for the reasons I&I was interested in him. A senior corporate, known for the number and variety of his Administration friends, was definitely more I&I's province than a lowly graduate student. Toreth recalled that Teffera's death had been reported in the news, with a bland, natural causes explanation he'd wondered about at the time. What was the connection to SimTech? A glance at the file provided the answer, but also a puzzle. "Found dead in his sim couch? I didn't think they were for sale yet."

"They aren't, except to corporate sponsors of the project and their close, influential friends." Tillotson checked on his screen. "The full list of who owns them should be in the file somewhere. I'd like you to make sure it's accurate, though."

"Of course, good idea," Toreth said, even though that had been the first thing

50

he'd thought of. Something else occurred to him, and he double-checked the date on the Teffera file. "Why has it taken so long to get to us?"

Tillotson's sharp nose twitched, a sign of irritation. "The Justice Department has been sitting on it. They called Teffera's death corporate sabotage, and then changed their minds to natural causes. This morning, some Legislature admin was at the . . . what is it?"

"Artificial Environments Research Center?"

"Yes. He arrived for an early morning meeting just after the student's body was found. He knew about Teffera and he started pulling strings before Justice turned up."

"Name of this good citizen?"

"Keilholtz. He's a personal assistant to one of the legislators—it's all in the file." Tillotson's way of saying "Get out there and get on with it."

"I have authority?"

"Yes. Justice is still on the scene. Kick them out, and be as rude as you like. Or maybe leave that until we have all their files. Take as many people as you think you need. I've sent out a priority for this to the whole department; if anyone doesn't cooperate with you, let me know. I want it dealt with and closed *quickly*."

Toreth left, grinning. A juicy case and a priority order on the resources to solve it. Chevril would be sick when he found out.

Back in his office, he drank cooling coffee and gave Sara an outline of the case, running through lists of things to do and people to get hold of. Then, leaving the arrangements in her capable hands, Toreth left to stake out territory.

In the car on the way over to the AERC Toreth considered the best approach to the problem of wresting his investigation from Justice. The student's death was the less important part of the case, except for any potential connection to Teffera, a question on which Toreth was keeping an open mind for now. However, it was the fresher crime scene—Teffera had been dead for a fortnight, and they would have to wade through the Justice investigation files before starting new inquiries.

Despite Tillotson's assurance, he half expected Justice to put up a fight. They wouldn't want to lose the case, especially not to I&I. Investigation and Interrogation had been two separate divisions within the Department of Justice before the great reorganization began. In the ensuing political turf war, they had been torn from their home and given to the newly created Int-Sec. The administrative problems caused by their separation from Justice were still a daily nuisance.

In the old days, the division which became I&I had worked on a broad range of crimes, from major fraud, to murder, to fomenting dissent, to active resistance to the authority of the Administration—anything, in fact, where the sentence might potentially be death or re-education. Now it concentrated on political or politically important crimes, leaving the more mundane investigations to the Department of Justice's civilian police. Inevitably, some cases fell into the no man's land between them. Toreth's new case, with one important death and one unimportant, and only a tenuous connection between them, was as halfway as could be imagined. Though loath to take Tillotson's advice on anything, a firm approach seemed most likely to succeed. Get his own people in and get rid of Justice quickly, before they put down roots.

When he reached the AERC, the half-dozen vehicles in dark blue Justice livery indicated the strength of the opposition. However, to his surprise, the first person he saw there was wearing the black I&I uniform. Harry Belqola, a recent acquisition for his investigation team, leaned against the wall in the hazy autumn sunlight, his eyes closed. Toreth approached silently, then coughed. Brown eyes opened wide in surprise, and the lean body jerked quickly upright.

"Keeping busy, Belqola?" Toreth asked.

The junior para-investigator's dark skin flushed a deeper shade. Looked good on him, although Toreth had a policy of not fucking inside his own team—the complications were usually tedious. "I didn't hear you arrive, Para," Belqola said, tugging his jacket straight.

"Obviously. What's going on?"

"Sara called me and told me about the new investigation in progress, so I came straight here."

Toreth calculated distances and times. "You weren't at work when she spoke to you."

"No. Sorry, Para."

Toreth smiled pleasantly. "Do you know how long a list of people I have applying for my team? I could find half a dozen new juniors—today, if I needed them. Maybe not with quite such impressive training grades, but I expect most of them could set an alarm." He waited to see if the man would produce some feeble excuse—or even a good excuse, neither of which would interest him.

Instead, he nodded and said, "Yes. I'm sorry, Para."

"Don't be sorry, be punctual. Why are you out here?"

"Justice wouldn't let me on the scene without a senior." Belqola waved to the assembled cars. "They look pretty well entrenched."

Toreth took a deep breath of the crisp air, enjoying the anticipation. "Do they indeed."

After a short but bracing discussion with the Justice guard on the main door, Toreth found reception crawling with Justice officers, most of whom looked as if

52

they had little to do. None of them challenged him, so he ignored them. Behind the reception desk, he noticed the same woman who'd been there for his last visit. She looked understandably unsettled by events, although when he strolled over, she collected herself. "Can I help you?"

"Very probably." He glanced at her nametag. Lillias Brinton. "My name is Senior Para-investigator Toreth, from the Investigation and Interrogation Division."

He paused, and a small frown creased her brows. Remembering Marcus Toth, no doubt. "You—" she began. Then the frown smoothed away to blank politeness. "Yes, sir?"

"We're taking over here. I'd like an announcement made throughout the building, please. By authority of the Investigation and Interrogation Division, all personnel are to stay in their offices until someone comes to speak to them. That shouldn't take more than an hour or two. More of my staff will be arriving soon— someone will look after reception while you're interviewed. Until then, ask any external callers to try again tomorrow."

She nodded. "Inspector Paris has already asked me to do those things for the Justice Department."

"Did he? Good." Pleasantly surprising competence on the part of Justice. "In that case, just stay where you are until someone takes a statement. Do you know where Paris is?"

"Right here." The voice from behind Toreth startled him, but he managed to turn slowly. One of the Justice officers in reception must have been on his comm. The man assessed Toreth with open dislike, pale blue eyes peering out of a heavily fleshed face. "Senior Para-investigator Toreth?"

"Yes."

Paris's eyes narrowed at Toreth's failure to add the "sir" the inspector rated, but with Tillotson's encouragement to be rude, he didn't see any percentage in diplomacy. "I understand that you've come to see if I&I have any interest in this case?" Paris asked.

"Then you understand wrongly. We have authority here. I'd like you to remove your staff from the building as soon as my team arrives."

"If you'd consider making it a joint investigation, my officers would be—"

"I have sufficient staff for the investigation, thank you." Through the glass of the main entrance, Toreth caught sight of two black I&I cars arriving. The first four out were all investigators on his personal team: Barret-Connor, Mistry, Wrenn, and Lambrick. Sara was on form. Turning, he waved Belqola over. "Para-investigator Belqola will liaise with you regarding the handover of documents and everything else you might have." That would make a suitable punishment for tardiness.

Toreth waited in reception until he saw the last of the Justice officers off the premises. His own small team was reinforced by temporary assignees from the I&I investigation pool, and he dispatched them through the building to guard the corpse and surroundings until the forensics specialists appeared, to patrol corridors, and to begin taking statements from the more junior staff. The important corporates he'd handle in person.

The Systems team also arrived to secure the SimTech security recordings and begin an assessment of what other computer systems they would need access to, though most of that would have to wait for warrants to overcome commercial confidentiality privileges. Brinton had already supplied him with a list of staff currently present in the building, along with times of arrival—a perk of a murder (potential murder, he reminded himself) committed in a secure access building. Exactly how secure was one of the questions he'd need to address soon.

Leaving Stephen Lambrick in reception to handle any new arrivals or unlikely rear-guard actions by Justice, Toreth headed for the lift. He noticed, as he hadn't on his previous visit, that the lift appeared to be the only way into the rest of the building, and that the recessed lift entrance was paneled in matte black plastic— detectors of some kind, or several kinds. He'd already sent his most senior investigator, Ainsley Barret-Connor, to speak to the head of corporate security as a priority.

Whom to speak to first, Warrick or Keilholtz? Did the head of a minor corporation rate a visit before the personal admin of a legislator? Too close to call, so he picked the nearest.

Keilholtz was waiting for him in a small office on the first floor. As Toreth entered, he stood up. Ten years' experience had taught Toreth that many people who saw an I&I uniform approaching under these circumstances appeared at least a little apprehensive. However hard the Administration pushed the line that the Investigation and Interrogation Division was a virtuous force for ensuring the safety of citizens against terrorists and other criminals, for those caught up in an investigation the second "I" tended to take on overwhelming significance.

Keilholtz looked positively delighted to see him. "Senior Para-investigator...?"

"Val Toreth. You're Clemens Keilholtz?"

The man nodded, and Toreth shook the offered hand. Keilholtz's grip was neutral, neither firm nor tentative, and his palm neither cool nor warm. It fitted the rest of him: smart but not expensive suit, neat hair in a hard-to-define medium brown, unremarkable face. He looked older than the thirty or so Toreth guessed him to be, but he would probably appear much the same in twenty years' time. A professional bureaucrat who would blend, chameleon-like, into any background.

Toreth tried not to hold it against him. "Thank you for calling us. Very public-spirited of you."

Keilholtz spread his hands, deflecting the dry compliment. "My primary motive was to act in the interests of the legislator."

Toreth sat and placed a small camera on the table—standard procedure for all interviews. He set it to record to his hand screen as well as transmit securely back to I&I, and checked the picture as Keilholtz sat opposite him. "And what is the legislator's interest in SimTech?"

"A professional one. The creation of virtual worlds also creates a requirement that new laws be drafted to regulate them. Legislator Nissim heads the Science and Technology Law Division."

"She doesn't like the sim?" Toreth asked.

"Ah, no. Far from it. She believes that this technology has great potential, both to provide something to prevent idle minds from entertaining unfortunate ideas, and to unite citizens across the regions of the Administration."

"People who'll be able to afford the sim can buy an air ticket. Or probably a private jet."

Keilholtz acknowledged the point with a polite smile. "In the short term, that is true, but Legislator Nissim prefers to take the long view. Eventually the sim will be affordable for all. A question of time, or so the legislator believes. You know what Dr. Johnson said about patrons."

Toreth didn't know, didn't much care, but felt obliged to ask. "Well?"

"Someone who watches a drowning man struggle, then burdens him with help when he reaches land."

A drowning—Toreth swallowed, a faint ringing in his ears. He mustn't start to think about it. "What's that supposed to mean?" he asked, his voice sounding harsh even to himself.

Keilholtz's eyebrow twitched at the tone, but he said, "That there's little point in taking a friendly interest in well-established technologies or large corporations. The legislator prefers to give whatever help she can to those who need it the most."

Whatever help she can. Such a powerful supporter at the European Legislature was...well, if not more than money could buy, then far more than a fledgling corporation could afford.

"Do you know the dead girl?"

Keilholtz shook his head. "To tell the truth, I don't even know her name, only that she was found dead in a sim couch. I've never visited the building before, so I know only the senior corporate figures here."

"Can I ask what today's meeting was about?"

"I, ah—" Keilholtz frowned. "I suppose that under the circumstances, the legislator would have no objection. I was supposed to have a demonstration of an upgraded version of the sim. The legislator has two units installed in her home."

Nice use of Administration resources. "Who did you speak to today?"

"The receptionist—I'm afraid I forget her name. I called the legislator immediately. Shortly afterwards, Justice kindly escorted me in here."

"You came to New London today?"

"Yes. I flew in first thing this morning." Keilholtz looked at his watch. "I had arranged for the demonstration, and after that I had a meeting with the directors. I was due to fly back to Strasbourg this afternoon. I imagine that my return will now be delayed?"

Toreth considered. Technically, he had every right to ask the man to stay in New London. On the other hand, inconveniencing the personal admins of legislators wasn't policy—Tillotson's or his. "I think you can go back. If we have any further questions, we'll contact you there."

On his way to see Warrick, he detoured to have a look at the corpse *in situ*. Toreth had vaguely wondered if he'd met the girl during his tour of the lab, but when he peered in through the doorway, he didn't recognize the body on the couch. A plain girl, thin, with artificially blonde hair. And, most noticeably of all, very dead.

It wasn't the room he'd used yesterday with Warrick; it was less cluttered and the sim setup itself appeared simpler. That could, of course, be his memory playing tricks. Over his career Toreth had learned not to rely on anyone's recollections, even his own; he had heard too many witnesses give honestly recounted but wildly inaccurate stories.

The newly arrived I&I forensics team was in the process of negotiating the handover from their Justice opposite numbers. The atmosphere was friendly enough. Slightly insulated from the interdepartmental politics, the specialty services tended towards better relationships than did the management. Technically, management included, at the bottom end, Toreth himself, although he would never have classified himself as such. He coughed to attract attention, then asked, "What's the story, ah—?"

The head of the Justice team stood up from beside the couch. "Muller, sir." Very polite, although addressing someone only a little over half his age as "sir" clearly hadn't improved his day.

"Call me Para. How, when—all the usual."

"Twenty-two hundred, give or take a little. How, you'll have to ask them." He gestured to the I&I team. "Although there are lots of things it wasn't. She hasn't been shot, stabbed, strangled, beaten to death, or poisoned with anything I can pick up here."

"Give me a guess."

The man looked pained. "I'm not psychic."

"Come on—you'll never have to see her again."

The man smiled wryly. "There is that, Para. If you insist—I'd say she stopped breathing. That's what it looks like to me. I know—that's only a symptom. But I'm not going as far as a cause; you know what's likely as well as I do."

Drugs of some kind, he meant. Had there been anyone else in the other couch when it had happened? Sim sex with extra spice? Toreth wondered, in passing, whether Kelly used the same body in the sim as he was looking at now. No reason not to try something a little more attractive in a fantasy world.

"Thanks." He turned to the leader of the I&I forensics team, hovering near the door. Backed up by Tillotson's priority order, Sara had found him the woman he'd wanted. Fifteen years older than Toreth, O'Reilly had worked with Toreth on his first case as a junior para-investigator and hers as a senior forensics specialist. That time, she'd stopped him from making at least three mistakes that would've fucked up the case beyond saving. A single brown curl peeked out from under the hood of her close-fitting protective suit, and Toreth reached out to tuck it away. She batted his hand away and smiled absently, as usual looking eager to get on with her job.

"Have everything you need, O'Reilly?" he asked.

She nodded, stepping back as the Justice team filed out. "Yes, Para. Luckily, there seems to have been minimal disturbance after the body was found."

"Great. Send the preliminary results along as soon as you can. Just the basics, before you start work on the fancy version."

Then, finally, on to Warrick.

Chapter Eight

❖

Outside the director's office he found an I&I security officer watching three admins, a middle-aged woman and two younger men. One of the men sat behind the largest desk, nearest the two doors at the back of the room, so Toreth addressed his question to him. "Is Dr. Warrick in his office?"

The man nodded and pointed to the right-hand door. "He left instructions that he wasn't to be disturbed." Clearly he didn't expect the request to be honored—he was simply carrying out his job.

Toreth nodded. "Don't bother calling through." He rather liked the idea of seeing Warrick's first, unprepared reaction to his arrival. Knocking on the door produced no response. Since the door was closed but not locked, he opened it and went in. The first thing he noticed was the surprising amount of mess in the large room. It was primarily composed of paper-copy files and printed journals, which had originally occupied the extensive shelving but had spilled over some time ago and were now arranged in piles around the room. In addition to that, pieces of hardware littered the place. Not how he'd imagined the territory of the man he'd met before.

Warrick sat at his desk, eyes fixed on a large screen. Two more screens kept it company on the wide desk. He didn't look up at the intrusion. "I said I didn't want to be disturbed until those idiots have finished—"

Toreth closed the door. "Good morning, Dr. Warrick."

Warrick's head snapped up, his eyes narrowing. Then he took in the uniform and made the connection. His expression smoothed into wary politeness. "Ah. An official visit. Part of the general disruption to the Center?"

"Yes."

"I thought I saw Justice Department uniforms in the building," Warrick said.

"You did. We're taking over their investigation."

"I see." Now Warrick's expression was as unreadable as it had been at any time during the game at dinner the night before. "May I ask what it's all about?"

"There's been a death here."

Warrick frowned. "Who?"

"I'm afraid I can't tell you that, not just yet." The frown deepened and he could see Warrick beginning to run through the list of people he had seen this morning, trying to work out who might be missing. Despite the lack of an invitation, Toreth shifted a pile of hardware components from a chair and sat down. "We have to speak to everyone individually," Toreth added.

"Before people start confusing each other with gossip. Of course." The explanation seemed to diminish Warrick's irritation slightly. "Hence why I was escorted straight to my office on arrival and politely ordered to stay inside."

"It's standard procedure for I&I and Justice," Toreth replied, using his best nothing-I-can-do voice.

"So I merit the attentions of a senior para-investigator? Am I a suspect?" Warrick sounded more intrigued than concerned.

"No, actually not."

"Oh?"

"You have a very good alibi."

Warrick raised an eyebrow. "I don't think anyone has even asked me for one."

"That's because the alibi is me. The girl died somewhere about ten o'clock, give or take a certain margin. That was about—"

"Coffee," Warrick finished for him. Actually, it hadn't been, but Toreth didn't feel like splitting hairs. Apart from anything else, the image of Warrick stripped and shivering wasn't conducive to professional concentration. For the first time, he noticed the faint bruises on Warrick's mouth.

"The girl?" Warrick added after a moment. Toreth shook his head slightly, which Warrick misinterpreted as a negative rather than an attempt to clear his mind. "Of course, you can't tell me."

Toreth weighed it up; he had to start somewhere. He set up the camera again, glancing at Warrick, who nodded, smiling slightly as he understood the implication. No mention of the night before.

"Her name was Kelly Jarvis," Toreth said, watching for the reaction.

"*Kelly?*"

Genuine-looking shock, Toreth thought, perhaps a little more than news of the death of an employee usually provoked. "Did you know her well?"

"Yes, I...she's...she's one of the students. University students. I—" Warrick wiped his palms together, repeating the gesture as he spoke. "No. Not very well, I suppose. God."

"When did you see her last?"

"I, er..." Warrick swallowed, pulled together a semblance of composure. "Yesterday evening. Just before I left, in fact, which was around seven p.m."

So much for "rushed over as soon as I could get away."

"I was due to review some of her work this morning," Warrick added.

Lucky early hit, Toreth thought. "Did she say or do anything unusual?"

"Nothing," Warrick said automatically, then, before Toreth could repeat the question, he held up his hand. "Sorry. Let me think about it." Toreth waited, content to give him the time. A helpful, cooperative witness was a rare enough find. "There was nothing that struck me at the time," Warrick said at length. A smile ghosted briefly across his face. "Although I must say that I was thinking about other things. She asked if we could postpone the meeting for a few days to give her a chance to do another experiment or two. I said yes."

"That was all?"

"Yes. No, wait. I offered her a lift home." Toreth raised an eyebrow and Warrick looked at him sharply. "When I said 'lift home,' that is precisely what I meant. A lift for her, to her home, where I would leave her. She lives off-campus, as you no doubt already know. Lived off-campus."

Address in the file, presumably, although Toreth couldn't recall it without checking. "Sorry. Why did you offer?"

"I was on my way out and I assumed she would be, too. I don't encourage the students to stay late."

"Why not?"

"I measure people's effectiveness by results, not hours worked—in my experience an expectation of long hours tends to encourage time wasting. Commercial security is another reason: predictable working patterns make it easier to spot aberrations. And the streets around the campus aren't the safest places for women—or anyone—to wander alone. Even the corporate-sponsored students at the AERC tend not to be able to afford accommodation in the more salubrious areas."

A comprehensive selection of reasons. Toreth made a mental note to return to the topic later. "Did she accept the lift?" he asked.

"No. She said . . . " He frowned. "She said she had something to do, but I don't remember what. Damn."

"Don't force it," Toreth said. "Can anyone else confirm the details of this conversation?"

The implication didn't produce even a flicker of emotion. "Probably not. Although I'd just left Marian's office. She may have heard us talking, but I doubt she would have been able to hear the exact words. Oh, yes, sorry. Dr. Marian Tanit—she's the senior psychologist here."

"And you didn't see or speak to Jarvis after that?"

"No." Warrick looked down at the desk, his palms stroking over each other again. Unconscious nervous habit, Toreth decided. "And won't, now."

"Do you have any idea why anyone would select Kelly particularly as a corporate target?" Toreth asked.

"Mm...no. I couldn't even venture a guess. Nothing she worked on was of great immediate commercial interest."

"I have to ask a standard question—nothing personal. Did you have any relationship with the victim, other than a professional one?"

"Meaning?"

He abandoned subtlety. "Have you ever had sex with her?"

Warrick frowned slightly—annoyance was Toreth's first guess, but then he realized it was a genuine effort to remember. "Not that I recall," Warrick said at length, "but I'd have to check the logs to be sure. If you mean outside the sim, the answer is definitely no."

The first sentence had riveted Toreth's attention to the extent that he barely heard the second. "The *logs?*"

Warrick smiled again, a fleeting glimpse of teeth before his expression sobered. "SimTech is a corporation, albeit a small one, but we aim to become a great deal larger and for that we need products—practical implementations of sim technology. Sex sells, Para-investigator. It is a historical truism that any technology that can be used for pornography or other applications in the sex industry will succeed."

"So what are the logs?"

"We test our hardware and software on as many volunteers as we can. Most of them are in-house, because of confidentiality issues. So it's possible that, during some test or piece of research, I might've had sex—in the sim—with Kelly. I don't think so, but I can't guarantee I would remember. However, everything is recorded, so it would be in the session logs."

"You get to fuck enough twenty-two-year-old students that you can't remember?" Toreth's professional control deserted him. "Jesus fucking Christ. Nice work if you can get it."

This time Warrick didn't smile. "It is not a free-for-all orgy. We're sensitive to the emotional dangers involved and the possibility of exploitation. All activities are covered by strict protocols and closely supervised. It is just a job, you might say." He tilted his head, eyes narrowing, making Toreth feel like a specimen under examination. "Tell me, Para-investigator, do you take pleasure in inflicting pain during interrogations?"

"I—" Toreth blinked. "Not in the way you mean, no. I like to do my work well, whatever it is."

"Mm." Warrick flexed his right shoulder, rubbing the wrist on the same arm, the implication clear: Last night you hurt me, and enjoyed it.

When the hell did Warrick start running the interview? Toreth thought with a touch of irritation. Still, better that than hiding behind corporate lawyers. He was all in favor of interviewees who were willing to talk enough rope to hang themselves. Toreth nodded. "Point taken."

61

"Is it?" Warrick shrugged. "Perhaps I forget how strange some aspects of SimTech must seem to outsiders. I apologize if I was a little sharp. I recommend talking to Dr. Tanit if you have any questions about the psychology of the situation here. That's her specialty."

Attack and retreat—the same game as last night. Toreth decided to change the subject. "You said you didn't encourage the students to stay late. What about other people?"

Warrick grimaced. "Ideally the same rule would apply. However, I long ago surrendered to the impossibility of imposing order on creativity. Besides, as I am among the worst offenders it would be hypocritical in the extreme. Provided that the work is done, employees have as much latitude as is practical in how and when."

"How much of the interior of the building is covered by cameras?" A question Barret-Connor would be discussing in detail with the head of security, but an idea would be helpful.

"Reception," Warrick said, and then stopped.

"And?"

"That's it. Reception. It's corporate policy. Elsewhere we have security logs which record entry and exit of people from secure areas and use of equipment, but no visual surveillance." Toreth couldn't keep the dismay from his face, and Warrick smiled slightly. "Unfortunate, from your point of view, I realize. However, security of that kind is a risk in itself—a greater risk than not having it, in our view. It's an easily transportable and saleable record of what goes on here, an open invitation to corporate espionage. We prefer to trust our staff, rather than spy on them."

Toreth would have preferred a little of the more normal corporate paranoia. He'd visited places that insisted on ID chip implants for their employees and monitored every inch of the buildings, right down to the toilets. "What about protecting the equipment?"

"Access to all areas of the building is controlled by security doors. ID cards are the baseline security. More authentication is required in some areas. All equipment is tagged—any attempt to take it out of the building will trigger the sensors you may have noticed on the way in."

Which meant no helpful footage of Kelly dying in the sim—or of any hypothetical murderer. "Kelly's body was found on a sim couch, with the straps and visor in place. No obvious cause of death."

Warrick looked at him for a moment, uncomprehending, before a flash of emotion passed across his face. Before Toreth could decipher it, a stony mask replaced it. "You think the sim killed her?" Warrick asked.

"It's a possibility."

"No, it isn't." If certainty were euros, Warrick could have underwritten the Central Bank with those three words.

"You might have wondered why I&I is here, investigating the death of a girl like Jarvis," Toreth said.

"Not worthy of your attention, you mean?" The corner of Warrick's mouth lifted. "The thought had occurred."

Toreth didn't miss the sour edge, but he ignored it. "We're here because of a possible connection to the death of Jon Teffera."

Warrick sat up. "Jon? What on earth does—ah." He leaned back slowly. "I see."

"Jon Teffera—"

"Also died in his sim couch. Yes. I heard the details. In fact, I attended his funeral, as a representative of SimTech and as a personal friend." Warrick leaned forwards, speaking slowly and clearly. "Para-investigator, the sim had nothing to do with either death."

Toreth looked at him curiously, trying to see even the faintest tinge of doubt on his face, and found nothing. "Thank you for your opinion," Toreth said. "However, I'm going to need access to data about the sim, to records of use by both Teffera and Jarvis. All the safety trials, and so on."

For a moment, he thought Warrick would repeat his denial of the possibility. In the end, he merely nodded. "Of course. Anything you require, naturally. If you want the very oldest pre-SimTech data, you'll have to apply to the appropriate Administration research division. However, you'll be wasting your time; you won't find anything."

"I'm afraid I'll have to look anyway. And I must ask you not to discuss the details of this conversation with anyone else, inside or outside SimTech, until the initial interviews are finished—particularly the circumstances of Jarvis's death."

Warrick nodded, although a wry smile suggested he had been thinking about that very thing. "You have my word."

"One more thing I'd like to know. Where were you on the evening of the twenty-seventh of September?"

"Let me check." Warrick consulted his screen, and then nodded. "At what time?"

"The whole evening, please."

"Very well. I left here around half past six and went home. Then about a quarter to eight—a little after, I think—I set off for Asher Linton's flat. I must've arrived about half an hour later. I used one of the SimTech cars, so the records will be able to give you the exact times. I had dinner with Asher and her husband, and I left about twelve. Lew was there, too—Lew Marcus."

Teffera had died at nine thirty, making a nice, tight alibi for all of the SimTech directors. It made him automatically suspicious, although senior corporates rarely did their own dirty work. Still, people planning a killing might prefer to have it occur when they themselves were definitely elsewhere. "Do you have dinner together often?"

"Yes. The last Friday of every month, at least, and twice or three times a month in addition to that isn't uncommon. We've managed to remain friends, despite working together."

"Do you remember anything unusual from the evening?"

"Nothing particularly." Warrick considered a moment. "We talked about the current refinancing, primarily. We're due for a new round of sponsorship talks. Routine." Warrick looked down at his hands, palms stroking meditatively across each other again. "Or it was then. With Jon's death, and now Kelly's, I suppose it will no longer be the case."

Toreth nodded. "If the sim turns out to be responsible for—"

"The sim didn't kill them." The confidence in his voice was still absolute.

"Then what did?"

"You're the para-investigator—you find out." Warrick smiled, perhaps an attempt to take the sharpness from the words. "And if you do, please let me know."

On that unpromising note, Toreth decided to leave it for the time being.

He found the second SimTech director also in his office, and in no better a mood than Warrick had been at his arrival. The first words he uttered were: "What the hell's going on?"

Toreth didn't reply at once, instead studying the man before him—older than Warrick, with short brown hair, thinning on top and receding at the temples. Thin, and, even when seated, obviously tall. He had a narrow, serious face, with deep-grooved lines and a beak of a nose that put Warrick's in the metaphorical shade. Probably literal, too, with sufficiently strong side lighting. Toreth kept up his scrutiny until the man looked briefly away. "Lucas Marcus?" Toreth asked.

He nodded. "Lew Marcus. You are?" The sneer in his voice matched the curl of his thin lips.

The attitude, unprofessionally, irritated Toreth. "Is that a registered name change?"

"It's a nickname. I don't like the one my parents saddled me with."

"Then we'll stick to a legal name, shall we?"

"If you like." While the exchange patently hadn't improved the man's temper, he did look at Toreth a little more carefully. "Sit down, please."

"My name is Para-investigator Toreth," he said as he took the indicated seat. Lower than the director's own chair, he noticed, and he marked the man down as someone who needed props to manage his interactions. "I'm investigating a death here at SimTech."

Marcus nodded. "Kelly Jarvis. Poor girl." He paused briefly, perhaps intending to convey distress, but actually making him look as if he were having trouble remembering who she was. "A loss to the corporation."

"How did you hear?"

"I found her." Still no emotion. "In a manner of speaking. I like to do a morning tour of the various sim rooms, to make sure that everything is in place and functional. A habit, although I have better things to do with my time these days. I opened the door and saw her on the couch. I assumed that she was using the sim, and I left again." He shook his head. "I even noticed that the sim was switched off—I thought she hadn't started yet. About half an hour later, around quarter to eight, I heard the fuss. One of the technicians had noticed she was dead. Anne Langford, I think."

"Wait—you saw Jarvis before anyone touched her?"

"Yes...I suppose so."

Another lucky break. "Was the mask in place? The straps?"

Marcus's eyes narrowed. "I think so. The visor certainly, or I would have known something was wrong. The straps I could miss, I suppose."

"What did you do when Langford found the body?"

"I went to see what the noise was about. The girl was clearly dead, so there seemed no point in calling an ambulance. I told everyone to clear out of the room and put a security guard on the door. Then I called Warrick and Linton."

A more typical corporate response. "Did you call Justice?"

Marcus shook his head.

"Do you know who did?" Toreth asked.

"No idea. Don't you know?"

The hint of contempt was back, and it made Toreth grit his teeth. "I'll have to check the records. Was it unusual for someone to be in the sim so early?"

"Not really. The sim is closed between midnight and six, except for emergency repairs. Then the next two hours are reserved for maintenance, systems testing, and psych evaluations. Official work bookings start at eight, but people try to squeeze in whenever they can. Between eight and ten in the evening is supposed to be for more maintenance and testing but, once again, it's usually overrun with people fitting in extra sessions."

"What time did you leave the building last night?"

Marcus frowned. "I'm not sure. It'll be on the security system, though."

"Give me a rough time and I'll confirm it."

"I, er—" Marcus stared past him. "It must have been...half past nine? Quarter to ten?"

"You tell me."

"I'm afraid I don't know. It must have been around then. I think I made it home around ten o'clock or quarter past, but I'm not sure about that either."

Toreth marked the point for later attention. "Did you have any relationship with Kelly Jarvis, beyond a professional one?"

65

Unlike Warrick, Marcus caught his meaning at once. "No, I did not," he said firmly.

"Not even in the sim?"

Marcus shook his head. "I work on hardware, not software, so I don't need to go into the sim very often."

"How about trials?"

The slight smile did nothing to soften his face. "I'm a married man, Para-investigator. I can assure you that my wife would have something to say about that."

"Was your wife at the Lintons' with you on the twenty-seventh of September?"

Marcus frowned, caught off guard by the change of track. "Was...no, she wasn't."

"Are you sure?"

"Yes. She rarely comes with me. It's shop talk, mostly, and the sim doesn't interest Lotte. Why the twenty-seventh?"

"That was the evening that Jon Teffera died."

"Jon Teffera?" For a moment, the name genuinely appeared to imply nothing to him, and then his face cleared. "Ah, that's why you're here, is it?" The knowing tone suggested that reality had resumed normal service. "I can't imagine the Investigation and Interrogation Division bestirring themselves for Kelly Jarvis."

Warrick had said more or less the same thing, but this time Toreth had to count to five before he could carry on calmly. "What time did you leave the Lintons'?"

"Ah—" He frowned again. "Let me see. I remember I arrived home at around midnight or...half past. No later than one, certainly. So I must have left the Lintons' about eleven thirty at the earliest. Somewhere around then."

Nothing interesting there, except that he was consistently bad with times. "Was there anything special about the couch Jarvis was found in?"

"No. Very unspecialized, in fact. That's the current prototype production model, the one used for the mandated safety trials."

That explained the relative simplicity of the design. "So, it would be very bad news if that particular version of the sim killed Jarvis?"

"Killed her?" Marcus stared at him, nonplussed. "Who says that it killed her?"

"It's one possibility."

"A rather remote one."

Not, interestingly, impossible. "Dr. Warrick said the same thing."

"And a lot more, I should think, if you suggested that to him. Good God." Now the possibility was sinking in. "But after Teffera...the sponsors won't like that at all. Corporate sabotage?"

"Another possibility."

"A damn sight more likely than the sim killing users, that's for sure." His confidence in that had firmed up.

"Did Jon Teffera own the same kind of sim that Kelly was found dead in?" Toreth asked.

"No. Teffera's sim was specially adapted for him; it's radically different to the basic design. He had serious spinal injuries—I assume you know about that?"

"Not in detail." Vague memories stirred. Toreth had absorbed the information at some point without consciously realizing it—he'd seen the man on some media broadcast, perhaps. An awareness of major corporate figures like Teffera was part of life. "Wasn't he partially paralyzed?"

"Quite seriously paralyzed. The adaptations were expensive and time consuming. Interesting, though—technically very challenging. Direct feeds into the brain mimicking lost nerve inputs, complete restructuring of the output analysis system and contact feedback." For the first time in the interview, Marcus became animated. "Ah, yes. It's a beautiful piece of equipment, if I do say so myself, although I don't know what we'll do with it when Justice finally returns it. A pity there aren't enough people in his condition with his kind of money to justify devoting more energy to it."

Back to money again. "Can you imagine any commercial reason for a corporation targeting Jarvis individually?"

"No. Although I don't have a clear idea of what the girl was working on. She was something molecular, wasn't she?" He shrugged. "To be honest, the commercial side isn't my strong suit. Warrick and Linton handle it. I have some knowledge, obviously, but my main role is staff management and technical expertise—the sim hardware and the biological interfacing, primarily."

"So you trust your fellow directors to have your best interests at heart?"

The answer came without hesitation. "Yes, I do. They are two of the most trustworthy people I have met in my life." Judging by the emphasis he put on it, two of the very few trustworthy people. "SimTech means a lot to me," Marcus continued. "I'm not going to pretend I have the same sort of—" He frowned, clearly looking for the right words. "I don't *believe* in it the way Warrick does, but it's as much my corporation as his or Linton's. And it's going to make me a rich man. I've always wanted to be rich."

"You think the sim will make money, then?"

Marcus smiled genuinely for the first time, a stretching of his thin lips that didn't reveal his teeth. "A great deal of money, Para-investigator. SimTech will be very big news indeed, I've always known that."

"You've worked at SimTech since the beginning?" Toreth asked.

"Since before that, as it were. I worked with Warrick at the Human Sciences Research Center."

"What was the original project?"

"It—" Marcus considered for a moment. "It was classified, medium security, but I suppose that doesn't apply here?" When Toreth nodded, he continued. "The

Department of Security funded the research group within the Neuroscience Section. The project was called 'Indirect Neural Remodeling'; the primary application Warrick and I worked on was the correction of neural defects by using stimuli sent through the patient's peripheral nervous system. It's probably easiest to think of it as very quick psychotherapy."

Toreth had a reasonable, if rather focused, understanding of psychology, particularly the practical applications. "Did it work?"

"Difficult question. The technology didn't do what the project wanted, no. Eventually the project was closed down after an unfavorable internal audit report." Marcus waved vaguely, the gesture suggesting unpleasantness beneath his notice. "There was a lot of internal politics after the big Department of Security reorganization—no one could agree who ought to pay for us. Or possibly someone in another department didn't like what we were doing. You know what it's like."

Fucking departmental politics everywhere. Toreth always enjoyed hearing that other people suffered, too. "So where did SimTech come in?" he asked.

"Although the INR was a failure, the technology wasn't. The brain is resistant to rapid, permanent change via peripheral nerve stimulation, but it's very interested in interpreting incoming signals. Warrick and I thought it had potential, far beyond the original project proposals. Or, to be honest, Warrick did. I was offered a reassignment, but he talked me out of taking it; he needed my expertise. We bought the intellectual property from the Administration and founded the corporation."

"Any trouble since? Corporate trouble?"

"Some. You'd be better off talking to the others for that." The suggestion seemed honest, rather than an attempt at evasion, so Toreth dropped it.

After taking Marcus on a second run though the events of the morning, Toreth moved on to the last of the SimTech directors.

This time the door was welcomingly open. When he knocked on the frame and entered, the woman behind the desk stood up to greet him. Around Toreth's own age, with short, neatly waved brown hair, she had a pleasant, if not especially attractive, face. There was a confidence in her movements and a sharp intelligence in her eyes, which belied the softness of her smile.

"You're the investigator in charge," she said.

"Senior Para-investigator Toreth." He offered his hand, watching her reaction to the title.

She seemed neither surprised nor disturbed. "My name is Asher Linton, as I'm sure you know."

"I understand that you're the director most concerned with the financial aspects of SimTech?" When she nodded, he said, "This will be a short initial inter-

68

view; a full set of financial disclosure warrants will be processed by tomorrow."

"Keir asked me to cooperate fully, in any case, without waiting for the warrants." He must have looked surprised at her use of the familiar name, because she offered him a seat and said, "I've been a friend of Keir Warrick's for a long time—since we were children. I met his sister Dillian at school; that's how I know him. Coffee?"

"Please." He watched as she made the coffee. Now that she was out from behind the desk, he had a chance to get a better look at her clothes: a smart jacket and trousers in lightweight beige wool, the flattering cut and natural fabric as unobtrusively expensive as any high-level corporate he'd ever visited. SimTech euros or independent wealth?

News of the death had obviously reached Linton already, and she'd clearly spoken to Warrick since his interview with Toreth. "Do you have any idea what happened to poor Kelly?" she said as she handed him his cup.

"We're investigating a number of possibilities." He took a sip of the coffee— decent coffee being a perk of corporate investigations—and said, "Do you have any comments you'd like to make about the circumstances under which she was found?"

She stared at him blankly, so Warrick had kept his word about not mentioning the details of the death scene. "She was found in the sim," he explained. "In the sim couch, rather."

Linton's reaction mirrored Warrick's. A pause while the significance registered, then quick calculation, ending up with dismay. "Like Teffera," she said, making it a statement, not a question.

"What's the financial significance?" Toreth asked immediately.

"We're in the process of gathering a new round of funding. Jon Teffera's death made many of the sponsors nervous. Not quite nervous enough to pull out, because Jon wasn't a well man and there isn't a shred of evidence to connect his death to the sim, but ... "

"What happens if the funding fails?"

"SimTech dies," she said simply.

If the sim hadn't killed Teffera and Jarvis, then here was as clear an impetus for corporate sabotage as he could wish for. "What happens to the rights to the sim technology?"

She frowned. "I'd have to check terms, but as far as I remember, they would revert to Administration ownership."

"Not to one of the sponsors?"

"No." Slight smile. "I'd hope we have better contract writers in the legal team than to do something like that."

That was a disappointment. Far better that the rights would go to a sponsor, giving him a solid primary corporate suspect. However, once they were back in Administration hands, a corporation with the right friends would have no trouble retrieving them. Justice might have been on the right track after all. "If corporate sabotage was involved, who would you suspect?"

"Me?" She frowned, and he waited for the usual hypocritical protests that she couldn't imagine any corporate she knew stooping to such appalling things. In the end, she surprised him. "There are various corporations. The first funding for SimTech was difficult to find, but when we released news of our initial successes with the technology, it became a quite different story. Competition to fund us was fierce, to put it mildly. There were a large number of disappointed corporations, any one of which could benefit from this. I'll arrange to have a list supplied to you. Do you want me to mark the most likely ones for you?"

He found the honesty pleasantly refreshing. "Please. And should you receive an approach from anyone offering to help solve your funding problems, especially if it's in return for concessions and decreased control..."

She smiled wryly. "I should shop our potential savior to I&I?"

He set his cup down. "I would consider it to be withholding evidence if you didn't," he said, letting just a touch of coolness into his voice.

"I see." When pressed, her mask was almost as good as Warrick's. "Of course I'll notify you of any such approach."

"Or any approach at all." He held her gaze until she nodded. "While we're on the subject, can you give me any reason why Kelly Jarvis would be chosen as a corporate target?"

Either she'd been thinking about it already, or the slight confrontation had disconcerted her, because she replied immediately, "None at all."

"Did you have any personal relationship with her?"

Linton shook her head. "I hardly knew her. To tell you the truth, I'm afraid that I had to look her up on the system before I could recall her face or project. I don't have much contact with the students."

"What's the difference between employees and students?"

Linton looked a little surprised. "All that information will be in the company files."

"Tell me anyway, if it's not too much trouble." Toreth kept his tone even and polite, because it wasn't necessary to put an edge on the question. His uniform did that for him.

She shrugged. "Of course. Employees are exactly that—direct employees of SimTech. Some university research groups occupy part of the AERC building. SimTech sponsors students—postgraduates—who work on the sim technology. Most of them subsequently join the company, but until they obtain their degrees they are registered as students at the university."

"Are there any practical differences?"

"Not a lot. Students have low clearance, and no access to sensitive areas outside their own research, but the same's true of many employees."

Toreth finished his coffee, and shook his head when Linton offered a refill. "I'd like you to tell me a little about SimTech," Toreth said. "An introduction to the company."

"Of course. We founded SimTech just over seven years ago, and we bought the rights to the technology from the Administration at the same time. I have a corporate background, and Warrick asked me to join to deal with the financial side of the business."

"Because you were a friend?"

"I should hope not." A touch of indignation, but at the same time she smiled, obviously confident in her abilities. "Warrick issued the invitation on merit, I assure you, Para-investigator. SimTech is always his highest priority."

A paragon of corporate virtue, in fact—something that Toreth was beginning to find annoying. "Why was SimTech established here?" he asked.

"We considered other sites across the Administration, but the university offered us a good deal—the building, and plenty of research money which came without conditions attached. That nursed us through the first lean years, so that when we sought our initial round of corporate sponsorship, we had a solid foundation of work to show them. Ultimately, the production facilities will be located elsewhere."

"How long before the sim units are commercially available?"

"Provided that we secure funding, and assuming all the tests and safety trials run to schedule, the first production run is due in three years. The cost will limit it to the rich and to commercial owners, but we expect a very healthy demand."

She clearly shared Marcus's confidence in the commercial prospects. From his own experience of the sim yesterday, he was willing to put more faith in that than most corporate pronouncements of future success.

"Who owns SimTech?" he asked.

"The directors. Warrick, Marcus, and I own around twenty-five percent each—eighty percent of the corporation between us. The university owns a further five percent, and the rest is split between various others. Mostly they're individuals who gave us money at critical early stages. Keir's sister Dillian, his mother, my parents, my husband Greg, a few other of the directors' friends. Jon Teffera was one—a personal investment, separate to his corporate interests."

"Does LiveCorp own shares?"

"No. We have an investment arrangement with one of its subsidiaries, P-Leisure. In return for development capital, they have exclusive options on certain aspects of sim technology, at preferential licensing rates."

"And are they happy with the deal?" Before the sim killed Jon Teffera, at least.

She shrugged, her expression neutral. "As far as they have ever told us."

They discussed a few more points and, as he'd expected, Linton confirmed

Warrick's story of a directors' dinner until twelve on the evening of Teffera's death. Finally, he asked, "Do you think it's possible that the sim killed the girl or Jon Teffera?"

After a moment's consideration, she said, "What does Warrick think?"

Warrick, not Marcus. "I asked for your opinion."

"I don't have one. The technology isn't my specialty. But I'd happily stake my reputation on whatever Warrick says. I have before, many times." A ringing endorsement of her fellow director, and a lot more positive than most corporate opinions Toreth had heard over his career.

Outside Linton's office, he found Jasleen Mistry, one of the junior investigators, sitting at Linton's admin's desk. She was reading a screen and replaiting her long black hair. When she heard Toreth close the office door behind him, she stood up at once. Mistry wouldn't be wasting time—if she was hanging around, it was because she had something important to tell him. "What is it?"

"We've found someone who saw Jarvis alive late last night, Para," she said, her fingers flicking through the last twists of the plait and snapping the band around the end. "Jin Li Yang."

At his nod, she set off along the corridor. "What is he?" Toreth asked as they walked.

"A software engineer. SimTech, not university."

"When did he see her?"

"Around nine fifteen. He was in the sim with her, running some kind of trial, and when he left the sim room she was alive and well."

"Or so he says."

"Of course, Para." She skipped to keep up with him and he slowed his pace a little.

"What's he like?"

"Frightened, but genuinely upset about the victim. The dead woman," she corrected herself immediately, and Toreth smiled.

"Up to talking to me?" he asked.

It was a serious question, and she took her time answering. "I think so, Para."

"Sit in, then."

Mistry took him down a level, and into a small conference room, where Yang was waiting for them. In here the décor was more gray than blue, reminding Toreth of I&I. Toreth introduced himself and sat down, deliberately relaxed and friendly. As they went through the introductions, he saw Mistry had, as usual, been dead on about the witness's state of mind. He was extremely nervous, which combined with his thin face to make him look even younger than he was—thirty-three, according to his security file. He had short, spiked hair and casual clothes, although he described his position as a senior level programmer, in charge of a team of ten.

"Did you know Kelly well?" Toreth asked as an icebreaker.

The man shook his head. "Not very. Only from trials. I've seen her in the cafeteria. We didn't work together." The phrases had a random, disconnected air.

"You were with her last night?"

"She was fine when I left her. She was absolutely fine." The statement wasn't an overt protestation of innocence—more an expression of disbelief that someone he'd seen alive only yesterday could suddenly be gone.

"Why were you there?" Toreth asked.

"For a trial. For her work, not mine. I'm on the volunteer list—the full list."

"Meaning?"

Yang stared at him, blinking rapidly.

"What's the full list?" Toreth asked patiently.

"Oh. There are—" He stopped. "I'm sorry. I'm not usually...it's shaken me up, that's all. It's—poor Kelly. She was *fine* when I left. Absolutely fine. I can't believe—"

"Take your time. Tell me about the lists." With any luck, talking about work would calm the man down a little.

"Didn't you speak to Dr. Warrick?"

"Yes. He didn't mention lists, but he said he wanted everyone to cooperate with the investigation."

That produced a slight relaxation. "Oh, right. Okay, full list. It means I'll do any kind of trial. There are different lists, depending on what kinds of trials people want to take part in. Whether you're prepared to participate in the sex-based research, basically. And what kinds of activities are acceptable, if you are."

A glance down showed a gold band on his wedding finger. Thinking of Marcus, Toreth asked, "Doesn't your wife mind?"

Yang almost smiled. "A bit, at first. But it's...well, it's completely voluntary, of course. No one has to do any trials at all. But you know how it is: people who volunteer are doing more for SimTech than people who don't. Anya wants me to do well here, for both of us."

Toreth nodded, knowing very well how that sort of thing worked. Employees always knew what was expected, what their superiors wanted to hear. All the sensitivity in the world to the possibility of exploitation couldn't stop those kinds of insidious pressures.

"When is the selection done?" Toreth asked.

"Oh, when the experiment is designed, normally. To give everyone a chance to arrange their schedules." He shrugged. "It's usually very tight, because everyone's so busy. The selection program picks a randomized pool of volunteers from the appropriate list, depending on the experiment."

Explaining a well-understood topic had had the desired effect, so Toreth decided to risk a more direct question. "How far ahead did you know you'd be there yesterday?"

"Only in the afternoon. A slot came free on the sim and Kelly—" He paused, blinking again, then pressed on determinedly. "Kelly was next on the list. She needed someone who could manage a two-hour time course. I think she tried a couple of people before she got to me."

"Are the sessions recorded? In—" It suddenly occurred to Toreth that he had no idea what a sim session would look like from outside the system. "I mean, is it possible to see what went on?"

Yang nodded. "Everything's recorded, at least short term. It can be, er...put back together to make a kind of recording, as if there was a camera in the sim room itself. The hypothetical observer viewpoint, it's called."

Toreth nodded at Mistry, and she made a note on her hand screen for the data retrieval team. "You said 'short term.'"

He nodded. "Until the raw data is analyzed—up to a few days, usually. The volumes involved are huge. After analysis, the data is summarized, and the important results are compressed."

"Now, did you notice anything unusual about Kelly's behavior yesterday?"

Yang stared down at his hands, fingers twisting together in his lap, and eventually shook his head. "No. If she was ill, I couldn't tell. She looked fine—in the real world, I mean. We arrived at the same time, and the session before overran by ten minutes, so we..." He shook his head again. "We stood outside and talked."

"About?"

Yang frowned. "I think...I think it was her report. Or was that what we talked about in the sim? She had a progress report coming up. She wanted to do a last experiment before it was due in, because she had the chance with the free sim slot. She'd okayed it with Dr. Warrick."

"Did anyone come into the room while you were in the sim?"

"Yes. Tara Scrivin, at least, quite early on. She's another graduate student— a friend of Kelly's."

Another nod to Mistry. "She came, er, into the sim?"

"No. But she spoke to Kelly over the link. She asked if Kelly wanted to go...oh, shopping, or something. Shopping for clothes, tomorrow lunchtime. Today lunchtime, I mean, of course. Sorry."

"No problem. Take your time. Did she say anything else?"

"Not that I heard. There could have been a private conversation, but I don't remember Kelly cutting out. Sorry, I mean, she didn't take her attention away from me to talk to someone I couldn't hear."

"Anyone else?"

"Not that spoke to us. But the rooms are secure access, so there should be a record of anyone who came in later."

"Thanks. How did Ms. Jarvis seem to you, during the time you were together?"

"She was...fine."

"There was nothing at all about her behavior in the sim that struck you as unusual?"

"No. She was fine. When I left her she was fine."

Toreth sighed and gave up. "Why did she stay on in the sim?"

"I don't know. It'll be on the booking system, though—everything's booked. I think it was personal time. All the trial volunteers have some; you can get up to an hour every six months, depending on how much you do. If you can find a free slot, of course."

"Can't carry it over?"

Yang shook his head. "Against the rules. Use it or lose it. Before and after official hours are about the only times you get a chance."

Toreth recalled the Justice forensic officer's suggestion. "Do you know if Ms. Jarvis ever took drugs when she used the sim for personal time?"

"Drugs? You mean, did she get sim sickness?"

The problem Warrick had mentioned yesterday. "No. Something recreational."

His eyes widened. "Oh, *no*. I shouldn't think so. That's completely against the rules. A serious disciplinary offense. Anyone caught doing it would be banned from the sim at once. I would've reported even a suspicion—anyone would."

Toreth shook his head slightly. What a place to work—fucking co-workers on billable time but getting bent out of shape over recreational pharmaceuticals.

Toreth left Mistry to finish the interview with Yang, in case her famed gentle touch might pull something useful out of him. He didn't hold out much hope, though. As a suspect, Yang was already eliminated; he'd left the building five minutes after the end of his sim session, while Jarvis was still forty minutes, give or take, away from death.

Outside the room, he looked at the list of names on his hand screen—long, and growing by the minute as his team picked out more key people to talk to. Already there were far too many to deal with personally today. He ran down the list, dividing up the names, until it became more manageable. He'd done the most immediate and important interviews; now he could return to I&I and begin on the no doubt monstrous piles of paperwork that would have arrived by now, if Belqola had done his job.

Chapter Nine

❖

Back at I&I, he decided to give Tillotson an update in person. The head of section liked to feel he was in touch with ongoing cases, even though (in Toreth's opinion) the only reason he'd been promoted so far was because he was an appalling investigator. He certainly wasn't para material—a widespread and persistent rumor circulated that he'd thrown up and fainted in the only high-level interrogation he'd ever witnessed.

When he reached Tillotson's office someone was already in there with him, so Toreth had to wait. Raised voices came indistinctly from Tillotson's office. He couldn't make out the words, but the meeting sounded heated. Someone who'd forgotten to complete his time sheet in ten-minute increments, no doubt. After a couple of minutes, curiosity piqued, he changed seats to one closer to the closed door. Tillotson's admin, Jenny, studiously ignored his eavesdropping.

From the little he could hear, it sounded as if Tillotson was getting the worst of it, for once. Unfortunately, before he'd had time to catch any detail, the voices died down to a low murmur of discussion. Toreth leaned on the arm of the chair, trying to hear, but got nothing. Go back to his office or wait? He pulled out his hand screen, deciding that he had enough work to occupy himself with here—it wouldn't hurt to look keen to talk to Tillotson.

Finally, twenty minutes later, the door opened. He leaned back in his seat quickly, staring at the ceiling, and then lowered his gaze to check out the exiting visitor. He needn't have bothered with the show of boredom, because the man didn't even glance at him.

For a moment, he thought it was Tillotson himself—the stranger shared his ginger hair and sharp features, although not quite Tillotson's infamous and apt resemblance to a weasel. However, he had a purposeful air quite at odds with Tillotson's habitual strategic defensiveness, and he was in his late twenties rather than early fifties. Surprisingly young, in fact, to have been giving Tillotson grief. If the man was an admin for an I&I higher-up, then Toreth didn't recognize him, and he had a good memory for faces. Could it be someone from Internal Investigations? If so, Toreth hoped fervently it had nothing to do with his new case.

"Senior Para Toreth?" The admin's voice cut the speculation short. "The head of section will see you now."

"What do you want?" Tillotson asked, before Toreth had even closed the door.

Toreth didn't bother to sit down. "To let you know I've been to SimTech and chased Justice off. It's all ours—they didn't put up much of a fight. And SimTech seems willing to cooperate."

Tillotson nodded sharply. "Good, good." He pursed his lips, staring past Toreth at the door.

"Sir?" Toreth prompted, after a moment.

"What?" Tillotson actually startled, his left hand jumping to grip the edge of the desk. "Ah. Is there anything else?"

"Not really. Just wanted to keep you informed."

"Thank you. Put it all in the IIP."

Toreth took the implicit dismissal and left without further comment. First time he could ever remember Tillotson not having *some* useless advice to give. In the outer office, he stopped to talk to Tillotson's admin. "Jenny, who was that in with Tillotson when I arrived?"

"No idea." She sounded rather put out. "He called the head of section directly and made his own appointment. I had to reschedule everything."

Toreth thanked her and left. Internal Investigations, he'd lay any money on it. In which case he could hardly blame Tillotson for getting sweaty over it. The appearance of the Int-Sec internal watchdogs—with their sweeping powers to question and punish, and famous incorruptibility—was about as welcome at I&I as the arrival of I&I was to citizens outside.

In his office, Asher Linton's list of potential threats to SimTech had already arrived, marked for his personal attention. His first thought was that despite her apparent cooperation, the speedy arrival meant it would be a whitewash. Far from it. SimTech had clearly prepared the file previously, for closely guarded internal consumption. Either Linton was clinically paranoid, or SimTech had more potential enemies than a corporation of its size had any right to possess. Every name had a detailed threat assessment, and Toreth suspected there was a wealth of supporting information he hadn't been sent. Even so, he paged through the document with growing dismay—the most cursory check into these names would require a fresh batch of investigators from the pool. A second file contained a similar evaluation on those corporations that had secured deals with SimTech and so were theoretically friends.

No way could his team handle this efficiently. A call to Chean in Corporate

Fraud and the collection of a favor owed secured him the loan of two finance specialists—Tillotson could sort out the official paperwork later.

Just as he'd finished a more detailed reading, Sara called through to say the specialists had arrived. When the door opened, he recognized Elizabeth Carey at once—tall, heavily built, and with an uncontrolled tangle of unnaturally vivid red hair—but not the slight, sallow young man lurking half-hidden behind her. He had white blond hair, his brows and lashes so pale as to be invisible. Toreth waved them in. "How're things going, Carey?"

"Great. Got something good for me?" Her voice had a rich, rough edge that Toreth had forgotten. Sexy, he'd always thought, although she was no beauty.

"You'll love it," he said.

She took a seat and then, without looking around, she snapped, "Don't hover, Phil. Sit!"

A dog-commanding tone of voice, and the pale shadow certainly jumped to obey. Toreth studied him with mild curiosity, wondering if he'd started out that nervous, or if it were due to Carey's soothing influence. Carey gestured in the man's general direction. "Phil Verstraeten."

Verstraeten bobbed his head at Toreth and mumbled, "Pleased to meet you."

"Just qualified," Carey continued. "I'm whipping him into shape."

Toreth raised an eyebrow. "Literally?"

Carey laughed. "They changed the rules since we were new graduates—can't even use shock sticks on 'em now. But he's good. *Very* good. To get the two of us, Chean must've owed you a chunk. So, what's the case?"

Toreth outlined what he knew so far. Not surprisingly, as a corporate finance specialist, Carey already knew about Teffera's death. "You think sabotage?" she said when he finished. She frowned, obviously doubtful. "LiveCorp plays clean—mostly, for a corporation its size—but hard. I wouldn't tangle with them. Phil?"

Visibly startled, Verstraeten glanced at his boss. "Clean but hard, yes," he muttered after a moment.

"I'm not sure what it is," Toreth said. He offered Carey his hand screen. "I've got a list of suspects for a death at a second corporation, and I want to know if any of them have reason to go after LiveCorp."

To his surprise, Carey glanced through the lists of SimTech's enemies and friends quickly, then handed the screen to Verstraeten and sat back, leaving him to study it. He took his time, the tip of his tongue peeping out from between his thin lips as he read. "Maybe," he said when he was done. He didn't look up from the screen. "Some LiveCorp rivals, but I don't remember any recent rumors of anything flaring up to killing levels. I'd need to check, though."

Carey nodded. "My first thought, too, but there's a lot to look at in there. If we need more help, which we will..."

"Open budget. Tillotson's authorized anything you need."

She grinned. "Now that's what I like to hear. We'll get right on to it." She stood up, and Verstraeten rose a lot more eagerly than he'd sat down.

When they had gone, Toreth returned to the main interest of the case. The first thing he read was the information on Jon Teffera. The security file took him an hour; the medical file took almost as long.

A skiing accident was responsible for his condition—the kind of injury of the rich and famous that always gave Toreth a glow of satisfaction. Damage to Teffera's spine and hemorrhaging in his brain had crippled his motor function and repair had proven beyond even the most cutting-edge nerve regeneration, grafting, and implants. After plowing through details of Teffera's subsequent medical treatment, Toreth hit the end point. After six years of near-continuous operations had restored only limited function, Teffera had rejected further attempts to improve his condition and settled down to live his life as best he could.

Despite his underlying conviction that most corporates deserved whatever they got, Toreth found it uncomfortable reading. After his taster in the sim, it was too easy to imagine himself in the same position, his body taken out of his control. The helplessness he'd felt in the sim kept returning as he read. Ironic that, to Teffera, the sim must have been a godsend.

Justice's information about the sim was scanty. Perhaps they hadn't tried, or perhaps corporate influence had defeated them. There was nothing at all noted about LiveCorp's connections to SimTech, or Teffera's personal interest in it. Of course, if Justice had been inclined to put the whole thing down to natural causes, it would explain the lapse in interest. Certainly the postmortem had nothing attention-grabbing about it. No sign of injury, toxin, or any other unnatural cause of death. The report was infuriatingly noncommittal, assigning the death to "respiratory failure," which didn't mean much at all.

When using the sim, Teffera took muscle relaxant drugs; these were mentioned as a possible contributing factor to his death. However, the suggestion was tentative and the old injuries were described as the probable ultimate cause of death. The body had been released back to the family—bad practice, even for Justice. He'd have to hope that Jarvis's corpse would prove more interesting.

Most irritatingly, although the man had enough personal medical monitoring equipment to equip a small hospital, most of it had been deactivated or removed from his body before he went into the sim, due to interference with the sim electronics. The sim itself had noticed his distress, and automatic alarms had called the resident medical staff. Efforts to revive Teffera were only abandoned six hours later, by which time his body was at an exclusive corporate hospital halfway across the city. Any amount of evidence could have been destroyed.

Justice had, Toreth noticed sourly, begun the investigation four whole days later. Pity no one had contacted them at once, as they had in the SimTech death. The thought reminded him of something, and he checked through the Justice files for the name of whoever at SimTech had felt suspicious enough of Jarvis's death to call Justice rather than a medic. A woman called Marian Tanit—the psychologist Warrick had mentioned in passing. He checked the interview lists, and sent Barret-Connor a note to ask Tanit about it when he saw her.

Toreth left I&I not long before nine o'clock. He'd sent Sara home a couple of hours earlier and he hadn't really intended to stay so late so early in the investigation. There would be plenty of opportunity for lost sleep later.

As he walked through the Int-Sec grounds, he considered the reasonably productive first day. The more he looked at the case, the more complicated he began to suspect it would be. The information from Justice alone—reluctantly delivered late in the afternoon—would take some untangling. Toreth had chased it up personally, after Belqola had proven unequal to the task, and the files were in the usual mess he'd learned to expect from Justice. The warrants to obtain disclosure of corporate information would hopefully arrive tomorrow, triggering another flood of files. He could only hope that Tillotson had meant what he said about freeing up as many resources as necessary.

Since Toreth was off-duty, he also considered Warrick. After the night before, he'd expected a different reaction from Warrick when he walked into his office. Toreth's extensive experience predicted defensiveness or embarrassment. He'd found neither—just calm intelligence, a touch of arrogance, and genuine distress at the news of the girl's death. That was telling in itself. Toreth had spoken to plenty of corporate types whose only interest in their employees was in terms of the bottom line. Of course, as corporations went, SimTech was barely a minnow, with more opportunity for the executives to know their junior staff.

Warrick had also been confident. Death had disrupted the high-tech haven, but it hadn't significantly shaken his faith in his employees, his technology, or his own abilities. Was he confident enough to be someone who thought he could get away with murder? Toreth decided on balance that he thought not. His instincts all said no, and on a more practical basis, Warrick seemed to have the most to lose from the killings. The commercial disclosure warrants would enable Toreth to be more certain about that.

In the meantime, with careful handling, Warrick could be useful—even necessary. If the sim was responsible for the deaths, Toreth didn't have complete confidence in the ability of the I&I computer experts to find the answer without full SimTech cooperation, to which Warrick was clearly key.

Chapter Ten

❖

The commercial disclosure warrants appeared early the next morning. Toreth took the time to check that they were all in order, because he hated the embarrassment of having warrants bounced by corporate lawyers because someone had misspelled a name. For once, he found no obvious errors. Time to begin arranging specialists for dispatch to SimTech to take the corporation apart for his entertainment and education. That part he would entrust to Sara.

On his way out to see her, Toreth paused with his office door open a little way, halted there by Belqola's voice, confidentially low. Sara's back was to the door, of course, but he could see Belqola's face in profile, and a glimpse beyond him of a figure with short blond hair—probably Barret-Connor. "I wondered if he'd said anything," Belqola said. "About my being late yesterday."

"Why on earth would he say anything to me?" Sara asked.

Toreth eased the door open another crack, because he suspected Belqola was about to make a serious tactical mistake vis-à-vis life on Toreth's team.

"Well—" The junior shrugged. "You two are . . . aren't you?"

"Are what?" Sara inquired in frosty tones.

"Together. Seeing each other?"

Her shoulders stiffened. B-C took a step back into plainer view, wincing in anticipation, and caught sight of Toreth. Toreth put his finger to his lips and B-C smiled.

Sara stood up. Twenty centimeters shorter than Belqola, she nevertheless managed to leave no doubt about who was intimidating whom. "Are you suggesting I'd be so unprofessional as to screw my boss?" she asked, dangerously quiet.

Toreth grinned. God, she had a lovely way of phrasing it. Yes or no were both disastrous, so Belqola won points for hitting on the only possible escape.

"I'm sorry, really, I am." Then he blew it. "You're always going out with him in the evening, that's all, so I assumed—"

"Assumed?" Heads were starting to come up around the office. Toreth noticed one or two people making comm calls, alerting absent friends to the show. "You just *assumed,* did you? Maybe I look like the type who has to screw around to get a decent posting?"

"Well, I asked a couple of—"

"So you've been gossiping about me as well?" Coming from Sara, the accusation would've left anyone who knew her helpless with laughter. Belqola, poor bastard, merely spent a while working on his fish-out-of-water impersonation. Sara left him to squirm until the moment he started to say something, then she said, "For your information, Junior Para-investigator, I have *never* slept with *anyone* I work for, and I never *will* sleep with anyone I work for. And *if* I did, you'd know without talking behind my back, because I'd resign the next day."

That was a lie, although Toreth wasn't sure if it was an intentional one. He and Sara had fucked, just once—five years previously and a couple of years after she'd begun working for him. It had happened at the end of a long and very drunken night, so drunken that Sara hadn't remembered anything in the morning, or at least had claimed not to. Between bruised pride and the worry that his indispensable admin might put in for a transfer, Toreth had never told her the truth. He'd always wondered, though, if she did remember. One day, he promised himself, he'd ask her. Just not today—he had far too much to do without Sara resigning on principle.

In the office, Sara was still in full flow, since Belqola kept trying to interrupt with what were either excuses or apologies. From past experience, Toreth knew that she could keep it up indefinitely, or at least until her victim surrendered unconditionally. Entertaining though it was, he did need to get on. He opened the door and coughed. Sara switched off in mid-rant, and turned to him at once, perfectly composed. "Yes, Toreth?"

"Specialists for SimTech—we've got all the warrants we need. Pick whoever you think is best, run the list past me if you have any questions." He looked over her shoulder. "Belqola, you're in charge of getting it all running smoothly over there."

"Yes, Para." Belqola took the offered escape with obvious gratitude.

When the junior was halfway across the office, Barret-Connor said in a low voice: "Do you want me to go along with him, Para?" To keep an eye on him, B-C meant. A surprising offer from the reticent junior investigator.

"No, thanks. You've got better things to do than hold his hand."

B-C took the hint. "And I'll go do them, Para."

When they were alone—not counting the rest of the attentive office—there was a long silence, with Sara trying and failing to suppress a grin. Finally, Toreth shook his head, keeping his voice serious. "Belqola is a junior para, you know. You should show some respect."

"Memo me," she said, unrepentant. "He deserved it. Oh, and I was about to call through to you when he slithered over. You've got an appointment this afternoon with the first corpse's brother and sister. At LiveCorp."

Good thing he'd put on a clean jacket this morning. Then something he hadn't done occurred to him. "Hell, I'll have to finish reading the LiveCorp files first. I thought they'd delay a day or two."

Sara shrugged. "They didn't sound eager—more like they were getting it over with. Oh, and they know all about Kelly Jarvis, don't ask me where from. Do you want to have coffee in your office, then?"

"Yes. And keep everyone you can away while I do my homework."

He had barely settled down with the mug and the Tefferas' personal files when the preliminary postmortem report for Kelly Jarvis arrived on his screen. Toreth read it through with growing dismay. On the plus side, it was the same cause of death as for Teffera. On the downside, it was no kind of cause of death at all.

O'Reilly answered the comm in her office, brown curls free of the protective cap.

"'Respiratory failure' is all you can tell me?" he asked.

"I'm afraid so, Para." At least the woman looked embarrassed. "We're still looking, of course, but at the moment all I can tell you is that she stopped breathing."

"No drugs at all?"

"Nothing yet, certainly nothing common or recreational. Something may show up on the detailed screens. And, of course, if it is corporate and if they put enough money into it, it could be something we won't pick up." She shrugged apologetically. "At least not without knowing what it is before we look, as it were. They know what we can screen for."

He cast around for something. "No sign at all of mechanical suffocation?"

On her face he caught a flicker of the same irritation he felt when Tillotson asked bloody stupid questions that were already answered in a file they'd both read. "Nothing, Para," she said. "I am sorry."

He nodded. "Well, let me know if you find anything else."

Half an hour later, Sara announced a call from the security systems specialist, too urgent to be delayed or a message taken. It proved to be the second piece of bad news about the case, and as disappointing as the autopsy. Toreth listened to the explanation all the way through and then started the futile search for a solution. "Aren't there any backups?"

"No, I'm sorry, Para. The fault was in the primary feed from the reception ID scanners. The backup system was recording nothing as well, from noon of the day the girl died."

"Didn't SimTech security notice?"

On the comm screen, the man shrugged. "Not that we've been able to establish. It's possible that the system didn't report an error, although it ought to have done."

"Deliberate? Wiped afterwards and made to look like a fault?"

"It's more than possible, Para. We're looking at it. The good news is that the rest of the building security is on separate systems, which includes the access records for the sim room. That seems to be all right, although we're going to go through it piece by piece to make sure."

"Good." Annoying news but not, on reflection, as bad as he'd thought at first. There were other, although more painstaking, ways of establishing who had been in the building, and proof of sabotage of that kind would be almost as good as a murder weapon.

Before he read the LiveCorp files, he set the I&I evidence analysis system to work on the witness statements taken at SimTech yesterday. It would cross-reference the statements to produce as definitive a list as possible of who had been in the building at the time of Jarvis's death. He called Mistry, who was back at SimTech for the morning, and told her to go through the list with any receptionists or security guards on duty at the appropriate times. Then, finally, he started on the files. To his amazement, he managed an uninterrupted run until he'd missed lunch. Then the comm chimed.

"Toreth? Sorry to interrupt." Sara, with her "there's a problem" voice.

"What?"

"There's a problem at SimTech. The new junior's been on the comm in a tizzy—not that that means much. But the technical people want to speak to you as well, so there probably is something going on."

The new junior. For no good reason Toreth could determine, Sara had never liked Belqola, even before his faux pas this morning, and her attitude manifested in a refusal to use his name. Toreth looked at his watch and sighed. "I'll go over on my way to LiveCorp."

They both turned towards Toreth as he opened the door. Warrick looked angry but under rigid self-control. Belqola looked frankly baffled by someone who simply refused to be intimidated by the I&I aura. "What's going on?" Toreth asked.

Instead of answering, Warrick walked away to his office window, leaving Belqola to explain. "The systems team say that he's refusing to hand the code over, Para," Belqola said.

If Warrick hadn't been present, Toreth would have asked why the hell the junior couldn't handle this on his own. "What do you mean, 'hand it over'? They don't need his permission—tell them to just take it."

Belqola glanced at Warrick, who didn't react. "According to the team, it's not that simple, Para. Apparently it's hidden somewhere, or protected—they can't get at it without his cooperation."

"Okay. Go and find the team leader and tell him to come up here and wait outside. When you've done that, check how the security team are getting on. They should've written a list of recommendations for places in the building to install I&I surveillance. Deal with that."

It was an excuse to take over handling Warrick, and Belqola clearly knew that it was. However, even though it was the second rescue of the day, he didn't make any kind of protest; he simply looked delighted to hand the difficulty over. It was enough to make Toreth wonder if the man had bought those impressive training grades.

Toreth joined Warrick by the window. "I have authority to demand the code. You've read the warrant; it's all in order. I don't want to start making threats, because we both know what I can do if I have to. Just do it."

"Not a chance." Despite his pale, set expression, Warrick didn't sound angry, only immovable. If Belqola had been hearing this all morning, Toreth could appreciate why he'd been so keen to leave. He spent a moment considering the most profitable approach.

"Why not?" he asked, eventually.

Warrick smiled his unfriendly half smile. "Do you know, I've been talking to your colleague for what seems like hours and he never once asked that?"

"Belqola doesn't care. Neither do I, actually, because you'll have to do it in the end, but I am curious."

Warrick turned away again and considered the question for a minute, looking out of the window at the gathering clouds. Then he sighed. "Sit down."

Not gracious, but Toreth accepted it as the concession it was. Warrick remained standing, pacing as he talked. "There are two reasons SimTech is still an independent enterprise. The first is that our sponsors know that ultimately they stand to make phenomenal amounts of money from the work we do here. We had sponsors cutting each other's throats—rumors suggest literally in one or two cases—to be the ones who gave us development capital. As a result, we were able to negotiate contracts which don't infringe on our control of the company." Warrick paused. "That is the first reason. The second is that I control the source code."

"Control it?"

"Physically control it. Only I have access to it. There is no way that another company can get at it, or force me to give it to them."

Warrick's corporate saintliness was getting harder to believe. "And the rest of the directors are happy with this?"

"It's in all our best interests to keep SimTech safe from corporate predation."

"And that's enough to keep it safe?"

"No." Warrick resumed his pacing. "It's part of a suite of measures to preserve our control. We use various techniques—short contracts, specialization, modular design—which make it difficult to hire the knowledge away from us. I designed the system architecture and wrote the core systems, and literally no one else knows precisely how they work. But it is the most basic and fundamental measure, yes."

"What happens if you're killed?"

Warrick smiled. "An excellent question. Briefly, I have a very long and detailed will, which is absolutely lawyer-proof. It releases all the sim technology into the public domain in the event of my death."

Toreth blinked. "What?"

"If I were to experience a corporate accident, then the company would be a far less valuable acquisition. I make it a policy to be worth more alive than dead. The release is automatic and time-controlled; there is no way of stopping it. The arrangement isn't widely known, but I've made sure that it's understood in the right places." Warrick leaned against the windowsill, folding his arms. "I'm sure you can appreciate that after going to all that trouble I cannot allow poorly paid 'experts' from your department to simply walk out of here with the heart of the company. The answer is no."

Toreth considered courses of action. He could force Warrick to cooperate and he could make that force as physical as necessary. However, permission to interrogate witnesses was difficult and tedious to obtain, and he was sure Warrick was more than capable of doing something dramatic to thwart the plan—destroying the code would be his guess. There had to be another way. Toreth spread his hands, smiled disarmingly. "Okay, say that I do appreciate it. Now, if you could consider my point of view for a minute. I have two bodies, and the sim might've killed them."

"No way in hell." The same unshakable confidence came without hesitation.

"If you want to prove that to me, I have to let the systems team see that code. That's the only way to clear the sim's reputation. So what do you suggest?"

Finally he caught Warrick off balance. "What?"

"There must be some kind of compromise. Tell me what it is and I'll discuss it with the systems team leader."

"Mm." Warrick nodded to the door. "You could ask him to come in."

Toreth had completely forgotten about Belqola's errand. A glance into the corridor revealed a patiently waiting man, slight and sandy-haired. As soon as he crossed the threshold, his face lit up. "Dr. Warrick?"

Warrick smiled politely. "Yes." This was obviously a regular occurrence.

"I'm Carl Knethen." Knethen brushed past Toreth and went to shake hands. "It's an honor to meet you. I'm terribly sorry about the circumstances. I've kept up to date with SimTech's progress—amazing stuff, really fascinating. I'm looking forward to seeing the system very much. We all are."

Warrick's smile turned sour and Toreth ground his teeth. This was exactly the reason that he normally went to great lengths to keep experts of any flavor away from the public. He coughed. "Excuse me?"

"I'm sorry?" Knethen turned, remembering Toreth's presence. "Oh, yes, of course. What did you want? Para," he added belatedly.

Toreth explained the situation to Knethen, who seemed remarkably sanguine considering that essentially Warrick had characterized his entire team as potential thieves. "I thought we had—" Knethen began.

"A warrant, yes. But forget that for the moment." Toreth turned back to Warrick. "So, tell me what will allow us to do this the easy way."

Warrick looked between them, then shrugged. "Very well. Firstly, none of the code leaves the building. It stays here, and your experts work on it here and nowhere else, in a secure room designated by us."

Knethen nodded. "Fine." He grinned. "The coffee'll be better, anyway."

Warrick didn't smile. "They take nothing out of here that isn't vetted by our systems security people. If anything capable of storing information leaves the room they work in, we see it first."

"No." Toreth didn't wait for Knethen's answer. "I can't expose I&I information to outsiders."

"Then don't have them bring any with them. Any special cases we can discuss later, but as a basic principle, I cannot let people walk out carrying anything that might contain this code. Not negotiable. No offense intended," he added to Knethen.

Knethen ignored the apology and stood, rubbing his chin, eyes downcast. "We can work with that," he said eventually. "If we have to."

"There must be no comms," Warrick said. "Personal or otherwise—I'll arrange an admin to handle messages."

Another glance at the systems specialist, and Toreth nodded.

Finally, Warrick smiled slightly. "Then, reserving the right to make minor modifications as necessary, I think I can see my way clear to allowing an inspection of the code."

Allowing—the arrogant fuck. Still, Toreth had to admit that the arrogance was justified in this case, since Warrick had just extracted major concessions from an I&I investigation. On the other hand, if it made Toreth's own life easier, why the hell should he care? Leaving the two of them to sort out the details, Toreth headed off for his next appointment.

LiveCorp occupied a classic corporate headquarters in the heart of the New London corporate district. Not a brand-new building, but all the more impressive for its air of old money. Toreth managed to be ten minutes early for his appointment, which he considered the perfect amount: early enough to look respectful, but not enough to seem pushy. While he waited, he watched the respectable corporates to-ing and fro-ing, and considered his approach.

Corporate sabotage was neither legal nor, always, subtle. Murders of high-level executives lay on the far end of a spectrum that began with disgruntled employees taking a few euros to steal information or delay a project. Relatively few corporations would take something as far as killing, because the unofficial corporate code dictated tit for tat action, attacks and responses carefully balanced. In Toreth's opinion, there were far too many game theorists in the corporate world. While he might hope that the surviving Tefferas would cooperate fully with the inquiry, it was more likely that they planned to deal with any threat to the corporation by themselves. If they'd wanted a serious investigation by outsiders, they would've pressed for an I&I involvement from the beginning.

Part of I&I's function was to enforce Administration law and (far more nebulously defined) Administration will over the corporations. At the same time, they were expected to ensure that the corporations, and most particularly the senior corporate figures, were allowed to go about their productive lives unmolested by resisters, criminals, or excessive corporate roughhousing. Defining "excessive" was one part of the problem. The customary flexibility in the law where the rich were concerned—labeled "corporate privilege" by resisters—was a murky area. Still, once corporate sabotage escalated to killing, the Administration preferred to step in and put a stop to it.

Except in the instances where they didn't. Generally, Toreth was adept at finding out which cases to pursue and which to close quietly, unsolved. Here there would doubtless be the usual mess of competing factors, and he'd have to poke around on the edges until he found a solid suspect, or until he received a clear cease and desist from higher up.

When his wait was up, an immaculate admin showed him into a lift, which rose so smoothly he couldn't feel the motion. The woman escorted him to a door which was flanked by a matched pair of two of the largest bodyguards Toreth had seen in his life. Unusually, they didn't seem to be simply for show—the inspection they gave the visitors was thoroughly professional, including a check on the ID of the admin accompanying him. They were also armed. Legal enough for corporate security, but the sight always irritated Toreth, because signing weapons out at I&I was such a tedious process.

The admin pushed open the door and waved him through. The room looked to be the antechamber to a main office beyond. Simple, pale colors were the current fashion in corporate design. This office, though obviously newly decorated, had dark, patterned wallpaper and carpets. An interesting statement for a company that pursued the cutting edge in entertainment technology. The beautiful furniture was also old, or rather antique—old was his own sofa at home.

A man and woman waited for him in chairs set around a small conference table. He recognized them from their security files and from their resemblance to one of his problematical corpses. Their files had given their ages as fifty-four for her and fifty-two for him, which made Jon Teffera the baby of the family at forty. Very young for a death in corporate circles, or at least for a natural death. Ordinarily, he would have spoken to them separately, but they had refused the suggestion. As Justice had already conducted all their interviews with brother and sister in the same room, he didn't see the point in antagonizing them over the question.

"Mr. Teffera, Ms. Teffera, my name is Senior Para-investigator Val Toreth."

The man nodded, and stood to shake Toreth's hand. "I'm Marc Teffera. This is my sister, Caprice. She is the official CEO of LiveCorp, as well as head of the legal department."

Toreth shook her hand, too, resisting the urge to make any comments about counting his fingers afterwards. "This is an informal interview."

The woman offered him a seat. "And we are here as Jon's relatives."

You're just choosing to do it here, where I won't forget what else you are. "Excellent. Well, I'll try not to take up too much of your valuable time, because I already have your previous interviews with Justice. First of all, then, is there anything you wish to add to your Justice statements, anything you've thought of since?"

"No," Caprice Teffera said with finality.

Toreth looked between them, meeting a united front of non-cooperation. "In that case," he said, "I have a few questions. One thing it didn't mention in the file was why you became interested in SimTech in the first place."

"I assume that you've seen Jon's medical file?" His nod seemed to annoy her. "Involvement in the sim was Jon's idea. It gave him back parts of his life he thought he had lost forever. However, he didn't spend corporate money recklessly; all the investments were reviewed by the finance division here and approved by the board."

Marc Teffera nodded. "Jon insisted on that. We—I, at least—would have been happy to support SimTech for personal reasons."

"So would I," Caprice agreed. "But it wasn't necessary. LiveCorp has interests in all areas of the leisure industry—it's the core of our business, the foundation on which our mother built the corporation. We have contracts with Administration leisure centers across Europe as well as extensive private sector business." And lots of powerful friends, she didn't need to add. "P-Leisure is our largest representative in the sexual leisure market." No flicker of emotion as she said it. "It's one of our most profitable subsidiaries, and SimTech is a natural partner for them."

The kind of person who'd say adult-themed entertainment when she meant porn. "You've been satisfied by the results?" Toreth asked.

"More than satisfied," Marc said without hesitation. "They have delivered ahead of schedule and fulfilled their side of the contract admirably."

"So you'll be reinvesting?"

Marc opened his mouth to reply, but his sister cut in. "That will depend, of course, on the formal financial assessment of P-Leisure's partnership with SimTech, which has yet to be completed."

"So there are problems?"

Caprice smiled coolly. "The question was already under routine review. With Jon's death we'll be reconsidering several of our associations."

Marc Teffera nodded, adding silent support to her statement.

Toreth decided to try something blunter. "And if the sim were proven to have killed him, then you'd pull out?"

"The situation is under review," she repeated.

"Do you think Jon's death was sabotage?" Toreth asked.

Now Caprice leaned across and, without making the least attempt to hide it, whispered something to her brother, who nodded. There was no point, Toreth knew, in asking what she'd said. "We are taking steps of our own to investigate that," Caprice said blandly.

Clean but hard, Liz Carey's junior had called them. "In any particular directions?"

"We're being guided by our security division." Caprice folded her hands on the table in front of her. "And, naturally, they will do all in their power that is both legal and proper."

Naturally. In fact, LiveCorp would already be devoting far more resources to discovering who might be behind Teffera's death than Tillotson would ever authorize. No doubt they'd take steps to deal with any culprits, too. Toreth closed his eyes briefly, opening them again before the vision of a spiraling corporate vendetta in the middle of his investigation became too disturbingly clear.

"Para-investigator," Marc said. "If I may ask something?"

"Of course."

"Do you have any evidence that this..." Marc glanced at his sister.

"Kelly Jarvis," Caprice supplied.

"Yes, of course. Do you have any evidence for a link between her death and Jon's?"

"We're investigating a number of possibilities."

He clearly took that as a negative. "But is there any reason to suspect her death was caused by the sim?"

The interest in Kelly was hardly surprising. The only real question was whether the Tefferas were more concerned about their brother's death, or the health of their investment in the sim. Caprice was watching him intently, waiting for his answer. He decided to try a direct approach. "Why do you want to know?"

Another whispered exchange, then Caprice said, "Internal security arrangements."

Of course—he'd missed the third possibility. "If any sabotage is aimed at SimTech rather than LiveCorp, you'll both be sleeping better than you have for the last few weeks?" She inclined her head. A likely enough reason. "There's no reason at all to blame the sim, as yet," Toreth said. "Beyond her body being discovered in the couch, with no other easily attributable cause of death."

"And do you expect to find anything more definitive?" Marc asked.

Let me check my crystal fucking ball. "I really couldn't say."

Caprice nodded, her expression closing again—obviously exactly the answer she'd expected, if maybe not what she'd hoped for. "If anything is resolved in that respect, we'd like to know at the earliest opportunity."

Toreth had an urge to ask why the hell she thought he ought to go out of his way to help them when they were doing their damndest to shut him out. "I'll keep you informed, of course. As far as is legal and proper." That drew a sharp glance from Caprice, and Toreth mentally put even money on getting a memo later from Tillotson about upsetting corporates. Fuck him. "Do you think that your brother's death was caused by the sim?" he asked.

"I'm a lawyer, not a doctor," she snapped. Then, as Marc Teffera shifted in his seat, her face softened very slightly. "I wouldn't blame the sim without some better evidence. We've known for years that there would be a limit to Jon's time with us. As I'm sure you read, he decided against further treatment, which was...perhaps not what the rest of the family wanted. But there was never any arguing with Jon when he made up his mind."

"He wanted quality, not quantity," Marc added. "In life and—" He tapped his fingers on the table. "In life and the corporation. And—"

He stopped, his voice hoarse, and Caprice reached over and laid her hand on his arm, squeezing gently. Unostentatious and, as far as Toreth could tell, perfectly sincere grief and sympathy. However, when she turned back to him, her expression was unreadable and her voice cool again. "Do you have any more questions, Para-investigator?"

Dismissed from the audience. "I'd like to speak to some of the LiveCorp staff, especially at P-Leisure," Toreth said. "Primarily the people who handled the contract with SimTech."

"Of course," Caprice said. "We'll help in any way we can."

The woman could give lessons in polite insincerity. He was wasting his time here, time he could have spent doing something more useful. Perhaps if he'd been here two weeks ago, he might've been able to pull something out, but they'd had too long to pick their positions and dig in to defend. To get anything now, he'd need the kind of damage waiver not normally available for people like the Tefferas.

Trying to hide his irritation, Toreth went through the ritual of goodbyes and

91

empty promises to call him if anything occurred, and went back to I&I. Maybe things would look brighter after the weekend.

Chapter Eleven

❖

Four days later, Toreth sat in the coffee room and pondered the unfairness of life. A juicy corporate sabotage case involving a major corporation would be a perfect addition to his case record. Right now, Warrick's protestations notwithstanding, he'd put his money on a malfunction of new technology and thus not I&I's concern. The investigation would be passed over to the Department of Financial and Corporate Affairs for an inquiry that would stretch out for months, even years; by the time they reached a conclusion, SimTech would be long bankrupt.

Toreth stared into his mug and sighed. The end of another long day spent wading through files—Justice files, corporate reports, medical reports, interviews from SimTech and LiveCorp, technical files—and for all the progress he'd made he might as well have stayed in bed. He'd found no clue as to who, how, or why. Normally Toreth preferred method over motive any day. Right now he would have accepted the slenderest hint of either with profound gratitude.

"It's unnatural, that's what it is," Toreth told his coffee.

Chevril looked up from his borrowed copy of the *JAPI*. "Must be something bloody odd if you think so." From his vantage point of long years of faithful marriage, he vocally disapproved of Toreth's lifestyle.

"No one can be as nice a guy as Jon Teffera and manage a successful corporation," Toreth elaborated. "It's not natural."

"Oh, right. Your case." He looked slightly relieved. "Figurehead?"

"Something like that." Toreth dipped a biscuit in his coffee and nibbled thoughtfully. "Except not quite. He didn't do the day-to-day stuff, but he was definitely involved. All the staff knew him, and they all, without exception, loved him. Not a bad word to say about the bastard. There's a brother and sister Teffera at LiveCorp, and they're harder, no doubt, but they're still nicer than your average corporates."

That didn't impress Chevril. "So are scorpions."

"Point. They liked him, though, and it seemed genuine enough. No rivalry

93

that I noticed, and the staff all said the same thing."

"Christ, you're right. It's not natural." Chevril laid the journal down on his knee. "Doesn't mean it's not corporate, mind."

"That's what the brother and sister think; they were fucking delighted to hear the sabotage might be aimed at SimTech. Right now they've got gun-toting security lurking everywhere in case they're next on the list. Mind you, if LiveCorp is the target then they're probably right to worry, because Jon Teffera's death isn't going to hurt LiveCorp that much." Toreth picked a bit of biscuit out from between his teeth while he thought about his interview with the Tefferas. "If it were me, I'd kill the sister. She's the smart one mummy made CEO."

"How'd he die?" Chevril asked after a moment.

"No fucking clue." He swallowed a mouthful of coffee, then shrugged. "Could even be natural causes. He had a medical file thick enough to beat him to death with."

Chevril eyed him, obviously perplexed. "So why the hell are you wasting your time with it?"

"I'm beginning to wonder the same thing." Toreth sighed. "I've spent five days digging for dirt on Teffera or LiveCorp, and I haven't got enough to fill a coffee mug. They're so clean there almost has to be something wrong somewhere."

"So what does that leave? Someone couldn't put up with his charming smile? Or how about an affair with someone's wife—that's usually a good one."

"Or husband," Toreth said, just to provoke the grimace of distaste from Chevril.

He duly obliged, nose wrinkling. "I suppose so. So was he?"

"Not in the real world. Paraplegic."

"Let me guess—not at all bitter about it?"

"You're getting the hang of it. You can add bravery and a helping of noble suffering to the all-round sugary niceness."

"I can feel my teeth rotting." Chevril stared at the ceiling as he considered. "Um, how about...good-looking nurse in the picture? He was about to marry her—okay, okay, or him—and disinherit the family?"

"No." Toreth gave the idea a moment's more consideration, then dismissed it. "And, you know, I don't think they'd mind if he did."

"Okay, I give up. So what have you got?"

"Fuck all. No, tell a lie; a ton of files and a fuckload of waspy little memos from Tillotson. Buzzing in every five minutes. I think he's got a nest of the fucking things in his office. Half of them are telling me to get a move on, half of them are telling me not to piss off any corporates while I'm doing it."

Chevril nodded, looking almost sympathetic. "I get Kel to deal with those."

"I told Sara this afternoon that if I see another one, I'm going to hard copy the lot, take them to Tillotson's office and ram them down whatever bodily orifice I find first."

Chevril snorted. "Let me know if you do, so I can sell tickets. What about your other corpse?"

Toreth had to think for a moment. "The girl from SimTech? No cause of death there, either. Could easily have nothing to do with Teffera."

Chevril nodded. "Right. LiveCorp's got to be the target, hasn't it? Killing Teffera would be a hell of way to get at a small corporation like SimTech."

Toreth thought the same thing, but habit made him argue Chevril's point. "It'll get the sponsors' attention, though. People like the Tefferas live with the threat of sabotage, but the key is risk versus reward. Right now, they can see either there's an active sabotage campaign in progress or the sim's a lousy fucking investment anyway because it's killing users. Either way, the Tefferas might not be the only ones deciding to play it safe by not reinvesting." Chevril nodded thoughtfully, and Toreth had to admit it didn't sound bad. Damn near convincing, in fact.

"At least the girl's fresh," Chevril said. "Fresher. I'd try her and see if you can get something from that. Actually, I'd kick the whole thing back to Justice and let them chase their tails over it." Chevril stood up. The journal slithered to the floor and he stooped to pick it up. "See you later," he said as he straightened. "Oh, listen to this first, though: my prisoner finally turned up. And guess what?"

"She's your long-lost sister?"

Chevril rolled his eyes. "No, of course not. After all that bloody fuss over the m-f, days of filling in forms and Tillotson sticking his pointy nose in, the silly bitch went and confessed, first session. I didn't even unwrap an injector. I could kill her."

Toreth grinned. "Is she annexed?"

"No, they want her alive for the trial." Chevril slapped his palm with the rolled-up *JAPI*. "I tell you, between the bloody prisoners and the bloody management, as soon as I find a decent job, I'm out of here."

As soon as he reached the office the next morning, Toreth read through the interviews with SimTech investors. Prior to Teffera's death, the sponsors and the personal friends of the directors all had sounded highly satisfied with the corporation's performance. Now, however, there was a sharp division.

The confidence of the personal friends in the corporation remained unshaken. The only sign of concern came from Warrick's sister Dillian, currently off-world on Mars. Judging by the transcript, she had spent most of the interview quizzing Barret-Connor about how serious the trouble at SimTech was, and whether her brother needed her to cut short her stay and catch a shuttle back immediately. Touching fraternal devotion, or whatever the hell the sisterly equivalent was.

Predictably, the corporates were showing less loyalty. There was a definite edge of wariness. Half of them had refused even an initial interview without sheaves of commercial confidentiality warrants. The rest had issued standard boilerplate stating that their relations with SimTech were commercially unexceptionable, and that they had no knowledge of the current situation that might be of the slightest interest to I&I. If Teffera's death was designed to make investors nervous, it was working.

Or perhaps the killer was selecting sim users genuinely at random, in which case the investigation was probably fucked from the start. Or the sim was killing users. Or one or both deaths were due to natural causes. Too many possibilities.

Much as it galled him to admit it, Chevril had been right. It had been a mistake to concentrate on the important name. Teffera's death had happened weeks ago and the sloppy Justice interview techniques had contaminated the witnesses. So now, hopefully not too late, it was time to look more closely at Kelly. For some reason, someone had singled her out to die. With luck, there would be a link, some evidence leading back to Teffera's killer.

Warrick seemed like a good place to start his new angle of inquiry. Toreth hadn't seen the director since the resolution of the code problem, or even had a message from him, which meant that the systems experts weren't making too much of a nuisance of themselves. This in turn probably meant they weren't getting anywhere. More bad news. He called SimTech and made an appointment to see Warrick. It wasn't strictly necessary, but it was tactful. Slightly to his surprise, Warrick's admin made the appointment without any fuss for eleven thirty.

Next Toreth pulled up the hypothetical observer record of the sim session and went through Kelly Jarvis's last hours in more detail. For fuck research, it was very dull. For two hours, Yang sat absolutely still at a table in a bare room that reminded Toreth of the interrogation rooms at I&I. Kelly sat opposite him, stroking the backs of his hands. Twenty strokes in each run, left and right mixed up at random, and then they would pause for five minutes, chatting about work, home and friends. Then Yang would draw his breath in sharply and tell Kelly the sequence of strokes. After another pause, they would repeat the process. It wouldn't make much money as commercial porn, or even adult-themed entertainment. Toreth skipped through the recording, watching the few sections marked for his attention, although they were nothing more exciting than office gossip.

Finally Yang vanished from the recording, and the room changed. Beautiful white sand stretched endlessly, sandwiched between tall palm trees fringing the beach and a glittering blue lagoon. Kelly's clothes transmuted into a skimpy bikini, which in Toreth's opinion rather unflatteringly emphasized her flat chest. She used the control panel to install a large beach towel and a low table with a selection of drinks. After a quick swim, she spent most of the rest of the hour building, with some assistance from an assortment of self-powering buckets and spades, a vast and impressive model of a castle in sand, complete with outer walls and a deep moat. Castle completed, she sat on the towel for a while, drinking the still cold-looking fruit juice and admiring her creation. Eventually she glanced at her watch, called up the control panel again and did something that was presumably the cause of the huge waves that, improbably, swelled up in the lagoon shortly afterwards. Toreth watched, a little uneasily, as they rolled fatly up the beach to break against the ramparts of the castle. A dozen or so and the castle was obliterated, the sand wiped clean as if it had never been. Kelly smiled, stood up, and the screen went blank.

Toreth sighed. He had a recording of the whole series of events leading up to Kelly's death, and there was nothing to find. Frustratingly, the death must have occurred almost immediately after the end of the recording, if the visor and restraints had never been removed. And, during those few seconds, the access system suggested that no one else could have entered the room. Despite Warrick's protestations to the contrary, it looked like a sim-generated accident rather than murder. The only evidence that argued against it was the fault in the reception area security system. However, technical specialists had refused to commit themselves to a conclusion of sabotage; the most they were willing to say was that it was possible.

Two deaths and a security failure couldn't be coincidental. Could they?

"Give me a moment, I'll just tidy up," Warrick said.

"Thanks for seeing me," Toreth said as Warrick attempted to clear space amidst the mess.

Warrick waved a folder, dismissing the thanks. "I left instructions that you were to be accommodated at any time. Annoying as it is to have every aspect of the corporation disrupted, I do realize that assisting you is in my—and all our—best interests."

"Thank you for your cooperation." Reflexive investigator response as he watched Warrick moving around the room. He'd forgotten over the last few days how attractive the man was. Not classically handsome, but compelling in a way Toreth couldn't define. Was it his confidence? Or maybe it was the contrast between his current self-assurance and the still vivid memory of Warrick asking—begging—to be fucked. How does it feel, Toreth wanted to ask, to look at me and remember how much you wanted it? Wanted someone you despise? However it felt, it apparently wasn't enough to ruffle Warrick's composure now. He appeared utterly at ease, secure in his kingdom. In control. Toreth never fucked suspects—not during the investigation, anyway—but the temptation tugged at him now, unexpectedly strong. Not lust so much as a desire to crack through Warrick's defenses. To see him for just a moment as he'd been in the room at the Renaissance Center. His cock certainly approved of the idea, waking and stretching.

"I'm not offering a general invitation, by the way," Warrick continued. "I don't want your less proficient subordinates eating up my time with inane questions." Pausing in his tidying, he gave Toreth a slight smile that didn't match his acid tone. "You, however, are always welcome."

He didn't give himself any more time to think about it, nor did he want to. As Warrick turned away again, Toreth took hold of him, pushing him back against the desk, stifling a surprised protest with a firm kiss. After a couple of minutes, Warrick pulled back, breathing raggedly. "Door. We should—the door. Lock it," he said, with flattering incoherence.

Toreth shook his head, not wanting to break the contact or give himself time to consider what he was doing. His hand slid between them, fumbling for fastenings. "We'll just have to be quick."

"I doubt—" Warrick's head went back and he gasped as Toreth's hand closed around his cock. "That's not going to be a problem," he finished in a rush, already reaching for Toreth in return.

It was fast, frantic and unexpectedly satisfying. Afterwards, as more calculating thought returned, Toreth watched Warrick wiping his fingers clean with a tissue and refastening his clothes, and wondered what the fuck he'd just done. It was one thing to fuck a witness—a witness who was technically also a suspect—before the investigation started. It was still against regulations not to have declared a personal involvement in the case. However, it wasn't a major disciplinary offense, so long as the investigation went well and Tillotson didn't have any other reasons to start hunting for ammunition. This was different. It was, in fact, insane. If Warrick gave any hint of the fuck to anyone . . .

Toreth was still trying to come up with a request for discretion without too much desperation in it, when Warrick spoke. "I take it," he said meditatively, "that lies somewhat outside standard interview techniques."

Toreth nodded, trying to keep his voice steady. "Somewhat."

"Then I shall be sure not to mention it to anybody." Warrick flashed a brilliant smile. "Although perhaps you should suggest it to your superiors. It certainly puts me in a very helpful mood."

"Thanks," Toreth said, covering both the offer and the compliment. That had been unexpectedly easy. He wondered where and when the payback would come.

Warrick moved around the desk and dropped rather heavily into his chair. "What did you want to ask me about?"

"What? Oh, yes." He took a seat opposite Warrick and set up the camera while he adjusted from pleasure back to business. "Whatever the dead girl was working on."

"Kelly," Warrick said, with a flicker of irritation.

"Yes, of course. Kelly. Tell me about her work." He knew a little about the technical bare bones of Kelly's research from the files, but it was always useful to hear what other people considered to be the important points.

If the sudden and somewhat belated interest surprised Warrick, he didn't show it. He paused, considering the admittedly broad request, then began. "Her research was funded largely by P-Leisure. They're a subsidiary of LiveCorp, as I expect you know."

Interesting that, from the sound of it, neither of the Tefferas had called Warrick to tell him about their interview with I&I. "Did she know Jon Teffera? Had she met him?"

"Kelly? I doubt it. Jon very rarely visited the building; as a courtesy we always went to him."

Toreth nodded. "The project—go on."

"As you might guess from the name, P-Leisure is largely concerned with the sexual leisure market. You may be familiar with some of their products." Warrick smiled, without looking at him. "So I'm sure you can see that the sim tech is something in which they're very interested. They're one of our largest sponsors, in fact, and they also fund several studentships. Kelly's project was originally titled, ah, 'Changes in Human Neural Cells Following Exposure to Sense-memory Stacking,' if I recall correctly. Unfortunate, really."

"Unfortunate?"

"Yes. There didn't seem to be any startling changes that she could find, compared to other types of sim experience. Unfortunate for her project, lucky for us. We're hoping to market SMS in due course, provided that we can eliminate all the safety concerns."

Safety concerns sounded interesting. "So what went wrong with the project? Why did the title change?"

"After the preliminary investigations showed essentially no effect, her university supervisor suggested a change of thesis title, and the sponsors agreed. The new one was 'Molecular Mechanisms of Memory Integration after SMS Experiences.' More scope for positive results. One of the staff scientists finished off the original project. Kelly was beginning to get some interesting data, although she'd only been on the new project for six months before she..." his voice trailed off and he made a helpless gesture. "Before she died."

Something nagged at Toreth's memory, then crystallized into a question. "Six months? There's a disciplinary note on her file from round then. What happened?"

"Ah, yes." Warrick sighed. "That was the other reason for the project change."

"Why didn't you mention it?"

"I didn't think it was important. And it seemed...inappropriate. The poor woman's dead, and it was all over and done with months ago."

"Warrick—" Toreth was about to launch into one of his practiced and mildly intimidating speeches regarding who decided what was and wasn't relevant, when something stopped him. Perhaps the oh-so-satisfying encounter on the desk only a few minutes ago, or the memory of the previous fucks. Or just the sound of his own voice saying Warrick's name—Toreth was fairly sure he'd said it earlier, too, as he came. He shook his head. This was getting ridiculous. "Just tell me. Anything might be relevant." Warrick didn't need to be intimidated; the point was valid, so Toreth guessed Warrick would accept it.

Which he promptly did. "Of course. My apologies. Kelly carried out the original project, along with a girl called Tara Scrivin. Kelly is—was—a neurobiologist. Tara is primarily a biochemist. A good combination for the research."

Tara Scrivin—the woman Yang claimed had spoken to Jarvis in the sim. "So what happened?"

"Tara became ill. Mentally ill. Dr. Tanit maintains it was an adverse reaction to the sim. Excessive immersion, as she styles it. She and I differ on the validity of her interpretation of the episode." Toreth knew enough to spot academic knives out when he saw them, and that Warrick's statement roughly translated to "I think she's talking shit."

"What's she like?"

"Dr. Tanit?" Warrick thought about the question for a few moments, longer than he'd had to think about other things. "She's highly professional."

Toreth smiled. "You don't like her?"

"We don't pay her to be likeable. We pay her to be an excellent psychologist, which she is." He smiled slightly. "However, as a matter of fact, I don't dislike her personally. We have some areas of disagreement, that's all."

Toreth thought back to his original question. "Why was Kelly disciplined?"

"Ah, yes. There are rules about sim access—how often and for how long people may use it, and so forth. Tara had legitimate reasons to use the sim for her work, but Kelly helped her to get extra time. Rather a lot of extra time." He hesitated, then continued. "There was an unofficial system in which people traded time, giving their allocation for one month to someone else in exchange for time at a later date, or for another favor. Senior staff, myself included, allowed the system to operate. It no longer does so."

"Because of Tara?"

"Because of the measures Dr. Tanit put into place with the directors' and sponsors' approval. I have to stress that there is no evidence that excessive sim use caused Tara's illness; the causation might just as easily flow in the other direction."

"What, exactly, happened?"

Clearly uncomfortable with the question, Warrick hesitated. "Perhaps it would be better to ask Dr. Tanit for the medical details. However, the practical consequences were that Tara was apprehended—fortunately—on the way to her ex-boyfriend's flat with a couple of large bottles of solvents, a box of matches, and a note explaining that they had decided to die together."

None of this had been in the personnel files Toreth had seen.

"The young man concerned very kindly agreed not to take the matter further," Warrick continued. "SimTech naturally paid for Tara's treatment, until she was fit to return to work."

"You let her come back?"

"Of course." Warrick sounded mildly offended. "Once her treatment was completed and Dr. Tanit was prepared to declare her fit, there was no reason not to. We arranged a more theoretical project—analysis and modeling—which doesn't require sim usage. We don't abandon our employees or students."

"A kinder, gentler corporation?" Toreth let the disbelief leak through into his voice, drawing a sharp look from Warrick.

"It's not our policy to throw fragile children onto the streets with a record which would render them virtually unemployable, no," he said precisely. "And she is a talented and hard-working scientist. The situation was unfortunate, and not her fault."

One word caught his attention. "Children?"

"Sorry. It's hard to think of her as a woman. Or rather... you haven't met Tara, have you? Someone once said to me that she made them think of fairy tales about changelings."

Toreth had never read any kids' stories, and had no intention of starting now. "What do you mean?"

"Well, she—when you meet her, you'll see what I mean." Warrick sat up suddenly. "You're going to ask her about this, aren't you?"

"Yes. She has a link to Kelly and possibly some reason to hold a grudge against her. She's tried to kill before—"

"That's ridiculous!"

"No, it isn't." Actually, it probably was. A desperate murder-and-suicide was a far cry from two carefully premeditated, passionless killings. However, Toreth was willing to follow any lead that offered itself. "It's my job."

Warrick looked at him expressionlessly, and then nodded. "Well, I can't stop you."

No, you can't, Toreth thought with an odd satisfaction, but there was no need to antagonize Warrick more than required. "I'll try not to frighten her. Tell me more about this... what did you call it? Her project."

"Sense-memory stacking? It's one of the fringe developments of the sex side of the sim program. P-Leisure has been very generous with funding for projects with a lower predicted success."

"So what's wrong with it?"

Warrick frowned. "Nothing. It's simply a highly technical application. It requires a greater degree of direct manipulation of the brain."

"Is it dangerous?"

"Not in my opinion. No more than any other part of the sim, which is to say that while it's in the development stage, rigorous safety precautions are perforce associated with it."

Sometimes Warrick sounded exactly like the corporate he was. "But you mentioned safety concerns?"

Warrick shook his head. "Nothing that could kill a user, if that's what you're thinking. Marian—Dr. Tanit—has raised concerns in the past regarding addictive properties, that's all."

"How does it work?"

"The SMS?" Warrick frowned again, thoughtful rather than annoyed this time. "I'll add an outline to the technical summary for you. But—" He checked the screen. "The problem is time and space on the sim . . . ah." He looked back with a hint of challenge in his voice and in his slight smile. "Perhaps it would be easier to show you than to explain. If you'd be willing to take part in a scheduled test, I could arrange a demonstration for the day after tomorrow—Friday afternoon."

Toreth weighed it up. He'd been in the sim before, of course, but that was before he knew about its tendency to produce dead bodies.

"I'll be in the sim with you," Warrick said. "I assure you that it's perfectly safe. No need to be afraid." Which I can see you are, he didn't need to add.

Toreth sighed silently. One day he was going to get himself into trouble. Maybe this was the day. "What time?" he asked.

Outside Tanit's office, Toreth read her statement through, and in the process found another reference to Tara Scrivin: she and Tanit alibied each other. On the day of Kelly Jarvis's murder, Dr. Tanit had left the building at seven forty, confirmed by both Tara Scrivin and the receptionist—a slightly later than average departure time, according to the security logs. She and Tara had gone to Tara's room on campus and Dr. Tanit had left there at ten thirty. Consequently, the interview with her had been brief, and information about Tanit in the case file was sketchy.

The main point in the interview was that Tanit had called Justice about Kelly's death. She'd told Barret-Connor she'd had no special reason for making the call; it had simply seemed like the right thing to do, which was no kind of reason at all. Apparently she hadn't felt the need to consult with the directors first. At the bottom of the interview Barret-Connor had added, "Don't let her ask you about your mother." Toreth had told B-C before that if he absolutely had to put jokes in case files, he could at least make them funny.

Finally the door to the office opened. He didn't know the woman who left—a SimTech employee, presumably—but the tall, spare woman who stayed in the doorway he recognized at once from her security file. She had light auburn hair, graying slightly, and pale blue eyes that now examined him thoroughly. He'd thought "arrogant" when he'd seen the picture, and he thought it again now as she studied him, taking her time, before she nodded him into the office. She took a seat behind her desk, sitting stiffly. The firm set of her mouth reminded him of War-rick—easy to imagine sparks flying between them.

"I understand you have some questions about one of SimTech's employees?" she said as he sat down.

"Yes. Or rather, students. I want to know the details of Tara Scrivin's illness: what caused it, exactly what happened, her treatment, her current mental state. I need a copy of her corporate medical file, and any additional information or opin-ions you have that would be relevant."

Tanit shook her head. "That is medically confidential information."

"We both know I can have a disclosure warrant issued right now, if I want it."

"Then get it." Tanit checked her screen. "You'll be glad to know that I have no more appointments today—I'm leaving an open door for anyone who wishes to discuss any personal difficulties, or concerns about the sim, following Kelly's death. Come back when you have the warrant. Otherwise, don't waste your time—or mine."

"Dr. Tanit, this isn't a game."

She stood up. "Patient confidentiality isn't a game, either, Para-investigator. I'm sure that you take your job seriously. Please do me the courtesy of believing I do the same."

Knowing a hopeless fight when he saw one, Toreth stood, too. "Can you at least tell me if we're going to get two sentences into the interview and come up against a commercial confidentiality problem I'll need another warrant for?"

Tanit smiled slightly. "There is nothing commercially sensitive regarding Tara's treatment. Unless, that is, you count her excessive immersion reaction."

"And do you?"

She spread her hands. "How can I, when my contract says otherwise?"

He decided to wait until later to find out what that meant.

Sara promised to get him the warrant within the next hour, a time lag that might have been designed to annoy. Too short to make a trip back to I&I worth-while, too long to wait and do nothing. There was no point in interviewing Tara until he had the information from Tanit. Toreth called I&I, asked Mistry to meet him at SimTech, and then filled the time by talking to the systems team.

He found them locked away in a stuffy room crammed with screens. A SimTech guard on the door politely requested that he surrender his hand screen and comm earpiece before entering, which grated even though Toreth had agreed to the conditions. The news from the team—that they had nothing yet to link the sim to the deaths, and no immediate prospect of progress—didn't improve his mood by the time the warrant arrived.

Tempted to walk straight into the psychologist's office, he opted for the politer route of knocking. No need to antagonize her unnecessarily. And, to be fair to her, with the warrant in order, she made no further protest.

The story she recounted was simply a more detailed version of the information obtained from Warrick and the released medical files, with the difference that Tanit placed the blame for the incident firmly on the sim.

As she spoke, he let his gaze take in her office—quite the opposite of Warrick's, with her desk clear and the few paper files neatly shelved. Personal touches, too, which had been missing from Warrick's office. Professional credentials on the wall, fresh flowers in an ugly vase that had the look of an impossible-to-refuse handmade gift. Probably a childhood present from her son or daughter. Their photographs sat on the table under the window—both now postgraduate students elsewhere in the Administration if he recalled Tanit's file accurately. It was unusual for a woman without a registered partner to be granted permission to conceive by the Department of Population. No doubt a psychologist would find it easier to pass the more stringent psych evaluation for solo applicants.

"Dr. Warrick mentioned that you thought the SMS might be addictive," Toreth said when she finished speaking.

"Indeed, although the SMS is only a more serious manifestation of a problem with the sim as a whole."

Finally, someone willing to admit the sim might be less than perfect. "Problem?"

"The sim is very..." her eyes narrowed. "Seductive might be a good general term, although too close a focus on the sexual element is counterproductive. It gives access to a world that can be absolutely controlled. Somewhere there is no danger, no risk, no chance of failure. All wishes can be gratified, without consequences. To vulnerable personality types it can be powerfully attractive."

Perfect place for a control freak like Warrick, too. "So what happened?"

"In her personal sim time, Tara created a room—her boyfriend's flat. It included a simple representation of the boyfriend himself, which required a restricted technology she shouldn't have had access to. With those, she played out certain fantasies: self-destructive impulses, and rage directed toward him. She obtained more sim time than she was entitled to, and eventually her understanding of the distinction between her experiences in the sim and the real world broke down. I've written an unpublished case study about it. 'Dissociative Disorder in a Young Woman Triggered by Immersion in an Artificial Reality.'"

"Unpublished? SimTech suppressed it?"

She shook her head. "Your word, not mine, Para-investigator. Its publication is not considered commercially appropriate."

"How would you characterize Tara's current mental state?"

"She responded well to treatment and I don't see any reason to expect a relapse now, although the stress placed upon her by current events is unfortunate. We've begun what you might call sim rehabituation sessions—supervised reintroduction to the sim. She requested it. She wants to resume her work. I may have to rethink it now, however."

"How did she feel about Kelly Jarvis?"

"She was devastated, of course."

"I meant before that. Did she blame Kelly for what happened six months ago?"

Tanit looked at him sharply. "If you are fishing for suspects, Para-investigator, then I won't supply them."

Toreth adjusted the camera slightly, a reminder of the official nature of the interview. "Answer the question, please."

"Very well." Tanit spoke directly to the camera. "Tara did not in any way blame Kelly for what happened. If anything, she blamed herself for persuading Kelly to help her obtain access to the sim and to the restricted code she used. Kelly was disciplined for her part in it and Tara felt guilty about that."

"Dr. Warrick mentioned that. And also that you suggested new measures to improve safety, which the sponsors approved."

"Indeed. They don't listen to my concerns very often—hardly ever, in fact. However, a psychotic episode finally caught their attention." She smiled sourly. "After I hammered the point home for some time. Perhaps they were worried about the mental health of their expensive investments. They twisted the directors' arms and persuaded them to make some concessions and give me more supervisory powers."

"What can you do?"

"I can interview any heavy sim user at any time, and suspend them from work in the sim if I find it appropriate. The standard interval is four weeks. I would have preferred to make it shorter, but the authority to insist on the sessions didn't come with a budget for the extra assistants required to make that possible. I interview and re-evaluate users of the off-site machines as well, at the same intervals. I try to speak to new recruits once every week at least, until I feel they are unlikely to be at risk. To compensate for this, the more experienced senior staff often slip to meetings every six weeks, or even longer."

"How often do you ban people?"

No hesitation in her reply. "Oh, there are usually two or three suspensions a month."

He blinked. "That many?"

"I prefer to operate on a precautionary basis. Most early signs of dependency or excessive immersion resolve spontaneously after a few days' or occasionally weeks' withdrawal from the sim. Easily manageable when I can control access to all the machines in the world."

Sparks flying from that grinding axe. "And is it enough? Could what happened to Tara happen again?"

"I freely admit the safeguards are adequate—if rigorously enforced—to prevent a repetition of the events." She smiled slightly. "Something I've learned here from working with programmers, Para-investigator—do you know why most estimates for project completion dates are underestimates?"

He considered. "Because people say what their bosses want to hear?"

That produced the first real smile of the interview. "Indeed. But apart from that excellent observation?"

The answer was obvious from the context. "Because only the time needed to solve the known problems can be included in the estimate. But there are always a host of unknown ones."

"Exactly. As with estimates, so with safety precautions." Tanit hesitated. "May I be present while you question Tara?"

"No." She nodded, clearly expecting the answer. The very fact that she accepted it without protest made him add, "I'll be as careful as I can."

"Thank you."

That over, he decided to pursue the question of the sim's safety with the one person who seemed willing to consider it. "What do you think of Dr. Warrick?"

Tanit hesitated—not as long as Warrick had, but long enough. "He's a very intelligent man, and he makes an excellent corporate. Many technical people don't."

"No flaws at all?"

Another silence before she replied, "If he has a flaw, I would say it was over-attachment to his own work. But that's a failing we all suffer from, to some degree."

"Do you think the sim is killing people?"

Tanit took a deep breath, held it, and let it out on a long sigh. "Do you know that there is a clause in our contracts with SimTech that prohibits us from discussing the sim, the principles behind it, the hardware, software, or, in fact, anything about it at all? Also from revealing, by direct description or implication or inference, the functionality of the technology or—" her voice slowed deliberately, "—any problems with it?"

Toreth nodded. Standard corporation contract terms.

Calling up something on her screen—presumably the contract—she turned the screen towards him. "The financial penalties are quite severe, and include unlimited liability for any damage to the corporation."

He didn't bother to read the screen, although it was interesting that she'd had it ready to hand. "That doesn't apply during an investigation."

Tanit turned the screen back towards her and leaned back in her chair. "I would be interested to see the legal basis for that statement, Para-investigator."

"I—" Toreth stopped. He'd said those words so many times with such confidence, but never in quite these circumstances. I&I cases didn't normally involve

106

questions of product safety. There had to be a legal instrument that put I&I over corporate contracts. Didn't there? He'd have to tell Sara to check it out.

Tanit continued, unsmiling. "So, you may find people unhelpful over that question."

"What do you think?"

"I think—" She glanced at the camera, but he didn't move to turn it off. "I think that, while we have made tremendous progress in understanding the functions of the brain and nervous system, there is still a great deal we don't know."

"You think it killed them?"

"I don't believe that all the safety aspects of the sim are being investigated as rigorously as they might be."

"But do you think it killed them?" Toreth repeated.

Her expression didn't flicker. "If that was your ultimate conclusion, it wouldn't surprise me."

Toreth shook his head. "They'll get you on inference, you know."

"Possibly." Tanit sighed again, and for a moment she looked older—tired and depressed.

If Toreth's job had that effect on him, he'd have started seriously scrutinizing the *JAPI* long ago. "Why are you still working here, if you think the thing's dangerous?"

That produced another hesitation, although a brief one. "Would it be good for SimTech if all its employees thought the sim was infallible?"

"I suppose not."

She shrugged. "I do what I can to promote the cause of safety. After all, it is in the long-term interests of the corporation for the sim to be safe. If it is to make a successful product."

"You think the sim will be successful?"

"Of course." She looked past him for a moment, as if contemplating the distant future. "It's a remarkable piece of technology, with a multitude of applications, and a multitude of corporations ready to exploit them. How could it not succeed?" Looking back at him, she smiled again. "Do you have any more questions?"

"No, not at the moment." Hands braced on the arms of the chair, Toreth paused and said, "Not going to ask me about my mother?"

Tanit looked at him blankly, and then laughed—honest amusement that almost startled him. "Ah, yes, of course. Your charming young investigator. He seemed to be expecting something appropriately psychological and I hated to disappoint him. Well?"

"Nothing to tell." Toreth stood up. "Haven't spoken to her for years."

Her thoughtful silence seemed to follow him out of the room.

Mistry met him outside Tanit's office and once more led the way to an office commandeered as an interview room. The camera was already in place, and Mistry left him there while she went to collect Tara. As soon as Tara entered the room, Toreth understood Warrick's reference to her as a child. She was tiny, less than one meter fifty tall, and lightly built. She had bright red hair, and pale, almost translucent skin, scattered with freckles. Overall, she looked incredibly delicate and oddly alien—there was something otherworldly about her.

And she was terrified.

Toreth saw a lot of frightened people in the course of his work, and he could judge the tenor of fear finely. His first assessment was that this wasn't guilt; she was simply afraid of him. It wasn't an uncommon reaction to the black uniform of I&I employees. Sometimes it was useful. Sometimes, like now, it was a major inconvenience. "Sit down, please," he said, putting as much reassurance into his voice as he could. "My name is Val Toreth and this is Jas Mistry."

"Tara," she whispered in response. "Tara Scrivin." After a moment she sat down, perching on the very edge of the chair, as though poised to flee.

"I know. And we have a few questions we'd like to ask you." Toreth found his voice slipping automatically into the mode he'd use for interrogating children. This is a smart adult, he reminded himself. Smart enough to win a prestigious studentship here, so treat her as such. "One of my officers already took your statement, but there are a few points we'd like to clarify. It won't take long."

The extra reassurance didn't seem to be helping. Then it hit him. She was almost certainly afraid he was going to do exactly what he was here to do—ask her about the breakdown. Something she had avoided completely in the interview he'd read. On balance, it would be better to go straight for it, rather than prolonging the anticipation.

"In your statement, you didn't mention your work with Kelly, or the reason you're having counseling from Dr. Tanit. Your previous illness."

Tara stared at him, her light brown eyes wide. "Who told you?"

Interesting question. "I've spoken to both Dr. Warrick and Dr. Tanit."

As he said the second name, she relaxed almost imperceptibly, shoulders loosening. "What do you want to know about it?"

Toreth waved Mistry forwards and took a seat further away from Tara. She watched him intently, openly relieved by the increase in distance between them.

Mistry sat down opposite Tara. "How long have you been back at work?"

"Two months, full time," Tara said after a moment, her voice back to a whisper. "I came in before for a day or two a week."

"And before that?"

"I was at home, with my parents. And before that . . . " Her gaze slid away. "I was in the hospital."

"How long were you there?"

"A month."

Mistry nodded. "Did you like it?"

Following the string of questions with known answers, all meant to soothe Tara with simple factual answers, Toreth thought it was a bloody odd question, and not one he would have asked. On the other hand, that was why he'd asked Mistry to do this interview, because Tara very nearly smiled. "Actually, yes. I know it probably sounds strange, but after the first few days, when I didn't really—" she waved vaguely, "didn't know quite what was going on—after that it was an okay place. Everyone was very kind. SimTech paid for it. There's a good corporate medical scheme, and it covers the students." She fell silent, but Mistry simply sat and waited. After a while, Tara nodded. "It was a good place. I had a lot of problems in my life. It could all... it could have ended very badly, but it didn't. It's in the past now."

She glanced at Toreth and then back to Mistry. "Before... I can't explain it. I can't even remember it that well, honestly. Everything was so mixed up, but very, very clear at the same time. I don't feel like that now. Ask Dr. Tanit, she'll tell you the same thing. I don't blame Kelly for anything that happened." Her voice strengthened. "And I wouldn't hurt her, or anyone else. That's what you want to know, isn't it?"

Mistry leaned forwards. "We just want to understand things a little bit better. How would you describe your relationship with Kelly?"

"We were friends. I used to share a flat with her."

"But not recently?"

"No." She edged back a little in the chair, sitting on her hands. "I live on campus now. Since I was ill. Dr. Tanit thought it would be better if we didn't see so much of each other."

"Did you mind?"

"Dr. Tanit thought it would be better," she repeated, as though that ought to be enough.

"And what did you think?"

"I'd—" She shrugged her narrow shoulders. "I liked living with Kelly, and she said it was okay for me to stay. But it was one of the conditions of keeping my studentship."

"What were the others?"

"Counseling with Dr. Tanit, changing the project, not going in the sim." Now her voice was almost normal—quiet, but calm. Either Mistry's magic touch, Toreth thought, or she wasn't hearing the questions she'd feared.

"So, did you mind having to leave Kelly's flat?" Mistry asked again.

"A bit. But—" She took a deep breath. "I'm grateful they let me stay. They didn't have to, and I wouldn't really have blamed them if they had kicked me out. I caused everyone a lot of trouble."

"What about the university?"

"Oh, them." She grimaced, freckled nose wrinkling. "They weren't so keen. But Dr. Warrick and Dr. Tanit talked to them and sorted it all out for me."

Toreth fought to keep the frown off his face. The amount of sheer bloody *niceness* in this case was beginning to piss him off. Maybe the resister-spread rumors were right after all, and the Administration was putting something in the water. In any case, there didn't seem to be much chance of finding an embittered homicidal maniac hiding under Tara's fragile exterior. Pity. Toreth coughed, and when Mistry looked around he said, "Before we finish, we might as well reconfirm her previous statement."

Mistry led Tara carefully through the day of Kelly's death, up to the time she entered the sim room at twenty past seven. No discrepancies with her previous statement caught Toreth's attention.

"What did you talk about with Kelly?" Mistry asked her.

"Nothing very...I think it was about shopping. The grants for the new quarter came through last week, you see. Then I went to Dr. Tanit's office and we went back to my room together."

"Why did Dr. Tanit go to your room?"

"We had a session booked for last thing in the afternoon, but she had to cancel it. I didn't want to miss the rehabituation session next morning, and we couldn't do it without the pre-session, so I asked her to come and have dinner at my room, and do it there instead. She said okay." Tara smiled. "She's always very kind to me."

Not surprising, Toreth thought, when Tara was Tanit's prize example of the danger of the sim.

"A shame you missed the sim, then," Mistry said.

"Oh, but we didn't. I mean, it was booked early. We were in the sim when..."

"When Kelly was found," Mistry said gently.

Tara nodded, hunching down in the seat. "It's horrible," she whispered. "We were in the sim and Kelly was only down the corridor. It's not fair."

It never is, Toreth thought. And it always amazed him how many people never came to terms with that. He examined his witness, tears beginning to sparkle in her eyes. Time to call a halt, since he'd promised both Tanit and Warrick that he'd be careful with the girl.

"Do you want me to stay?" Mistry asked when they were back outside.

"No. If you've got things to do, come back to I&I with me."

He'd thought about sending Mistry to have a crack at Dr. Tanit, and attempt to uncover more details of her worries about the sim. However, that would probably be a waste of everyone's time; outside an interrogation room Tanit would reveal no more or less than she wanted others to see.

They shared a car to I&I, but Toreth passed the journey staring moodily out of the window. The day at SimTech had provided an enjoyable fuck, but he'd come up depressingly short on useful new evidence or leads. He felt unpleasantly out of his depth with the case—technology wasn't his specialty, and he found himself wishing he'd never heard about the seminar at the university. Maybe he'd get a better feel for the sim from the SMS demonstration on Friday.

Chapter Twelve

❖

Toreth lay in absolute darkness. In fact, lay wasn't the right word—he simply existed. He could feel nothing, not even an awareness of being inside his body. He tried to blink, and didn't know if he had. He was a mind, adrift in an endless emptiness. Apart from his own thoughts, the only thing he was conscious of was Warrick's voice, giving a running commentary on the body Toreth couldn't feel. "God, you're hard," he murmured, from an unguessable distance.

"What the hell are you doing?" Toreth couldn't even feel his lips and tongue as he spoke. The words got out, though, because Warrick answered him.

"Right now? Fingerfucking you. The virtual you."

"I don't see what the point is if I can't *feel* anything."

"You will. Don't you trust me?"

"For some reason, yes, I seem to."

Warrick laughed.

"What's so funny?"

"You. Listening to you talk and watching you move. So disconnected." He laughed again, low and hungry. "Actually, it's not funny. It's the most incredible turn-on. You have a spectacular body, if you don't mind my saying so."

Not at all. "Then let me out and I can get on with something more enjoyable than sensory deprivation. Like fucking you through the mattress. If there is one," he added.

"Mm...tempting. And I can always call up a mattress. Not yet, though. You'll thank me afterwards." There was a pause, absolute isolation, before Warrick said, "Say something else."

"How long have I been here?"

"How long does it feel like?"

Toreth tried to think back, difficult as it was with no frame of reference other than Warrick's voice. "An hour?" he guessed. "Two?"

"A little over fifteen minutes."

"How much longer?"

"Until the protocol says we're done."

"Warrick, I'm supposed to be working."

"And so you are—as in fact am I. I'm running an SMS trial on a new volunteer. You're investigating the sim. Didn't you say your boss was convinced it was responsible for the deaths?"

"I don't think Tillotson will be impressed if I file an IIP saying I spent all afternoon here in the dark with your virtual fingers virtually up me."

The warm laugh again. "So ask me a question, Para-investigator."

Toreth sighed—or tried to. All interviews were supposed to be recorded, although the breach of protocol was hardly significant compared to rest of the experience. On the other hand, technically this was being recorded, so . . . "Dr. Tanit told me that you suppressed a paper about the dangers of SMS."

"The case study?" Warrick sounded surprised. "Suppressed isn't the word I would choose. Personally, I had no problems with submitting the paper for publication. However, it was commercially impossible—the paper revealed too much about the sim and broke a number of confidentiality agreements. We would have been sued from here to Mars and back. The sponsors concerned received copies, naturally, as part of the report into the, ah, incident."

Toreth considered the differences between Warrick's version and Tanit's. The point about sponsors receiving copies would be easy enough to check out, and so probably was true. "What did they think?" Toreth asked.

"That it was an unfortunate incident that didn't affect the commercial potential of the sim. Or, indeed, of SMS." Warrick paused, and then said, "You're about ready now, as this is a first run through the protocol."

Warrick fell silent and Toreth waited for whatever was about to happen. He tried counting seconds but the nothingness made it impossible. He searched for a contact with the sim reality somewhere out there, with Warrick, with himself, with—

Without any sense of change or transition, Toreth's body flamed back into life. At the same instant, the sensory awareness of twenty minutes of Warrick's careful handiwork exploded into his mind with perfect clarity. If he could have drawn breath, he would have screamed at the overwhelming intensity—he felt as though he had spent hours on the brink of coming. He held on to the sensation for seconds that seemed to stretch into forever, before it peaked into a blaze of ecstasy, which finally burned out back into darkness.

Toreth woke to the sound of gently lapping water. Woke, or came around, he wasn't quite sure. He felt gentle heat on his body from above, and a soft, ticklish touch beneath him. The scent of flowers and warm earth filled his nose as he

113

breathed in deep. He guessed at the water meadow and opened his eyes to discover he was right. Warrick lay on his back in the grass to his right, eyes closed against the sun. He spoke without moving. "So, what do you think?"

Toreth sighed. He felt too good to be bothered with this. His body still tingled with little aftershocks of sensation. "Can't we leave the postmortem 'til later?" Toreth asked. "You said it's all recorded anyway."

Warrick turned his head to look at him, shading his eyes with his hand. "Subjective accounts form a very important data set," he said in his lecture voice. "The sim is largely a subjective experience and that was, after all, an official trial. Debriefing is required in the protocol."

"And you get off on hearing about it, don't you?"

"Mm." Warrick smiled. "That would be extremely unprofessional." His much warmer tone of voice seemed to stroke over Toreth's nerves.

"Okay, I'll tell you." Toreth stretched, pressing his hands and heels down into the thick grass. First official interview he'd ever conducted lying stark naked in a field. "But first, you tell me how it works."

"Very well." Warrick sat up. "Simply put, there is a temporary disconnection between sensory input-stroke-processing and conscious awareness of the same."

The sun slipped briefly behind a cloud, and Toreth wondered if the jargon had scared it away. "Any chance of doing this in English?"

"Of course. In fact, I can do better than that." Warrick snapped his fingers, and the grass by his feet morphed into the control panel. He reached down and ran his hands over the screen. "Now," he said after a couple of minutes, "a simple example. Watch and feel."

Warrick licked his forefingers, and then ran them over both of Toreth's nipples at the same time. To Toreth's surprise, he felt only the contact on the left; on the right side of his chest he felt nothing, although the virtual flesh clearly responded to the touch.

"You didn't feel that, did you?" Warrick asked. "Except that you did. The sim fed the sensation into your nervous system, it traveled up into your brain, was processed there, and you now have the memory of being touched on that side. It's merely not consciously accessible to you yet. I said it was a simple example—actually, that was technically rather more sophisticated than the protocol we did before because of the hemispheric—" Warrick paused. "We were doing this in English, weren't we? Sorry. Anyway, to complete the demonstration..."

A touch of the controls, and memory returned. Toreth gasped. It wasn't that he felt the touch now—although he did—it was that he quite clearly remembered the simultaneous caresses, at the same time as he remembered looking down and feeling nothing. The disjunction between seeing two touches, feeling one, and then remembering two left him disoriented and struggling for words. "Fucking hell. That's ...Christ, that's—that's so fucking *weird.*"

114

Warrick grinned. "Isn't it just? Fascinating effect. Now you see why the sensory deprivation is required. It's a question of temporally intersecting memories. Watching the process creates a disharmonic memory that—"

Toreth tuned out, struck by a possibility that was so obvious and so commercially viable that he knew there had to be a reason why they hadn't done it. "Why do you have to bother fucking me?" he asked, interrupting Warrick in mid-flow. "Couldn't you just stick in the whole memory in one go?"

Warrick nodded. "Theoretically. The sim is potentially capable of that, given access to the right preparatory techniques and drugs, although it wouldn't be a trivial process. It would certainly require a great deal more training than SMS. However, artificial memory implantation is highly restricted technology. There are some strictly controlled therapeutic uses, and," his voice became sharper, more precise, "beyond that, you probably know more about other applications than I do. We are legally limited to real-time input and no historical modification. SMS slips through a loophole in that regard, because the memories are there all along, but hidden."

"I see." Shame. He'd rather fancied the idea of being able to hook up to a sim machine and download a memory of having had a fantastic fuck the night before. Of course, if he'd actually spent it finishing paperwork, and he remembered doing both at the same time...

"So?" Warrick asked.

Mind-fucking tricks. Toreth shook his head, dismissing the unsettling idea. "So what?"

"Tell me what you thought of the SMS," Warrick said.

"I've never felt anything even remotely like it."

"Good. Go on..."

When the session finished, Warrick insisted on walking him out of the AERC. It was a rather more pleasant journey to the exit than after their last sim session. At the exit, Warrick halted, uncharacteristically irresolute. Toreth waited for whatever it was—nothing to do with the case, he suspected. Sure enough, Warrick eventually said, "If you would be interested in any more sim sessions, I'm sure I would be able to accommodate you."

Toreth smiled, enjoying, as he always did, the feeling of being pursued. Of having the power to refuse. Enjoying it enough that, rather than responding with one of the more final retorts from his repertoire of rejections, he said, "I'll think about it."

That drew not a flicker of emotion in response. "Well, let me know."

Piqued by the lack of reaction, Toreth said, "Aren't we due a real-world fuck, in any case?"

That got a response, if only a small one, a catch in Warrick's breathing before he said carefully, "I suppose so, if you wish to keep score."

"No point playing if you don't. We could do a hotel again. Tomorrow night?"

"That would be delightful." Mask back in place again, which made shattering it with the next sentence that much more fun.

"Should I bring something this time? Cuffs from work?"

"Well, I—ah." Warrick licked his lips, and then grinned, suddenly abandoning all pretense of detachment. "Yes. I'd like that a great deal, I expect. Shall we say eight? The Anchorage is very nice, and quite out of the way."

When Toreth nodded, Warrick turned and left at once. Toreth watched him go, mildly irritated to find himself smiling. The man refused to react as Toreth expected, and that was perversely intriguing. No time to dwell on it; he had a meeting scheduled with Tillotson, which was more joy he didn't need.

As he waited for a taxi back to I&I, Toreth thought about the SMS. It certainly beat interviews and paperwork as a way to spend the afternoon. In fact, he had to concede it had been one of the best sexual experiences of his life. No wonder Warrick was keen to add it to the commercial version of the sim. On the other hand, he could now see where Marian Tanit's concerns about addictiveness came from. If he personally had free access to something like that, would he ever leave the house again? Forget that, would he even leave the sim long enough to eat? It took two people, though—at the moment—and presumably required a certain amount of expertise on the part of the . . . what would the word be? Dominant and submissive didn't seem to apply, although there was a certain passivity to the experience. In that way it had been, on reflection, a little unsatisfying. Perhaps it wouldn't be so very addictive, at that. For him, anyway.

Warrick had mentioned that they hoped eventually to have the sim take on the role of the active participant, although he'd been vague about the details. In any case, until then the SMS would require the services of professionals or well-practiced amateurs. It all created employment. If SMS was a taste of its potential, the sim would indeed make a very great deal of money, and that was nice because he always liked money as a motive. However, it led him no closer to finding the theoretical corporate sabs.

The taxi drew up, and he stood for a moment, hand on the door, trying to find some kind of bright side to look on. At least the dearth of live leads meant that he could take some time off over the weekend. It was Friday, and provided the interview with Tillotson didn't take too long, he might even be able to get away in reasonable time. Maybe he'd ask Sara if she had any plans for this evening that she couldn't cancel for beer and Thai.

116

Chapter Thirteen

❖

One year, just *one* year, Tillotson would approve his grade increase and bonus recommendations without quibbling. When it happened, the shock would probably kill both of them.

With so many other things he needed to do before he could leave, the meeting took forever, or felt as if it did. Toreth checked his watch surreptitiously. Fifteen minutes, and they'd only just made it through the part where Toreth agreed that, yes, he had significantly more recommendations than the section average, and then carefully explained to Tillotson, in small words, that this was because his team was significantly *better* than average. There was no arguing the section head's genius with budgeting, and from that point of view, they were lucky to have him. General Criminal didn't have the cachet of some of the other sections, and Int-Sec was always looking for somewhere to cut a little something. However, Tillotson still shared the normal management conviction that, where salaries were concerned, "average" meant "maximum" (and that when it came to results, "average" was "minimum").

Tillotson finally reached the end of a monologue. "Understand my position, if you can. I have to justify the overall budget." When Toreth shrugged but didn't comment, Tillotson frowned and scanned down the list on the screen. This was the point at which Tillotson traditionally tested his resolve by picking what looked like a weak case and demanding an on-the-spot defense. "Mistry. I'm sure she's a good enough investigator, but a promotion to level three and a third of the way up the pay scale? I don't see any outstanding cases credited to her."

"She's very sympathetic."

"Sympathetic?"

Look it up in the fucking dictionary. "Yes. She's good with people. Witnesses, particularly. People tell her things they didn't mean to, and it all adds up. If the witnesses don't talk to someone, we don't get any evidence, and then we don't close *any* cases. Unless you'd like me to run a lot more witness interrogations with damage waivers and all the rest of the trimmings."

Any chain of logic he could complete with a threat to spend more money was usually a winner. In this case, Tillotson sighed. "Oh, well. If you say so. Why is the jump on the scale necessary?"

"She's been approached by another section. Corporate Fraud. They're offering her level three, bottom of the scale, if she'll put in for a transfer. And a housing upgrade."

Tillotson frowned, tapping the edge of the desk. "Corporate Fraud, eh? Are you sure? How did you find out?"

"Mistry told me, Sara checked it out. It's a legit offer." All except the housing upgrade, which he'd made up, but odds were Tillotson wouldn't bother to verify the details.

"Hm. Why does she want to stay?"

Because I'm not quite as much of an arsehole as you and most of the others here. Toreth smiled. "She likes me."

"Oh." Tillotson looked back at the screen. "Maybe we should let her go. Then CF can pay for the psych discharge."

He laughed politely. With Toreth's reputation, most people would've come up with a different comment. However, Tillotson's mind didn't work like that. As far as Toreth could tell, it was mostly filled with numbers and division politics, with people existing only in relation to the wages they cost, the expenses they submitted, and the kudos they generated. Sex had no budgetary implications.

While he watched Tillotson studying the screen, Toreth wondered how section heads bred. Probably went down to Accounts and divided. He was still working through the filthier permutations of double entry bookkeeping when Tillotson looked up, apparently reaching a conclusion. "I can't justify a housing upgrade for a single employee."

"Then I'll have to try and sweet-talk her with the grade increase. Can I make it midpoint instead of a third?"

Tillotson hesitated, then shrugged and changed an entry on the screen. "If it's that or lose her to CF. Now, what about Parsons?"

Here he was on more solid ground, because there was a nice, numerical assessment to back this up. Tillotson must be desperate. He started with a feint. "He worked for me before I went to Mars, if you remember. I promised him a bonus if he'd wait in the pool until I came back."

"I am under no obligation to fulfill promises you made without—"

"And if you'll look at his interrogation record since I took him back on, you'll see he's more than earned it."

Tillotson studied the screen and frowned. "I suppose so." He paged through a few more screens. "Above average raises for Lambrick and Wrenn, too, I see." His lips pursed, then he shrugged. "The rest looks fine. I'll approve them and send them on."

Toreth blinked, caught off-guard by the sudden curtailment of their annual combat. "Right. Thanks."

"Just go away, and get on with finding out whatever's behind the mess at SimTech." Tillotson sat back, still frowning. "Is there any progress with that?"

Halfway out of his chair, Toreth sighed silently and sat down again. So much for a quick escape. "It's all in the IIPs."

"I'm catching it from all directions—Legislator Nissim called personally yesterday. Twice. And people are questioning the use of resources when we don't even have a definite crime—something I have wondered about myself. Do you think there's really an I&I case there?"

"I still think murder is the most likely possibility."

Tillotson's nose twitched at the disagreement. "Is there any actual evidence that it's not this 'sim' itself? Untested technology? That's not an I&I matter."

Why the hell did he bother filing IIPs at all? "There's the wiping of the security records at SimTech. Systems is eighty percent sure it was deliberate. There's no reason for that to have happened if a sim fault was to blame."

"Hmm." Another twitch. "I've had memos inquiring whether it wouldn't be better to take the case out of your hands."

From whom? Nissim? Departmental friends of the Tefferas? Suddenly cold, Toreth sat up straighter. "I beg your pardon, sir?"

Tillotson smiled sourly at the unusual politeness. "I told them you were my best senior, and you have the best—or at least the most expensive—team. So I suggest you get out there and start justifying *this*." He gestured irritably at the screen.

Toreth stood up, his stomach still fluttering from the shock. "Yes, sir."

"God, this place is disgusting!" Sara's voice came from the tiny kitchen of his flat. "There's stuff decomposing in the fridge that even the forensics lab wouldn't touch."

Toreth swept an assortment of clothes, weights and pizza boxes off the sofa, looked around, and dropped everything in a corner. "It's only six months since you cleaned it."

"You should let me do it again."

"I can't afford you. The night out after the last time cost enough to pay for a monthly cleaning service for the whole year."

Sara reappeared, with two newly washed glasses and a handful of beer bottles held expertly by the necks. "So get one," she said.

Old, comfortable argument. "I don't like having strangers messing round with my things."

"How the hell could you tell?" She put the beer down on the coffee table and frowned at the room. "I can't leave it like this."

"The food's getting cold."

"Five minutes."

Toreth sat down, opened a couple of bottles, then leaned back to watch Sara cleaning, or at least moving the mess around. It always mildly amused him, because her own flat was barely any tidier. The mess didn't matter anyway, since she was the only one who ever saw his flat. He never brought fucks here, and it wasn't as if the place was large enough to invite more than a couple of people around. In the living room, the sofa—scene of his and Sara's one and only fuck— and the coffee table were the only items of furniture that had survived the gradual encroachment of Toreth's collection of exercise equipment.

When Sara had satisfied her domestic urge, they sat together, ate take-away Thai and drank beer. Most of the meal passed in a thorough discussion of Tillotson's faults, personal and professional, which was always a reliable way to pass the odd hour or so. Meal over, they moved on to more enjoyable topics. Sara lay on the sofa with her head in his lap, looking up at him while he recounted his first visit to the sim with Warrick—edited to his advantage—and then on to his evening with Warrick at the Renaissance Center. Normally he'd have passed the news along over morning coffee, but coffee times had been short since the case started, and the encounters were too good to rush through. The cuffs and kink made it a bit different from his usual fuck stories, so he found he had an attentive audience. When he'd finished, Sara helped herself to another beer, and said, "Does Tillotson know you screwed him?"

"Fuck, no. I fudged his alibi to 'with a lover, confirmed by surveillance and interview.' Identity concealed on request, not relevant to the case, et cetera. I got a security recording of him going in and out of the RC, so I'm in the clear. Tillotson never wants to upset corporates, so he won't ask who it was."

She shook her head, which felt rather nice, but she didn't say any more about concealing personal involvement in cases. "Was he good, then?"

"Yeah, he was. Very—" He snapped his fingers, hunting for the word. "Responsive. Didn't hold back. Maybe it's to do with all that fuck research in the sim. He was worth making a bit of an effort for, anyway. And he'd never done that kind of thing before."

She raised her head for a mouthful of beer. "I didn't know *you* did that kind of thing."

"Sometimes." He shrugged. "Not very often."

"Can't find anyone to do it with?"

"No, that's not a problem. Good tops are hard to find."

She laughed at the immodesty. "And you're good, are you?"

"I've had compliments." He leered down at her. "Want to find out?"

It wasn't a serious question, and Sara didn't take it as one. "I don't do kinky. So why don't you do it more often?"

"Usually it's all too, I don't know...friendly. Organized. It's a whole social scene—bores the fuck out of me." He leaned back, resting his arms along the back of the sofa. "You meet people who know what they want; they've got a list as long as their arm. What they like, what they don't like. All discussed in advance. Takes all the fun out of it."

"And respectable corporate guy doesn't have a list?"

Toreth grinned. "Exactly. Doesn't even know he ought to have one. Not yet, anyway. He'll learn, I suppose."

"You're going to do it again, then?" She sounded mildly surprised, as well she might. Toreth had rather surprised himself at SimTech when he had arranged another real-world evening with Warrick.

"Yeah, I am."

"Not while the investigation's in progress, though?" Then her eyes narrowed. "You didn't screw him again *already*?"

"A couple of times." He finished the bottle. "And I'm seeing him tomorrow."

"Oh, Jesus. Tillotson'll blow a fuse if he finds *that* out."

"He won't. Warrick's not going to tell anyone." He tapped her on the nose with his beer bottle. "And it's not going to get onto the network, is it?"

Sara sighed, and made zipped lips gestures. "You know I wouldn't. I hope he's worth it, that's all." She sat up, burped loudly, and grinned. "Sorry. Chilies and beer."

He laughed. "It's a good job you don't want to fuck your boss, because that's not a turn-on." Toreth couldn't help deliberately testing her alleged memory lapse, trying to provoke a readable reaction, so he'd know without having to drag it into the open and risk her leaving his team. He'd tried it plenty of times over the years, often on this sofa, and he'd never got a rise out of her.

This time, her smile turned into a more thoughtful inspection, before she pointed her bottle at him. "You know, I never thought I'd see you of all people getting into an interrogator junkie."

"A what?" Toreth blinked, distracted from his fishing expedition. "No fucking way!"

"No?" She arched an eyebrow. "Screwing him with his arm up his back? Sounds like it to me."

"Bollocks does it." Taking the piss was one thing; this was something else. "Do I look that desperate for a fuck?"

"You should be careful with him, that's all." Toreth couldn't tell whether she was serious or not. "Next thing you know, respectable corporate guy'll turn up outside your flat with your name carved in his chest. Remember Helen the psycho stalker?"

"Oh, fuck, yes. Thanks for reminding me." Toreth opened a new beer and downed half of it, trying to wash away the faint embarrassment the memory always stirred up. It was a well-known rule at I&I that anyone who went through a genuine high-level interrogation and came out the other end wanting to fuck interrogators was guaranteed to be certifiably nuts. Of course, he'd insisted on learning that lesson the hard way.

"He's nothing at all like her," Toreth said. "Exactly the opposite, in fact. Doesn't even want to hear about it. He's..." Not a junkie. Not a typical submissive. Not anything Toreth could easily put his finger on, and all the more interesting for that.

His mind went back to the hotel room, to Warrick's shivering expectation and uncertainty, and then his wholehearted surrender. It made an intriguing contrast to the first dominating fuck in the sim, and to the untouchable confidence he'd shown during the interviews. Hard to believe that they were the same man. Toreth hadn't found the idea of a repeat fuck so appealing for a long time—if he ever had. Although, counting twice in the sim, he'd already had Warrick four times, which really ought to be enough for anyone. He shook his head, dismissing the idea. "Anyway, he doesn't know where I live, so don't worry about it." He leaned back and patted his thigh. "Come here, and let me tell you about this SMS sim thing."

Chapter Fourteen

❖

"Sara, could you come in here for a moment?"

"I'll just be a minute or two."

Toreth cut the connection and stared at the message on his screen. It said simply, "Lucas Marcus destroyed the security records." No name or address attached. Who had sent it? Warrick was his first suspect, although the tone of the note felt off for him. No guesswork required, no clever phrasing or possibility of misinterpretation.

Maybe Toreth's fantastic fucking technique on Saturday night had inspired Warrick to send the note later. Or maybe not. Had Warrick seemed any different on Saturday? Toreth leaned back, considering. It had been an interesting evening. Very interesting. Topping was more fun than he'd remembered. He'd planned for half an hour or so after dinner, and they'd taken nearer two.

Tell me what you want. An entertaining question to ask someone who had so much practice at analyzing his own sexual responses and who could produce clear, descriptive requests. Or at least had started off able to do so. Maybe that was why it had taken so long—pushing Warrick past that into shuddering incoherence had been the most enjoyable part of all. Kneeling, flushed and panting, cuffs pinning his arms. Everything distilled down into one desperate need.

Please. Fuck me.

Respectable corporate guy, indeed.

"Is this a private moment? I can come back later." Sara stood in the doorway, one eyebrow raised. Fuck. How long had she been there? "Did you want me?" she asked.

"Um, yeah." He sat up and cleared his throat. "Where the hell did this message come from?"

"I don't know. It was on the system when I got in. Arrived yesterday, but because it was Sunday nobody looked at it. It's as anonymous as it can be. The systems people say there's no chance of tracing it back to wherever it came from."

"Okay, thanks. That's it."

She grinned and left, closing the door pointedly.

Since the security specialists hadn't been able to find anything incriminating in the SimTech security system on their first pass, Toreth doubted whether having an anonymous note would chivvy them into an inspired discovery. However, with a suspect to concentrate on, there were other approaches. He pulled up the evidence analysis system's records for Marcus. Last positive sighting of him in the building was made by another engineer, who'd visited Marcus's office at eight thirty and spoken to him in person. A security guard by the name of Alicia Dean remembered Marcus leaving, but couldn't swear to a time. A look at the duty roster showed that she was off-duty, so he called her at home. It took a while before she appeared on the screen, puffy-eyed and wearing a dressing gown. After a brief introduction, he asked, "Do you remember what time Lew Marcus left the building?"

The woman frowned. "I'm not sure—on my shift, I think. Didn't I say that before? It was later on. I said goodbye to him, and he didn't answer, just waved. I'm pretty sure that was that night."

No point in pressing someone who was honestly doing her best to remember. Perhaps it would be enough to use against Marcus. Briefly, he considered bringing Marcus in to I&I, but the director wasn't the kind of man who would intimidate easily. Better to go around to SimTech and ask him there, where he might feel secure enough to be a little off his guard.

In Marcus's office, Toreth didn't take the low seat offered. Instead, once he'd set the camera up, he remained standing in front of the desk, forcing the man to look up at him. "What time did you leave SimTech on the night of Kelly Jarvis's death?" Toreth asked.

From Marcus's wariness, Toreth knew he'd found something. Marcus gazed around his office, as if seeking inspiration from the carefully shelved hardware. "I still don't remember, I'm afraid," he said eventually. "Didn't I give you a guess? Half past nine or later, I think."

"Well, do you remember noticing who was on duty in reception when you left? Because they remember you leaving."

Marcus licked his thin lips. "I, ah...no."

"Alicia Dean. I asked her what time you left."

"I—well, there you are, then." He was looking everywhere but at Toreth. Finally, he forced his gaze back. "Ah...what time was it?"

Toreth smiled. "I'm going to ask again if you remember. Before you answer, I'd like to remind you who you're talking to, and why. Impeding the conduct of an investigation is in itself a minimum category two offense—higher if the seriousness of the case merits it."

It was a reminder he'd often found useful, and it worked in this case. Marcus's eyes narrowed, resentment at the show of authority temporarily displacing his unease, and then he said, "Quarter to nine."

Setting the time back to an hour and a quarter before the murder—no good. "Try again," Toreth said coldly.

"It's true!" Open fear showed on his face now. "I'm telling the truth. It was eight forty-five. I looked at my watch as I was waiting for a taxi."

"And what time did you arrive home?"

"I don't—" He stopped, staring at the camera recording the interview, and Toreth watched as he ran through the lies, failing to find one that would stand up to pressure. Eventually, he looked down to where his hands were clasped together, resting on the edge of the desk. "It was about ten fifteen, just as I told you before. I honestly don't remember exactly, so it could be ten minutes either way."

Too early to have been here killing Kelly Jarvis ten or even twenty minutes earlier. "That's a long time to get a taxi from here."

"Yes. I saw someone else on the way."

Toreth's heart sank—a month's salary said it was a lover. "You'll have to do better than that. I need a name."

Marcus shifted his gaze up, looking past Toreth. "I was with a girl. A woman."

"A regular thing?" Who would hence make a bad alibi, and keep this lead alive.

Marcus shook his head, still not looking at him. "A prostitute."

Which made her an alibi with no interest in covering up for Marcus. "Was she registered?"

"I didn't—I don't remember."

"In other words, you didn't ask." Since money wasn't likely to be a concern, he considered briefly and picked a likely kink. "How old was she?"

From the flash of panic, he knew he was right. Marcus took a deep breath and said, "S—eighteen. She had ID."

"Of course she did. You checked her ID, but not her registration." He took a small step sideways, forcing Marcus to meet his gaze. "Listen. I don't care who you fucked. I don't care if she isn't registered. I don't care which side of legal she is. I do care that you're making my life difficult. Give me a name—if you can't give me a name, give me a place, a time, and a description of whoever the hell you bought her from. Then I can check it out and just maybe I won't have to go and explain all this to your wife."

Marcus actually flinched at the threat. "Jana. That's all I know. The place is registered. They . . . they'll remember me. They know me there. I'll give you the address, but—"

"Yes?"

"There's something else." He leaned his elbows on the table and rubbed his eyes with the heels of his hands. "Oh, God. All right." He looked up. "I was the one who trashed the security records."

"I know," Toreth said, enjoying the dismay on Marcus's face. "I'm afraid it's too late in the day for honesty to help."

"But I have the backup!"

Toreth blinked. "What?"

"I kept the backup." Color flushed into his pale cheeks. "It's not been tampered with—your security people will be able to tell you that. I wasn't here when Kelly died."

The idea of Marcus keeping a copy of the records seemed improbable, to put it mildly, or at least it did if Marcus had wiped the surveillance to cover up the murder. But if he hadn't committed the murder, it was simply more evidence that the director's story was, infuriatingly, true. "Fine," Toreth said. "The system specialists will take it."

He nodded. "What will happen?"

"To you? Well, as I said, what you've done is a category two offense. A fine rather than prison, but it's automatic revocation of corporate status. And a category four on top, maybe, if the girl comes in underage. The Justice system might issue a re-education order for that, for a noncorporate. If I asked for it, of course. Or I may not charge you with anything—it all depends on what kind of mood I'm in." He smiled coldly. "Not very good at the moment, I have to say."

Marcus simply stared at him, all arrogance gone.

Toreth picked up the camera, wringing what little satisfaction he could from the situation. "I promise I'll let you know when I make my mind up."

Back in his office, he passed on the details of Marcus's alibi to Lucia Wrenn and sent her to check it out, although Toreth was pretty sure the investigator would find it was solid. There might be enough minutes' leeway somewhere in the middle to squeeze in the murder, but he knew that was clutching at straws.

However, as he considered the situation further, he called up a picture of Kelly, looking at it in the light of the new information. While obviously no longer a teenager, Kelly had a light build and short, boyish hair. Could she have been involved with Marcus? It depended on whether Marcus indulged his tastes at work, or whether he was happy to pay for it. Come to think of it, Tara would probably appeal more to someone like Marcus, and she was Kelly's friend. Blackmail of the respectable corporate by the two women was an outside possibility, but maybe worth considering. Toreth could construct any number of scenarios that might lead to murder. If the security specialists came up with evidence of tampering on the backup recordings, he might be able to show that Marcus had the opportunity to kill Jarvis.

Superficially attractive as the conjecture was, he found it hard to get excited about. A liking for fucks of dubious legality didn't make a murderer, and he'd have a hell of a job getting a damage waiver from Justice with that as his only evidence. Worse, it didn't provide Marcus with a motive to kill Teffera. Proving that Marcus had killed Kelly would at least have eliminated one death from the inquiry. Leaving him with...what? Teffera's murder as an unrelated event that Marcus had exploited to distract attention from his own crime? Or maybe not even murder after all? Just an unlucky coincidence that had left him with two corpses to which the labs were infuriatingly unwilling to ascribe *any* cause of death. Tillotson wouldn't like to hear that.

For a moment, he envied Justice, investigating their unimportant, nobody crimes. Easy enough to get a witness interrogation waiver when the witnesses couldn't snap their fingers and call up a pack of corporate-trained lawyers. Not to mention that Warrick wouldn't appreciate having his fellow director interrogated. Regretfully, he abandoned the idea of applying for a waiver unless any more evidence turned up. The way things were going with the inquiry, that was optimistic to say the least.

So what were the options? Tillotson was right—he had nothing. Thanks to the anonymous tip-off, he had less than he'd had on Friday, as the possibility of murder had receded still further with the resolution of the lost security records. Proving the culpability of the sim seemed unlikely. The systems analysts were up to their necks in code and hardware, and muttering about timescales that Toreth refused to believe. Not that disbelief would make any difference, because Systems always took as long as they took.

Right now, finding someone else to pass the case to looked like an attractive option. He had no how, no why, no who. He didn't even have a definite murder. All he had was a coincidence. The timing of the deaths, this close to the reinvestment negotiations, looked so much like corporate sabotage. How long was he willing to plow on before he gave it up? The investment deadline would at least put an end to the case, if not an optimistic one. Once the nervous sponsors pulled out and another corporation snapped up SimTech, the ever-more hypothetical killer would've achieved their aim. After that there would be no more fresh corpses. A pity, since another body or two could only help.

Toreth leaned back in his chair, considering that idea more carefully. More bodies... Maybe he could do something about that, and at the same time test the theory that the deaths were an attack on SimTech. A little provocation might bring him the evidence he badly needed.

At coffee time, he caught up with Sara and said, "I'd like something dropped into the admin network, please."

She grinned. "Sure. What?"

"The sim didn't kill our corpses—it's just a very odd coincidence. Two cases

127

of natural causes. We're sitting on our hands for a while to annoy Justice, and then closing the whole thing down."

Now she looked disappointed. "It's going to be hard to float that one. It's not exactly gripping, is it?"

"It doesn't need to get very far—just round the section." Any corporate sabs big enough to tangle with LiveCorp would have friends at I&I to pick it up from there.

"Warrick?"

Startled, Warrick looked up from his screen. He hadn't heard the office door open, but Lew Marcus stood there, hands behind his back, stance suggesting he'd been there for some time. He looked worried and harassed—he had since Kelly's death, now that Warrick thought about it, but who among the senior staff hadn't? Warrick checked his watch: half past nine. "You're here late."

Lew didn't answer. He closed the door behind him, then stood by it, hands by his sides now, opening and closing nervously. Warrick waited, wondering. Finally, Lew crossed the room with rapid, jerky strides, and sat down. "Warrick, I'm afraid I've done something stupid. Very probably unforgivably stupid. Do—oh, God." He squared his shoulders. "Do you remember the trouble six years back? The girl?"

"Your amateur blackmailer?" He tried to keep his tone light, although dealing with the incident had been one of his less enjoyable lessons in corporate management.

"Yes. I did…" Lew looked down at his hands, long fingers clasped together, knuckles white. "I've been doing it again."

Oh, hell. Lew's predilections weren't a subject Warrick had any wish to discuss, even when there was a legitimate concern as to how they impacted on SimTech. On the other hand, Warrick had spent a fair portion of Saturday night kneeling on the floor of a hotel room in front of the para-investigator in charge of the case, discovering how good it felt to have to beg for every touch. He was hardly in a position to take the moral high ground over sexual practices occasioning threats to SimTech's image. Absently, he rubbed the faint cuff-mark on his right wrist. "You should talk to Marian about it," he suggested, trying to sound sympathetic. Now was the worst possible time for a repetition of old problems.

"I already have. That's not it. Rather, it is, but—" Lew took a deep breath. "I was with a girl on the night Jarvis died." He looked up. "I thought she was over legal age, Warrick, I swear. She had ID."

Warrick nodded, keeping the distaste locked inside. "How much does she want?"

Lew shook his head, his expression grim. "It's worse than that, I'm afraid. I was the one who wiped the security records."

A pity that he couldn't have misheard that. All sympathy was blasted away by the sudden magnification of the threat to SimTech.

"I—" Lew shook his head. "After the last time, Lotte said she'd leave me if I did it again, that I'd never see the boys. God knows I suppose I couldn't blame her, but . . ."

"So you wiped the records, so no one would find out when you left the building? Oh, you damn . . ." Perhaps it wasn't too late to tell Toreth and sort something out.

"I knew they'd check with Lotte to confirm the time I got home." His mouth twisted into a parody of a smile. "And I was right, so far as it went."

"Lew, you have to explain this to I&I, right away."

"That's what Marian said. And I'd been thinking about it, trying to work out how. But it's too late; the para-investigator already found out, somehow. He was here today."

Better and better. "What did he say?"

Lew's expression soured even further. "He made a lot of unpleasant threats and thoroughly enjoyed himself, as far as I could tell. The man's revolting—I'd always heard that that place employed sadists, but I didn't believe it until now."

Keep still, or I'll break your fucking neck. Ghost words distracted him with a remembered thrill. Warrick forced his attention back to the problem. "But did he believe that you had nothing to do with Kelly's death? That's the important thing."

"Oh, yes." Lew waved the question aside. "Or he will. I gave the backups to the I&I people this afternoon."

"You kept backups?"

"Yes." A hint of a smile lightened his expression. "Old habits, eh? And even when I wiped the records, I knew deep down that it was an idiotic thing to do."

"Yes, it was." Anger hardened his voice. "I don't need to tell you what this could do to the finance renegotiations."

Lew returned his gaze, all traces of humor gone. "I know. That's why I had to tell you what I'd done. In case—" He sat up straighter, his shoulders stiff. "In case you wanted to invoke the founders' clause to remove me from the board. I think you could legitimately consider me a fatal liability to the corporation at this point. I won't fight it, if you do, and I'll give up my shares right away."

Warrick nodded. It was something they'd all agreed to when SimTech was founded—an instrument to cut the corporation quickly and cleanly free of a disgraced director. This was certainly the closest they'd ever come to a qualifying situation. Tempting to say yes, to tell Lew to get the hell out of the building right now. Wiping the records had been beyond stupid. However, Warrick knew that threats to SimTech tended to set off a disproportionate defensive response in him. Both his sister and Asher had often teased him about it, over less serious issues.

129

Anger still tightened his throat, but he tried to keep it under control. What was best for SimTech? As the current dire situation made Lew's action so much worse, so it dictated the necessary response.

"Have you spoken to Asher?" Warrick asked.

"Not yet. If you want to wait to make a decision until you've talked to her, I understand."

"No. There's no need. I know what she'll say, so I can tell you now that we'll stand by you." To his surprise, the pronouncement didn't seem to bring much relief. "Lew?"

"There might be charges." Words dragged reluctantly out of him. "Obstruction, anything he can come up with about the girl. I want to be sure you know that. If you need to change your mind later, I'll understand."

"No. If I&I charges you, with anything, you'll get the best lawyers SimTech can find you."

Clear relief washed over Marcus, and he sagged slightly in the chair. "Thanks. You have no idea what that means to me. And, Warrick, I am sorry."

Not sorry enough that you couldn't stay away from the girl in the first place. Warrick bit back the retort. Personal feelings had no place here—SimTech must come first, as always. "We have to stick together," Warrick said. "If someone is trying to kill SimTech, the last thing we need is for the directors to fall apart. That would be the last straw for our chances with the sponsors." He closed the screen down and stood. "Come on, I'll give you a lift home."

"I can get—" Lew stopped. For a moment, Warrick thought he would protest the unsubtle escort, then he nodded. "Of course. Thanks."

Chapter Fifteen

❖

Sitting at his desk, Toreth stared at a screenful of analysis of the financial reports on SimTech, which told him nothing that he didn't know already: time was slowly running out for the fledgling corporation. More fool Warrick if he were looking to Toreth to solve the problem.

The next week promised to be as dull as the past two. Eleven days had passed since Toreth had dropped his bait into the gossip pool and the less-likely-by-the-day murderer hadn't responded. The list of disappointed investors supplied by Asher Linton was generating its own mountain of files, none of which had so far produced a substantial lead. Carey had interviewed the Tefferas and extracted no more from them than Toreth had managed. She seemed as disappointed and frustrated by the lack of progress as Toreth, although she professed herself to be impressed by SimTech's number of potential corporate enemies.

Toreth had filled his time with specialists' reports, technical details, and security files, out of which the evidential analysis systems had pulled nothing. On the Monday of the second week, Toreth had asked Tillotson to let him take back personal charge of the interrogations for his old cases. There wasn't much left to do, but level D would make a change from his office. Tillotson had told him curtly that he could have them back when he closed the SimTech case. By yesterday morning—Thursday—Toreth had been so bored and frustrated that he'd called Warrick to take him up on his virtual offer. A sim session that evening had been a welcome distraction: fucking that he could charge as overtime, which cheered him slightly.

The whole case, he decided, was an evidential black hole, rapidly sucking his career in past its event horizon. He should've dumped the whole fucking thing when he had the chance—Justice would never touch it now. At least it was the end of the week again. With a sigh, Toreth closed the reports on his screen and went for a coffee.

In the quiet of a Friday afternoon coffee room, he found Chevril, sitting alone.

131

That brightened his day; it was a chance for revenge for all the times he'd sat through Chevril's bloody irritating whinging. He went through the case in grim and depressing detail, and by the time he'd finished, he discovered he'd managed to make himself feel worse. Chevril's expression revealed no hint of sympathy. "So, no skeletons in the closet at SimTech?" he asked.

"If there are, I can't get the fuckers to rattle." Toreth sighed. "Like I said, one of the directors likes teenage girls and that's it. Turned out in the end that she was legal age after all. She hit fifteen *two days* before he fucked her, so the best I've got there is obstruction, and I can't be bothered processing that, not with corporate lawyers swarming all over. I let the bastard sweat it out for a few days, then I told him I was dropping it." That had been a necessary preliminary to yesterday's sim-fuck; otherwise he was certain Warrick would only have used the opportunity to bore him about his fellow director. "Other than that, it's a respectable minor corporation full of respectable minor corporates and respectable, well-published academics."

"But are they well cited?"

"Huh?"

"Well cited." Chevril waved vaguely. "It's something Elena's editor friends say at dinner parties. One of them says, 'So-and-so's very well published,' and then someone else says, 'Yes, but are they well cited?' and then they all laugh a lot and open another bottle. Alcoholics, the lot of 'em. Anyway, it means, does anyone actually read the stuff they churn out?"

Toreth blinked. "You have dinner parties?"

"Uh, yes." Chevril shifted in his chair. "Or at least Elena does. People from work."

"How come I never get invited?"

"*You?*" Chevril laughed derisively. "Well, let me think about it. Would it be good for Ellie's career if you seduced the wives of half her colleagues, causing broken hearts and messy divorces? Um...no."

"I wouldn't necessarily."

"You—"

"It could be their husbands."

"Oh, God." Chevril grimaced in disgust. "You always have to, don't you?" He drained his mug and stood up. "And that is exactly why you don't get asked to dinner."

That, Toreth thought, and the fact that Chevril had a notoriously attractive wife.

Back in the office, Sara had gone home early—ridiculously early, even for a Friday and even given their recent long hours. Toreth left her a note asking her to find him complete publication and citation records for SimTech staff past and present, and all the university staff who had ever been associated with the AERC.

There might be some useful tidbit in them somewhere, and it might teach her not to be absent when he was handing out work. The thought of her expression when she found it on Monday morning gave him his first smile of the day.

Warrick was late for the Friday afternoon session. Marian knew why, of course—showing his irritation both that she had interrupted his schedule and that she had the power to do so. In this matter, she had the authority of the sponsors on her side.

She had last spoken to Warrick officially nearly eight weeks ago, and he'd kicked up a fuss about her demand for a session today. However, she had the ultimate threat: she could stop him working in the sim. She could, and she would. As she'd told the para-investigator, she took her responsibilities very seriously. Here, in her office, she put all other concerns and worries aside and focused only on her job, as difficult as that had become to achieve lately.

Eventually Warrick walked in without knocking, making no comment or apology, and took a seat. "Well?" he asked, before she could even say hello.

"Well, what?"

"You must have a reason for dragging me in here. What is it?" He stared at her directly, challenging her.

If that was how he wanted it... "The senior para-investigator in charge of the inquiry here." She felt her lip curl on the title, but couldn't stop it.

His eyes narrowed. "Toreth? What about him?"

"Why are you interested in him?"

"What makes you think I'm interested?"

"The strategically placed bruises on your face recently, for one thing." She'd briefly considered asking him if he thought he was in danger; that might shake him a little. However, she opted for the more direct opening gambit. "I wouldn't have thought you'd go in for pain, Warrick."

"It didn't hurt," Warrick said with the trace of a smile. "And he did it with his mouth, not his fist."

"I'm not joking. I'm concerned about you. To do his work properly, he has to have at least one, possibly two, personality disorders. It's in the general psych profile of para-investigators."

He brushed a speck of fluff from his trousers. "You seem to think you know a lot about it."

"People like him are selected as interrogators. Psychologically he's barely an adult. He's a case of arrested development. A type," she said precisely. "He'll never do anything surprising. They've written books about him. I can lend you some if you want to see what you're getting into."

"A book might be useful, at that." Warrick tilted his head. "I don't suppose that you have anything about persuading cases of arrested development to pay their share of bar tabs?"

Distancing himself from the discussion. "He's not interested in you, you know. He can't even see you as a person—you or anyone else. He's only interacting with his own projections."

"Don't we all?"

"Beside the point. He—"

"If I may remind you," he interrupted, "you are the one who once told me to interact more with people outside the sim or I would require your professional help. And now that I am, you're telling me to stop, or I will require your professional help." He raised one eyebrow in mock inquiry. "Is there any possibility of you establishing a consistent position on this particular topic?"

She couldn't help being irritated by his willful refusal to take her concerns seriously. "How about, you ought to spend more time outside the sim interacting with nonsociopaths? Is that really so much to ask, Warrick?"

Having been provoked into the careless phrasing, she expected the answer, and the ironic quirk of his lips that accompanied it. "Apparently."

No sign that the word sociopath meant anything to him, or stirred any doubts. "People like him are dangerous. They charm you and make you think they're something they're not."

"Oh, I know what Toreth is. Don't concern yourself about that."

"Then you've got to realize he's using you." There must be some angle to exploit, for everyone's sake. "You've got something he wants. Any idea what it might be?"

His smile flickered into life again. "Now you're wounding my ego."

She had the grace to smile. "Sorry. I understand sexual attraction. And he's a handsome, healthy specimen, I'll give him that. And if he's any good, then good for him. But he's a predator, Warrick. Sooner or later, you'll find out why they recruited him. A relationship with someone like him isn't a question of playing with fire; this is Russian roulette. The gun is loaded. I'd hate to see you get hurt."

"Your concern is very touching, I'm sure, but we don't have a relationship. We just fuck. Does that make you any happier about him?"

"Fucking is a relationship, even if you don't want to admit it." She looked at him thoughtfully. "Frankly, if sex is all it's about, I do wonder why you would choose someone like him. Some day you'll have to tell me about your parents."

"You can overanalyze these things, you know." Warrick looked at his watch. "Not to hurry you, but what does any of this have to do with work?"

"My job is to assess the fitness of SimTech employees to use the sim. You've been going into the sim with him."

Warrick tilted his head, looking at her with curiosity. "He has a name. Why don't you use it?"

She hadn't even noticed. "You've been in the sim with Toreth. And at that point he, and his relationship with you, become my concern."

He leaned back in his chair, pointedly relaxing. "Everything has been booked and logged. The computer passed his psych test. He won't do enough hours to qualify for your attentions. It's all been done according to the protocols."

"I'm sure it has." Warrick wouldn't lie about something so easily checked. "Have you had sex in the sim?"

"Yes." The quick, confident answer didn't match up with the resentment in his eyes that she had the power to ask these questions.

"Which protocols?"

He crossed his arms. "P-Leisure. And, before you ask, yes, it was SMS—he wanted to know about it for the investigation. He signed the release."

She sighed. "Warrick, you know how I feel about sense-memory stacking. It's dangerous."

"It's nothing of the kind. With the proper screening and supervision."

"It's addictive," she said firmly.

Warrick shook his head, his fingers tapping on his biceps. "One student over-doing things doesn't make an addiction."

"Tara developed an addiction to the sim, and the excessive immersion precipitated her breakdown. Those are facts, Warrick, and your personal feelings about the sim do not change them."

"We have precautions in place. It won't happen again." Tacitly conceding the point, without acknowledging it.

"And what happens when the technology is sold to the general public?"

"Other precautions will be put in place." He shook his head, again half smiling. "Marian, the world is full of things that are dangerous if people misuse them. SimTech can't be held responsible for the irresponsibility of others. If we avoided technology because some people *might* hurt themselves with it, then we'd still be in the caves, worrying about burning our fingers."

"Sex is hardly a necessity for survival." Then, as his eyebrow arched, she quickly added, "Exotic virtual sex, I meant."

"I realized. But the sim isn't simply about SMS, as you well know."

"Of course not. No doubt Para-investigator Toreth has some suggestions for other uses."

Warrick froze in the chair, absolutely still. Marian cursed herself silently—such carelessness was unforgivable, however angry his obstinacy made her. Odd and infuriating in itself that he could effortlessly cut through years of training and hit a nerve every time.

"I won't sell technology to I&I," Warrick said, icily precise. "They will never have it while I'm alive and in charge of SimTech."

That she didn't doubt. "I know. I'm sorry, Warrick—truly I am. I misspoke. But addiction is a danger, and it will do SimTech no good to face the problem later, rather than now."

He nodded. "I appreciate that. You know we're always working on safety improvements. Besides—" His voice sharpened again. "You can always go around me and speak to P-Leisure directly, as you know."

As she had about Tara. Marian was poised to launch into the results of her last attempt to talk to P-Leisure when she suddenly realized that he'd very neatly sidetracked her from the real reason she'd called him in. She tried to find a route back to her concern. "If you are going to use an SMS protocol with a non-employee volunteer, I want to talk to him, to make sure he understands the risk."

His eyebrows went into action again. "That's a rather sudden concern for Toreth's health."

"I'm still worried about you. You didn't get those bruises in the sim. What happened to Tara can happen to him, and you'll be the one who gets hurt in the fallout. I don't think you understand the risk you're running by pursuing this."

"I'm not 'pursuing' anything. Or anyone, come to that. We met, we fucked, we liked it. That's it. If it weren't for the sim, once or twice would have been enough for him. He's far more interested in it than he is in me."

"And what about you? How interested are you in him?"

To her surprise, he cocked his head, seeming to genuinely consider his answer. "From a sexual standpoint," he said at length, "he's without doubt the most talented partner I have ever had. Personality-wise, he's really not my type." He stood up. "I hope that answers your question, because I have a meeting to get to. With P-Leisure, as a matter of fact. I'll tell them you said hello."

"We're not done."

"Yes, we are." He straightened his sleeves. "If you have any more questions, Dr. Tanit . . . well, you know what you can do. I can't stop you. Good afternoon."

She could have stopped him. She could have told him to sit down and actually listen to her concerns, or she would cancel his sim access. However, what would it have achieved beyond increasing the distance between them? Some people, she reflected ruefully, simply refused to allow themselves to be helped the easy way.

After informing her admin that she would be busy, Marian locked her door and pulled out the session records. This was something else she had the authority to do; Warrick's parting remarks had pointedly demonstrated that he knew. Therefore, she was utterly unsurprised to find that everything was in order, labeled, and properly annotated. There was a link to the protocol they had followed, analyses of responses and experiences, signed consent forms for the participation of a non-company member.

She doubted she would find anything in the visual reconstructions, but it was worth skimming for signs of anything amiss. Turning down the office lights, she skipped through the session, her face illuminated by the changing images on the screen. As usual, it was an uncomfortably voyeuristic experience, even given her professional detachment. As she expected, the SMS session matched the filed protocol. Some of it was interesting enough, but none of it surprised her. She noted that they briefly discussed the lack of progress in the investigation into Kelly's death, but nothing else about Toreth's work. The professional reticence of a para-investigator, or something more?

There was a second session yesterday, which hadn't followed an established protocol. That had been properly booked as part of Warrick's allocation of personal sim time. He'd even made notes on it and booked a working session next week, on his own, to test out some modifications.

She started to run through the hypothetical observer record of the session. There were no sensory tricks involved, nothing but a straight simulation of reality, in a low-lit, bare, nondescript room. She watched it through carefully, rewinding parts and occasionally freezing the digital flow into still images, which she left scattered around the edges of the screen. The pictures slowly built up, overlapping.

Warrick, naked and with his arms bound behind him, kneeling in the center of the room. The blindfold bisecting his pale face. Dark hair disarrayed and curling with virtual sweat. Fingers spreading wide against the small of his back as his shoulders arched. Sharply defined lips caught open in the middle of whispered words. "Please, don't."

Toreth standing by him. Kneeling. Touching. Admiring the realism of a hand mark flushing red against white skin. His fingers in Warrick's hair, pulling his head back. Smiling as he looked down at him.

"Please."

Just a game. A game for which there was so much scope in the sim, where it would leave no telltale bruises. Marian tapped her finger against her chin, watching the intent, absorbed faces of the players. She hadn't lied to Warrick—she'd never imagined this would be something he wanted. A sign of how little she knew him.

At the end of the session, they lay together, panting, almost laughing. She cut off the visual reconstruction, leaving only the words. Her gaze wandered over the collection of images as she listened.

"It doesn't work, does it?" Toreth asked.

"No. Don't get me wrong, though. It was good—very good—but not like it was outside. I wonder why?"

"Because it's not real enough," Toreth replied immediately. "It's much too safe for you."

"Yes. Yes, of course." Warrick's breathing became regular, his tone more analytical. "Not as intense. Yet everything is mechanically fine. There has to be a way of making it work."

Silence, then Toreth suggested, "You should try taking out the disconnect code. Would that have helped—if you couldn't have stopped me? No easy way out."

"Mm. Perhaps. But it's not possible. The disconnect has to be available at all times. It's a fundamental part of the design."

"Couldn't you let people choose to turn it off?" Toreth asked.

"Absolutely and categorically no. Safety is paramount."

Marian sighed, frustrated. Still blind to the true risks of the thing—she'd tried so hard to tell him.

"It's too dangerous," Warrick continued in an odd echo of her thoughts. "Users have to feel secure, not trapped."

"Yeah, but that's what you want."

"Yes," Warrick said, his voice cool and measured. "So I'll have to look for another way around the problem. There'll be an approach that will work; I just need to find it."

"Why bother?" Toreth had begun to sound a little impatient, or maybe just bored. "Why not stick to what the sim's good at? All your fucking weird games, all the things you can't do outside. Memory stacking whatever. And we can play *my* game in the real world. Or aren't I a good enough fuck out there?"

Warrick laughed. "God, no. Or rather, God, yes. Whichever—more than good enough. But the sponsors would like it. There's a market, you know. I'm hardly unique. Although I'm not denying I would like it, too."

There was a silence for a few seconds, then Toreth laughed as well, suddenly breathless. "Stop it. Ah—you've got to show me how to do that."

"You'd need a lot longer in the sim. I've been practicing for years. Shall we get out and go for a real coffee?"

"Sure."

The recording cut out, and Marian played the scene over again with the sound off, watching the body language. Professionally, she found nothing to worry about. There was no sign of adverse effects, nothing that would justify banning Warrick or the interrogator from the sim. However, it did confirm her opinions and, to her surprise and personal distaste, Warrick's. Toreth was manipulative and dangerous, and Warrick understood him perfectly. They were . . . comfortable together. Somehow, Warrick's unexpected insight into this only further strengthened her conviction that he would never willingly accept the dangers of the sim. And so neither would the sponsors, not unless another disaster forced their hands.

Marian sighed, and closed the files. She had an appointment scheduled with Tara Scrivin that she couldn't miss.

Chapter Sixteen

❖

The call for Toreth to go in to I&I came just after four on Monday morning. When he arrived, he found Sara already there. She stood up when she saw him, her eyes wide with excitement.

"Is it really Pearl Nissim?" he asked her, and she nodded. "Legislator Pearl Nissim?"

"One and the same," she said.

Stupid question. It was hardly a common name, and the woman was connected to the investigation already. From now on, SimTech would have to sink or swim without their patron in the European Legislature. He felt an unaccountable urge to laugh, although it wasn't funny at all. "Fucking hell," he said.

"Found dead in her sim machine, just like the other two." Sara waited for a comment, before adding, "Do you want to go out to Strasbourg or send someone from the team?"

Toreth pulled himself together. "For a legislator? I think that merits a personal appearance. Besides, one of the local bastards will claim it if I don't show. Send a message to I&I and Justice over there and tell them it's *mine*. And get hold of Tillotson or Jenny and get something saying the same sent in his name."

"He's done it already."

"What?"

"Tillotson left a message before I got in. You've got full authority over there."

"Right. Find me a flight as soon as possible and I want O'Reilly and her team as well. I'll dig out an investigator to go with me."

Sara nodded and Toreth went past her into his office and closed the door behind him. He sat down at his desk, half his mind running through what needed doing and the other half stunned by the news. Teffera had been one thing, but this was in a new league. The murder of an Administration higher-up—damn near highest-up, in fact—wasn't something a para got a chance at solving every day. Even less frequently when it was their fault. When he'd thrown out his bait, he'd expected another death at the AERC. Another student, or maybe one of the more senior staff. Legislator fucking Nissim? Better hope Tillotson never found out about *this* one.

Shaking off the distraction, he called Barret-Connor. When the investigator finally answered the comm he was wrapped in a startlingly pink duvet. Possibly not his own—in the background Toreth could make out female legs, from the knees down. B-C's cropped blond hair was far too short to rumple, but his bleary-eyed face made up for it. "Um...Para?"

"We have a new body. Get in here, and bring some clothes; we're going to Strasbourg."

"Now, Para?"

The legs behind him stirred, and Toreth heard a faint, sleepy protest over the comm. He understood B-C's reluctance—they were the kind of legs he wouldn't like to be torn away from himself. "Yes, now." Toreth grinned. "Look on the bright side: we'll get there just in time to start work."

On the flight over, with Barret-Connor sleeping in the seat beside him, Toreth read the legislator's security file. Not something he often saw, although it actually made disappointingly tame reading. Nissim was in her early sixties, although from the picture she could have been ten years younger. Her family background was respectable Administration; her father had also worked for the European Legislature, although his career had ended at a rank below his daughter's. After a brief stint in the Department of Science, Pearl Nissim had transferred to the Legislature. Over the next forty years she had progressed smoothly and unremarkably through the ranks until, to no one's surprise, she had reached her current position in charge of Science and Technology legislation.

In theory, laws were drafted at the direction of the Council of the European Administration, a body made up of ministers appointed by Parliament, senior bureaucrats, and corporate representatives. Those laws were even under the nominal, ineffective scrutiny of the elected European Parliament. However, the European Legislature, as the body that actually wrote the laws, had more than its share of power.

The Legislature was one of the more powerful of the departments that kept the Administration running. A not-so-secret cabal, sharing power under the umbrella of the Bureau of Administrative Departments. In theory, it had purely bureaucratic function. In practice, when the Bureau spoke, even the Council listened. The heads of departments, united, exerted almost unstoppable power. Almost. When the stranglehold of the Department of Security had been broken by the reorganization, there had been rumors that the Bureau also planned to split up the Legislature. It never happened. Who, so the joke ran at the time, would have made the necessary changes in the law?

The Legislature was also a point of contact (or collision) between government and corporations. Although it happened very rarely, the Legislature was one of the departments where corporate sabotage killings occasionally spilled over into the Administration. Normally, Toreth would have had no trouble thinking of a handful of reasons why someone might want a European Legislature head of division dead. However, Nissim's security file produced no obvious suspects. No scandals, no mysterious backers, no overt ties to any major corporation.

After he'd read the file again, Toreth called up the files for Teffera and Jarvis and paged through them. At first glance it would be difficult to find files more different—a major corporate, a graduate student, and a division head. However, looking past the details, they gave him a strong feeling of similarity. All highly respectable. All almost unnaturally well liked by their peers. Jarvis had the most exciting black mark against her, and that was the unforeseen consequence of trying to help a friend.

Toreth stared out of the plane window at the dawn sky. Everything about the deaths screamed either natural causes or technical fault. It screamed it so loudly, in fact, that it only strengthened Toreth's belief to the contrary.

At Strasbourg airport, two local branch I&I cars and an investigator met them and took them straight to Nissim's residence. On the way, he discovered that, as with Teffera, the body had been moved to a hospital for futile attempts at resuscitation. Worse, the local forensics team had already swept through Nissim's home. Tillotson's note clearly hadn't been explicit or emphatic enough. As soon as they arrived at the house, Toreth sent O'Reilly and her team on in the cars to the local I&I office to wrest control of the evidence and at least supervise the postmortem and sample analysis.

Senior Administration officials didn't achieve the same luxury of accommodation as senior corporates, but the house was in an exclusive residential area close to the Legislature complex. The place was crawling with investigators and security: private guards, Legislature guards, and Service troopers. They all had the desperate busyness of people well aware that the horse had long since departed, and that whoever had left the stable door unbolted was about to catch all kinds of holy hell.

Toreth recognized the first man they met inside—Clemens Keilholtz. The recognition, however, wasn't instant. The legislator's death had hit him hard. However, while shock and grief tended to dull people's expressions, in Keilholtz's case they had supplied some character to his previously nondescript face. His suit was rumpled; yesterday's clothes, in Toreth's experienced judgment. Once again, he looked pleased—or perhaps this time relieved—to see Toreth, and Toreth had the impression that the man had been waiting for him. Keilholtz's first words confirmed the guess. "I heard you were coming."

"When did you find out about the legislator's death?"

"I was there when it happened." He said it with the unconscious ease of some-one who hasn't thought through what that might mean.

"You were in the room?"

"No. Or rather, yes. Next door. We'd both been in the sim—" And now he hesitated.

It couldn't have been more obvious if Keilholtz had worn an advertising screen. "Go on."

"Ah, there isn't an easy way of explaining this, Para-investigator."

Easy enough: you were fucking her. Toreth looked around the busy hallway. He wanted to take control of the situation here, but he also wanted to get a clear story from Keilholtz in person and as soon as possible. "Excuse me, Mr. Keilholtz."

Toreth took Barret-Connor by the arm and moved him a few steps away. "Go around the place, find out who the hell everyone is and get rid of anyone we don't need. Try and cut it back to I&I only."

"Yes, Para."

When B-C had gone, Toreth returned to his witness. "Shall we go somewhere quieter?"

Keilholtz nodded gratefully and showed Toreth through a doorway into a small, sparsely furnished sitting room. An open door showed a kitchen, and another led into a tiny hallway off which two more doors were visible. "My flat," Keilholtz said. "Can I get you anything?"

Toreth let him fetch them both a drink while he set up the camera and had a brief snoop around. The other doors revealed a bedroom with a single bed, and a bathroom with dust on the shower floor. A place to give the illusion of propriety, not a home. After Keilholtz set down the coffee pot and cups and sat opposite him, Toreth said, "I think you were about to tell me that you and the legislator had a relationship?"

A little of the tension eased from his shoulders. "Yes."

"For how long?"

Keilholtz poured the coffee, his hand steady, and offered Toreth a cup. "Nearly four years. It would've been our anniversary next month. Before you ask, few people know about it. A handful of people at the Legislature, one or two close friends..." He rubbed his eyes—tired, not tearful. "It's inevitable it will come out now, though, isn't it? Pearl hated gossip."

He'd dropped the "Legislator." "Why did you keep it a secret?"

"Why do you think?" He smiled wryly. "It would've drawn a great deal of prurient attention. Neither of us wanted that."

"How old are you, Mr. Keilholtz?"

Keilholtz clearly expected the question, even if he didn't welcome it. "Thirty-

142

one," he said tonelessly. "Exactly half Pearl's age."

There wasn't an easy way of asking his next question, so Toreth didn't try to be too tactful. "Is that why you were with her in the sim?"

He nodded. "I should say—I want to say that *I* had no problems at all with the situation. I much preferred sex in the real world, to tell you the truth. If you haven't been with someone in the sim, it's difficult to explain it. It lacks intimacy. Perhaps it's just me, but I'm always aware that my body is elsewhere, and alone. But outside the sim, Pearl was, well, self-conscious. It spoiled things for her, and I hated that. So we compromised: we alternated between the two."

Taking turns in the real world and the sim. It gave Toreth a twinge of unease, thinking of his own recent dabbling. He pulled his mind firmly back to the case. "Yesterday evening. Was there anyone else in the house?"

"No. The usual security people, that's all. We tried to keep Sunday nights for ourselves. Pearl was always so busy, it was hard to make time. I was with her at work, of course, but that's not the same."

"Could anyone else get into the room while you were in the sim?"

"No. The security is quite extraordinary; it has to be, for commercial reasons. The sim room has no windows, the walls, floor, and ceiling are reinforced, and there is an access security system; the door opens only for the two of us. I'm sure someone will be able to give you the details. In any case, the only entrance is through Pearl's bedroom—" He stumbled over the words, and then cleared his throat and carried on before Toreth could comment. "And the door to the bedroom was locked. It was still locked afterwards. No one could have got even as far as there."

"Except for the security officers, presumably?"

"Well... well, yes, I suppose so." Keilholtz flushed faintly. "I'm sorry, I didn't think of them."

Toreth smiled. "You'd be surprised how many people don't. People are the weak point in any system. What time did you go in?"

"After dinner. About eight thirty." Keilholtz glanced at the watch on his left wrist. Expensive make, Toreth noted, and wondered if it were a gift. "One of the security guards helped us into the sim. It was the usual routine, I think—I let him into the sim room, and we settled into the couches right away. All he did was tighten the straps and lower the visors, and then he left."

"How can you be sure he went?"

Keilholtz paused, then smiled wryly. "I'm making assumptions again, yes. I don't know, because I was in the sim. But the security system will have recorded everything."

"Do you remember his name?"

"I—" He narrowed his eyes. "Byrne, I think. I don't know his first name. He's a Legislature guard."

Toreth paused to call B-C and pass on the name, watching his witness while he did so. Keilholtz filled their cups again, slowly stirring a spoonful of sugar into his own, spending too long on the process. Hardly suspicious: a killer and a bereaved lover would both have reasons to be uneasy as the time to recount the death approached. Call completed, he said, "Go on."

"We were in there for three hours, maybe a little more. Do you—" Keilholtz looked down at his cup, then up again. "Do you need to know what we did?"

"I'm afraid so."

"Why?"

It was hard to take offense at the soft, plaintive question. "We're investigating the possibility that the sim itself caused the deaths of Jon Teffera and Kelly Jarvis—and now the legislator."

"I see. Very well. There was a room she especially liked, a garden..." He went through the session in surprisingly clear and careful detail, not looking at the camera, and with only occasional questioning required. A slushily romantic evening, but Keilholtz seemed to have genuinely enjoyed it. To Toreth, it sounded dull enough to bore a user to death. On the other hand, he reflected, he wouldn't be fucking a sixty-two-year-old legislator in the first place. Marian Tanit would probably have some choice questions for Keilholtz about his mother.

"I left first," Keilholtz said when he reached the end of his account. "She liked—" He shook his head, smiling slightly, although his eyes were bright with incipient tears. "She liked to tidy up in there. I used to tease her about it, because of course everything resets when the program ends, unless you save it deliberately. I unfastened my own straps, stood up, I went over and—" He stopped, swallowing hard. Toreth waited. "I went over and loosened Pearl's straps, so she'd be able to get out easily. Then I left her and went through to the bedroom. I started running a bath for her. Then I sat on the bed for a few minutes. I felt a little sick, from the sim; I often do. When the bath was full, I turned the sheets down, put the lights on by the bed, and—" He was crying now, making no attempt to hide it or wipe away the tears.

"By then she'd usually come through, so I—I went back to the sim room. Her eyes were open but she wasn't breathing. She was so still. I couldn't—I didn't know, right away. Or I couldn't believe it, maybe. I touched her face and then—" He stopped. The only sounds in the small, sparse room were his rough breathing and the muffled voices from the rest of the house.

"Then?" Toreth prompted.

"Oh. Yes. I—oh, I called security first, I think, and then the medics, or maybe it was the other way around, and I tried to do something—to get her heart started, to make her breathe." Keilholtz wiped his cheeks with the palm of his hand. "I'm afraid I'm not sure about the exact order. I usually have a very good memory but— no. It's all confused. I'm sorry."

Toreth drank his cooling coffee, giving Keilholtz a moment to compose himself while he considered the story. "You said that her eyes were open?"

Keilholtz nodded.

"Does that mean that the visor was up when you entered the room?"

However hazy his recollections of later events, he answered that without hesitation. "Yes. And her left hand was," he let his arm dangle over the arm of the sofa, "like that. The rest of the straps were in place, I think, because I had to undo them to—to get her free."

So similar to Kelly. This was stretching the realms of coincidence too far, and the sim room here was as secure as the one at SimTech. "Could anyone have come through the bedroom while you were running the bath?"

He shook his head. "All I did was start the bath and then I went straight back into the bedroom. Besides, as I said, the sim room opens only for Pearl and myself. I had to leave—I had to leave her to let security in."

"So you're quite certain there were only the two of you there?"

"Absolutely." Then, before Toreth could speak again, Keilholtz said, "Do you know what was in the legislator's will, Para-investigator?" Toreth, who had been considering asking Keilholtz something very similar, blinked, then shook his head. "I do." Keilholtz's voice was cold. "Pearl had three children, a daughter and two sons, by her estranged husband. Everything goes to them."

"Nothing at all to you?"

"A handful of personal gifts, nothing extravagant. Our letters. My gifts to her. Otherwise, not a thing." He gestured around the room. "I don't even have any right to stay here. I'll start packing up my things here as soon as your people have finished. I have a flat of my own, although I'm renting it out at the moment."

"You don't get on with her kids?"

"As it happens, we get on very well. They had no objections to our relationship." He lifted his chin. "But I always wanted to make it clear why I was with Pearl, to her more than to anyone else. I couldn't prove it wasn't career ambition—although it wasn't—but I could very definitely prove it had nothing to do with money. I never took a cent from her and I won't start now that she's gone."

"I didn't—"

"No, but you were about to." Keilholtz smiled slightly. "I spend a lot of time in meetings, Para-investigator, watching people think. It's one of the reasons I was happy to keep our relationship secret. It's not pleasant knowing that people are looking at you and wondering. Assuming an ulterior motive. I had none. I loved her; that's all there was to it."

Oddly, Toreth believed him. Of course he'd still verify the will story, and then he'd run a credit check on the man to make sure he hadn't received any unexpectedly large payments from unknown sources lately. Time to get back to the rest of the house. "Does SimTech have any other champions in the Legislature?" he asked before he put the camera away.

Keilholtz smiled sourly. "Not that I know of. And certainly not right now. Para-investigator, Pearl Nissim had a great many friends there. If the sim had anything at all to do with her death, I can promise you that SimTech is finished."

The emergency meeting at SimTech took place after lunch. News of Nissim's death had spread quickly around the building. The directors had discussed making it an open staff meeting, but in the end they agreed that it would be best to speak to the senior staff first. When they had assembled, rather cramped, in the sound-proofed conference room, Warrick opened the meeting with a blunt question. "Do you think that we ought to suspend work in the sim?"

He had expected a rush of responses, but the room stayed silent except for the low hum of the air conditioning, switching itself on to deal with the heat of so many bodies. Warrick looked around the table, finding all eyes on him. Almost all—Lew was staring down at the table, frowning. "Three people have died," Warrick continued. "Personally, I do not believe that the sim had anything at all to do with their deaths *directly*. I say that not because of pride in my work, or because we can't afford a delay in the program, but because I think it's safe. I know it's safe. My personal belief is that SimTech is suffering a particularly unpleasant corporate sabotage attempt. Closing the sim is tantamount to unconditional surrender to that attack."

Asher cleared her throat. "A suspension now would be a disaster from the point of view of the sponsors. I've been reassuring them that there is no problem, that we're confident it's corporate. If we close everything, we're as good as admitting that we think the sim is at fault."

"Would another death be any better for them?" Jin Li Yang asked.

Lew looked up. "We've taken all the units outside the AERC offline, and from now on, no one here will be allowed to use the sim without at least two other people in the room and not in the sim. We've put a security guard on all the sim suite doors and installed surveillance. No one can get into a sim room or once inside do anything unmonitored."

Nods and murmurs of agreement rippled around the table, although Yang didn't join in. However, these were the long-serving senior staff—those most committed to the corporation. How the junior staff and students would feel about continuing to work in the sim was another question. Looking around, Warrick noticed Marian also assessing the room. Odd that she had made no objection, no comment at all, when she was the one person he'd expected to say something. "What do you think, Dr. Tanit?" Warrick asked.

"Me?" She looked a little startled by the question.

"What do you think would be best for morale?"

"Morale?" Now she smiled slightly. "Overall, I would recommend re-empha-

146

sizing that sim work is voluntary. Forcing people to work in it would be damaging. From a commercial point of view," she added, placing the words with precision, "continuing on a voluntary basis is clearly the best option. If all work is suspended and staff believe that SimTech is going to fold, they'll start looking for other jobs." She shrugged. "Nothing you didn't already know."

Warrick nodded. "Thank you. And I think the idea is a good one. Is it acceptable to everyone?" General nods. "Very well. We'll send around a message to the staff reiterating the directors' confidence in the sim, and making it clear that they are free to refuse to work in it, with no stigma attached to refusing. Asher, if you could inform the sponsors of that decision."

The difficult part over, Warrick looked around the room. Not the happiest gathering he'd ever seen, but things could have gone worse. Now for a brief demonstration of corporate director hypocrisy. "One more thing, while you're all here. I have evidence that someone—or more likely several someones—have been accessing test data." Evidence he'd found while examining the supposedly closed files himself. "As you know, I&I has sealed all the data for the duration of the investigation. I do very much appreciate the efforts everyone is making for SimTech, but I don't want anyone to end up at I&I answering unfriendly questions." Beside him, Marcus shifted in his chair. Warrick looked from face to face as he talked, searching faces. Yang, for one, glanced down at the table as Warrick caught his eye. "So," Warrick finished, "if you could pass on to your staff that while I&I is here we play very much by their rules. Thank you."

The three directors sat at the table as the rest of the senior staff filed out. Yang stayed behind, still seated. When the rest had gone, Warrick asked, "Well?"

"Uh. I wanted to talk to you about—" With their undivided attention on him, Yang colored slightly, then sat up straighter. "Are you sure the sim is safe?" he asked, a little too loudly.

"Absolutely," Warrick said. He glanced at his fellow directors. Lew nodded firmly, and Asher a little less emphatically. "There is no danger from the sim. I meant every word I said."

Yang hesitated, then said, "Still, I'd like to stop work in the sim. If it was just me...but I have to think about my family."

Warrick waited for any comments from the others before he spoke. However, as he expected, they stayed silent. Yang was a programmer, and hence his to deal with. "I understand completely. The decision is yours, as I said."

Yang smiled with relief. "Thanks. I don't mean I won't work in the sim again. I just—I thought about taking some time off. A few days. Then I wouldn't need to mention anything to anyone."

Warrick shook his head. "That's not necessary. If you want time off, take it. But don't do it for that reason alone."

He nodded. "Even so. I have to think about things. And, well, my wife would prefer me to stay at home. It's just for—" He shrugged and stood up, not looking at any of them. "Thank you, again."

They watched him go in silence. When the door had closed behind him, Lew sniffed. "He's going to leave."

Warrick's own thought, spoken aloud. "Yes. At least if things aren't cleared up soon. And he won't be the only one, whatever rules we pass about the sim, and whatever Marian says about morale." He turned to Asher. "How much longer can we last financially?"

She expanded her hand screen, opened a page, then abruptly collapsed the screen and dropped it onto the table. "In two months we'll have run out of money," she said bluntly. "After that, we can't pay the staff. At that point we fold, or we take whatever deal we can get."

"Anything new from the sponsors?" Warrick asked.

"Yes. Three messages this morning withdrawing their current terms. Two of them say that they'll submit something new. The proposed terms were already un-acceptable and our position is only weakening."

Lew nodded. "So even if SimTech survives, we'll lose control?"

"Yes, and that's assuming that anyone wants it." Asher sighed. "The rumor that the sim is killing users is everywhere. Not so much rumor as well-known fact, now."

"P-Leisure?" Warrick suggested. Their biggest hope.

"I called before the meeting. They're still 'reviewing their options.' It's so—" She slapped the table with the flat of her hand, and even Lew jumped slightly at the un-Asher-like display of anger. "It's so damn *frustrating*. Caprice asked me twice whether there was any evidence that the sim was responsible. Unfortunately, the contract doesn't require them to submit anything for another six weeks."

Warrick shook his head. "Too late."

"That's about the size of it. We are, as Greg would say, thoroughly fucked." Asher slumped in her seat, and Warrick noticed for the first time how exhausted she looked. He'd been too preoccupied to see it before.

"How much sleep have you had recently?" he asked.

She smiled, which only emphasized the tiredness. "Not a lot."

"Then go home and get some now, once you've told the sponsors about the new arrangements. Everything else will wait until tomorrow. We don't want to make any quick decisions, anyway."

After a moment, she nodded. "I might, at that. Maybe things will look different in the morning."

Lew rose. "Well, they'd better look different soon, or it'll be too damn late."

Chapter Seventeen

❖

It took them two days to finish in Strasbourg. Toreth barely noticed the hotel—a place to grab some food and not enough hours' sleep before he and B-C went back to work. Interviews, reinterviews, and the first, depressing forensics report that confirmed Toreth's fears—or rather expectations—by finding nothing. Late afternoon of the second day, and they were still in the temporary office, reviewing the last of the surveillance reports provided by the Strasbourg investigators. At least the high security around the legislator's flat meant that no unauthorized persons could have entered the building, and all authorized people were recorded. An exhaustive test of the security system for the sim room only confirmed that everything was also functioning fine and the story given by both Keilholtz and Byrne was as rock solid as it could be.

"Do you read much, B-C?" Toreth asked.

Barret-Connor looked up from his own screen. "I'm sorry, Para?"

"Fiction, I mean."

The investigator shook his head. "I'm afraid not."

"Me neither, much. I used to read thrillers, until I noticed they weren't. And mysteries. Of all the setups, you know which ones really pissed me off? Sealed room murders. They're always so contrived, and yet here we are, with three of the bloody things."

B-C looked back at his screen. "Yes, Para."

As he was considering calling it a day, the detailed postmortem report on Nissim arrived. Toreth skimmed through it, then called O'Reilly. "*Nothing?*"

On the screen, O'Reilly nodded, looking distinctly uncomfortable. "I'm sorry, Para."

"No need to be, assuming you didn't screw it up somewhere." She didn't respond. Toreth paged down through the report, then paused, hand raised. "What's that? Page seventeen, first line of the table."

O'Reilly glanced to the side. "Er... traces of an anti-nausea drug. It was pre-

149

scribed to Clemens Keilholtz. He suffered from what his medical file calls 'sim sickness.' What's in her body isn't enough to kill her, not by a long way; the amount suggests it was a low dose, or she took it three or four hours before she went into the sim. There's no sign of an allergic or any other adverse reaction. No genetic susceptibility."

"Do we know where the drug came from?"

"Um...yes." O'Reilly paused, her eyes flicking from side to side as she scanned a screen out of his view. "It was prepared at SimTech and delivered by courier to the legislator's home in sealed, single-use injectors. Part of the service contract. We looked at the remaining doses in the batch, and they're clear of anything noxious."

"The used injector?"

"No sign of it in the room—probably already in the recycling system, Para."

He nodded. "Thanks. Good work."

"Thank you, Para."

"But still, I'd like you to do another screen on the body. Everything toxic the system can think of." Catching sight of her expression, he shook his head. "I'm not saying you weren't thorough the first time. Humor me—give me a straw to clutch at."

She smiled slightly. "Yes, Para."

As soon as O'Reilly closed the connection, Toreth called Keilholtz. When the man answered, Toreth asked, "Why didn't you tell me you gave Pearl Nissim an anti-nausea injection?"

Keilholtz stared at him. "I'm sorry? If you mean...I must have forgotten to mention it. She gave me the injection every time we used it. The sim makes me queasy if I stay in for more than an hour or so, and we planned to be in there all evening, so—"

"We found the drug in her body, Mr. Keilholtz."

Keilholtz frowned. "I don't... " His expression cleared. "She had an ear infection a few days ago. It's something she was prone to. Another reason she liked the sim—she could go swimming without earplugs."

"You're saying that she took it herself?"

"If I'd known she'd taken it I would have told you, Para-investigator." His voice held a touch of irritation at Toreth's deliberately disbelieving tone. "I didn't even think about it. I asked her if she was all right before we went in, and she said she was fine. She'd used it before, once or twice; just a half-strength dose to stop her feeling sick if her ear was bad. She'd cleared it with the medical staff at SimTech."

"Wait there, please."

Blanking out the comm, Toreth pulled up Nissim's medical file. It took only a few seconds to find details of recurrent ear infections, confirmation of anti-nausea

150

drug compatibility tests courtesy of SimTech, and the record of an infection treated a few days ago. All of which Keilholtz could've known and used as a cover. Toreth reactivated the comm. "When did the legislator take the drug?" he asked Keilholtz.

"Just before we went in, or rather, that's an assumption. That's when she gave me mine. I was already sitting in the couch. Just after I'd had the injection, the guard strapped me in."

He paused, and Toreth prompted him. "Yes?"

"I don't remember seeing her take another injector, but I can't swear she didn't. She would've had time to take a shot before the guard finished with me."

"And dispose of the injectors?"

"Oh, yes, Para-investigator. Pearl was always very tidy."

"Thanks for your help, Mr. Keilholtz. I'll be in touch if we have any further questions."

Pity the injection wasn't provably linked to the legislator's death. The only progress the information provided was evidence that Nissim had been given (or had given herself) an injection immediately before entering the sim. After which she had spent an allegedly happy three hours fucking her toy boy before dropping dead. Given that Keilholtz already had ample opportunities much closer to the time of death to kill his lover, nothing had changed. "How is it possible to have so many bodies and so few suspects?" Toreth wondered aloud.

Barret-Connor had been listening to the conversation with Keilholtz. "They are a bit thin on the ground, yes, Para."

"People always get more popular when they die, B-C. Fact of life." Toreth pushed his chair back from the desk and stood up to pace. "I've never met a corpse yet who wasn't saint material if you believe what people tell you. Then you open their security file, and they're exactly the kind of bastard that someone would want to murder. Or they've got 'natural victim' stamped all over them and it was only a question of who got to them first. Either way you've got to dig through dozens of suspects to find the right one. But these three . . . what do you think?"

The younger man frowned, rubbing his fingers through his short-cropped hair. A nervous habit Toreth was familiar with—B-C wasn't good at producing opinions on the spot. However, he was methodical, thorough, and a superb observer. "Well . . . if it's corporate sabotage, they are natural victims," B-C said at length. "At least two of them are, I mean. Teffera and Nissim both supported SimTech strongly."

"Killing a legislator is a hell of a risk, though. If there is a killer, they must know that. It won't get covered up now, however big the corporate behind it. The Administration doesn't like to encourage corporate sabs targeting legislators—the idea might catch on. They'll be found and nailed for it, however long it takes us."

B-C nodded. "So, we're back to square one: why pick Nissim?"

Why indeed? "Maybe they didn't."

B-C frowned thoughtfully. Toreth waited, and eventually the junior said, "You mean, if it was something in the injector—"

"Two gets you ten there's nothing in the body, however many times O'Reilly looks."

B-C smiled wryly. "I don't think I'll take that bet, Para. But assuming that's how it was done, then the target was Keilholtz, wasn't it?"

"Exactly. Unless someone knew...no, the last batch was dispatched from SimTech before her ear flared up. Even then, the odds are in favor of a single contaminated injector getting him, not her. And it makes more sense. Killing Nissim brings you big trouble, killing her boy toy and blaming the sim gets you an avenging angel ready to take down SimTech. Hmm." Toreth thought it over. "Teffera took drugs for the sim. Maybe he had a contaminated injector, too. And that would make Jarvis the odd one out again because, as far as we know, she didn't take anything at all."

"Although Jarvis makes sense if it's an insider looking for an easy target. Or..." B-C rubbed his fingers through his hair again.

"What?"

"Maybe it was the sim." B-C glanced at him, looking back to his screen when he caught Toreth's gaze. "I mean, there's nothing to say that it wasn't, is there, Para?"

Toreth didn't answer. His conviction that the deaths weren't due to the sim was obviously developing a reputation as an obsession. For a moment, he forced himself to look at the idea head on. Was he fixated on the sabotage idea? He didn't think so, but then, if he was, he wouldn't, as it were.

Toreth sat down at the desk again and read through the postmortem results slowly. Anti-nausea drugs. Not the same as the drugs used by Teffera; however, it was as close to a clue about method as anything they'd found so far. Somewhere in the mounds of case files might be additional clues. Feeling oddly optimistic, he connected through to the main I&I evidence analysis system, and started constructing queries. Did Teffera, Nissim, and Jarvis share any genetic predispositions that would make a particular toxin effective? Were there any shared genetic traits that had no previously known damaging effect, but might somehow make them vulnerable to the sim? Could the sim affect susceptibility to toxins?

Were there any injectors at Teffera's home that hadn't been tested for toxins? Could the sim induce users to injure themselves, as Tara had tried to, without producing any obvious change in behavior?

He kept working, trying more unlikely suggestions as the answers began to come back as negative or insufficient data. The sim was an unknown quantity that the analysis program stumbled over repeatedly. Teaching the system to understand the properties and limits of the sim would take longer than the investigation could last. Worse, the only people who understood the sim well enough to do that worked at SimTech. Asking witnesses and suspects to modify I&I systems was even less standard procedure than fucking them.

Toreth spent a minute or so cheering himself up by imagining applying for high-level damage waivers on the entire SimTech staff, half of P-Leisure, and all known professional corporate sab teams, and then cranking through the interrogations until someone said something helpful. Start with Warrick and the Tefferas, and work his way down the social scale. It might be worth proposing the idea simply to watch Tillotson turn purple. Pity that he wouldn't get the waivers. Maybe he could arrange to have a few more Administration higher-ups killed. So far, producing a big-name corpse seemed to be all he'd achieved in the case. He snorted with laughter, and B-C looked up. "Para?"

"Nothing." Time to get back to work.

To get any results from the system at all, he had to relax the criteria so far that it was only one step up from drawing cards. When he told the analysis system to assume undetectable poisoning as the method, it did spit out a name, although Toreth would've sworn the screen had a slightly apologetic air. Tara Scrivin. Of course—she was a biochemist. She probably had access to the area where the drugs were prepared and possibly the knowledge to make up something the forensics lab couldn't detect. Unfortunately, Toreth would bet any amount of money that she'd told him the truth in her interview. If she'd been faking, she'd done it better than anyone else he'd interrogated. Not to mention her solid alibi for Kelly's death.

While he had nothing better to do, he should at least consider an interrogation. The idea certainly had potential, although Justice (or at least SimTech's lawyers) might make trouble over her mental state. However, with Nissim dead, he had a feeling that waivers of all levels would be a lot easier to come by. Though admittedly tenuous, the possibility of her possessing the skills to create a poison would certainly be enough to get him a low-level waiver. Toreth checked his watch. He could pick Tara up on a witness warrant tomorrow morning, and that would give him twenty-four hours before Warrick's lawyers could possibly wrest her out of custody. He'd tried nice, with Mistry. Now it was time to try a different approach. He could start the interrogation on a level two waiver while they waited for a higher level to come back from Justice.

He called through to Sara, finding her diligently at her desk. The hint with the publication search had paid off, although he doubted it would last. "Sara, I've got a few things for you to do. Start by finding Parsons, and tell him to see me first thing tomorrow."

"You'll be back here?"

"Yeah. Tell him he's got a witness to interrogate—give him Tara Scrivin's file to look over. And apply for a witness warrant for her."

"Okay. See you."

Toreth's stomach rumbled, reminding him of missed meals. Not a good idea, when he needed to concentrate. "Come on," he said to B-C. "Let's get something to eat and then see if we can catch a flight home."

"Tonight?" The junior looked dismayed.

Toreth checked his watch. "Why not? We'll be back in New London by one."

Barret-Connor's narrow shoulders slumped. "Yes, Para."

Chapter Eighteen

❖

The initial interrogation took Parsons an hour and three quarters. Toreth resisted the urge to spectate on the screen in his office—watching other people doing his job, even very talented people like Parsons, always drove him mad. "Anything?" Toreth asked, when Parsons came up to his office.

"No, Para." Parsons wasn't apologetic, simply matter-of-fact. In the eight years he'd known the man, Toreth couldn't remember hearing him sound anything other than calm and cold. His lined face and deep-set dark eyes were equally expressionless. "The same story as in the file, bar variations for errors in recollection well within standard limits."

Sign of someone telling the truth rather than well-rehearsed lies. "Damn. Well, there'll be a level three waiver coming through, so you can see if she'll loosen up for that."

Parsons nodded. "Yes, Para. However, I should tell you that I'm sure I'll be wasting a room booking. I can do her, no problem there, but she doesn't know anything she isn't already talking about."

Fuck. Exactly what he'd thought himself. "Are you sure?"

Parsons nodded again. "Positive. And for once, Justice is right that she's a fragile witness. She isn't a wreck, but she isn't so stable that I can fill her full of drugs and be sure she'll come out the other end exactly the same as she went in. If she's got good lawyers rather than a Justice rep, I'd prefer a level four, maybe five, before I'd even try the top-end level three drugs. Just thought you'd want to know, before I got started."

Toreth nodded. "Thanks. If that's your opinion—?"

"Yes, Para, it is."

"Then I'll try something else." Exactly what that would be, he thought as he watched Parsons leave, was a different question.

While he thought about it, he called up Tara's medical file, scanning through the psych section. Fragile fucking witness indeed. Just the kind of irritation he didn't need on a case that was already looking set to give him ulcers. Particularly annoying that Marian Tanit had pronounced her patient fit enough to return to work and to the sim. Shame she couldn't have glued the girl sufficiently back together for a decent interrogation, too. Not much of a cure, from that point of view.

Poised to page down to a new section, he stopped, attention caught by the diagnosis summary. Not much of a cure. But how much was not much? Toreth spent fifteen minutes searching through the I&I system, read a lot of things that stirred uninformatively hazy memories of interrogator training psychology courses, and decided he needed another opinion. He opened the door to the outer office. "Sara, do you know what a dissociative state is?"

Sara looked around. "Nope. No idea."

"Me neither. Comes from being hung over for most of the nine o'clock seminars, I expect."

She frowned. "Sorry?"

"Nothing. If anyone wants me, I've gone down to Interrogation to find a psychiatric specialist who can explain it to me in words of two syllables or less."

At the time of the merger with Investigation, Toreth had been at the Interrogation Division for a year and he'd enjoyed his work. However, it hadn't taken him long to see where the brighter future lay. He'd worked hard to win a place in the first round of appointments for the newly created post of para-investigator, a job that theoretically combined the skills of both investigator and interrogator.

Interrogation was a profession that had certain basic requirements. Primarily, the ability to hurt people, sometimes kill them, and not care. Plenty of interrogators had applied for the para conversion course, and few had made it. The successful ones were on the more socially adept end of the spectrum—those who could be let near citizens of the Administration without the precaution of a damage waiver. At the time, Toreth had heard the term "high-functioning" used.

Or, as Sara put it in her less tactful moments, the difference between paras and interrogators was that the former weren't quite so dead behind the eyes.

Parsons was a classic example of an interrogator, but they weren't all so icy. As Toreth explained his question to Psychiatric Specialist Senior Interrogator Warner, he found his mind drifting back to Sara's words. To be fair, the man was working—a prisoner sat slumped in the chair, head forward and hands limp in the restraints. Toreth himself was known to be tetchy when interrupted mid-interrogation. That said, talking to Warner was still hard work. He had a combative stance, legs apart, heavy shoulders braced, leaning a little forward. At the same time, his gaze kept flicking away from Toreth's face, searching the interrogation room, before returning to glare for a few seconds. Overall, it left an odd impression of aggressive disinterest. "Who's feeding you that crap?" the interrogator asked when Toreth had finished.

"Crap?"

"That's corporate lawyer-spawned bullshit, that is." Warner snorted. "'My client wasn't in control of his actions, he didn't know what he was doing.' Tossers."

"Can it actually happen, though? Could Scrivin do things without knowing it? Several times. Complicated things, with a long-term plan, and then forget about them afterwards?"

"Now *that* sounds like a DID. Dissociative Identity Disorder. An even bigger pile of steaming lawyer crap." He spat the words out. "'My client embezzled a million euros and used it to fund a resister cell, but he did it in his sleep.' Pah. Bullshit."

Toreth sighed silently. "But is it possible? I was told you were the expert in this sort of thing."

Warner's eyes narrowed, and for a moment Toreth thought he would start demanding names. Then he shrugged quickly. "Sure, it's *possible*, in theory. Have you got the list of symptoms? Usually they wheel them out like they got them from the manual—that's how you know they're talking shit."

"So? What are they?"

"Presence of multiple distinct identities or personality states that recurrently take control of the individual's behavior, accompanied by an inability to recall important personal information that is too extensive to be explained by ordinary forgetfulness." Warner produced the definition in a monotone, staring past Toreth, before he looked back again. "And very expensive lawyers. That's usually a clue."

"It does happen, then?"

"Sometimes," Warner admitted reluctantly. "Rare as rocking-horse shit. I've seen maybe four in thirty-five years, and I get lumbered with all the real basket cases. Ninety-nine times out of a hundred it's someone spinning a line to get out of here."

"How do you tell the difference?"

The man shrugged again. "Send 'em down here on a high-level waiver and I'll tell you in a couple of days."

Visions of SimTech lawyers rose like malevolent ghosts. "If I can't get a high waiver?"

"It'll take us a while longer. We're interrogators, not diagnosticians. Or—" Warner glanced away again. "If you're that keen, send the prisoner to Psychoprogramming and get a deep scan done. DID is only nature's version of the fast re-education crap they pull over there, anyway." His gaze slid back. "But with the waiting lists they've got, you're better off here."

The prisoner stirred, and Warner looked over. "Looks like I've got company again."

"Thanks," Toreth said, taking the hint.

"Send her down," Warner repeated. "*If* she's a real DID, I can shove the results through the expert system when we've finished with her. They're so rare we're short of comparison data."

Toreth sat on his hands outside Tillotson's office, trying to keep still, until the section head called him back in. It had taken so long that he'd begun to think Tillotson must be getting somewhere. However, one look at Tillotson changed his mind about that. "No luck?" Toreth asked.

The section head smiled sourly. "No. Psychoprogramming says that their priority is political, not corporate or ordinary criminal, so the request would have to be put through the system in the usual way."

"This case *is* political. Didn't you tell them that we have a murdered legislator?"

Tillotson frowned. "Of course I did. Or rather, I told them that we have a dead legislator. Murdered is a matter of speculation—unless you have some information you haven't shared yet?" Toreth had to shake his head. "I'm sorry, Toreth. I'll do what I can to shift them, but I can't promise anything."

Toreth sighed. "Thanks, anyway."

The man was a waste of good oxygen, Toreth mused on the way back to his office. In fact, you could take every Administration official at Tillotson's level or higher and sink them in the North Sea and it would only improve Europe. Not to mention violate a slew of intercontinental treaties regarding toxic waste. The idea generated a small smile of satisfaction, not least because, if you had the right kind of petty mind, it was treason. If he'd said it out loud in the coffee room, it could be incitement to discontent. It wasn't, of course. He was anti-moron, not anti-Administration. Not his fault if the two often coincided.

Tillotson probably would try his useless best. However, Toreth didn't have weeks to hold Tara Scrivin until Psychoprogramming could get around to formally rejecting his application because it had a spelling mistake in the prisoner's name on page ten. He'd have to see what a little sweet-talking could achieve.

Psychoprogramming had been created at the time of the reorganization, stealing experts away from many divisions. Int-Sec made a natural home for them, but they were one of the more clandestine divisions. Unlike I&I, they had no public contact numbers, nor access for private legal representatives to bother them over the fate of the majority of the unlucky citizens who crossed their threshold.

Toreth scanned his ID at the unmanned minor entrance and was let through the heavy security door. The solid sound of the door closing behind him gave

Toreth no more than a momentary twinge of unease—Mindfuck might be departmental rivals, but they were Administration colleagues. Colleagues who were doing very nicely, or so it looked to him. None of the buildings in the Int-Sec complex was more than a dozen years old, so there was no reason that the place should seem so much sprucer than I&I. Toreth suspected that one reason Mindfuck was so secretive about their techniques was to hide the fact that most of the time they did fuck all. If they were really so fucking busy, where did they find the spare budget for fresh paint and new carpets?

Certainly it was quieter than I&I. Still, like I&I, the detention levels were underground, and they were probably noisier than the admin areas. He passed a door marked *Research,* where a serious and heavily armed guard watched him pass. Toreth's lip curled. Pretentious wankers. Who the hell were they expecting, here in the middle of the Int-Sec complex? Packs of armed resisters come to find their friends? Finally he reached his goal and stuck his head around the office door. "Ange, my darling, can I have a word?"

The senior administrative assistant to the head of the Psychoprogramming Division was putting her coat on.

"What do *you* want? Make it quick, whatever it is—I've got an appointment."

Not a promising opener. Toreth made it a policy to keep on the good side of senior admins, whatever their division, and he'd been hoping for a better reception. Ange was a favorite because, as well as making a useful contact, she was married but not very married. That gave him an easy way to keep her friendly, as well as to fill the occasional lunch hour. Had he remembered to call her after the last time? He sat on the edge of her desk, to get his eyes lower than hers, and gave her his patented admin-melting smile. She looked resolutely unimpressed. "I wanted to talk about booking an m-f—about booking a psychoprogramming session with one of your esteemed and preferably discreet colleagues," Toreth said.

"So fill in a request form and send it to Scheduling."

"Ange, sweetheart..."

"No form, no session. Anyway, they're booked up two months ahead for externals."

By which time the SimTech funding would be history and the case effectively over. He inched closer and cranked the charm up a notch. "I'll make it worth your while, I promise. Dinner? Somewhere nice?"

"Well...there might be a couple of cancellations, I suppose." A smile indicated a slight thaw as she sat down at her screen and switched it back on. "Of course, Scheduling will play hell about me messing with dates over their heads, but they'll live. Let me see...all right. There's an afternoon slot in three weeks' time—that's absolutely the best I can do."

Still too late. "I need it now. First thing tomorrow I'm going to have corporate lawyers crawling all over me."

Absently, she reached out and rested her hand on his thigh. "Lucky lawyers. But I can't do any better."

"Okay." If that was the best he could get, he'd have to take it. He hoped Tillotson could come up with something better, and that SimTech's lawyers wouldn't be too tedious. Neither of those sounded like good bets.

"What's the prisoner ID code?" Ange said.

"She's not a prisoner, she's a witness."

She smiled archly. "And you mean to say your silver tongue's not silvery enough to get her to talk?"

He grinned briefly and touched the center of his top lip with his tongue. "What do you think? Anyway, that's not the reason. She's talking, all right, but I think she's not remembering what happened."

Ange's eyes narrowed. "Illegal memory blocks?"

Not quite what he'd meant, but he liked the reaction. "Just a suspicion. If it's not a memory block, I don't want to waste weeks chasing it up. All I need is a scan to look for a block or other evidence of tampering—no deep poking round or reprogramming."

She gave an exaggerated sigh. "And I suppose you don't have a damage waiver?"

"Indeed I do. Level three witness."

"Is that an I&I witness waiver or anything good for over here?"

"Ah."

She sighed again. "All right. *If* you can get her to consent—signed forms, mind, and no drugs before she signs them—then I can squeeze in an extra session later today. I'll book it in as a recalibration, so no one will ask any questions about queue jumping, and I'll ask Seiden to stay and do it. But you might want to consider taking him out for a meal as well."

Toreth laughed. "I'll think of something else."

She patted his leg and began to enter the booking into the computer. "This is just for you, Toreth. I don't want you telling anyone else I'm a soft touch."

"Cross my heart. You're an angel, Ange."

She smiled without looking up. "This dinner had better be good, that's all."

On his way back to I&I to collect Tara, Toreth made a mental note that hinting about a threat to Psychoprogramming's fiercely guarded exclusive rights to mindfucking was a technique he'd have to remember in future.

Up in the observation gallery, Seiden worked over a screen, grumbling occasionally about the unexpected extension of his shift. Toreth kept the length of the room between them. At the end of a long day, Seiden's body odor could strip paint.

Setting the machine up took forever. Through the window, Toreth studied Tara's pale, elfin face. Lying on the platform in the enclosed room below them, sedated and surrounded by the m-f equipment, she looked horribly fragile.

A level three I&I damage waiver didn't explicitly cover memory scans. The risk from the procedure was small, but if he ended up damaging a technically un-waivered witness, he'd be lucky to get away with a reprimand. SimTech's lawyers would raise hell, no doubt, with Warrick encouraging them every step of the way. Tara had signed the consent to the procedure eagerly enough, once he'd explained she'd be released after the scan, but a lawyer could so easily twist it into her sign-ing under duress. Toreth might even be sacked, particularly since he'd deliberately circumvented Tillotson's authority to get her here.

"This is safe, isn't it?" Toreth asked.

Seiden didn't look up from the screen. "Yes. As safe as it can be for someone with a history of mental instability."

"Oh, hell."

"If you don't want to know, don't ask. If she has been tampered with, then it's possible that messing around without knowing what was done to her could be un-fortunate." He scratched the back of his neck, and then added, "That's why the prisoners we get here have high-level waivers."

"She's a witness, not a prisoner, so be careful."

Seiden looked around, offended. "I'm always careful. Even with the low-life resisters that get passed through for reboring. Of course," he added more thought-fully, "that's different. We don't need a waiver at all after they're convicted."

"If she breaks down, I'm sunk."

"She won't. She's not even going to get a headache." Seiden flipped a plexi-glass cover up from a small panel and pressed a button. "Activating."

The platform slid smoothly into the tunnel, the upper half of Tara's body van-ishing into the maw of the machine, and Toreth waited. After a while, Seiden said, "If there was any justice in the world, you'd need a waiver to do that to music."

It took Toreth a moment to realize Seiden was addressing him. "What?"

"To hum like that. If it's in a key, it's one I don't recognize."

"Sorry." Toreth hadn't noticed he'd been doing it.

"I play the cornet; bet you didn't know that, did you? Jazz. Nearly professional standard." Seiden peered at the screen, then nodded. "Right, I've finished the calibrations. First, I'll do the scan. Then I'll take the interviews she gave you and play them back to her, to stimulate her memory. If she has memory blocks, that should show them up."

"Don't forget the DID."

"I told you already, it's in the program."

From the gallery, Toreth could see nothing except the smooth metal casing of the large scanner and the blinking lights of the computer systems. He thought that, compared to the sim, it was a lot of tech to achieve something that was on the surface less impressive. Like the sim, it was dull to watch, but if it produced both a result and an undamaged witness it was time well spent. His slanted view of Seiden's screen showed samples of the scan results flicking into life and vanishing again. Complex 3D traces, like multicolored tangles of thread, represented the activity of neurons. A light touch, for the m-f. With more invasive and potentially damaging scanning and a lot of expensive computing power, the results could be processed into fragmentary thoughts and memories. That was the reason that mind-fuckers were widely considered to be a threat to I&I territory. More by Interrogation than Investigation, but that was half of Toreth's job.

Psychoprogramming's specialty was brainwashing, not mind reading, but the m-f still gave a direct link into the brain. At the moment, it made for a ridiculously expensive alternative to real interrogation, but Toreth had to admit, reluctantly, that in some cases it was better. For one thing, it was capable of extracting memories that couldn't be deliberately retrieved by their owner. Even when pressed to the point of desperation, most people knew more than they could consciously call to mind. For another, as it worked on unconscious subjects, the m-f couldn't be lied to. Nor was it as susceptible to the anti-interrogation drugs and vaccines that kept I&I locked in a pharmacological arms race with resisters and criminals. Still, as he'd told Chev, it would be a long time before the equipment below him displaced people like Warner and Parsons. Cost wasn't the only factor. The m-f was a perfect tool, as long as you ignored the failures: the partial and complete amnesiacs, the psychotics, catatonics, and other oops-we-fucked-up results.

Toreth leaned against the glass of the observation gallery and stared down at his valuable, vulnerable witness. Neural scanning, direct stimulation and manipulation of memories—the basic technology here wasn't so different to the sim. Yet, while Seiden was willing to admit to the dangers of the m-f, Warrick was unshakable on the safety of the sim. On the other hand, if the sim were as dangerous as the m-f, SimTech would be full of highly paid expert vegetables. There was no evidence the sim could injure. Not counting, of course, three corpses.

Time passed slowly, almost an hour and a half. Eventually, Seiden said, "Done."

"Is she all right?"

"Fine, as far as I can tell at this stage." He looked over his shoulder and grinned. "'Course she could be completely fucked when she wakes up."

Probably just trying to wind him up. "Did you get anything?"

"Well..." Seiden paged through screens of numbers and complicated 3D mappings that meant nothing to Toreth. "Nothing glaringly obvious. A few anomalies are flagged here and there."

"What the hell does anomalies mean?"

Seiden shrugged. "It means something odd or irregular. Probably just a glitch

162

in the scanner. Things like that usually go away once the program analyses the data and hammers it into shape. I can't tell you for sure until these results have gone through the program." The screen went black, and Seiden blew out his cheeks, looking at his watch. "And that's going to wait until tomorrow morning. Results by the afternoon, and only because Ange said to be nice to you. The systems are swamped. Send one reformed citizen out of here, we get two bad ones back in."

When the Psychoprogramming medic pronounced her fit to leave, Toreth arranged a taxi to take Tara Scrivin wherever she wanted to go. He already had three messages from SimTech's legal department waiting on his comm. It gave him great satisfaction to send replies, all polite variations on, "You can fuck off, because we don't have her anymore."

He was back in his office, reading through Tara's files again, when a knock on the door attracted his attention. "Yes?"

Sara appeared. "If there's nothing else, I'm off."

"What time is it?"

"Nearly seven."

Toreth blinked. "Really? Okay, fine." As Sara turned to go, Toreth remembered something he ought to have checked already. "One minute. First thing tomorrow, can you get me the surveillance recordings for the SimTech pharmacy? Probably no go, but if there was something in that injector it must have come from somewhere."

She paused. "I'm sorry?"

Other people might simply have forgotten about something like that. However, since it was Sara, her blank expression gave him a sinking feeling. "There should've been surveillance equipment installed at SimTech. I told Belqola to arrange it weeks ago."

Sara regarded him in eloquent silence. She hadn't approved of Belqola's appointment in the first place, and remembering that didn't do anything for Toreth's temper.

"Where the fuck is he?" he snapped.

"At SimTech," she said promptly. "Talking to the technical people. Or he was ten minutes ago. He called me and made a point of saying he was still there. Trying to look keen, if you ask me. Do you want me to ask him to come back?"

"No. I'm not hanging round here. I'll find him and then go straight home afterwards. Call him; tell him to wait there for me."

By the time he reached the AERC, Toreth was in a steaming bad temper. Knowing that he should have checked that the surveillance was in place himself only made it worse. However, nursemaiding idiot juniors wasn't Toreth's job. Toreth didn't make many mistakes when selecting for his team, and the failure was another irritation. So much for high fucking training scores. As he slammed the car door, he vowed he'd never again make the mistake of relying purely on those when picking new team members.

He found Belqola waiting in the entrance, looking apprehensive. Good. "Where's the surveillance for the pharmacy?" Toreth asked.

"I've arranged for it to go in now, Para."

Sara had obviously taken pity on the idiot, for what little good that would do him. "Using your time machine, are you?"

"I—I'm sorry, Para."

"Sorry is no fucking good to me. And no fucking good to Pearl Nissim, either." Toreth stepped closer. "Why the hell wasn't it in place a month ago?"

The junior shifted his feet, but didn't back away. "I forgot to arrange it, Para."

That won him one point for not coming up with an excuse, but only one. "You can tell that to the disciplinary board. I'm sure Tillotson'll be sympathetic." He waited, but Belqola had decided that silence was the best approach. "Do you know what?" Toreth said. "I can't be fucking bothered with disciplinary reports and turning up to hearings when I should be running my cases. I don't need to waste any more of my time on you." Belqola brightened very slightly, before Toreth continued. "Because tomorrow morning, you're out of my team. And I promise you that with the reference I'll put in your file, no senior will touch you with a fucking shock stick. You'll be doing investigative grunt work and level one interrogations 'til you fucking retire."

Belqola's stricken expression provided at least some satisfaction. "Please, one more chance." Belqola's gaze dropped, and then he looked up again, taking a deep breath. "I'll do whatever it takes, Para. Anything."

With the metaphorical axe about to fall, Toreth paused. Was that an offer? It was hard to tell from Belqola's expression—he'd looked desperate since the beginning of the conversation. Not that Toreth intended to change his mind about throwing the man out. His team were worth far more to him than a quick fuck. However, it might be entertaining to see how far the junior would go for the sake of his career. He could postpone the reassignment for a little while. Until the end of the investigation, say. Toreth smiled slowly, watching the hope kindle in Belqola's eyes. "Okay. Come out for a drink, and we can discuss your future performance."

Toreth picked a nearby bar at random, and let Belqola buy him a drink. Then he listened with a fragment of his attention as Belqola talked, explaining how much his job meant to him, how proud his parents were of his career, and a lot of other probably fictional crap Toreth wasn't interested in. The underlying message was clear enough. After they'd finished their drinks, Belqola checked his watch. "I ought to get home. My—my wife was expecting me an hour ago."

First time he'd mentioned his wife. Just testing Toreth's intentions—it was quite clear he'd stay if required to do so. Toreth smiled indulgently. "All right. But first—" He looked over towards the toilets. After a moment's hesitation, Belqola stood and led the way.

The toilets were fortunately empty, and equipped with sufficiently spacious cubicles to make things, if not comfortable, then at least not too awkward. Toreth leaned against the wall of the cubicle, hands behind his back, and said, "Well?"

Belqola started to kneel, then obviously thought better of the state of the floor and settled for squatting. Once there, he hesitated; Toreth wondered if it was second thoughts or a desire to set the deal out in more concrete terms. No chance of that. "Done this before?" Toreth asked. Belqola nodded. "Good. So I won't need to give directions." Resting his head against the wall, Toreth closed his eyes and waited as Belqola unfastened his clothes and freed his cock, already hard with anticipation. Another pause, then Toreth heard one deep breath before Belqola took him in.

Toreth was willing to concede that, with the decision made, the man wasn't bad. Seven out of ten, he'd give him. Nice and deep, not rushing things despite the uncomfortable position. Putting enough effort into it that Toreth could feel him gagging from time to time. Not Toreth's problem, nor Belqola's for much longer. He clenched his fists, toes curling, pressing himself back against the wall as, for long, delicious seconds, his orgasm wiped out the irritations and stresses of the case and everything else in his life.

Belqola spat into the toilet, the sound nudging Toreth out of the pleasant post-orgasm haze. As usual, Toreth enjoyed the soothing flood of endorphins. And, as usual, he felt an urge to get away from the person responsible for it as soon as was practical. He zipped himself up and then opened the door without offering the junior a hand up. The toilets were still deserted, making an uncomplicated end to a very satisfactory ten minutes.

Back at the table, Toreth sat. Belqola hovered by his chair for a moment, then said, "I'll see you tomorrow, Para."

"Don't be late. And give my love to your wife."

As he watched Belqola leave, Toreth caught sight of Warrick leaning against the bar. There was no reason Toreth ought to be surprised—they were only a few minutes' walk from the AERC. However, the idea of Warrick watching him—as he clearly had been—was peculiarly unsettling. Toreth wondered briefly if Warrick had followed them there. As soon as he caught Toreth's eye, Warrick picked up his drink and strolled over. "Good to see the forces of law and order working so hard," he said as he dropped into the chair vacated by Belqola. He settled in with a comfortable casualness that didn't disguise the curiosity in his glance.

"Just getting to know my staff," Toreth said. "Harry Belqola. He's a new junior—finished his training this year."

"Ah. So how's he enjoying the investigation?"

"I don't care. It's a job, not a hobby."

His sharp tone didn't scratch Warrick's poise. "And how's he enjoying the investigator?"

Toreth blinked. "I have no idea what you're talking about," he said, and hid his smile in his drink.

"Oh, please. Don't tell me he turned you down?"

Toreth looked up, nettled. "Of course not!" Then he caught Warrick's smile. "Bastard. You should come and work for us, you know. You can have Belqola's job."

"Not my field. Besides, it was hardly challenging. Or do you choose your juniors on qualities other than deductive skills?"

"He came highly recommended." By fucking idiots.

Warrick snorted. "I'm sure he did."

To Toreth's relief, Warrick apparently found the whole situation funny rather than...what? Threatening? A reason for jealousy? Not the kind of shit Toreth wanted to deal with when he was fucking a witness in the middle of a case.

Warrick sipped his drink and eyed Toreth appraisingly. "You didn't really want him, anyway."

"How the fuck would you know?"

"He was too keen to go along with it," he said judiciously. "Not putting up enough resistance. You could've had him over the table if you'd wanted to—more comfortable than your ten minutes in the toilets probably were."

He noticed an attentive silence at the next table. "He's married," Toreth said, as if it made a difference to how willing the junior had been.

Warrick snorted, unimpressed. "I know. He hadn't even bothered taking his ring off. Which probably means he isn't feeling guilty about it, either, and that makes him even less interesting. To you."

"Big assumption from someone who's known me for what, five weeks? I thought scientists were supposed to consider the evidence."

"And the evidence tells me you like to play games. Particular games, at that. Tell me something, how often do you have sex with the same person, on average?"

"Once." Toreth shrugged. "Twice, maybe, if—"

"Well?"

Another fucking interrogation, but what the hell. "If they regretted the first time. You've been spending too much time with Tanit."

166

Warrick ignored the comparison. "You're only interested as long as your target is putting up resistance of some kind—my point exactly."

"You don't exactly play hard to get," Toreth pointed out.

"No." Warrick smiled slightly. "No, I don't, do I?"

A pause, while Toreth considered this exception that proved the rule. It edged dangerously towards a silence before the explanation occurred to him. Or rather an analogy: Ange, with her useful influence in Psychoprogramming. "You've got the sim," Toreth said.

"Ah, yes. Of course." There was a moment of probably mutual hidden relief before Warrick said, "Why did you arrest Tara?"

Not surprising that he'd heard about it; from his calm tone, he'd heard about her release as well. "She wasn't arrested. We reinterviewed her as a witness, regarding the evidence she gave before."

"You couldn't do that at SimTech?"

"No."

A long pause, then Warrick nodded. "I see."

"Did you speak to her?"

"No. I understand she's at home. She called Dr. Tanit."

That explained why Warrick was taking it so well. Once he'd heard Tara's account of her experiences with Parsons and at Psychoprogramming, he'd be less sanguine. Still, his good mood upped the probability of a fuck this evening. Toreth wouldn't mind keeping up the buzz he'd got from Belqola's efforts. With that in mind, Toreth asked, "Would you like a drink?"

Warrick shook his head and raised his half-empty glass. "I'm fine. I try not to drink too much during the week. Are you making any progress with the investigation? With Legislator Nissim, I mean?"

Toreth shrugged, wondering if the change of topic was a refusal. "Big mess of nothings and dead ends. No suspects, no method, no opportunity. Tillotson still thinks the sim killed her and the others."

"Then he's an even bigger idiot than you said he was," Warrick said emphatically. "It's not possible. And I bet your so-called computing experts who've been thrashing around in my code say it's impossible, too."

"No, they say they haven't yet found a way the sim could kill. They also say it'll take weeks to be sure."

"Months," Warrick predicted with relish. "If not years. There are thousands of man-years of effort in it. And in the end they won't find anything that would kill a sim user." He sipped his drink. "While we're on the subject, may I ask why you still have so many of the files at SimTech sealed? It's making work very difficult, and it's upsetting the sponsors. You have copies, why stop us using them?"

"It's procedure, I'm afraid." Then, one eye on the rest of the evening, Toreth modified the automatic response: "But I'll have a word with Tillotson about it."

"Really?" Warrick sounded genuinely surprised. "Thanks. Can I do anything in return?"

"Such as?"

Warrick sighed. "Or, in the less subtle version, do you want to fuck? Or was your staff management session too taxing?"

A woman at the next table spluttered red wine all over her white and silver skirt. A man Toreth guessed was her boyfriend started to stand up with intent, took a better look at Toreth's uniform, and sat down quickly. Toreth stifled a laugh, because there was no point in starting trouble. Warrick looked openly amused. "That's a handy perk of the job."

"How the hell do you avoid getting beaten up in bars?" Toreth asked with genuine curiosity.

"Well, normally I don't say things like that. It must be the company I'm keeping." Warrick stood up. "Coming?" he asked in a pointed voice which made white and silver skirt giggle again. Toreth winked at her as they walked past, and the boyfriend looked daggers at them.

They had reached the door and were discussing hotels when Toreth's comm chimed. "Damn. Excuse me."

Warrick leaned against a pillar and waited. Toreth listened, and sighed, and agreed, and finally finished the call. "On my way."

"I sense impending disappointment," Warrick said.

Toreth opened his hand screen and flicked through numbers. "I have to go in to work."

"Why?"

"Sorry, can't tell you."

"Then I hope it's good news. For someone." Without a farewell, Warrick pried himself away from the pillar and walked out of the bar.

Toreth felt slightly aggrieved. It wasn't *his* fault. Someone had very inconsiderately found a body.

Chapter Nineteen

❖

When he reached the morgue in the Justice complex, he discovered it was actually two bodies.

A Justice officer waited at reception for him, a woman in her midthirties who looked tired—probably from life in general rather than anything that had happened tonight. Justice officers had plenty of experience in dealing with corpses. She also looked less than pleased to see him, which was no surprise. Better funding, better facilities, and a reputation for arrogance made I&I unpopular in the Justice Department and considering the time, she might well have been going off shift when someone ordered her to wait for him. "Senior Para-investigator Toreth, sir?" He could almost hear her teeth gritting.

He nodded. "Just call me Para. No need for the sir."

"Officer Lee." She sounded surprised, but slightly friendlier. As they walked through the dingy corridors, Toreth amused himself by wondering how she'd look with her severely pinned-up hair let down, and a couple of weeks' sleep.

Once they reached the vast morgue, the officer told him to wait by the empty reception desk while she tracked down assistance. Her footsteps echoed as she walked away, the sound distorted by the tall ranks of preservation units. It was still relatively early in the evening, a quiet time down here, Toreth guessed. Eventually she reappeared with a scrubbed-looking young man in a spotlessly white uniform and a nametag identifying him as Pathology Officer Kirkby.

"Evening, sir," Kirkby said. His smile was a disconcerting on-off flash, like a torch, leaving the impression he had consciously to operate it. "This way, please," he added, leading the way across the room. Eventually he stopped by one of the racks and pulled a flat control screen from his pocket. "Let me see . . . yes. These are the two."

He touched the screen and first one unit opened noiselessly, then a second, spilling chill wisps of condensation into the already cool air. Toreth recognized one of the corpses at once: Jin Li Yang, his usually pale face now stark white and

169

his spiky hair matted and filthy. His ID must have been the reason Warrick had had his evening spoiled; the man's file would be tagged with his association to a high-priority I&I case, making the call to Toreth automatic. The other body was of a man of indeterminate age—anywhere between thirty and fifty. He had scruffy clothes and long, tangled hair and a beard that were probably brown. Indigent, judging by the smell if nothing else.

"Where did you find Yang?" Toreth asked Lee.

"We pulled him out of the river and—sir? Are you all right?"

Toreth had turned away quickly, but not quickly enough that Lee hadn't seen his face. Out of the river. The body hadn't looked it. Obviously drowned corpses were bad enough, but surprise intensified the reaction and it slipped beyond his control. He could *feel* the water choking him, the hands holding him down as he struggled and his treacherous lungs fought to pull more water in. Drowning. He was—

"Sir? Para?"

Slowly, Toreth became aware of a hand on his shoulder. Lee peered up at him, her face creased with concern. "I just—" Shit, he'd have to say something, much as he loathed admitting the weakness. "I had a bad experience once. Some fucking idiot tried to drown me." Leave it at that.

Lee nodded. "Close the unit," she said to Kirkby.

"No. I'm fine." He forced himself to turn, to look down at the bodies, focusing on the questions he had to ask. "Who's the other one?"

"An indig. We'll get his registered name from the Data Division as soon as the DNA check comes back, but his friends called him Tracker."

"Friends? What's the story?"

"Seven of them, counting this dead one, sitting round a fire. Tracker disappeared; one witness said he thought Tracker might have heard something, one of the others said he thought he had a meeting arranged with 'a friend.' Probably a supplier. I wouldn't rely on either of those statements. Then—a few minutes later, half an hour later or an hour later, depending on who you ask—they heard a yell."

Lee shook her head. "They must have really counted him a friend, 'cause they went to look for him. They looked down the alley and saw a shape bending over what turned out to be the body." Forestalling his question, she added, "Too dark to get many details. Three say a man, one says a woman, two honest 'don't know's.'"

Toreth nodded. Lee was almost certainly right that the "don't know's" were the more honest witnesses.

"Then, and this is a shame, a couple of our witnesses shouted out. Mystery figure saw them and ran. When they got there it was clean gone and Tracker was dying. He'd been shot in the chest at close range with a silenced weapon—no one heard a shot."

"Did Tracker say anything to them?" Toreth asked.

She shook her head.

"So how did you find Yang?"

"The officer on the scene—that was me—spoke to the indigs there. Two of them mentioned hearing a splash just before they turned the corner. I ordered a search of the river and we found him—" She hesitated, gaze searching his face, and he gestured impatiently for her to continue. "He'd been pushed, or had fallen, into the water. The river's deep and fast-flowing there, but the body snagged on some railings underwater; the tide would have washed it clear within the hour."

"How did you get there so quickly?"

"The indigs called Justice." The officer shrugged in response to his expression of surprise. "They called the Administration indig medic service and they called us at the same time. It happens more often than you'd think." She gave Toreth a sly smile. "Of course, you wouldn't know about that up in the rarefied heights of I&I."

Toreth acknowledged the jab with a smile of his own, but it annoyed him that the woman was right. He didn't know much about Justice work and although normally he didn't care about the good opinion of Justice officers, he found himself bothered by it now. Perhaps it was because Lee had displayed a higher degree of competence than the run-of-the-mill Justice employee.

"What killed Yang?" he asked, not wanting to hear the answer.

Kirkby's smile clicked on again. "Drowning." He said it with a relish that made Toreth's fists clench involuntarily.

"He just—" Fuck. "Just drowned? That quickly?"

"It can be almost instantaneous. Vagal inhibition from the shock of hitting the water can stop the heart, especially if they're drunk." Kirkby nodded at Yang. "He'd had a glass or two of something. Normally people hold their breath until elevated carbon dioxide forces them to breathe." Flash of teeth, his eyes intent on Toreth's face. "But they can panic and inhale right away."

Toreth turned away, bracing one hand on the cool metal of the preservation unit. He could barely hear Kirkby's voice over the pounding in his ears. Jesus, he was going to be sick—he didn't dare open his mouth to tell the bastard to shut the fuck up. *Inspiration of fluid by the lungs induces choking and vomiting. Unconsciousness and death follow quickly.* Memories flooded back, so vivid, of sitting through the pathology lecture, held back from bolting only because then everyone would see him, everyone would *know.*

"Or there's laryngeal spasm," Kirkby said. "Sometimes—"

"That's enough," Lee said sharply.

"He asked," Kirkby said, sounding hurt.

"Get back to reception," she said.

He heard the hiss of the units closing, and then footsteps retreating. Toreth breathed deeply, trying to think about anything other than his roiling stomach. A

171

light touch on his shoulder was followed by Lee clearing her throat. "I'm sorry about that, Para."

After a final swallow, pushing down the nausea, Toreth turned around, forcing himself to meet her eyes. "Forget it. I'll need all your interrogation—interview— transcripts and I'll need to speak to the witnesses. Are they still here?"

Lee nodded. "We held the witnesses because of the flag on Yang's file. Do you want to do it now?"

"No, it'll wait until tomorrow," he said, and smiled slightly at her expression of relief. "I'd like to look through the transcripts now, in case there's anything I need to check right away, and then I'll send a couple of investigators around to-morrow morning. Investigator Stephen Lambrick will be in charge. They can... may they use your interview facilities? It'll save us both the transfer paperwork."

The change of phrase from a demand to a request didn't impress her. "What-ever you need, Para."

While she made the arrangements, Toreth called I&I and sent a forensic team along to the murder site. With luck, Justice wouldn't have done too much damage up there. The bodies could go to I&I—more business for O'Reilly.

He sat in Lee's small office—obviously shared with two other officers, but empty at this hour. The descriptions of the figure were infuriatingly vague, although four out of the six were positive it wasn't Jin Li Yang. Two said they saw reddish hair, one said dark, three didn't know. No one could agree on a height. All six were either drunk or had systems filled with assortments of drugs that raised even Toreth's eyebrows. Needless to say, there were no security cameras near the scene.

Toreth considered Yang's possessions as they lay spread out on the desk in their protective plastic sheaths: a hand screen yielding nothing on a quick inspec-tion, ID, and credit card. No indication Yang had expected trouble, nothing out of place at all. No gun, either. It could be lying at the bottom of the river—people were searching for it now—but Toreth didn't expect them to find it. No fucking *ev-idence.* Story of his life, at least on this case.

Chapter Twenty

❖

The end was always mercifully fast, the unrelenting grip pinning him, forcing his head down. The horror of the water flooding into his lungs and his body's desperate, involuntary reactions. Choking and vomiting. Unconsciousness followed quickly. Yes, it had. But not quickly enough to avoid leaving the memory, a seed for the nightmare.

Toreth woke at six thirty a.m., jerking awake for the third time that night as the water-distorted noises in his ears faded into silence. He fought his way free of the tangled sheet and sat up, sweat stinging his eyes. If you died in a dream, supposedly you died in the real world too, heart stopping in sympathy. Sara swore that it was true; Toreth knew it was bullshit. He'd drowned in dozens of dreams, and he always woke. Nauseous and with muscles aching from the phantom struggles, but he always woke. Toreth took a deep breath as his heart rate settled down. He was already starting to shiver in the cool air.

In the bathroom, it took him a minute before he could make himself step into the shower, and another two before he could put his face under the spray. He stood under the water, fighting down the rising panic until it was over, and the fear settled down. Back to normal again. He'd expected to have the dream, although three in one night was bad. Fucking Kirkby's fault, Toreth thought sourly as he toweled himself dry. Without his little performance it would have been one—none, if he'd been lucky. If he had another tomorrow, that meant at least a week of them. Maybe even carrying on until the case closed and he could forget about Yang. Unpleasant as the dreams were, Toreth was used to them. Knowing them, understanding their rhythm, gave him an illusion of control that he welcomed. It was the next best thing to never having another one in his life.

They'd come up once during his yearly psych evaluations. The division psychologist had seemed more interested in discussing them than suggesting any way of making them stop. He'd spent a long time talking about the symbolism of water and fear of death, until Toreth could barely breathe for the tightness in his throat.

Eventually, he'd told the psychologist that unless he shut the fuck up, Toreth would fetch a couple of friends and demonstrate just how fucking symbolic it felt to have your head held underwater until you drowned. No doubt the outburst had produced an interesting entry in his psych file, but at least it had brought the interview to an end. He hadn't failed the evaluation, of course. It took a lot more than threats to kill for a para-investigator to fail an I&I psych assessment.

Toreth jogged in to work, and then spent an hour in the gym. No swimming, though, not just yet. Combined with the lack of sleep, the unaccustomed early-morning exercise left him tired, but at least it banished the leftover tension from the nightmares.

When he arrived at his office, Toreth found a message from Tillotson waiting for him. Sara gave him a sympathetic look and promised him a quadruple-strength coffee when he got back. However, as soon as Toreth walked through the door, Tillotson offered him a cup of his own coffee, which was unusual enough to arouse instant suspicion. Still, he accepted gratefully—section heads received a far better grade of coffee than the lower ranks.

"You're sure it wasn't suicide?" Tillotson asked when Toreth had run through the events of the previous night.

"Positive. Can I—?" Toreth waved the cup, and Tillotson nodded. Toreth re-filled his cup and sat down. "The SimTech man went in the river and someone left the scene in a hell of a hurry. And we didn't find a gun. Even if it had gone in the river the detectors should have found it. On the positive side, it does help the cor-porate sabotage angle. Rather than the sim killing them, I mean. It was an awfully real bullet in that indig."

Tillotson frowned, clearly irritated by having his pet theory mocked. "Any one of the indigs could have killed both of them."

"Justice is holding them for a few days—I can interrogate if you like. But if they did it, why call Justice? Why not—" Toreth set the refilled cup on the section head's desk, because he hated to let anyone see his hands shaking. "Why not just drop both bodies in the river? Odds are they wouldn't be found for weeks, if ever. And they all saw someone, even if they can't agree on the details." And two of them said they'd seen red hair. He thought about asking Tillotson where he had been last night, but refrained. Deliberately inducing apoplexy in a section head was probably a disciplinary offense.

"Indigs aren't what I would call quality witnesses," Tillotson grumbled.

"They were clear enough about the order of events, though. A splash, then they saw someone standing there."

"I see." Tillotson nodded slowly. "It certainly puts a new spin on the investigation."

Toreth had expected Tillotson to be overjoyed at the prospect of getting a re-turn on the time and euros invested so far. Worrying that he wasn't. However,

Toreth hadn't had enough sleep to manage the steps to the political dance. "Do you want this whole thing buried? If you do, don't f—" He caught himself. "Just tell me."

"No. If it's corporate, with the legislator dead it needs wrapping up ASAP." After a moment, Tillotson added, "But don't forget to follow up other possibilities."

"Sir?"

"If the sim killed Nissim and the others, then this could be an attempt to divert attention from that. There's a lot of money at stake. The killer might hope that if you have one corpse definitely not killed by the sim, you'll assume all the deaths are corporate sabotage."

And without my wise guidance, you'd be falling for it. Yeah, right. Toreth bit his tongue and considered the idea, trying to take it on merit. Possible, he supposed, but hardly the first thing that sprang to mind. Certainly not a plan he could imagine any of the SimTech directors devising. "It's a theory, sir," he said politely.

"Hmm. In any case, keep the whole thing as quiet as you can—no one outside the division hears about it. If it's a cover-up or corporate, better not to let whoever's behind it know what the witnesses saw."

"Thanks for the suggestion, sir. I hadn't thought of that."

Tillotson looked at him sharply, but didn't pursue it. "Do you have any leads on the mystery figure?"

If he were less tired, he would've been able to come up with something vaguely positive. "Not really."

"Then why are you sitting around here?"

Back in his own office, Toreth called Mistry, whom he'd sent in search of the other redhead in the case. From the gray and blue decor of the office behind her, Mistry was at SimTech. "Have you spoken to Tara Scrivin yet?" he asked. "Where the hell was she last night?"

"At home in bed, Para." Mistry sounded apologetic. "Building security confirms that she was in the building. It is a student building, though, and there are plenty of potential unofficial exits. However, she was sedated; she was still a little groggy when I spoke to her this morning."

"Who sedated her?"

"Dr. Tanit. She went to see her yesterday evening at home, and she visited again this morning. She arrived while I was interviewing Tara. I've spoken to her too, Para—I thought you'd want me to."

He nodded.

"Tanit said—" She glanced down. "Scrivin was distressed and panicky as a result of the interrogation. Parsons upset her."

175

"It's his job. When was this relative to the time of the murder?"

"Dr. Tanit left about twenty thirty." A bare fifteen minutes before the indig disturbed a killer by the river. "She called a taxi at Tara's and went straight home; that's confirmed by the taxi record and the surveillance at Tanit's home. She offered to stay the night, but Tara apparently didn't want her to, so Dr. Tanit put her to bed and left."

"How's Tara now?"

Mistry considered. "Badly upset by the news—she liked the victim. He volunteered for her trials, I think. I'm at SimTech to check that. She was virtually incoherent in places. It took me a long time to get the story out of her, and not because of the doping. When I left, Dr. Tanit was talking to her about the hospital—the psych ward she was in before. Sounded to me like they'd discussed it last night as well. She was trying to talk the girl into a voluntary admission, and in my judgment, she'll probably manage it."

Funded by SimTech's generosity again, no doubt. "Thanks. Let me know if Tara goes anywhere." Toreth cut the connection and went over to the window to think.

On the face of it, the idea was ridiculous—Yang wasn't a large man, but Tara was tiny. How could she have thrown him into the river? Still, if he'd been drunk... A glass or two, Kirkby had said, which was probably not enough. Then there was the indig. Difficult enough to imagine Tara killing Yang—calmly dealing with an unexpected interruption and killing Tracker seemed even more improbable. Where would she have got hold of the gun? Not a trivial thing, even with connections he couldn't see her having. Fifteen minutes might be long enough to get from Tara's room to the river—he'd send an investigator to run it and check out cameras on the route. The alternative was that Tanit was covering for her. Would she do that?

Toreth called up everything he had on the two women. When he examined Marian Tanit's files, he found three he didn't recognize: one was a moderately impressive list of her published papers, the other two were both lists of the papers citing her work. Sara had found time to fulfill his citation search request in the midst of all the excitement. He flicked through them, then stopped and went back, comparing the duplicate citation documents more closely. Then he called Sara into his office.

"Why are there two of these?"

She peered at the screen. "I don't...oh, wait, yes I do. The system produced two records with the same ident number. Probably a mix-up with the name, although you wouldn't think there would be two Marian Tanits with PhDs in psychology. I shoved them in the case database and then I didn't get back to working out which is the right Tanit. Sorry."

"No, don't be. They're both the right Tanit. Look at the papers cited and tell me what you think."

Obediently she scrolled down the lists, then frowned and did it again more slowly. "This one is a truncated version of the other," she said. "Except not quite. It looks like the shorter one is an older version—the last citation on the list is twenty-five years old. Same year as the last time the short file was modified. But there are citations on the short one that aren't on the longer one."

"And if you look, the extra citations are for papers not on her publication list."

Sara checked the list again and nodded. "Maybe it got cross-indexed with someone else's record. That happens sometimes."

"Or... how did you do the search?"

Sara kept her eyes fixed on the screen, guilt stamped plainly on her face. "I, er... what do you mean?"

Toreth sighed. "Don't forget what I do for a living. Whose code?"

"Well, I... I'm not sure." She straightened up, and then sat on the edge of his desk. "I wouldn't have done it, except that there was so much going on and it takes forever to do the need-to-know justifications for the restricted stuff. There's a high security level code I got from—" She stopped. Toreth raised his eyebrows and waited. "Kel." She put her hand on his arm. "Don't bust him, Toreth, please."

Chevril's admin. "Of course I won't. But you could've shared the goodies, you know."

She grinned with relief. "Sorry. I'll add it to your collection."

"Good. Now do the search again, using your own code."

Toreth watched while Sara did it. The screen displayed only one file—the longer, up-to-date version, with a few restricted-access papers now marked as unavailable.

"You're right," Sara said. "Someone frigged the files. I wonder why?"

Toreth considered the papers cited. The titles of those missing from the start of the longer list meant nothing to him. He recognized the names of the three journals, though: *The Journal of Re-education Research, Neuromanipulation,* and *Social Pathology and Psychology.* All restricted circulation. If this file had been modified, others belonging to Tanit could have been tampered with as well. "Give me that code," he said.

Sara stood behind him and watched as he used Kel's stolen code to call up all Tanit's files. Only the citations file came up with two versions. He tried a couple of other high-security codes he kept for emergencies, with the same result. When he'd finished, there was an expectant silence. "Well?" Sara asked eventually.

"No idea. Could be a glitch in the system. Could be someone rewrote her files and took her name off those papers, but missed this version of the citation file when they were tidying up the databases. A full-clearance citation record is fairly obscure, so if they were going to miss something, it's a good candidate. This is the first time I've ever asked for one."

"So why did you this time?"

Mostly to annoy you. "It was Chev's idea." He studied the screen again. "If the date of the last entry is any guide the alterations are twenty-five years old, so it's probably not important. Still..."

She sighed. "Someone needs to waste time finding out who did it. Any ideas before I get my lamp and helmet and start delving in the archives? Or can I ask one of the investigators to do it if I don't tell them about Kel's code? Wrenn's good with the systems."

Toreth didn't answer. He was thinking about a restaurant. *The files are* always *supposed to be secure.* Warrick smiling, boasting a little without admitting anything directly.

Time to get over to SimTech.

When the admin showed Toreth into Warrick's office, Toreth thought Warrick looked surprisingly calm. He wondered whether he even knew about Yang. However, as he neared the desk he noted the tight lines in Warrick's face. Warrick watched coldly as he sat down and placed the camera on the desk. "Can I assume that you've heard the news?" Toreth asked.

Warrick nodded sharply. "And to answer your next question, I spent yesterday evening at home. Alone—except for the SimTech security guard outside my flat door, that is. The building security will confirm that."

"Thanks. Sit down and let me tell you the details."

Halfway through the reiteration of last night's events—just after he'd steeled himself and said "in the river"—Warrick stood up abruptly. "He committed suicide?"

Toreth couldn't help noting how damn fuckable he looked, pale with anger, his eyes bright and intent. "If you'd sit down and listen, Doctor—"

"I don't believe it. Not for a moment. If you're trying to say that the sim was responsible for this, somehow, then you're a fool."

Warrick's hands clenched, his body taut with tension—easy to translate the image to a bedroom, and ascribe the slight baring of his teeth to a different emotion. Then Toreth banished that unprofessional line of thought. "I know he didn't kill himself. He was murdered."

First reactions always interested him. Color flushed back into Warrick's face, and he leaned on the desk. "Oh, thank God." Then, as he realized what he'd said, he paled again and sat down. "I'm sorry," he said. "I didn't mean... I told you all along it wasn't the sim, that's all. I knew it couldn't be and I'm—God. Have you told his wife?"

"I sent Mistry round last night. We're keeping the details of the murder quiet for now."

Warrick nodded. "What did happen? I won't tell anyone else."

Warrick had held to a previous promise to keep quiet. "We're not sure yet. There was no sign of violence, no drugs. Your first guess was suicide—maybe the perpetrators hoped that's how it would look, if the body was ever found."

"Corporate sabotage," Warrick said. "It has to be. A professional team."

"That's one alternative."

"There are others?"

Ironically, Warrick's reaction to the news of Yang's death, with his relief that Toreth was treating it as murder, not suicide, meshed nicely with Tillotson's improbable suggestion that the directors were behind the killing. Toreth still didn't believe it. "That's where I was hoping you might be able to help."

"I wish I could." Warrick stared past him, palms stroking together. "He hasn't been at work since Monday."

"Why?"

"Well . . . after the legislator's death, we tightened sim security and instituted a policy that anyone who felt uneasy was free to refuse to work in the sim, no questions asked, no stigma attached." His mouth twisted, half smile, half grimace. "The kinder, gentler corporation, as you would say. Most people elected to keep working, but Yang wanted to take some time off."

Interesting that Warrick would tell him about a senior employee's misgivings. Either for once he hadn't thought through the implication or he was banking on Toreth discovering the programmer's doubts and taking the chance to put the best spin on it. "He thought the sim was dangerous?"

"He didn't want to take a risk." Another grimace. "He was thinking of his family."

"You don't think he had any proof, then, that the sim caused the other deaths?"

Warrick frowned at him, uncomprehending, until his expression cleared. "And he was killed to suppress that information? By whom? Am I top of the list, or are you going to accuse the directors in order?" His tone was mildly amused, but Toreth could hear the undercurrent of anger. "Do you really think I make a habit of killing my staff and friends?"

Genuine anger? Or evasion? "That's not the question I asked."

His eyes narrowed. "No. I don't think he had any such evidence, because it doesn't exist. The sim doesn't kill. It can't kill."

"So you've said."

Warrick leaned back, mask firmly back in place. "And if you have any evidence to the contrary, then I would love to hear it."

Back to stalemate because, as Warrick damn well knew, he had nothing. "I'll let you know if I find any. Now, I have another question. You used to work in the Data Division?"

Warrick nodded. "That's right." His face showed only curiosity, slight wariness, but nothing that looked like guilt. Not that reading Warrick was an easy task.

"Doing what, precisely?"

"Security and encryption. It was my first job—I had a part sponsorship at university."

"Did you ever work on citizens' security files?"

"Int-Sec or Central Records?"

Interesting distinction; the fact that Warrick mentioned the Int-Sec records at all told Toreth that he must have had access to sensitive areas. "Either."

He half expected Warrick to ask, "Isn't it in my file?" Instead he merely said, "Central Records, primarily, although some of the same encryption and transfer systems were adopted for the Int-Sec files. Or so I understand."

"I have a question about security files. Are they often lost? Or rather, is it possible for someone to lose that kind of information?"

Warrick studied him carefully. Toreth waited, saying nothing. Warrick must know that the ins and outs of security files were hardly a mystery to a senior para-investigator, and so he must also suspect why Toreth was asking. "Accidentally lose...perhaps," Warrick said at length. "Mistakes are made all the time; it's inevitable with so many records. In the vast majority of cases, something as major as losing an entire file would be caught by the crosschecks. The system is quite robust. If you mean the kind of losing that takes a great deal of effort, then also 'perhaps.' With skill and time. Is there a reason for asking me this?"

"It's possible that someone has altered Marian Tanit's security file."

A pause, before Warrick made the obvious connection. He smiled slightly. "If someone has, it wasn't me. And however you ask the question, the answer will be the same."

Toreth sat and scrutinized Warrick's face, letting the silence stretch out. Lying, or not?

After a while, Warrick raised his eyebrows. "Well?"

"When you gave Tanit the job, how far back did you take the background checks?"

Warrick didn't react to the implicit acceptance of his denial. "The actual checks would have been made by Personnel and the security department. However, I spoke to her previous employer myself—I always do for senior appointments."

"And?"

"And everything was fine. If not, she wouldn't be here now."

Toreth nodded. "Thanks. I won't take up any more of your time, Doctor."

He switched off the camera, but didn't stand up. Warrick waited. Dare he risk this? Toreth wondered. He looked at the desk, close enough to touch, thinking of the fuck they'd had there. It would be stupid, when he'd already compromised his relationship with Warrick so badly, to risk anything more. Warrick was still watching him, slowly spinning a pencil around on the desk. He appeared willing to give

Toreth however long he needed to make up his mind, and the thought came again: when did Warrick start running the interview? Any time Toreth gave the bastard a chance, like all the other corporate fuckers who thought that the world ran on their time.

"If her file had been changed," Toreth said, "could you retrieve the original version?"

Warrick's right eyebrow twitched very slightly. "I think you are rather better placed to access security files than I."

"Hypothetically, then, if for whatever reason I couldn't manage it at I&I, do you think that y—that someone else with more experience of Central Records security systems could—?" Toreth wasn't sure how best to put it, so he left the question dangling.

Warrick sat, head bowed, apparently intent on the pencil. "Hypothetically, then," he said at length, every syllable distinct, "perhaps. There are extensive archives and backups. It would depend on how thorough the initial, ah, losing had been. For an ordinary civilian file it may be possible, at least for someone who understood the system on, shall we say, a fundamental level. Someone who knew how to examine files without leaving traces that they had done so." He glanced up, eyes hooded, expression giving nothing away. "Would you think that was a good thing?"

"A good thing? In what sense?" Toreth asked.

Warrick looked back down. "If someone could do that, would you want them to? Considering that such an action would be manifestly illegal, I would imagine that you'd be very much opposed to it."

"I wouldn't care, frankly, as long as I saw the file. I certainly wouldn't ask any questions about where it came from—hypothetically or actually."

"Mm." Warrick smiled, rather distant. "I do so admire flexibility." He picked the pencil up, examined it for a moment, and then dropped it into a drawer and smiled. "Was there anything else you wanted?"

That was, apparently, that. Had he agreed to look, or hadn't he? Trying to crack Warrick was like trying to get a purchase on polished marble—an impervious, reflecting surface.

"I—" Toreth stood. "No. I've got lots to do. You'll be seeing me again, I expect."

Warrick nodded, half smile still in place. "Good luck, Para-investigator," he said as Toreth crossed the office.

With the door open, Toreth stopped and turned, leaning on the frame. "One more question, if you have time."

"Of course."

Letting the door swing closed, Toreth strolled back across the office and leaned against Warrick's desk. "Do you deep throat?"

The pure surprise on Warrick's face was a gratifyingly immediate payback.

After a few seconds he said, "When the occasion demands."

"In the sim?"

A short nod.

"And out of it?"

One corner of Warrick's mouth quirked as he recovered his poise. "Is this an official inquiry, Para-investigator?"

"Not at all."

"In that case, I tried it several times, a long time ago. I never got the hang of it."

Another few slow steps took him behind Warrick's chair. He leaned on the back. "It's easy," he said, lowering his voice to not quite a professional tone, but definitely with an edge of threat. Or promise.

"Is it?" Warrick didn't look around, didn't move at all.

"Oh, yes. You need to learn how to relax, that's all. To accept. To be taken. To be used. I bet you could do it with one hand tied...with *both* hands tied behind your back." His mouth was now only a few inches from Warrick's ear. "With some training and a sufficient incentive."

"Mm. Which you think you could, ah, supply?" Warrick was struggling to keep his voice level.

"I'm sure I could." Despite the risk of the partly open door, he couldn't resist lowering his head the last short distance to nip at Warrick's throat. Warrick shivered, marble crumbling like clay.

When Warrick spoke again, his voice was a whisper. "Tonight?"

"No." Toreth stood up. "Far too much to do. I'll call you, maybe."

Outside the door, he ran into Belqola, looking eager to be useful. "We've got all the staff accounted for and interviews scheduled, Para."

Toreth left the SimTech staff interviews to his team. He returned to I&I and read the reports as they came in. Some of the staff alibied each other, although this time the directors did not. Asher Linton was confirmed by AERC security to have been in the building. Marcus had been at home with his wife—being a good boy, obviously. Most of the rest of the staff had also been at home at the time of death— quarter to nine—or in other places that excluded them from being at the river. Times were listed for checking with movement records, credit usage, and security recordings; alibis, weak, strong, or nonexistent, were noted for corroboration.

Toreth studied a map of the city, watching as the system traced routes for him, highlighting those of the staff whose alibis left them a large enough window to have been at the murder scene. The place itself wasn't too far from the edge of campus; quiet and unobserved, it would've made a convincing enough place for a suicide but for the intervention of the luckless Tracker. Most of the staff who came up as possibles had alibis for Kelly's death, and of the ones remaining, none had any special connection to Teffera or Nissim. Frustratingly, by the time the last of the interviews came in, there was no clear SimTech suspect. That left a team of commercial sabs as the strongest possibility. Toreth hated chasing professionals—I&I tended to come up against the expensive ones, which meant the good ones.

Only one point argued against pros. Yang had left his house at eight fifteen, captured on security camera leaving the building and heading in the direction of the river. He'd been alone, but walking quickly, like someone late for a meeting. That suggested he had an appointment—hopefully, the man hadn't been stupid enough to meet someone he didn't know in such an isolated spot. Still, Toreth couldn't assume that, so he had to consider professionals. That meant more names to pull up, of known and suspected contractors. More whereabouts to discover, credit reports and movements to analyze, and names to eliminate. It also meant a lot of very long days. Saturday tomorrow, but he'd no doubt be working through the weekend. Long days and, probably, bad nights.

With a sigh, Toreth called Sara and asked her to arrange to have something delivered to his office for dinner. I&I security didn't like random take-away food delivery staff arriving at reception but, frankly, screw them.

Chapter Twenty-one

On Monday, Toreth had hoped to get away from work early, meaning before seven o'clock. With ten minutes to go, a call came through.

"Para-investigator Toreth?" To his surprise, it was Officer Lee, looking tired but cheerful.

"What can I do for you?" he asked, knowing that the early getaway was doomed.

"I have another body for you, Para. I think you might like to come and have a look at it."

For a moment, Toreth considered sending Mistry instead, or even Belqola. He'd had only the one nightmare last night, and he didn't fancy another visit to the morgue so soon. On the other hand, Lee looked to have good news and he could do with some of that. "I'll be right over."

❖❖❖

To his irritation, Kirkby was waiting for them in the morgue. Toreth didn't bother to respond to his greeting, which earned him a dark look from the pathologist. The preservation unit slid open, and Toreth looked at the body. A man in his late thirties, unkempt, bearded, and vaguely familiar. "Who is he?"

"One of the indigs from Friday night," Lee said. "We released them a few hours ago. They'd been gone for about two hours when the indig medical service got another call. Only this one was there when the medics arrived—I expect the others didn't fancy our hospitality again. He was already dead; the body lay only a few hundred meters from where the first one was found. The medics called me in because I'd flagged all the indigents' files."

There were no obvious marks on the body and, thank fuck, no sign it had been anywhere near the river. "Any idea what killed him?"

Kirkby's smile lit up. "We certainly do, sir. An engineered biotoxin, delivered

184

by a cell-type specific immunotargeting system."

Toreth blinked. "A what?"

"Genetically engineered poison, and a sophisticated one, according to the lab. A full report is being prepared, but in summary, it attacks the breathing control centers in the brain in a very specific fashion. Death would take somewhere between one to twenty minutes, depending on the dose. And it had, um—" He consulted the screen. "A postmortem self-catalyzing destructive element. Probably a conformational change triggered by pH changes in the cerebrospinal fluid due to carbon dioxide acidosis; the lab is still working out the details. That means it cleared from the system very quickly once he stopped breathing—we were lucky to catch it."

The summary didn't help much, but the last sentence caught Toreth's attention. "Why did you look?"

"Because of the injector." This time Kirkby's smile looked almost natural. "Otherwise we'd have bedded him down for the night, processed him in the morning, and found nothing."

"Injector?" Toreth queried.

Lee nodded. "A disposable injector with a three-quarters-empty drug ampoule was found in the nearest recycling unit; luckily, the unit was out of order. A sterile wrapper by the body caught my attention and made me look for the injector, because a wrapper's unusual for the quality of drugs indigs take. Fingerprints from the indigs all over the wrapper and injector. I had an immediate pharm work-up on the contents of the ampoule."

Toreth seriously considered kissing her. Or Kirkby. Or maybe both of them and the corpse as well. "How much of the toxin did you find in him?" he asked the pathologist.

"None. As I said, the stuff starts to degrade as soon as it's finished its job. The lab managed to get some diagnostic breakdown products from the body."

"I have tissue samples from Yang over at I&I," Toreth said urgently. "And from three more bodies, all dead for days or weeks. Is there any chance of showing that the toxin killed them?"

Kirkby considered. "Maybe. I could have a word with Pala—she's the senior immunologist—in the morning. She might have some ideas."

"Do it. Not in the morning. Now. Get her back in here—charge her a taxi to I&I. Deborah O'Reilly from I&I Forensic Pathology will be getting in touch with her."

Kirkby looked at Lee, who nodded slightly. "Yes *sir*," he said, and hurried off back towards the reception desk.

Lee said, "I've got all the files ready to send over to I&I, sir. And I've put out a detaining order for the rest of the indigs. My guess is that the injector came from the previous scene. The indigs hid it before we arrived, then picked it up after we let them out; they probably assumed Tracker bought it from whoever shot him. One of them dropped it into the recycling unit when they realized it had killed this one."

"Sounds likely enough. Pull them back in and send me the interviews." Time to get back to I&I and start trying to locate a creator for the drug. "Thanks for everything—you did a good job. I'll let your boss know how helpful you've been."

She grimaced slightly as she closed the unit. "Thank you, sir."

"Don't fancy a commendation from a para?" he asked Lee as she walked him to the exit.

"No offense intended, sir, but it's not the best thing to have on your file."

Career ambition over all—even in a dump like Justice. On the other hand, someone with Lee's obvious ability ought to shine here. "Were you at Justice before the reorganization?"

"Yes, for four years."

He didn't remember her from the year he'd worked at Justice before Interrogation became part of I&I, but it had been a big place. "Didn't apply to be an I&I investigator?"

"I didn't think I'd enjoy it, back then."

"And now?"

Lee shook her head. "Sometimes I think it was the biggest mistake of my life." She looked at her watch. "Usually when I'm working overtime without any chance of getting paid for it."

And as a favor to an outsider at that. "You could apply for a transfer. We take people from Justice, if they're good enough." She'd be a hundred percent improvement over bloody Belqola. "I could put a word in for you—I'd be glad to have you on my team."

"Thanks. But no thanks." They reached the foyer, and she stopped in the center of the quiet space. Two guards stood by the door, with two others behind the desk. All four watched them.

"Why not?" he asked.

"Ninety-nine percent of the cases we see here are routine. No idealists, just ordinary criminals. Then every so often we stumble across part of something big and dangerous. Like this—restricted biotech, corporate connections, politics, and God only knows what else. And when that happens, people like you breeze through those doors and take the case away before we really know what's going on." She smiled. *"That's* when I know I made the right choice."

186

Chapter Twenty-two

Toreth was so deeply asleep that it took several minutes for the insistent chiming of the comm to awaken him. Even through a thick haze of sleep he felt certain that he'd set it to take messages, so he knew who it was. Moving on autopilot, he reached out and fumbled for the earpiece. "Sara?" he croaked.

"Where were you?" Warrick's voice demanded.

"W—" Was this a bad dream? "Where the fuck do you think? Asleep. What the hell do you want?"

"Come over to SimTech." He sounded disgustingly awake.

Toreth finally pried his eyes open and looked at the clock; it took him a moment to focus, and then another to believe what he was seeing. Tuesday the thirteenth of November looked right, but the time—Jesus fucking Christ. "No. It's three o'clock in the fucking morning. What is it?"

"Get up, get dressed, get over here."

The comm went dead. Toreth closed his eyes and buried his head in the pillow. Every bone in his body protested the idea of leaving the loving embrace of the sheets. Then he forced himself out of bed and started hunting for clothes. Warrick would only call back if he didn't show up. As he stood on the street in the biting wind, waiting for the taxi, he decided he really hated this fucking case.

❖ ❖ ❖

At the AERC, the security guard let him in without asking for an ID and told him Dr. Warrick was in his office.

Toreth voice-activated lights in the corridors as he went; the building echoed emptily and he felt a stab of apprehension. There had been five murders already. If he hadn't been half-asleep in the taxi on the way over, he might have thought more about it. Had it really been Warrick's voice over the comm? Had Yang received a similar summons? Wishing he'd detoured to I&I and checked out a gun,

187

Toreth hesitated outside the office, and then opened the door. No one there. He stepped inside cautiously and moved over to the desk. All three screens were active, showing pages of complex-looking coding. On the other hand, most code looked complex to him, especially right now.

"There you are!" Startled, he looked up to find Warrick in the doorway, carrying a tray with two mugs and a large insulated flask. "Coffee," he said. "My machine in here's empty, but I dredged this up in the cafeteria. I thought you might need some, and I sure as hell do."

Warrick did look as if caffeine might help. The dark hollows under his eyes made Toreth feel a little better about his own haggard appearance. However, Warrick's eyes shone with what Toreth recognized as sim-related excitement and he was practically bouncing on the spot. How, Toreth wondered, could he get so excited about his job at this time in the morning?

Warrick set the tray down and poured the coffee. Tepid, and with the consistency of gritty soup, it tasted wonderful. "So, what is it?" Toreth swept a pile of papers away and dropped into the chair, slopping coffee onto the floor and not caring. "And why the fuck couldn't it wait until tomorrow?"

"Because I didn't want to risk waiting 'til the morning and talking myself out of it." Warrick sat down at the screen. "And also because I thought you might like to know that I found out how they did it."

"What?" Toreth blinked. "But we know—" He bit the sentence off, but Warrick didn't seem to have noticed.

Warrick started bringing up new screens of code. Toreth pulled his chair up beside him and tried to ready his brain to keep up. The first words surprised him. "Yang sent me a file," Warrick said.

"Sent? When?"

Warrick glanced at him. "This afternoon—Monday, rather. Time-coded. I think it was something along the lines of health insurance."

"Not very healthy."

"No. But he's—he wasn't a corporate, just a programmer. All I was once, but I've learned. Blackmail-style insurance only works if the right people know about it. Clearly, they didn't."

"So what was in the file? And why didn't you send it to me straight away?"

"Well, for one reason, because you already have it. It's a log of the session where Kelly died."

"All that was supposed to be with the division investigators downstairs," Toreth felt obliged to point out. "And the files have been sealed."

Warrick waved a dismissive hand, and Toreth snatched his coffee out of danger just in time. "Yes, well, pretend he found a copy on a machine they overlooked. It hardly matters now, does it? He thought—" Warrick hesitated, then plowed on. "He thought it was evidence that the sim was responsible for Kelly's death."

188

Toreth blinked. "And was it?"

"No. Quite the opposite. But first, look at what he sent me: it's a comparison of the homeostatic control module activation log from the fatal session here with some approximately equivalent data." One of the expansive monitors on the desk displayed a section of code. Another showed line after line of numbers and letters, each with a time attached, accurate to microseconds. Occasional lines were highlighted in red, and that was all Toreth could see. "Yang misinterpreted it," Warrick continued. "And your systems experts probably haven't even found it. Not their fault—I&I didn't write this stuff, and it is complex. I didn't write most of it, either, but I created the system architecture and I did write the homeostatic monitoring and the associated feedback code."

Now a caffeine buzz overlaid the fatigue, concentrating it into the beginnings of a splitting headache. "Could you run that past me again, only a lot more slowly and in English?"

Warrick frowned. "Did you even read the summary material I sent you?"

"Let's say that I did, and that I've somehow forgotten it over the past three days during which I've had about five hours' sleep a night." Three hours short of what he needed to stay civilized.

"Sorry." Warrick endeavored to look contrite. "All right. Slowly and in small words. Broadly defined, homeostasis is the body's ability to regulate itself. It's very complicated and the biochemistry behind it isn't really my field. It covers blood chemistry, breathing, temperature, that sort of thing. It's relevant because if, to pick an example, you get into a hot bath in the sim, your body feels hot but the heat isn't real. In that case, the sim has the potential to interfere with the mechanisms that maintain body temperature."

"And kill you?"

"Very unlikely. Detailed modeling suggests not. However, there is a miniscule outside chance, theoretically, that it could cause some minor, non-fatal damage. The sponsors didn't want to take the risk and neither did I. Even if it did no harm, it could be unpleasant for the user. Actually, it's one of the potential causes of sim sickness, so we were very interested in eliminating the smallest effect." He hit a key and the code scrolled smoothly past. "This is the homeostatic control module—HCM. It takes real physiological and biochemical readings from the sensors and feeds them into the homeostatic control centers, bypassing all the other parts of the sim. A direct link to the real world. And the HCM can modulate autonomic nervous functions to smooth out confusions caused by the sim environment." Warrick frowned, obviously looking back over the speech. "The autonomic nerves regulate involuntary body functions," he added. "That's the important feature in this case."

Toreth knew exactly what autonomic nerves were, but that didn't make him feel any less stupid. "So you could kill someone by fucking with this HCM?"

"No, of course not," Warrick said witheringly. "There are so many failsafes in this system that the moment the body chemistry was pushed beyond acceptable limits, the sim would disconnect. It's impossible to turn those failsafes off and have the sim operate at all. There is no way on earth the HCM could kill someone." He smiled triumphantly. "But it could keep someone alive. If a user had a defect in his homeostatic control, even a serious one, the sim could compensate for it and he wouldn't die straight away. Think of it as a very expensive life support system. Actually, it's similar to standard nerve induction systems in a hospital intensive care unit; like those systems, the sim would make him breathe, bypassing the damaged portion of the brain."

Surprise temporarily banished sleepiness. "Make him breathe?"

"Yes." Warrick scrolled up to the point where the red highlights began. "If you look at the log, the respiratory control module was called repeatedly after a certain point. That alone should have tripped an alarm, but it's a secondary level one and it can be disabled—remotely, if necessary, like everything else. And the only plausible explanation is a drug, a poison."

Toreth stared at the screen, not really seeing it. One line of characters looked very much like another to him, but if Warrick said that it was possible, then he was willing to believe him. The real question was why Warrick was showing this to him now.

"What do you think?" Warrick asked impatiently.

"I thought the pharmaceutical side wasn't your field?"

"It isn't, but the exact biochemical mechanism doesn't matter." Impatience sharpened his voice again. "Gross damage, even a localized stroke, would've shown up in the autopsy, so it requires something capable of destroying the body's ability to breathe in a highly targeted way. You're the damn investigator. There must be some evidence to find, some trace in the bodies."

It was too much of a coincidence. "Warrick, how the fuck did you know?"

"It's all in the files—your systems people will be able to confirm it." Warrick frowned at the screen with disapproval. "It's almost disappointing, really. It requires no technical skill at all; it's simply a question of spotting the potential loophole in the system. My code does all the work."

"No, I mean how did you know about the toxin?"

"About—" His head snapped around. "You mean you've already found something?" Anger flared up. "Why the hell didn't you tell me before?"

That was a step too far over the line. "I file my IIPs with Tillotson, not with you."

Warrick's expression closed down. "I apologize. If you could share some details, I'd be grateful."

"I don't know anything for certain yet. We found an injector with a toxin engineered to target breathing—we're checking the bodies for traces of it now. You

190

did know, didn't you? That's why you called me now."

"I had no idea. None at all." Warrick sat back, then laughed—a single, short sound before he shook his head. "I was expecting to have to convince you this was evidence of sabotage rather than the sim. That's why I spent so long checking it out before I called you."

"Actually, I thought all along it was probably corporate. Not that you ever bothered to ask me." Toreth considered the new information. "Wouldn't the person in the sim feel an injection and come out?"

"No. That's the whole point of the sim, to block out perceptions of the real world and replace them with the virtual. If the program stops early for any reason then the person dies sooner, but that's all. It would even be possible to fix the time of death with a preprogrammed or remote shutdown, if you had the authority to do it."

Another consequence of the revelation occurred to him, and Toreth groaned. "Fuck. Alibis. All the bloody alibis are worthless."

Warrick nodded. "The victims could have been injected with the toxin at any time between starting the sim—or even just before—and the time of death. Or earlier, with a slow-release system."

Toreth looked at him curiously. "And you knew I'd think of that?"

Warrick waved the question away impatiently. "I should hope you would, Para-investigator. It's obvious."

Toreth found truthfulness somewhat difficult to handle at the best of times. It made him suspicious. "Why did you tell me?"

Warrick looked at him with genuine surprise. "Apart from the intellectual dishonesty of not telling you, it's important. Those people were friends—I want you to find who killed them. And who's killing SimTech by extension." He shrugged. "Anyway, once I'd realized what it meant, hiding it would look highly suspicious. Yang may have sent copies to other people, and your division friends should have found it eventually."

He never got just one explanation with Warrick, although Toreth couldn't imagine anyone other than Warrick coming up with a dislike of intellectual dishonesty as a reason to make himself a murder suspect. Of course, the last one Warrick had given was the obvious reason he would've called Toreth, were Warrick really the murderer. "Did you kill them? Any of them?"

Warrick looked at him narrowly. "What do you think?"

"I'm asking you."

"And if I don't answer, you'll take me down to the Interrogation Division? Strap me down and hurt me for real?"

"Warrick, I'm being serious here."

One side of Warrick's mouth lifted in a non-smile. "So am I. You would, wouldn't you?"

191

"Of course." Toreth shrugged. "Or, rather, I'd take you there. I'd have to hand you over to another interrogator because I'd have a personal involvement with the prisoner." The conversation, in fact the whole experience, had begun to feel unreal, far more unreal than the sim.

"Personal involvement. Mm. No, I didn't do it. I could have, but I didn't. You'll have to look elsewhere, I'm afraid."

Toreth stared into the sludgy remains of his coffee until he decided that, on balance, he believed him. He'd never really thought Warrick had done it. He had a very good instinct for lies, probably because he told so many himself. One instinct he did trust.

Confrontation over, Warrick's manic energy had drained away. When Toreth looked at him again, he was staring at the screen, watching the lines scroll past. "It's ironic, really. A system we put in place because of probably unfounded safety concerns is the one used to kill. I just wish Yang had come to me," Warrick added quietly. "I would've worked it out and brought it directly to you. He'd still be alive now."

Toreth yawned. "Probably thought you wouldn't listen."

Warrick looked around, his fatigue-ringed eyes seeming darker and larger than usual. "Why do you say that?"

"People tell their bosses what they want to hear. You do go on about how safe the sim is."

"I suppose I do. I have a responsibility to the corporation." He shook his head. "I seem to be doing better on that front than with responsibility to my employees."

Toreth downed the last bitter mouthful of cold coffee. "Don't worry about it. Unless SimTech contracts don't limit corporate liability for sabotage damage, that is."

Warrick winced slightly. "Hardly the point."

"Bet they do, though, don't they?" When Warrick nodded reluctantly, Toreth grinned. "And looking on the bright side, he trusted you enough to send you the file, so at least now we know."

Warrick stared at him, but tiredness took some of the edge off his usual icy glare. After a moment he nodded. "Indeed. Now we know. And, to be equally and grimly practical, once the sponsors hear—"

"No. I can't allow that yet. You'll have to keep it quiet for now." Warrick started to protest, but Toreth spoke over him. "Once the sab team discovers that we know about the toxin, they'll pull back and we'll never find them. News will get out soon, but the longer it takes the more chance we have of catching the bastards."

"Please, couldn't we at least—" Warrick took a deep breath, and Toreth couldn't help admiring the effect. Pleading must just about kill him. "Would it be possible to reassure a few of the major sponsors?"

"When any one of them could be responsible? No."

Warrick looked at him, dark eyes hooded, then nodded. "Of course, Para-investigator. I would appreciate it if you could let me know when the news can be released."

"Of course."

Warrick reached out for the screen and closed it down. "Now I think I'm going to rest on my laurels for a while. How did you get here?"

"Taxi."

"I'll give you a lift back." He raised an eyebrow, half smile slipping into something more sardonic. "If you don't mind a murder suspect knowing where you live."

"Right now I'd give you the code for the door if it'd get me back to sleep any faster."

They sat in silence as the car drove them across the quiet city. Warrick seemed to be thinking, and Toreth was already imagining his bed. As Toreth let himself into the building, he heard Warrick call his name. He went back to the car and leaned down to the window. "Yes?"

"There's something—" Warrick stopped.

"What?"

"Nothing. Or nothing relevant. Ah—I thought I should mention that I'm not planning to be at SimTech first thing tomorrow. I need my beauty sleep."

Toreth, who knew that he himself would have to be at work in less than four hours, glared at him.

Warrick smiled slightly. "So, the answers to the questions are that there was no homeostasis log on Jon Teffera's machine, but we installed full logging on all the external machines, including Pearl Nissim's, after Kelly's death. Also, no one has authority to alter the logs, and that all the data recording is tamper-proofed." He spread his hands. "Although if someone understood the security system on a fundamental level..."

Before Toreth could say anything, the car drove away.

193

Chapter Twenty-three

When he arrived at I&I Toreth called the division computer experts at SimTech and informed them that Dr. Warrick had suggested checking the control call logs against a comparable data set. There was no point in prejudicing them with Warrick's conclusions. It took them two hours to find the homeostatic control evidence, another two hours to work out what it meant, and half an hour on the comm to explain it to Toreth. Warrick had told him the unvarnished truth. Almost a pity—he would have liked an excuse to drag Warrick out of bed and ask him some searching questions.

Once Knethen finished explaining things Toreth already knew, he promised a more thorough analysis. Toreth nodded. "And—" Tillotson's suggestion rose in his mind. Better to cover all angles. "Check for a mechanism for the sim to cause the neural damage in the first place. If there's any possibility, no matter how small, I want to know about it."

"Yes, Para. While we're doing that, could someone find out for us whether the sim machines not in the AERC building had session logs and who, if anyone, had the necessary security permission to alter the logs?"

Feeling slightly better disposed towards Warrick, Toreth spent an hour asleep in his office while he pretended to hunt down the information.

❖ ❖ ❖

The short day at work had made a pleasant change of pace, Warrick reflected. At least it did until he allowed himself to think about why it was pleasant. He'd always loved SimTech, and looked forward to waking up and coming in to work. His sister had teased him about it for years. Now, waking up to the knowledge of how close they were to losing everything made every day an ordeal. Over the last few weeks, he'd found himself searching for excuses not to get up. Leaving the flat was the worst part: setting off, knowing that there would probably be more bad news waiting for him when he arrived at the AERC.

Now, finally, there was hope of a way through the nightmare.

Before he went home, Warrick looked at the file for the fiftieth time and wondered what to do with it. When he'd first found it, he'd been reluctant to say anything to Toreth because the man was so clearly ready to clutch at straws. Anyone who was willing to pull in and question someone like Tara Scrivin would certainly go a lot further with Marian Tanit. He'd told the truth to Toreth when he'd said that, personally, he had nothing against Marian. He respected her, on many points, and he'd always made an effort to accept criticism within the corporation—it was healthy, in fact, as long as it wasn't out of control or commercially damaging.

He'd almost mentioned the file to Toreth in the early hours of this morning, but he'd stopped himself. The logic he'd used then was that he'd done his duty as a loyal citizen by bringing the murder method to Toreth's attention, and that made the omission acceptable. It had worked at the time. In the cold light of day—or the fading light of the November afternoon—it sounded hollow. The thought of Marian at I&I still held him back. The thought of anyone in that place. The techniques of the Interrogation Division weren't public knowledge, but the Administration found rumors to be a useful way to remind people of the penalties for open defiance or serious crime.

However, unlikely as the information was, he had to check it out for SimTech's sake, never mind any theoretical obligation to Toreth. Short of telling Toreth, he could find no way of doing that except talking to Marian. As he opened the office door, he realized how infrequently he visited her without a summons. The surprise on her face reflected that, but she offered him a seat without comment.

"I have a question I must ask you," he began. "I received some information about your qualifications."

No flicker of a reaction. "From the para-investigator?"

"No. I'm talking to you now because I'm trying to decide what to do with it. Whether to tell him."

"Is it relevant to the investigation?"

"I can't imagine that it would be. It's a suggestion that you once worked for Psychoprogramming, or at least for their predecessors. That they sponsored your training. Is it true?"

"Yes."

He'd been so confident of a denial that he couldn't think of a response.

"They sponsored me through university," she continued. "Then they employed me for four years, and after that I left. I've had no dealings with them since. I want to tell you now, before you say or decide anything, that I never wanted to work for them."

The defensiveness might have sounded odd except that she was well aware of his feelings about psychoprogramming, interrogation, and other allied arts. "So what the hell were you doing there for four years?"

Marian looked down at the desk with a slight frown. "I wanted to be a psychologist. To help people. To do that, I had to get into university and I couldn't afford it without finding a sponsor. So...I faked my psych test to give myself a psychoprogrammer profile." She smiled sadly. "I thought I'd spend a few years there, find a corporation to repay my training debt, and then I'd be free."

"And?"

She looked away. "I couldn't do it. I stuck it out through the training, but when I qualified, when I was assigned, I couldn't do it any longer."

"What happened?"

"I tried to fake my way out again. I had a 'breakdown.' I was hoping for a re-assignment, but I'd have been grateful enough if they'd dismissed me and thrown me out onto the streets. I was lucky, in a way. They saw right through it, and then it all came out—how I'd got there in the first place. They didn't want the embarrassment of dismissing me officially, because that would have meant acknowledging that I'd beaten the psych tests. Instead they found me a university post and wiped the records. A clean parting of the ways. It was the only time I felt grateful to them." She looked down at the table for a moment. When she lifted her head, the desperation in her eyes shocked him. "Warrick, you don't know what goes on there. Most of the psychoprogrammers are barely human. I've never forgotten the things I saw there. I won't for the rest of my life. The things they do to people..." She actually shivered. "But more than that, it's the way they do it. Their technology isn't so different from the sim, you know."

So much about her hostility towards the sim was becoming clear now. "The sim is safe."

"So you keep saying. I was there when the first neural manipulation machines went into service. I've seen people destroyed by them—*destroyed*, Warrick. Not just a single memory blocked or implanted here or there, but their entire lives torn away from them, piece by piece. Broken down and rebuilt into different people who'd willingly betray their families, their friends. They call it 'fast-track re-education.' It takes days, even weeks for every victim who survives. Months, sometimes, back then. Cliché or not, the people who die in those places really are the lucky ones."

"Marian..." No point in repeating the assurances she'd heard so often. "It's too late now. Even if I agreed—which you know I don't—the sim exists. We can't uninvent it. We can only make it as safe as possible. Besides, as you say, it's not new technology, in a way. They can do...what they do, already." She didn't answer. This was the unbridgeable gulf between them. "The sim can't be used like that in its commercial form," he said. "And I have no intention of making it easy for Psychoprogramming or any other part of the Administration to get hold of it. They can't afford it, and as long as the directors have control of SimTech we won't drop the price."

196

She looked at him for a long moment, eyes narrowed, then said, "Are you going to tell the para-investigator about it?"

"I—" He'd been so confident that the file was a mistake that he hadn't thought it through. It took him only a few seconds to decide—his first loyalty was to his employees, not to a man he'd known for only a few weeks. He'd failed Yang; he wouldn't fail Marian. "No, I won't. It doesn't have anything to do with the investigation. I'm happy to keep it as our secret. Now that they know for sure it's murder—"

Marian stared at him. "It is?"

"Oh, Christ. I shouldn't have said."

"I'll treat it as confidential, of course. What have they found?"

"They suspect poisoning. No, they're sure of it. They've found a bioengineered toxin. The sim was used to keep victims alive for a while, but that's all the connection it had."

"Not the sim." Marian leaned back, slowly, her face pale. After a while, she nodded. "Not the sim."

"Definitely not. It was Yang, actually."

Her brows knitted. "What was?"

"He found the evidence in the data logs. He left a time-delayed copy for me. He must have been worried that something would happen to him."

"He didn't say—" She stopped abruptly.

"What?"

Marian shook her head. "He came to see me last week. About stopping work in the sim—about leaving the company, really. He never said anything about logs."

"Don't blame yourself. I had exactly the same thought—if only he'd told me. But it's no use dwelling on things like that." Odd to be giving her advice. If it were someone else, he might have gone over to touch her, comfort her, but he had no idea how she would take such an approach. Instead, he stood up, brisk and professional. "Hopefully they'll clear everything up soon. I'll instruct the legal department to press I&I for a preliminary release of the findings, if they don't make a quick arrest. It should be enough to reassure the sponsors. Toreth thinks it's corporate sabotage, and the sponsors will unite in the face of that; if the sim is valuable enough to kill for, it's valuable enough to invest in."

She nodded again. "Yes. Yes, I'm sure they will."

He'd never seen her so subdued. Had she placed that much hope in her theory about the dangers of the sim finally being proven true? Healthy diversity of internal viewpoints was one thing, but perhaps, when it was all over, he should speak to Asher and Lew about finding a new senior psychologist.

"Marian? Can I get you something? A drink?"

"No, I'm all right." She checked her watch. "Goodness, I'm afraid I have some calls I really must make. Was there anything else?"

"No. And don't worry about your—about it. Not a word to anyone, I promise."
She smiled, relief evident. "Thanks. But..."

"What?"

"Perhaps—" She closed her eyes briefly, and then carried on. "Perhaps you ought to tell the—to tell Toreth what you found out. Better to have things like that out in the open. It's certainly better to be as honest as possible with people like that." Another smile, more like the usual Marian. "Aren't I always telling you that repressing the past is unhealthy?"

Late in the afternoon, Toreth was snatching another nap at his desk when Sara woke him to announce the arrival of the lab results for the first three bodies. They were better than he had hoped. Despite a list of technical problems that filled most of the report, O'Reilly had finally produced clear positive traces in Nissim and Kelly, although nothing for Teffera. Even Tillotson would have to drop his sim theory now.

By taking the time of the first red line on each log, he also had definite—and now hopefully correct—times of "death" for both Kelly Jarvis and Pearl Nissim. Nissim's was half an hour into the sim session, when she had been alone in the room except for Keilholtz, and both of them were in the sim couches. That made a low dose of the toxin contained in the anti-nausea injection a perfectly plausible theory.

The red lines in Kelly's session started at seven thirty-three and some seconds, which was when Toreth had been changing in his room at the Renaissance Center, and Warrick would have been in the SimTech car on the way there. That appeared to put Warrick in the clear. He must have known that last night, and Toreth spent a few minutes wondering why he hadn't said anything. Then he remembered the second question the techs had asked. The logs could've been altered, and Warrick had the ability to do it.

At least now he had an indisputable suspect for Kelly's death—Tara Scrivin. The respiratory control whatever-the-hell-it-was had activated fifteen minutes after she had entered the room to speak to Kelly. Jin Li Yang made a technical second suspect. He had been in the room, too, and he could have administered the drug after Tara's departure. However, his sim record showed he'd been in the couch all the time. That left only the possibility that he'd faked the records. Given that he was a programmer, Toreth wasn't about to discount that possibility. If Yang had been the killer, however, who had killed him?

No, Tara was the obvious suspect. Infuriatingly, she was probably the best-interrogated witness in the case, and he and Parsons were in complete agreement over her honesty. That left only the extremely thin straw of Tara committing the killings in some kind of autonomous state. He could just imagine what Tillotson would have to say about that suggestion. Still, her mental fragility wasn't in doubt. As Mistry had predicted, she'd been admitted to the hospital on Friday, and without some better evidence, it would be a hell of a nuisance to pull her out of there. Pity he hadn't done a more thorough interrogation of Tara while he had the chance. Except—

Toreth sat up suddenly. Except he had. He'd put her through the m-f scan, and with the distraction of Yang's death he'd never bothered to get the results from Seiden. When he put the call through, Seiden looked surprised to see him. "I thought you'd forgotten about her."

"Hardly." Out of sight of the screen, Toreth crossed his fingers. "Did you find anything?"

"Not a lot. She's not a DID, I can tell you that. She's got emotional spikes all over the place in response to pretty much everything, but underneath she's well integrated."

Another lovely theory shot down in flames. "Nothing else? Nothing in the interviews?"

"Nothing definite, since it was just a preliminary scan, but a few anomalies persisted once the system had finished smoothing things out."

Still fucking anomalies. "In what?"

"Uh..." Seiden peered at something away from the comm. "Recollections of her movements from the night of the eighteenth of October."

The date of Kelly's death. "Can't you be any more specific?"

"Not unless you bring her back in and let me do a detailed check on the memories. Put a request in."

"Could be a problem. She's in hospital."

Seiden grinned. "And you told *me* to be careful. Unlucky drug reaction, was it? Accidental overdose? Fell down the stairs a few times?"

Fucking idiot. Toreth cut the connection before he did anything to radically worsen relations between I&I and Psychoprogramming.

Leaving his desk, Toreth went to stare moodily down at the courtyard. The palm trees had gone, and he wondered vaguely when that had happened. Was it worth trying to wrestle Mindfuck into providing a more thorough scan on Tara? No chance of bypassing the system again so soon, unfortunately. At least Tara was safe and sound in the hospital. He could fill in the m-f form, shove it into the system, and wait. By the time it came through, the girl might be stable again. He could wait. Masses of information were still being gathered and sifted and something could come from the sab team inquiries at any time. With this level of biotechnology, a sab team was more likely than a deranged girl. He had a definite method and he should be grateful for that.

Toreth sat down at the screen and stared at the files displayed for almost ten minutes before he acknowledged that he couldn't do it. He'd been pushing too hard for too long. Switching the screen off, he pulled on his coat and stood. Home and bed was tempting, but he could use some stress relief first. Not Belqola—he wanted more than five minutes, and he didn't think he could bear the useless bastard's company for any longer than that. Toreth smiled. Plenty more fish in the building.

Chapter Twenty-four

❖

When he got to work in the morning, Toreth found that Warrick had called yesterday evening, missing him by fifteen minutes. He'd left a message asking Toreth to meet him for lunch at SimTech. Toreth rather hoped there weren't going to be any more revelations. Or that they would lead somewhere immediately useful, if there were.

The cafeteria at SimTech was a considerable step up from I&I's, including such luxuries as fresh salads. Toreth filled his plate, to Warrick's apparent amusement. "What was he or she like, then?" Warrick asked, as they took seats at a corner table away from other diners.

"Who?"

"When I called your office yesterday, your charming admin was very cagey until I told her who I was. Then she said, and I quote, 'He's got a hot date, don't expect him back tonight.' From the relish with which she said it, I suspect she had some privileged information about me and was hoping for an amusing reaction." During the course of the speech, his voice crept from cool calm to simmering anger. "Or maybe not such privileged information, as I'm not au fait with torturers' coffee room gossip."

Torturers—sign of a bad temper. "It's just Sara." Keep it casual. "She likes gossip, but she doesn't spread it if I've told her not to, which I have. Come on, am I likely to be broadcasting the fact that I'm fucking a murder suspect?"

"I suppose not." Warrick sounded somewhat mollified. "In that case I withdraw my slur on her character."

"So have you found something out?"

"That it was someone from Accounts and that they'd only been married for a fortnight. I gathered that was what piqued your interest. Although Sara hinted it might also have something to do with getting your expenses through faster."

"About the investigation," Toreth said patiently, making a mental note to have a stern word with Sara later. Gossiping with a suspect was . . . well, a lot less serious than what he'd been doing. Moreover, he didn't entirely blame her—he could just imagine Warrick's smooth voice coaxing out the information. Probably best not to mention it to her. "It is about the investigation, I assume?" Toreth asked when Warrick still hesitated.

"Not as such, no. It's the question you asked me about Marian Tanit's background."

"Yeah?"

"I came across an old file, which doesn't match her career history as given in her application to SimTech." Warrick stopped, eyebrows raised, waiting for a question.

"Go on."

"After she finished school, she was given a scholarship by the Psychocorrective Institute, which became the core of the Psychoprogramming Division after the reorganization. And after university, she went on to train there."

Psychoprogramming. There was no getting away from the bastards. "Shit. Really?"

Warrick nodded. "I can send you the file. It contains nothing more than I've told you—no details of what she did after training, or how the file came to be altered."

"How long have you known?"

"Not long."

Which could mean practically ever since he'd first asked about it. "How *long?*"

"I did the search shortly after you left the office."

"Why the hell didn't you tell me before?"

Warrick shrugged. "I didn't think it was relevant."

Toreth took a deep breath, managing to keep his voice low. "Didn't I already explain that it's not your job to decide what's relevant and what isn't? Impeding the course of an investigation is a minimum category two offense."

"I see." Warrick put his knife and fork down, aligning them precisely against the edge of his plate. "And, purely out of interest, what category is conspiring with a civilian to illegally access Administration files?"

"Conspiring—" He blinked at Warrick. "You have no fucking evidence I did anything of the kind."

"Don't I?" The soft, dangerous voice matched the light in Warrick's eyes.

On reflection, it was unlikely that Warrick would have tried to locate the file without some security—and he could easily have recorded a request made in his own office. Toreth broke eye contact, taking a sip of water, and then said, "Okay. Want to call that one a draw?"

"Why not?" Warrick smiled suddenly, the display of teeth nothing but friendly. "For one thing, you're right, and I apologize. Perhaps you can understand a feeling of loyalty towards my employees. Particularly after..."

After Yang. "So what changed?"

Warrick hesitated, and then picked up his fork, returning his attention to his plate. "As you said, it is an investigation, and it's not my place to make those decisions."

Toreth didn't entirely believe him, but for the moment he was willing to let it go.

As he crossed the office after lunch, Toreth saw Mistry talking to Sara. To his surprise, when the investigator saw him approaching, she finished the conversation and left before he reached the desk. "What did she want?" he asked Sara, looking after the retreating figure.

"To know whether or not you were screwing Belqola," Sara said equably, eyes on her screen.

Toreth grinned. The circumstances under which he did fuck team members were well known to the old hands. "What did you tell her?"

"That it probably wasn't worth adding him to her New Year's card list." She looked up. "Do you want me to file a transfer for him?"

"Yes. Or at least put it in the system. I'll authorize it when the case is over. If it ever is."

Back in his office, Toreth looked at the new information, sent by Warrick as promised, and wondered how the hell it helped. Toreth had never liked psychoprogrammers or their division. Few people at I&I did. Still, in this case, he'd be acting on reflex prejudice if he pretended the revelation made much sense. There were the interesting questions of who had concealed Marian Tanit's past, and why and how. Tanit's version might be the truth. Alternatively, a corporation could be responsible, if they could afford the substantial bribe to someone in the Data Division. However, the answers all lay a long time in the past. If the alteration had been recent, he might have been able to make something of it, but twenty-five years ago was long before SimTech's founding, before the sim had been conceived.

Tanit was a technical suspect for the murders of Nissim and Teffera, as was the rest of the solar system, but she had a cast-iron alibi for Kelly's death and the deaths by the river. Unless Tara Scrivin had been lying for Tanit, which struck Toreth as highly unlikely. He would have staked his reputation on Tara having told the truth as she remembered it, and Parsons had said the same thing.

He paused, struck by the thought. The truth *as she remembered it.* That was the bane of interrogations, because however cooperative the prisoner that was the best that they could give. Tara didn't have to be lying, or in a dissociated state—at least not a natural one. Warrick had told him that theoretically the sim was capable of memory implantation. Not a trivial thing, he'd said, and with the proviso that it would need the right drugs and the right training.

Toreth forced himself to think it through before the excitement overwhelmed good judgment. He didn't know a great deal about the mechanics of psychoprogramming or the intricacies of the sim, but nothing he did know made the hypothesis impossible. Marian Tanit had the training to do it. If her corporate employers could buy access to tailored biotech toxins, then they could sure as hell supply her with mindfuck drugs. The sim contained copies of rooms and corridors in the AERC. Everything Tanit would need to create and implant a false memory was there. Seiden had found anomalies in Tara Scrivin's recollection of the night of the eighteenth of October.

He pulled up the sim summary files Warrick had provided, found the list of available sim rooms, and compared the AERC interiors to the floor plan of the building. When he found the room number of the sim suite where Kelly's body had been discovered, and also the corridor leading to it, he couldn't contain the yell of triumph. A method and a suspect, when this time yesterday he'd had neither. Best of all was the prospect of eventually telling Psychoprogramming that they'd produced a rogue who'd killed a high-profile corporate and a legislator. They would never live it down.

Tillotson approved without quibbling Toreth's request for a waiver to pull Tara out of her hospital haven. However, by the time she was delivered to I&I two hours later, SimTech lawyers had found out about the request and begun lodging protests. Toreth didn't bother reading them.

Whether it was a piece of unusually forceful persuasion on Tillotson's part or—more likely—fear that their techniques were loose in the big wide world, Mindfuck was so cooperative it was disturbing. Tara spent barely an hour in the I&I holding cell before Ange called from Psychoprogramming to confirm that a slot was available. Toreth escorted the sobbing Tara over to the Psychoprogramming building and waited while she was sedated and placed into the machine once more. Officially booked in and waivered this time, which made the experience far more enjoyable—at least for him.

Seiden was waiting for him in the gallery, unusually animated. "What the hell are you up to? There are higher-ups doing headless chicken impersonations all over the building."

"Just get on with it."

Seiden sniffed. "Aren't you going to tell me not to break her?"

"She's waivered for anything short of taking her apart with a scalpel. Do whatever it takes, just get me a result."

"That's funny," Seiden said after an hour.

Two of the best words to hear during an investigation. Taking a deep breath, Toreth crossed over to peer at the screen over the mindfucker's shoulder. Figures and multicolored images that meant nothing to him filled the screen. "What?"

"I'm not sure. It looks like something... not just a block, though. It's—"

"Wait a minute. You said, 'not *just* a block'?"

"That's right. You can see the block here. See?" He pointed to an incomprehensible mass of colored peaks on the 3D map. "Or at least that's what it looks like on the preliminary scan. She's a mess—worse than the last time I saw her." The screen changed to a more complex map. "But when it's processed... if anything, it looks like an implant." Seiden turned to another screen. "It's concurrent with this part of the statement. From 'I finished my work' until 'we left together.' The retrieval patterns for those memories are different to the segments before and after. If you look at this trace—"

"Hang on. You're saying it's not real?" Toreth had forgotten about holding his breath.

Seiden shook his head. "I'm saying it's an anomaly. If it's an implant, it's a bloody good one. Better than I could do."

The sim. It had to be the sim. "It's like a real experience, slotted in afterwards so the edges don't quite join up."

Seiden looked around. "Something like that. Where the hell did you learn to read retrieval traces?"

"Nowhere. I'm a lucky guesser. Can you stick it all in a report and send it to me? I need a one-page summary simple enough that a head of section will sign an arrest warrant on the strength of it."

Warrick put up more resistance than Tanit. The director pushed his way into the psychologist's office only minutes after Toreth, B-C, and a pair of I&I guards arrived. Toreth continued to read the warrant out, simply raising his voice to make sure that Tanit could hear it over Warrick's protests. When he'd finished, and asked her if she understood, Tanit nodded and turned to Warrick. "Don't worry," she said. "I don't have anything to hide."

"Don't—" The guards started to move forwards and Warrick stepped quickly in front of Tanit. "She's not going anywhere until I get her a lawyer."

"Arrange it with the Justice rep," Toreth said. "I'll send you the name as soon as one's appointed." He turned to the guards. "B-C, get her back to I&I. Process her, put her in the cells."

"Yes, Para."

"You can't—" Warrick began.

Toreth caught Warrick by the arm and pushed him back a few steps, holding him as the guards escorted Marian from the room. Warrick tried to jerk his arm free, then hissed with pain as Toreth dug his fingers in strategically. "Listen to me," Toreth said, his voice low. "I'm doing my job here. Just because I've had my cock in you a few times doesn't mean that I give a fuck about what you think—about Tanit, about I&I, or about any other fucking thing. One more fucking word out of you, and I'll arrest you for obstruction."

Warrick stared at him, his mouth open. Then it snapped closed, and he nodded sharply. Toreth released him and turned to find B-C and the guards still waiting in the outer office. Tanit was watching them through the door with a slight smile. Her calm was mildly unnerving. "Go on, get her out of here."

As the guards started to lead her away, Warrick took a step forwards, then stopped himself. Silence in the office, until the sounds of footsteps had faded, and Warrick turned to him. "She didn't do it," Warrick said. Toreth noticed that he made the statement with the same confidence that he usually applied to pronouncing the sim completely safe.

"That's what we'll find out at I&I."

Warrick's lip curled briefly, contempt familiar to Toreth from a hundred previous cases, and then he left without another word. As Warrick walked out, the forensics team walked in. Toreth hung around outside, waiting for them to finish the first pass of the room. They found only one thing, but it had the potential to be all he needed: two ampoules, in a box marked *Sedatives*, pushed to the back of a drawer. Why the hell Tanit had kept them—if they were the toxin—and why they were here to be found, Toreth didn't know. Still, it gave him something with which to open the interrogation in the morning.

Chapter Twenty-five

❖

Down in the interrogation room, Tanit kept up an impressive front as she read through the analysis of the ampoules in her desk drawer, which perfectly matched that of the toxin in the injector found by Lee. After reading it carefully, Tanit shook her head. "I have no idea at all where those came from," she said calmly. "They're not mine, and I didn't put them in the drawer."

"Your own office records show that Yang came to see you last week. Twice."

Tanit looked at the copy of the record with equal composure. "Indeed he did—about his future with SimTech. And, regrettably, that was all he talked about. Perhaps I should have guessed that there might be more to it."

"He told you nothing about his suspicions that the sim might be killing people?"

Her lips quirked. "If he had, don't you think you'd have been the first person I would have told? How long have I been trying to tell you that the sim isn't safe?"

He flicked the screen to the third item, and she looked down again. Her expression froze. "Is she all right?"

Toreth shrugged. "I didn't ask. No one mentioned that she died."

"Tara was in no condition for a deep scan!" Her hands tightened on the edge of the screen, knuckles whitening, and when she looked up, her eyes were blazing. "You knew that—they must have known that, too. She was in the hospital. That's why—" She stopped dead.

"Why you sent her there?"

She stared past him, lips pressed together.

"Look at the summary. Look at the scan results. Who else at SimTech could do that?"

Composure returning, Tanit simply shook her head slightly.

"I know about your training. I have a file that proves you have the necessary skills." No response. Toreth shrugged. "Well, if you won't do this the easy way." He stood and gestured to the interrogation chair.

Tanit was already rising, setting the screen down with a sharp click. "You have a noticeable theatrical streak in your nature, Para-investigator Toreth," she said as she crossed the room and took the seat, settling her wrists into place as he came over. She looked up at him as he fitted the restraints, her pale eyes clear. "One might almost call it playful. An uncommon trait in the personality disordered. Someone should write a paper."

Straps secured, he dismissed the guards and cut out the external feed. He didn't like an audience, and with a commercially sensitive case and the possibility of a corporate sab team still in his mind, he couldn't risk information leaking.

Popular rumor gave I&I wonder drugs that made subjects talk instantly and truthfully, and scanners that could read minds. Toreth had never understood how people could believe both that and the horror stories of brutality and maiming. The truth was, as usual, somewhere between the two. They had drugs, and they often worked if given enough time and experimentation. Neural monitors and behavioral analysis gave a high probability of detecting lies, but they couldn't pluck out the truth. If the drugs didn't do the trick, or if someone needed the information quickly, there were other methods available. Toreth worked carefully, adjusting dosages and adding extra compounds to the mix, until Tanit's denials trailed off into confusion and stumbling half-confessions. It took him five hours before he found the right combination to keep his prisoner both truthful and capable of stringing together a useful sentence. He started with his entry point to the whole case. "How did you kill Kelly Jarvis?"

"I went into the room with Tara, when she opened the door." She spoke slowly, concentrating. "Then, while she was using the mike, I injected Jarvis. Next morning, in the rehabituation session, I altered her memory so that she didn't remember I was there."

"Warrick said that the sim can't do that."

"It can't. Not—" She frowned. "Not without drugs. Right drugs."

"Which were supplied by?" She shook her head. Toreth crouched down beside the chair. "Come on. You had help—to get hold of the drugs and the toxin, you must have had. Who?"

Another shake. Standing up, he considered. Another dose might send her over the edge of coherence, but he was too frustratingly close not to risk it. He could always wait for her to come down and resume later, although every lost minute gave whoever was using Tanit more time to get away. She watched, unreacting, as he gave her the injection. He sat down, tapping his fingers on the edge of the table, while it took effect.

When he repeated the question, she answered at once. "I was contacted. Three months ago. Four."

"Why you?"

"Don't know. Because I'd made objections, maybe. Maybe they'd seen the paper on Tara's episode."

"Who?"

She shook her head, the gesture exaggerated. "Corporate. No names. They wanted to cripple SimTech's funding. I arranged everything with them. I wanted people to know the sim is dangerous. It damages users—not all users, but some. Warrick won't *accept* it. None of them will."

Justifications that didn't interest him. "So you killed Jon Teffera?"

"No. Jon Teffera died." She smiled, relaxed in the grip of the drugs. "Just died. Coincidence. Or the sim—it would serve him right. I warned him. Said it was dangerous. I didn't know what to do, and then, when he died, I saw the way."

"What was the plan?"

The smile became almost mischievous, oddly out of place on her usually austere face. "Which one?"

"What do you mean?"

"I told them I would kill users, one or two. I picked them—Jarvis and Keilholtz. Do you want me to tell you about Keilholtz? They said you were going to call it natural causes, so I contaminated one ampoule in the batch. That's all. Easy." She giggled. "It was all very, very easy."

"Why Keilholtz?"

"He had no children, no family. No one close except Nissim. Nissim was dangerous. She backed the sim. She could have helped them—SimTech. I'd sent her information about it. Anonymously. She wouldn't listen. I had to neutral—neutralize her. Better than killing her—that was a mistake. Wanted to make her hate us. Them. SimTech."

"And Kelly Jarvis?"

For the first time, Tanit looked away from him. "I needed someone. She was Tara's friend—the one Tara went to see in the sim."

"You could've picked Yang."

She nodded. "I had to pick one, didn't I?" Her face was bleak. "One of them. And he's married and Kelly was Tara's friend. Her only real friend. The shock. Isolation. Makes it easier to implant. To get close. To—God . . . such a long time ago when I learned it all. I'll never forget it. I see their faces in my sleep, all of them."

It took Toreth a moment to realize she must be talking about her psychoprogrammer training. "You said there was more than one plan?"

"Plan . . . oh, yes." She shook her head. "Corporates. They wanted the sim. No good if it's been killing people, yes? You understand?" He nodded. "I told them when SimTech was gone, I would give Tara the memory of carrying out the killings. She'd confess. They could have the sim, cleared of blame. Easy to do. She was ideal. So vulnerable. All those rehabituation sessions . . ." She smiled bitterly.

"Best work I ever did. So well prepared—putting the memories in would've been easy."

"But you weren't going to keep your promise?"

She giggled again. "No. Wasn't that naughty of me? Let them blame the sim— it would never be sold." The humor disappeared abruptly. "I never planned to hurt Tara. She should've been fine. You. It was your fault. You were supposed to blame the sim." She looked almost angry now. "I made it easy for you. I told you it was dangerous. It *is* dangerous. I sent the note about Marcus. I knew about that—about his girls. He told me he'd tampered with the security system. It was *obvious* it was the sim."

"Not obvious enough. Or maybe too obvious."

She nodded, biting her lip. "I never wanted her to get hurt."

"So what about Yang?"

She shook her head emphatically. "It wasn't me. No. Not him. He'd—he'd done nothing." Her voice sank to a whisper. "Or maybe...I don't know. Maybe it was me. I didn't want anything to happen to him, but it was my fault. He came to me with the sim logs. I knew what it meant, that it could lead you to the toxin. He trusted me because I doubted the sim. I shouldn't have told them."

"Who?"

"No names. Anonymous contact. I didn't think. Should've seen it, that they'd try to silence him. So...yes. That's my fault. As much as the others. I killed him. Price—" She stopped, breathing quickly, obviously trying to pull herself together. "The sim is dangerous." Her voice strengthened. "People will—people will suffer. People will die. It's damaging. Neuro...neurological damage. When there are enough users, for long enough, it'll show up. But do you think they'll let that out? When it's making money? I had to stop it now. Kill a few and that would stop it now."

Her conviction, in the face of all the evidence he had about the safety of the sim, made him ask, "Tell me how you know the sim is dangerous."

She took a deep breath. "Original data, from the Neural Remodeling. In—Indirect Neural project. He destroyed it."

"Who?"

"Warrick."

"Keir Warrick destroyed data demonstrating neurological damage from the sim?" He had to say it out loud because it sounded so unlikely.

"Yes. He thought...I don't know. Maybe he thought he could correct it, make it safe. I don't know." She shook her head. "I like him. Warrick. I like him, but he's so *blind*. Fixated. He loves the sim." Her expression grew distant. "Displacement, I think. I don't know. He won't talk to me. Can't do therapy in an antagonistic... he said he knew what you were. He has no idea. No idea."

The prisoner was losing focus, so Toreth ignored the digression and pressed on. "Why didn't you tell the sponsors?" She blinked up at him. "Why didn't you tell the sponsors that the sim causes neurological damage?"

"*Oh*. Yes. Why would they believe me? I told Warrick first. I thought he might not know." She laughed. "Naive, yes. I showed him the file and he said he'd look into it and then—" She snapped her fingers clumsily, hampered by the restraints. "Gone. Couldn't find it again. I had a copy and that was gone, too. No hard copy. Stupid. There might be other copies somewhere. I couldn't find them. But he knows, Para-investigator. He's always known. Must have."

He walked away, listening with a splinter of his attention to his prisoner's breathing, as he thought it through. Warrick loved the sim; that was an indisputable fact. Toreth didn't believe that he loved it enough to kill for it, still less kill people he knew, but Tanit's accusation was a different matter entirely. Destroying data showing a fault he hoped he would be able to correct—that was more than plausible. How would intellectual honesty stand up to the threat of SimTech's destruction? Warrick might not have flat-out lied at any point during the investigation, but he'd withheld information twice that Toreth knew about—on Tanit's background and Yang's doubts—then brought the information forward only after he'd examined it and apparently decided that it would not harm SimTech or its employees.

He thought back to Warrick's ready cooperation over the trials data. *Of course—anything you want . . . But you'll be wasting your time. You won't find anything.* Confident as ever. Because he believed in the sim, or because he had made sure there was nothing to find? There was no way of telling. If anyone at SimTech had the expertise required to make the information vanish, it was Warrick. If this long-standing deception of SimTech's corporate partners got out, the chances of finding further funding for SimTech would fall to almost zero. Reason enough for Warrick to conceal the truth. Case closed.

Lots of things he ought to do next. He ought to strip any remaining information from his prisoner. He ought to submit the transcript of the session to Tillotson. He ought to start a hunt for the vanished trial data; Warrick had proven with Tanit's security file how difficult it was to lose a file completely. A witness interrogation order for Keir Warrick should be the first thing on the list. He listened to Tanit's breathing, almost subconsciously, alert for the changes that might signal a reaction to the interrogation drugs, for the telltale signs that something was wrong. However, it had stayed regular and even. It was—

Something *was* wrong.

As soon as he'd called the guards and had Tanit taken back to her cell, Toreth went down to the medical labs. To his relief, he recognized the man on reception: his own ex-admin from pre-Sara days. Useless, but at least usually friendly.

"How're things going, Les?"

Del Lesko smiled at him. "Using my famed psychic powers, I'm going to deduce that you need a favor."

Les had always had a talent for spotting and avoiding incoming work. "You should be an investigator. I want a sample put through quickly."

"For?"

"Full drug resistance sweep—all the exotics, pharm blockers, and vaccines, whatever you've got."

"You don't want a standard set first?"

"You did that already. Unless you screwed it up, the prisoner's clean for those."

The admin sniffed, mock-insulted. "If we say they're clean, they're clean. When by?"

"This evening?"

He laughed. "The wait's two days for the samples to go into the machine on a priority screen—Monday now. Do you have a section head's authorization on the request? If not, it's four days."

Fuck. "It's urgent."

That cut as little ice as he'd expected. "Find me a senior whose cases aren't."

Toreth sighed. "Okay. How much?"

"I beg your pardon?"

"Don't fuck around." Toreth fished a crumpled sheaf of notes from his breast pocket and started smoothing them out onto the counter as Lesko watched. Cards paid adequately for almost everything these days, but the Administration had never quite managed to stamp out the demand for less traceable currency.

When he had put down three, Lesko said, "First thing Monday?"

"Results first thing tomorrow. We both know you can do it if you get on with it."

Four more notes, and then the pile disappeared under the desk in one smooth sweep. "They're doing a run in fifteen minutes. If someone comes looking for you, wanting to know why their sample got bounced, you can tell them it was probably a cock-up in the system."

Toreth handed over the vial of blood. "Just get me the results and I'll tell them anything you like."

Something else to put through on expenses.

Chapter Twenty-six

❖

Lesko delivered, as promised. At nine in the morning, Toreth sat at his desk and reviewed the results of the screen for interrogation drug resistance. Perversely, the results cheered him. A lone murderer might just be able to whip up a metabolic bullet in her spare time without outside help, but there was no way in hell Tanit could have come up with this kind of sophisticated anti-interrogation arsenal without a lot of very expensive friends indeed.

I had a copy and that was gone, too... There might be extra copies somewhere. I couldn't find them. Yes, no doubt there would be copies, somewhere. Carefully planted files, to be dug out and displayed as part of an I&I investigation. Officially endorsed evidence designed to deal the final deathblow to SimTech. Toreth hated being played, most especially by corporates. However, corporate privilege stretched only so far. This time, with the death of Pearl Nissim, they—whoever they were—had well and truly crossed the line, even if the prisoner had been telling the truth about Teffera's death being natural.

Tanit, he was sure, could give him names. From those he could generate more interrogations, naming the same names, and eventually he'd have whichever of SimTech's rivals or possibly sponsors lay behind it. Best of all, however many friends they had, with Nissim in the morgue they wouldn't be able to buy a way out. For that happy, if accidental, choice of victim, he was grateful to Tanit. Taking down a major corporate—a big, beautiful case that would really make his name.

He called Sara into his office. "If I asked you what's the biggest waiver I could apply for on the SimTech case, what would you say?"

She pulled a chair around. "What's the new evidence?"

He showed her the results. "That's conspiracy," he said, "and the illegal use of plenty of restricted substances and technology on top of a confession of the murder of a legislator. Nothing solidly political I can point to, though, so it still looks corporate."

She considered the question. "Um... six? Seven, if you want to push it."

"Six sounds about right. Put it through, will you? And listen, this is the important part: don't put anything in about why she says she did it. No mention of Warrick or the flaws in the sim. I don't want whoever's behind it getting wind that I don't buy it. At the moment, no one's seen the confession except you and me. She's lying, and I want to know why, but tell them to hurry it up."

Sara nodded, but in the doorway, she hesitated. "Are you sure you want to do this?"

"Why the hell wouldn't I?"

Coming back into the room, she closed the door. "Toreth, this sounds like big stuff. Restricted tech isn't cheap. And if it isn't corporate it—"

"Of course it is," he interrupted. "It's one huge corporation going for a small one. But if I can get names and prove it, then it would be a hell of a coup. How often do we get a chance at a really big corporate arrest?"

She nodded reluctantly. "I suppose so. What does Tillotson think?"

"I haven't told him yet. You know what he's like; he's got no fucking spine when it comes to corporates. I'll tell him when I have a name for Tanit's employer. He'll be keen enough when he sees there's a solid case."

"And if there isn't?"

He'd wondered the same thing himself, but the doubt in her voice stung him. "Then it'll be a good thing I didn't go spreading accusations around. Sara, I know she was lying. Warrick didn't hide any evidence about the sim—I'm absolutely sure about it."

"How can you be?"

"How can I...?" He stopped, unaccountably stuck for a way to explain it. "It's not the way he's put together." Her skeptical expression didn't alter, so he changed tack. "There's nothing to get excited about. It's typical nasty corporate sabotage, only with big-name bodies. Why the hell should they get away with it on my case record?"

"Well, you said it before: expensive friends. She's confessed; the case is closed. Is it really worth digging any deeper? Just for Warrick?"

"What the hell has Warrick got to do with it? I want the score, that's all."

She looked at him oddly, and then shrugged. "If you say so. I just thought I'd better mention it. I'd hate to have to break in a new boss when you get demoted to running level ones down in Interrogation." After she shut the door once more, he sat looking at it and wondering what the fuck that had been about. Sometimes he didn't understand the woman at all.

Two hours later, while Toreth was tidying up the backlog of IIPs, Sara showed the Justice rep into his office. Toreth had been half expecting to see Marian's rep; whoever was protecting her would fight like hell over the application for a higher-level damage waiver, and no doubt the man was here to argue him out of it. Well, he'd be disappointed, because Toreth wasn't dropping it now. However, after Sara had closed the door, the man refused Toreth's offer of a seat, and simply produced a hand screen, transferring the authorized waiver to Toreth's screen. Toreth frowned at it, perplexed, then at his visitor. "Level eight? I applied for—"

"The Justice Department has reviewed the case as requested and in view of evidence presented has issued a waiver as deemed appropriate by the system."

Toreth stared. Textbook answer, and quite obviously there would be no explanation given. Equally obviously, that wasn't all. "And?"

The man smiled faintly. "Annex A," he said, and left.

Annex A. An unofficially official addendum to a maximum level waiver—the prisoner talked, then died. The mystery corporation must be getting nervous about the prisoner's apparent silence so far, when she was clearly supposed to be feeding him her line about Warrick's duplicity.

Back in the interrogation room, Tanit looked angry and sullen—the near-perfect picture of a proud woman forced to betray herself. However, now that Toreth was paying closer attention, he wondered how he'd managed to miss the signs before. The prisoner hadn't broken—far from it. She had delivered every sentence with careful thought and for maximum effect.

"Good morning." He looked at his watch. "I hope today's session won't take too long—if you're willing to cooperate this time, it can be very short indeed."

"I told you everything I know." She was a damn good actor, but not quite good enough.

He shook his head. "I don't think you did. In fact, I'm sure you didn't. I had some interesting lab results this morning. Regarding your resistance to interrogation drugs." A flash of suddenly real emotion showed in her eyes, which made him even more sure that yesterday's performance had been precisely that. "It leaves me with a dilemma. Most of the pharmacy isn't going to be very effective. And what's left would probably kill you before you said anything."

Stark fear showed in her eyes now, although her physical control still impressed him as he paraphrased the relevant section of the Procedures and Protocols. "Under most circumstances, pain isn't a very effective questioning tool. But for some prisoners, under some circumstances, it can work very well."

She collected herself. "It doesn't matter what you do. There's nothing else I can tell you."

"Well, we'll see which of us is right about that." He picked out a nerve induction probe from the bench. A level eight lifted all restrictions, but it was always better to start out on the basis of no tissue damage.

"Please."

After two hours of stubborn (and impressive) near silence, a significant moment at last. Some prisoners would've started pleading straight away, but that was the first time she'd said it. Toreth gave her a moment's respite, enough for her to think that it had stopped, and then carried on. That first time she had been sufficiently in control to ask. By the time he stopped again, she was begging, sobbing.

"Before we begin, these are the rules." He leaned on the back of the chair and spoke in a low voice, filling in the time while she regained enough control to produce a coherent narrative. "It can start again whenever you want it to. If you don't answer a question, if you hesitate, if you tell me a lie, if you try to hold something back, I'll know about it and we'll go back to the pain until I'm satisfied you've learned the lesson. Do you understand me?" She nodded, pleas held back now, but still shaking with tears. "Good." He moved around in front of her, to where he could see her face. "Now, did you tell me the truth yesterday about how you carried out the killings?"

"Yes." A whisper.

"Think very carefully about that." He shifted the NI probe from hand to hand, and she flinched in the restraints.

"It was all true."

"Good. Did you tell me the truth about why?"

"No."

"Tell me what the lies were."

"There are no old results. No proof. Not really. They said they could create them, that they would be found. By you. Warrick would be disgraced. If the sponsors believed the sim could cause harm, that I was sure enough to kill to prove it, they'd pull out. But the sim . . . the sim *is* dangerous. I know it is. I had to stop it."

"The story about old results was a fallback, in case the killings weren't attributed to the sim?"

"Yes."

For procedure's sake, he ran through the previous day's answers again, getting nothing different at first. Eventually he asked, "Who picked out Keilholtz?"

"Me. His death was supposed to drive Pearl Nissim away from SimTech. She would have blamed the sim, because there was no way it could be anything else." She almost smiled. "They weren't very happy about the legislator. Not what they wanted."

As he spotted the mistake, he caught the simultaneous flash of realization on her face. "Who wasn't happy?" he asked. "Who was behind it?"

"I—I don't know."

When he moved forwards, she closed her eyes and clenched her fists. Ready

216

to resist. Toreth smiled. It was only a matter of time. He waited until she opened her eyes again before he activated the probe.

Only a matter of time, but still more time than he'd expected. Toreth changed the angle of questioning repeatedly, trying to chip through the stubborn resistance, and cursing the useless pharmacy. Eventually he risked a low dose of one the newer additions to the pharmacopoeia, an antidote to which had presumably been beyond the expertise of whoever had supplied Tanit. He'd never tried the drug before and he didn't have much faith in it. It was supposed to increase susceptibility to pain, and he'd always felt that could be more easily and reliably achieved by turning up the probe. But at this point, he was willing to take a risk on something new.

After twenty minutes, he thought he might owe the pharmacist an apology. The prisoner had a worryingly pale and clammy look, from fear rather than from an adverse drug reaction—the monitors showed nothing drastically wrong. More importantly, the prisoner was finally becoming more cooperative. "Your fallback plan was to confess to murder and taint Warrick in the process?"

She nodded, shivering.

"You expect me to believe that you were willing to be executed to destroy the sim?"

Another nod, but accompanied this time by a glance at the probe. Pitifully easy to read. Toreth shifted his grip again, and at once she was talking. "They promised me a way out. When it was over—I wouldn't be tried."

"Who are they?"

"I don't know."

He shook his head, lowered his voice. "That is a lie."

"No! I promise, I—"

Two minutes this time, as she struggled in the chair, screaming, all pretense of control gone. "Psychoprogramming! *Psychoprogramming.*"

A name at last, but not one he expected, or wanted to hear. Toreth clicked off the probe and stepped back. "Say that again."

"Psychoprogramming. They wanted the sim. They knew where I was. They knew I was there, they knew I was trained; they knew about the paper on Tara, they knew I wanted to destroy it, they...please. Please. It was Psychoprogramming."

Distantly, he heard himself say, "A name. Give me a name."

"I don't know." She was crying again. Toreth watched with more than normal detachment. Psychoprogramming. "I had one contact, a man with ginger hair. After my time. I don't *know* his name, I swear. Please."

"Fine." Psychoprogramming. Fuck.

"I don't—"

217

"Shut the *fuck* up!"

She stared at him, eyes wide, tears brimming on the lower lashes.

"That's enough. You've said enough." He threw the probe back onto the instrument bench. "More than fucking enough."

The next fifteen minutes were a blur: calling the guards, having Tanit taken back to her cell, going back up to his office, and locking the door. Sara was away from her desk, thank fuck, so she wasn't there to ask what was wrong. That would have been an easy question, though—everything.

Psychoprogramming, obviously looking for a way past budget restrictions to get hold of the sim tech. He knew all too well what it meant: he was thoroughly and totally screwed. Of course, there was always the chance that Tanit was lying. A slim chance, given that her description of a ginger-haired contact from Mindfuck matched the indigs' description of Yang's killer, but he'd take whatever chance he could get. A few minutes' consideration produced a possible way of confirming her story. He called Carey, and got Phil Verstraeten. Over the comm the man was more confident. "What can I do for you, Para?"

"Is Liz there?"

"I'm afraid Investigator Carey is out of the building."

Fuck. Toreth debated, but couldn't bring himself to trust a trainee he'd met for ten minutes. "Where? I need to talk to her now."

"I'll see if I can get hold of her, Para. Shall I ask her to call you?"

Of course, you fucking idiot. "Please." He cut the connection and stared blankly at the darkened comm screen. Toreth knew how these things worked. Mindfuck would never risk any hint of this escaping. Hell, the Administration top ranks would suppress it no less keenly. While corporates normally displayed the same sort of group loyalty as starving sharks, they would go berserk at such a blatant attack on corporate sanctity. That sort of thing brought down heads of department, or even more than that. Idealistically motivated resisters were less than nothing compared to a united corporate front.

Tanit would be dead as soon as the mindfuckers responsible for the mess found out she'd talked; he was the only living witness to her doing it, which gave him a life expectancy just marginally longer. The fact that heads would undoubtedly also roll at Psychoprogramming was no consolation at all. The reason behind the unexpected annex was clear now. According to the plan, Tanit should've confessed quickly. The request for the higher-level waiver showed that either she hadn't yet, or that Toreth didn't believe her. The Annex A ought to have ensured that in either case Tanit would die without Toreth examining her faked confession too closely. He cursed himself for the stupidity that had landed him here. Tillotson should've given the case to Chevril, who had the dedication and animation of a whelk. In Chev's hands, Tanit would already be annexed and cremated.

The comm screen flickered, and Toreth composed himself in time to greet Elizabeth Carey. "What's so urgent?" she asked.

"I need a file. A list of"—not too specific—"everyone who's tried to license sim tech. Successfully and unsuccessfully."

Luckily, she made it easy for him. "Corporate and Administration?"

He pretended to hesitate. "Sure. Sling in the internal budget requests while you're at it. Might as well collect the set."

"Don't go away, I'll only be a minute." She looked away, talking as she worked. "Verstraeten could've done it for you, you know. I think you hurt his feelings by asking to talk to me."

Toreth forced a smile. "I admit it—I just wanted to hear your voice. It's pure aural sex."

She chuckled. "Keep that up, I'll be applying for a transfer to General Criminal. Okay, it's all on its way to your screen."

"Thanks, Liz." He skipped quickly through the summary file, praying not to find what he was looking for. On the first run through, he somehow missed it, but he'd barely had time to enjoy the first rush of relief before his eyes caught the link, and his stomach backflipped.

The details of the requests to purchase sim technology filled pages. Psychoprogramming had tried every damn thing they could to get hold of the sim. The Treasury must've had to take on an admin just to bounce the requests. When he looked at the sums involved, he couldn't believe they'd kept trying. Warrick was clearly stretching the licensing rules to the limit to keep Mindfuck at bay. Why hadn't the stupid bastard given them what they wanted? The requests had kept coming in until—what a fucking surprise—four months ago. The same time Marian Tanit claimed to have been contacted. Since then, they'd sent a couple more, just for appearances. No new justifications and no appeals. It was—

It was evidence. Solid evidence and a motive. Money. He'd always liked money as a motive.

One more thing to check. Where, specifically, did ownership of the sim technology revert? All he knew was Administration. He called up Asher Linton's carefully written files, and began tracing the links. The Human Sciences Research Center fell under the umbrella of the Department of Medicine, and had been basically untouched by the reorganization. However, as Marcus had told him, the Neuroscience Section project had been funded by the now-defunct Department of Security. On that basis, the rights would revert to somewhere within Internal Security, External Security, or the Service.

That made him think of something else Marcus had said: that it was possible someone elsewhere in the Administration had deliberately killed the project after the reorganization. Perhaps, even back then, it had been an attempt to gain control of the technology. Could that be traced to Psychoprogramming? Was it worth trying to find out? It might take days to track the information down in the wake of the reorganization, and he didn't even have hours. In the end he decided to try. It took only one call to locate the former head of the project; the man was still at the Human Sciences Research Center.

"Dr. Le Tissiet? My name is Senior Para-investigator Val Toreth. I have a question about the Indirect Neural Remodeling project, if you remember that."

"Of course," he said, polite but wary. "I'll do anything I can to help."

"When the project was canceled, did you think it might've been deliberately squelched by another department?"

Le Tissiet's expression closed down. "We had our suspicions, yes."

"Who?"

"I really can't remember." Open evasion now. "It was a long time ago, and it was nothing more than the usual rumors."

Toreth changed tack. "The rights to the technology were sold. Do you know where they would end up if the corporation who owns them now failed?"

"To you, of course. Don't you have that information already?"

To I&I? "I'm sorry?"

"Para-investigators are Psychoprogramming, aren't they?"

For a moment, he couldn't answer. Gold. He'd struck a great big shining vein of gold. "No. Part of Int-Sec, yes, but we're Investigation and Interrogation. Are you saying Psychoprogramming asked the same question?"

"Yes. A few months ago. Took us a while to trace the information, I can tell you. But I have all the details to hand now. Or closer to hand than they were."

"Do you remember the name of the person who put the request in?"

Le Tissiet frowned. "Ah . . . no, I'm afraid not. In fact, I didn't speak to anyone in person. The request arrived on a general information code. Shall I send it all along to you?"

With the "please" on his lips, Toreth reconsidered. "Maybe later. And I'd be grateful if you didn't mention this to anyone." Le Tissiet's eyebrows lifted, but he merely nodded. The I&I reputation was very good for deflecting inconvenient questions. "Thanks for your help." Toreth closed the connection and sat back.

A case. An actual, solid case. A good confession and nice circumstantial evidence to back it up. Now what the fuck was he going to do?

One option was to take it directly to an Administration higher-up. Now he regretted Nissim's death. He could try one of her friends in the Legislature, or even the Int-Sec head of department. What was the man's name? Toreth had once seen him on a tour of the building. Shaken his hand, in fact, and thought he looked like exactly the kind of untrustworthy political scum that rose to the top. Of course, if the first person Toreth approached was involved, or reported him to someone who was, or thought the whole thing was best covered up very comprehensively, he'd be just as fucked as if Psychoprogramming found out what he knew. On reflection, Toreth decided he'd rather have a plan where an optimistic outcome wasn't "maybe they'll kill me quickly." Evidence of Psychoprogramming's involvement or not, what he really needed was a way to bury the whole mess deeper than the I&I waste recycling level.

His first impulse was to go back downstairs and kill Tanit and then try somehow to wipe the recordings. However, there were too many backups and safeguards that he had no idea how to circumvent. Nor would Sara, and she was the only person in the building he could trust to do it and keep quiet. Tillotson might be able to fix it, or at least refer the question up to find who could. With a high enough level of authority behind it, transcripts could certainly be erased and altered. However, that meant trusting Tillotson not to sacrifice him if things went badly. He'd rather trust corporates. That unlikely sentiment gave him pause. He knew one person who might be able to erase the confession.

On the face of it, trusting Warrick, an outsider, looked insane. Fortunately, trust wasn't required. Warrick stood to lose from this, too. The confession that went back to Justice with Tanit's corpse wouldn't be the one he'd extracted today but rather her first faked confession, which would destroy Warrick's personal reputation and take SimTech out of his control. Toreth wasn't sure which of those two Warrick would hate more, but either on its own ought to buy his help. He locked the records up as completely as he could, as would be expected anyway with such commercially sensitive results. Thank fuck it was Saturday tomorrow and he could justify not showing the recordings to anyone until Monday. Then he called SimTech.

With the surveillance he'd had installed at SimTech (not to mention whatever private arrangements Warrick had in his office), Toreth didn't want to risk a meeting there. Warrick was waiting by the lake on the main university campus when Toreth got there, staring out over the water. He didn't look around as Toreth walked up. "If you're here to ask for Tara back, then you're wasting your time," he said coldly, before Toreth could speak.

"Back?" Last thing he'd heard they had her in the cells.

"She's in hospital again—we finally managed to retrieve her from I&I this morning. Don't tell me that you didn't know." His voice chilled even further, which Toreth would have said was impossible. "Or do you lose interest once you've broken your witnesses?"

"I missed the memo, and you're welcome to keep her. Listen, Warrick, I need your help."

Warrick laughed. "Oh?"

"It might interest you to know that Tanit has made a confession. To two of the four deaths."

He turned slowly. "Really? Well, I have to admit that with the methods available to you, the only real surprise is that she didn't confess to all of them."

Hardly an original accusation. "You want to try Justice for that. I'm not in the business of extracting false confessions." Or at least not in this case. "Please, just hear me out."

Warrick said nothing, which Toreth was willing to take as encouragement. He had debated his approach and had decided on honesty because, as at the bar in the Renaissance Center, he only had one shot at convincing Warrick. He outlined the problem quickly and straightforwardly, trying not to let his nervousness show. Halfway through the explanation he felt certain Warrick would simply not believe him. The last thing he'd said at SimTech was that Tanit hadn't done it. When he finished, Warrick stayed silent. Having gone this far, Toreth saw no point in not taking the extra step and pleading. "Warrick, I swear it's all true—I checked the Mindfuck budget requests. And they approached your old boss, Le Tissiet, about the license reversion. He—"

"Yes, I believe you."

Toreth stopped, relief and surprise fighting for his attention. "You do? Why?"

"I told Marian that you knew about the toxin." Warrick held his hand up. "I'm sorry, it was an accidental slip of the tongue. However, once she'd heard that, she suggested that I should tell you about her old file. About her connection to Psychoprogramming. She must have known that you would make the link between that and—" His voice flattened. "Tara's scan results."

Toreth nodded. "She wanted to be arrested before you could tell the sponsors the sim was in the clear. It's all to fuck SimTech. She wants to give the sim to Psychoprogramming. You understand that?"

"Of course. However," Warrick added, "I fail to see what you expect me to do about the situation."

"I don't know. Something. Anything." Panic surfaced briefly. "If anyone gets hold of this I'm dead. Literally and pretty fucking soon. And—" And you're almost as fucked as I am—but it was obvious that Warrick had realized this.

"All right," Warrick said. "Be quiet and let me think."

They walked around the edge of the lake in the thin sunshine. Eventually Warrick stopped and stared into midspace. Toreth watched the ducks pulling up underwater weeds and tried not to scream with impatience. "I think I have an idea," Warrick said slowly. "Perhaps. I'll need to know a few things first." When Toreth nodded, he continued. "Do you have any names for the people behind it? Someone at Psychoprogramming?"

"No. A one-line description of Tanit's contact, that's all. I could get more from her, but I daren't risk putting it through the ident system. I might have blown it already by getting the Psychoprogramming budget requests."

"I see. Now, has anyone else seen the interrogation?"

"Not yet. Soon. Monday at the latest."

"Excellent. Is there tamperproofing on the recording?"

"Yes."

"Mm. Is your office under surveillance?"

Toreth blinked, then said, "I don't think so."

Warrick looked at him sharply. "Think isn't good enough."

"Well, then . . . no, it isn't. I'm sure." If it had been, then some of the things he'd done in there over the years would definitely have ended up in the edited highlights of life at I&I, screened every year by the head of security at the New Year's parties.

"All right," Warrick said, "here's my idea. We mock up the interrogation room in the sim, record a version of the interrogation where she doesn't confess, and then substitute it for the real record in the I&I system. I should be able to fake the tamperproofing if you can give me access to the system. Will that work?"

Toreth considered it. Okay insofar as it went, but it only solved the immediate problem. If only the rep had given him an Annex B—dies without talking. "It's not enough. What we need is a short confession with a good motive, and then for her to die without getting a chance to say anything else."

Warrick stared. "*Die?*"

"Yes. I can't leave her alive. They'll give her to someone else if I don't get a result. And she will talk—she wants to. She only held out as long as she did at first to make it look good."

Appalled silence, then Warrick said, "If I could talk to her, convince her to keep quiet—"

"It wouldn't matter. If she doesn't come through for Mindfuck, she's dead and she knows it. Besides—" This wasn't the time to consider Warrick's squeamishness. "You haven't seen her. She's broken. She'll break again, even if you or I could talk her into trying not to. There won't be any questions about the death— I can guarantee that."

Warrick shook his head, but his next words weren't a refusal. "How can you be sure?"

Toreth hesitated, then decided that it wouldn't make any difference. Not with the kind of trouble he was in already. "I've been told to make sure she doesn't get to trial."

"There has to be another way," Warrick said.

Toreth clenched his hands behind his back, fighting to keep his voice calm. "Fine. You think of one. Because at the moment the only other way is that she confesses and dies anyway, SimTech loses the sponsors, and you're out on the streets or in prison. Psychoprogramming gets the sim to do whatever the hell they want with, and I'll be dead." Warrick turned away, looking out over the lake, and Toreth fought down the urge to grab him, to shake him into agreement. "What does it matter?" Toreth said. "Christ, they'll execute her anyway, even if we don't kill her at I&I. She killed Nissim, and the Justice system won't give a fuck that she claims it was a mistake."

Eventually, Warrick nodded. "Very well. Get me the plans for the room, pictures if you can, and a copy of the recording we need to replace. Marian is on file at SimTech, or we wouldn't be able to do it in time."

He collected the things as quickly as he could, managing to avoid Sara, and delivered them to SimTech. He didn't see Warrick—his admin said that he was in the sim and that he'd left a message saying he would call—so he put everything in Warrick's office, waiting until he knew that Warrick had been told they were there.

Sara had left already by the time he got back to I&I. She usually went a little early on a Friday, although Toreth thought that a full two hours was taking the piss. He filled time by writing an informal disciplinary note for her to ignore. After four versions came out vitriolic enough to require apology-flowers, he decided to give up and leave early, too.

On the way to the lift, Toreth remembered the surveillance he'd had installed at SimTech. He sent a security team out to remove it right away, and they were happy enough for the overtime. Still, the incident left him cold. If he hadn't thought of it, God knows what might have been recorded and left lying on file. At the very least the surveillance would show himself and Warrick at SimTech, working together for hours. It was just the kind of thing to interest Internal Investigations. He remembered Marian talking about estimates. One pitfall in the plan he'd barely avoided. Could he possibly miss all the rest he hadn't yet even considered?

Leaving instructions that his prisoner could speak to no one except him, Toreth went home.

Chapter Twenty-seven

❖

He woke up early on Saturday morning, the sheets drenched in sweat, his ears still ringing, and his shoulders aching from fruitless struggles against the dream hands holding him under the water. Once the worst of the sickness had abated, Toreth lay back, trying to calm his breathing. When he looked at the clock, it read six a.m. Too early to get up, but he'd be lucky to sleep again now. Kirkby's fault for bringing the old nightmares back so vividly. Fucking sadist. Toreth had always thought that spending too much time with the dead couldn't be healthy.

Abandoning any idea of getting back to sleep, Toreth showered and dressed, and settled down on the sofa to consider the contents of Marian Tanit's final confession. Warrick might have his own plans, but the result needed to be satisfactory for Toreth's career, as well as for SimTech. But for Warrick's involvement, he could use the first, fake confession verbatim and make Psychoprogramming into happy little mindfuckers. Much as he disliked Psychoprogramming and the know-all shits who worked there, it would be by far the safest path. However, he'd still need Warrick's help to erase the second confession, which named Psychoprogramming. Warrick would never agree to anything that would damage SimTech and Toreth had no leverage over Warrick. No power over him at all.

Pushing that nasty idea firmly out of his mind, he got to work. After several elaborate starts, he went for the simple and unverifiable. Tanit was paid to discredit the sim by one of the numerous disgruntled corporations that had been disappointed in its hopes of investing in the sim. Unable to partake in the spoils, it had resolved to destroy the fledgling corporation instead, and buy back the rights from the Administration. Tanit had been contacted by an anonymous third party—she knew no names. An ordinary tale of corporate sabotage, exactly, ironically, as he had always maintained it was. It would be nice to be proven right, even by an illusion.

When he'd polished the story to his satisfaction, he sent the file to Warrick, receiving a terse note of acknowledgement a few minutes later. Then he could do no more except wait for Warrick to call.

225

❖ ❖ ❖

By late Saturday afternoon, Toreth was almost frantic with worry. If Warrick was unable to set up the mock interrogation room soon, it was probably too late to think of another plan.

Then the comm chimed. Not Warrick in person, simply a message reading "Come." When he reached SimTech, a technician met him in reception and showed him straight up to the sim suite, where Warrick was already in the sim. To Toreth's surprise—and relief—there were no security guards in the sim room. He hoped that their dismissal wouldn't cause comment. Setting up the sim seemed to take three times longer than normal. He almost yelled at the technician to hurry up as he checked the straps, ran the calibration, and finally lowered the visor.

Opening his eyes, Toreth found himself somewhere very familiar indeed. Warrick sat at the table, working on the virtual control panel, which was the only incongruent thing Toreth could see except Warrick himself. "How is it?" Warrick asked, without looking up.

The room was creepily like work, and he said so.

"It's not finished. Many of the items on the bench over there you can't pick up. You can handle the items you used in the interrogation but they aren't all fully interactive. I couldn't find sufficiently close templates for some things. Let me know if there's anything else you need functional and I'll see what I can do."

Toreth looked at Warrick, busy with the control panel, speaking so calmly and matter-of-factly about interrogation. At any other time, the subject disgusted him. Now it had become an interesting technical problem and he was utterly caught up in it. He must have watched the interrogation through if he knew which instruments Toreth had used. "What about the prisoner?" Toreth asked.

"Wait."

As Warrick worked, Toreth checked through the instruments and drugs. Then Marian Tanit appeared, seated in the chair, staring blankly ahead. Toreth moved over, reached out, then paused and looked across at Warrick. He nodded permission, and then went back to the screen. She felt alive, warm and pliable. Toreth lifted his hand and touched her eyeball. The figure blinked and flinched very slightly away, then returned to her—its—former position. Not convincing. Not good. "Will she react properly?" he asked.

"No, she won't. But I will."

"What?"

"I'm going to be inside."

"*Inside?*"

Warrick looked up and smiled tightly. "It's the only way to make it look real. I don't have time to train up an expert system to play the part realistically. Believe me, I'm not suggesting this for lack of trying to think of another option."

"Warrick, it's going to take eight hours. Eight hours recorded."

"Not at all. As I understand it, you require three interrogation sessions—the two already conducted and one tomorrow where Marian will die." No waver in his voice. "Is that correct?"

"Yes. And they all have to be in the system by Monday. After that it'll be too late to do anything. Once Tillotson sees the real interrogations we're both fucked."

"We should have everything completed in time to clean out the system before anyone gets here tomorrow. Even leaving a margin for any necessary processing, the recordings will be ready to install in the I&I systems by tomorrow afternoon." Warrick stood up and began pacing—lecturing voice and illustrative gestures. "In the first interrogation, she says nothing dangerous until the last ten minutes. So we simply duplicate the record up to that point. I've already prepared that. Then we have only to remove the section where she alleges that the sim is dangerous and that I hid the safety data. That leaves just ten minutes which need to be filled with new material."

That sounded almost reasonable, except for one thing. "And you'll play her part?"

Warrick paused and smiled. "I'm not a bad actor. You'll see. I suggest adding the ten minutes in bits and pieces near the beginning of the interrogation, when she isn't saying much anyway. Less likely to attract scrutiny there."

There was no point arguing now—he'd simply have to wait to see if Warrick could do it. "Okay, say that works. What next?"

He resumed pacing. "In the second interrogation, the damaging content is again at the end, where Marian names Psychoprogramming. It's only a few minutes long. Again, I've already duplicated the sections where she says nothing and we can pad the recording near the beginning."

"What about the interrogation for tomorrow?"

"You'll be in the interrogation room, and I'll feed the recording into the system as if it were coming through the cameras in the room. Even if anyone watches it live, they'll see our recording."

All very neatly planned. God, it was never going to work. "But there's nothing to edit that interrogation out of."

Warrick nodded and sat down at the screen. "That will be the most difficult part. How long does the recording need to be?"

Toreth thought about it, looking at the silent Marian. "Twenty minutes is the shortest—half an hour would be better. I need time to prep her and then get on to an accidental overdose." Traditional for an annex death. "That'll look most convincing. I can screw the calibration on one of the injectors while I'm in the interrogation room with her and you're running the recording." No response to his words. When he looked around, he saw Warrick staring down at the controls, his hands still. "There's no other way," Toreth said, guessing what was wrong.

"There must be."

"Jesus fucking Christ, how many times do I—" Toreth caught hold of himself. Trying to browbeat Warrick was an exercise in futility. "If you can think of something else, I'll happily give it a try. Fucking with I&I systems isn't my idea of fun, anyway. I don't think there's a chance in hell this is going to work."

Warrick looked up sharply. "Of course it will! There is absolutely no technical reason why—" He stopped, then smiled, lopsided. "Very good. However, you're right. There is no other way. Shall we proceed?"

Things did not go as smoothly as Warrick had predicted.

It took them nearly three hours to produce the material to pad out the first two interrogations—fifteen usable minutes of nothing more exciting than Marian saying nothing. Still, by the time they were done Toreth was willing to concede that Warrick was indeed a pretty good actor.

It took another hour for Warrick to splice the new pieces into the material from the original interrogation recordings. Toreth watched the two doctored recordings. To his surprise, they looked pretty damn flawless. An I&I interrogation analysis program might still pull out discrepancies in the prisoner's behavior. However, as there was no reason for anyone to run one, he allowed himself to feel moderately confident about it.

Then they moved on to the final session—thirty minutes of original interrogation—and the real problems began. Neither he nor Warrick were patient men at heart; his attempts to coach Warrick into responding correctly to the ineffective drugs and neural induction probe, on top of matching Marian's speech patterns, brought them virtually to blows. Eventually, after two hours had yielded no usable recording, Marian went limp in the chair and Warrick reappeared by the controls. "Wait here," he said, then vanished again.

Toreth sat on the virtual chair and waited as patiently as he could. He wished—not for the first time—that he hadn't applied for the higher-level waiver. Ten years at I&I should have taught him about the dangers of ambition. If he started running, what were the odds that he could make it beyond the reach of the Administration?

For some reason he never trusted his watch to tell the right time in the sim. However, it said nearly an hour passed before Warrick reappeared. "Where the hell have you been?"

"Recalibrating neural induction settings and tearing out safety overrides. I'll deal with the SimTech security footage tomorrow." He walked over to the array of equipment and picked up one of the neural induction probes. "This one is now fully functional up to about half power. That's as high as it'll go before it trips safety systems that I can't disable."

"What about the drugs?"

"The pharmacy is locked; unfortunate, since relaxants would appeal right now. I've set up a response filter to mimic the physical effects of the drugs." He looked at Toreth's expression and added, "That means—"

Lecturing again. "I'm not interested, as long as works."

"Very well." Warrick vanished and Marian lifted her head. "Let's try it."

Toreth shrugged, then moved over to where a ghostly outline of himself indicated the place the recording ended. A disorienting moment passed as the sim translated his body into the exact position, and they were ready. He picked up the live NI probe. Wishing to test the realism, he set the control to the right level, then activated the probe. The prisoner arched back in the chair and screamed once, badly out of character. When Toreth switched the probe off there was a silence before she said, in Tanit's voice but with Warrick's inflection, "Christ, that *hurts*."

"That's pretty much the point. I don't think this—"

"No. I wasn't expecting it, that's all. How many times are you planning to use it?"

Toreth considered the fewest that would look passably convincing. "Maybe three or four."

"That I can handle. Start again."

This time he started with a question. "Who paid you to discredit the sim?"

"A corporate. I don't know who."

"I want a name and verifiable details."

"I can't tell you what I don't know."

Tanit writhed in the chair as the probe activated, and Toreth found it hard to remember it was really Warrick he was hurting. "You're lying. Who paid you to discredit the sim?"

"I don't... please. I don't *know*."

"What do you know?"

"I've told you, I... please."

"Tell me again."

He listened with half an ear to the stumbling words, impressed by the performance, watching the mock monitors displaying their convincing results. Those readings too would be faked and fed into the I&I system. Could Warrick really do it all?

"I don't know who he represented. I *don't know*."

Toreth used the probe far more than four times, and he had to admit a grudging respect for Warrick's persistence. Or was Warrick enjoying it on some level? Toreth had never consciously focused on that element of the game they had played. However, Warrick was satisfyingly responsive to slaps and arm twisting. Perhaps he would appreciate a little more pain for its own sake, as well as a tool to emphasize control.

"I'd tell you if I knew. Please, I swear—I'd tell you if I knew."

229

On and on, like so many interrogations he'd conducted, except that from time to time they'd stop and repeat a section. Finally, Warrick called a halt and Toreth laid the nerve induction probe down on the instrument bench. As he did so, Warrick stood up from the interrogation chair, his body separating from Tanit's, and strolled over to the table to check the console. A minute or so later Toreth realized that the restraints were still fastened. The sim, and Warrick's control over it, didn't often disturb Toreth, but for some reason that did it. Warrick was fucking with sim reality, but also with something so familiar to Toreth's own reality, without even noticing he was doing it. Maybe Tanit had a point after all.

"Toreth?"

He turned to find Warrick standing by the table, obviously impatient. Had Warrick said his name a couple of times already? "What?"

"Check this through. It's only a rough cut. I'll do it in detail later."

A few adjustments, and Toreth pronounced it acceptable, and then they reached the final hurdle.

Marian's death.

When the moment came, he thought Warrick would balk, but in fact it was almost the easiest thing they'd done. A convincing hiss from the fake injector, a few seconds for the drug to take effect with Marian growing still in the chair, and then a few more for it to stop her heart while he turned his back long enough not to notice. Turn around again, register the scene, fake a little shock for the record. A classic annex death, if only Warrick had known it. Toreth hit the comm, called for the medical techs, and was almost surprised to realize that meant the performance was over. They wouldn't come; there was no corridor outside the door, no I&I.

"Warrick?" He waited, seconds stretching out, then touched Marian's still face. "Warrick?"

"Over here."

He spun around to find Warrick sitting next to the control panel, checking the screen. He looked absolutely calm and composed, but then there was no reason he shouldn't. Toreth wondered what he looked like outside the sim, under the concealing mask. "Did that do it?" Toreth asked.

"Have a look for yourself."

It was perfect, thank God, meaning that there was nothing left for him to do. He left the sim while Warrick was still splicing together bits of the recording. The technician had long gone, so he had to work his arms out of the restraints to free his legs and remove the visor.

Standing over Warrick's still body, he thought briefly about exactly how much trust he was placing in the other man to pull this off. Briefly was all he allowed himself. Before today, if pressed, Toreth might have conceded to trusting Sara. Chevril was something like a friend, as were one or two of the other paras, but trust was a rare quality at I&I. The very idea of depending on an outsider unnerved him. An outsider, and a corporate at that, whom he'd known for only a few weeks. Not merely trusting him, but trusting him with his career and—no denying it—his life. However unpleasant it felt, he could still see no alternative.

Chapter Twenty-eight

❖

U nlike much of Int-Sec, I&I was a public building in the sense that it was possible for citizens to visit it. They simply rarely did so voluntarily. However, as the respectable face of Administration internal security, I&I was equipped with a reception desk, publicly available contact numbers and, indeed, entire sections devoted to dealing directly with the people to whose protection it was dedicated. An appointment was usually advisable, but during the week, if a visitor had the name of someone they wished to see or some information they wished to give, even that could be bypassed.

On a Sunday, however, an appointment was mandatory, so Toreth was forced to book Warrick's visit in officially. When Toreth arrived at lunchtime, the office was reassuringly quiet. The fewer people around, the better. However, after consideration, he called Sara in. He didn't like to involve her, but he needed her to ensure Warrick wasn't disturbed. As he sat on her desk, letting her description of the wonderful day he'd ruined pass over him without hearing a word she said, he saw Belqola across the office. Had he decided to try working for a change? Too late, if he had.

"Belqola!"

The man looked around. "Para?"

"My office."

In the office, Toreth sat down behind his desk, leaving Belqola standing. "I thought I ought to give you some notice—when this case wraps, I'll be sending you back to the pool. With the reference you deserve."

He watched Belqola's face slipping from shock to disbelief to anger. "You're throwing me out? You can't!"

"Really? News to me. I've sent the order down already."

Belqola's eyes narrowed. "I did exactly what you wanted."

"Hardly. I wanted a junior para who didn't mess up all the damn time. I gave you more than one chance. You screwed them up."

"You know what I mean."

"The fuck was your idea, not mine. Incidentally, I'm not disputing that you suck cocks like a professional. But I'm running an investigative team, not a brothel."

Belqola flushed, with anger rather than embarrassment. "You said—" And he stopped dead.

Toreth smiled. "Yes? What did I say?"

"Okay, you implied."

"I'm not responsible for your assumptions. A tendency towards making assumptions is a bad habit for a para-investigator. You ought to keep an eye on that."

"You fucking—" The junior clenched his fists, and then slowly relaxed them. "I know I screwed things up, Para. Give me another chance. A real chance. Please. You can have... well, anything. Whatever you want."

"I already have. Once was more than enough. You'd need to be a lot better than that to fuck yourself a place on my team."

"You'll be sorry you did this. Sir."

Toreth always loved the empty threats. "If you want to make yourself a laughingstock, go right ahead and lodge a complaint. Tell everyone why you thought the only way you could keep your assignment was taking it on your knees in a toilet. Seniors will be queuing up to sign you on after that." No answer from the junior, but there didn't need to be. The rage and humiliation, plain on his face, said it all—and warmed Toreth's cock nicely. Pushing his chair back from the desk, he smiled. "I'll tell you what, one more blowjob and I'll write you a nice transfer reference. How about it?" Belqola hesitated, and then shook his head firmly. "Suit yourself." Toreth turned his attention to his screen, dismissing the junior. "If you change your mind before the end of the case, you know where I am."

Without another word, Belqola stalked out of the office.

Reception called up at twenty past two to tell Toreth that he had a visitor. The call produced an unexpected kick of relief—he'd begun to worry whether Warrick would go through with it or not. Toreth told Sara Warrick was on his way and then kept the comm open. After a few minutes, he heard his voice. "You must be the inestimable Sara. My name is Dr. Keir Warrick."

A pause, then Sara said, "I'll tell him you're here."

When the door opened to admit Warrick, he looked completely and reassuringly calm. Exhausted, though—far more so than that night at SimTech when he'd shown Toreth the key to the murder contained in the computer code. His face was hollow-eyed, with deep lines around his eyes and mouth. He couldn't have slept much the night before, if he'd slept at all. "I'll need as much access to the system as you can give me," Warrick said without preamble, as he sat down at Toreth's screen. "It will save a great deal of time if I don't have to find my own way through the security."

Toreth had already drawn up a list of his own access codes for the I&I systems, as well as an assortment of other people's codes that he'd acquired here and there. He handed the list to Warrick. Might as well be hung for a sheep as for a lamb. Not the most comforting of metaphors right now. Warrick looked down the list, his eyebrows creeping up as he read. "Is that going to be enough?" Toreth asked.

"Oh, certainly." Warrick glanced up and smiled. "More than enough, I should say. Now, if I could have a little peace and quiet, I'll see what I can do."

Warrick worked quickly, intent and absorbed. Toreth managed to sit still for a couple of minutes, then gave up and paced aimlessly, trying not to hum. Warrick didn't seem to mind, or even to notice. This was it. Up until now the danger had been theoretical, if he ignored the basic stupidity of involving Warrick at all. Now they were creating the evidence that could see both of them arrested, and in all probability annexed. With half of his attention on Warrick's face—his eyes locked to the screen, the occasional frown gathering, then clearing—Toreth passed the time cataloging all the crimes they had committed or were about to commit. Unauthorized access to I&I systems, attacks on systems security, perjury, falsifying evidence, conspiracy to do all of that, and murder to top it off.

Finally, Warrick sat back. "Everything is in place."

"Right. I'll get downstairs."

"You should check the recordings first. If the doctored ones pass muster, then today's should work, too."

Trying to delay the inevitable? "We don't have time."

"At this point I could probably undo what I've done and leave the system none the wiser. It would be a pity to—to go through with the plan, and only then discover that the tampering was obvious. Rather too late at that point to consider other options."

Toreth checked his watch, and then shrugged. "Okay. Move over."

He ran the recordings through the highest level of the interrogation analysis systems, while Warrick watched over his shoulder. The system would pull up any discrepancies in the prisoner's behavior or indications of tampering in the record. If anyone questioned him, Toreth could claim he ran the analysis to check for telltales of interrogation resistance aids. After an agonizing wait, the recordings came back clean. What he would have done if they hadn't, he had no idea.

The feeling of relief was short-lived; they still had most of the plan to go. Toreth stood up and headed for the doorway. He paused there for a last run through the plan, as much to steady his own nerves as because he thought Warrick needed the reminder. "You don't have to watch it all," he said, "but keep the audio link open until it's done. I might need you to check that everything looks okay when we sync up. I'll be back as soon as I can afterwards, but I'll have things to do first—don't panic if it takes me a while. Whatever you do, don't go anywhere. Right?"

Warrick nodded, already back in his place at the screen. "Good luck," he said absently.

The silence stretched out in the room.

Marian sat in the chair, twisting her wrists mechanically against the restraints, which made her think of the sim. How many times had she watched the technicians tightening those straps, on herself or others? She saw her hands moving, but they felt distant, unconnected. A stranger's. It reminded her too of her training days—of standing by, listening to the direct neural re-education guinea pigs pleading for their memories, for an end to the pain, or simply for death. Perhaps there was nothing she could have done even if she had tried to help them. She hadn't tried. She'd run away, grateful to Psychoprogramming for the easy escape. Maybe this was her well-deserved punishment.

A night and a day and a night. It hadn't occurred to her that she would be back here. It ought to have done. She had told the para-investigator everything, but of course he didn't know that. The idea of what had to come—of how long it might take to satisfy him—intensified the fear that had kept her awake since the last interrogation, until she felt herself beginning to shake.

Twisting against the restraints. Stupid and pointless. What would she do if they broke? There was no way out. The para-investigator stood not far away, filling injectors and occasionally glancing up at the watching cameras. Where had he been for all this time? Checking her story? How? Eventually, unable to bear the silence any longer, she had to speak. "What do you want?"

Toreth finished the last of his preparations, moved to sit at the table. "Nothing. I'm just killing time." She heard the smirk in his voice. "So to speak."

She lifted her head, curiosity sparking. "What?"

"We're all done with confessions now. You put on a good show—even if you'll never know."

She thought about it for a minute, but after three sleepless nights, she couldn't focus. Memories of her shameful performance kept intruding. She had blown her last chance. Psychoprogramming would leave her to twist in the wind now, and she deserved it. "I don't understand," she said eventually, hating to admit it, wanting to know.

He looked back at her, bored on the surface, tense as strung wire underneath and she knew he was debating whether to explain. She felt a tiny, improbable surge of hope. Why would he be nervous? "It's nothing that you need to worry about," he said. "You made the wrong confession, that's all. Two of them, in fact. So I fixed that, with a little help, and now you're not going to have a chance to make them again."

"Help?" she asked, forcing herself to think, to try to see how it could be done. The image came back to her of Warrick and Toreth in the sim. So comfortable together. "Warrick," she said, and as his eyes narrowed she knew she was right.

Then he shrugged. "Yes, Warrick. It doesn't really matter if you know now, does it?"

If he didn't care about that, if he was willing to tell her what he had planned, then there really was no way out. All she could think to say was, stupidly, "You're going to kill me?"

He nodded. "We already did, in the sim. Accidental overdose. It looks very good. Very convincing."

"Warrick wouldn't use the sim like that."

"It was his idea." He looked up at the camera. "Wasn't it?"

For a moment she didn't understand what he meant to show her, perhaps because the idea was too horrible to accept. For all Warrick's faults, for all his overattachment to the sim and his blindness about it, she'd always respected him. She felt bereft at the mere idea that Toreth could have persuaded him to do this. Warrick wouldn't have thought of it himself. Not even to save SimTech and his own neck, and the neck of the sick, twisted excuse for a human being who sat here and watched her and smiled. But if it was true then Warrick really could be somewhere nearby, looking at a monitor, waiting to see her die. "Bastard," she whispered, hopelessly, not even sure which one of them she meant.

He laughed. "Don't get all fucking morally superior with me, Dr. Psychoprogrammer. Don't tell me you never killed anyone before you took it up as a hobby, because I've read your file. The only difference between us is that you lost your nerve and bottled out into a nice, cushy corporate job."

The contempt, the careless cruelty, gave her back some focus. "Psychoprogramming is a perversion of medicine, like this place is a perversion of justice. You—"

"Save your breath"—brief grin—"for what it's worth. I've heard it a hundred fucking times from resisters. Your version pays better, though. What did Mindfuck throw your way to bring you back into the family?"

Anger flared. "That wasn't why I did it."

"No?" A tell-me-another tone of voice.

"No. I had to stop the sim being commercialized—Psychoprogramming provided a tool to do it. People are going to get hurt, badly hurt." Was Warrick watching them now? If he were, this might be the last chance she ever had to try to make him see reason. "The tech isn't safe for everyone. There are vulnerable people out there who will suffer. Lots of them. Addiction, lives destroyed by overdependence, and the Administration doesn't give a damn because it will keep people trapped in fantasy worlds that won't threaten *them*. And more serious effects—Tara won't be an isolated case. There will be illegal copies of the sim, probably even more dangerous. By the time it's recognized, it will be too late to stop it. I didn't want to kill innocents. I didn't want to kill anyone, but sometimes the price of saving lives is—"

"So you decided to hand it over to the kind hearts at Mindfuck instead?"

Yes. That was what she'd decided, although she'd seldom forced herself to look at it so starkly. All she had in her defense was the justification she'd used for all these months. "Better a tool for them than damaging indiscriminately. Once they have control of it, they'll never let it into general use."

He shrugged. "Actually, I don't care."

He didn't, of course. She hoped Warrick would see that, at least.

The para-investigator looked at his watch, came over to the bench. "Time to get started. Or finished."

He pressed the injector against her arm. She felt the brief pain and then the icy heat of the drug flooding through her, making her stomach heave and her vision swim. Someone else might have said, "it won't take long," or "it won't hurt." He simply watched her dispassionately. The strength drained out of her and her head dropped forward. Toreth lifted her chin, tipped her head back against the chair.

"How's that?" he asked.

A moment before she realized he wasn't speaking to her. He nodded, answering an unheard instruction, and moved her head a fraction to the left. Posing her. She tried to fight it, to ruin their plan, but her muscles weren't responding to her commands and she could manage nothing more than rasping breaths. She tried to focus, eyelids suddenly heavy. He wasn't even looking at her now. His gaze moved steadily between his watch and the monitor beside her as he counted out seconds under his breath.

"Fifteen."

Slowly suffocating, every breath a desperate struggle. "Please, no...please, God...don't...I don't...Warrick...Warrick, please."

"Twelve."

"Warrick, please, you have to..." Warrick, listening and watching somewhere. What could he do for her now, even if he finally heard her?

"Ten."

So many important things that she'd never told him, that she had never been able to make him hear.

"Eight."

And now she never would, because she couldn't breathe, not noticing the moment when it finally became impossible. This is how it must have been for them, how they must have felt.

"Five."

237

Silent terror, her heartbeat stuttering to an end and the room graying to a narrow tunnel focused on him—

"Three."

—on his lips shaping the words.

"Two."

The final words, going down with her into the darkness at last.

"One. Kill it."

Chapter Twenty-nine

❖

It took him almost an hour to get away from the interrogation room. Toreth called for an emergency team, started the resuscitation he knew would be futile, waited around as the medics took over and finally pronounced the prisoner dead. Then there were the initial reports to file, a statement to make. All standard procedures, marking out an agony of waiting and worrying about what Warrick might be doing.

When he made it back to his office, Sara looked anxious. "I heard what happened." Of course she had, even on a Sunday. Sometimes he wondered how the admin gossip network functioned so efficiently.

Wanting to go right past and into his own office, he stopped, sat on the edge of her desk. "No big deal," he said calmly. "Everything by the book. Everything inside the waiver. No need to look for another boss just yet."

She grinned. "Thank fuck." Suddenly she looked over her shoulder. "He's still here. Dr. Warrick. I haven't told him anything because you said not to go in until you..." The sentence trailed off and she looked back at him, her eyes narrowing. "What's going on?" she said quietly.

"Nothing."

"Don't give me that. I know you. What's going on?"

"Sara, don't ask. I mean that. It's much better that you don't know." He saw the mutiny in her eyes. "I wouldn't want you to have to lie to anyone about it. Do you understand?"

Then he saw that she did. "You k—" Her voice rose, then dropped again. "Wasn't she annexed?"

"Yes. That's what the rep was here for."

Calculation on her face, trying to work out what was wrong if it wasn't the death itself. Then she glanced at the door to the office. "He *knows*?"

"*Sara.*"

She sat back in her chair, staring at him in bewilderment. Then, like a seamless computer morph, she was Admin Sara again. "Do you want to me to take your comms?"

239

"Yes, please. And do me a transcript of the interrogation—just up to the prisoner's death. Send it through as soon as it's done. Get a couple of coffees first." Warrick would probably need one, and so did he. What he really wanted, in fact, was a huge fucking drink. Maybe later. Toreth took a deep breath and went into the office.

There was a horrible moment when he saw the empty desk and thought that, somehow, Warrick had gone. That maybe the session hadn't been fixed. That he'd been recorded talking to Marian and—

All that went through his mind in the second it took him to register the vacant chair, and then Warrick standing by the window, looking out into the courtyard. Warrick didn't look around, and after a moment Toreth went over. "It's done. All we need now is—"

"I should have listened to her," Warrick said, almost too quietly for Toreth to hear him.

He moved closer. "What?"

"I should have listened to—to Marian."

Not good. "About what?" After a long silence, Toreth cautiously put his hand on Warrick's arm, with a view to turning him around, but Warrick pulled away sharply. In the brief contact, Toreth could feel him shaking. Really not good at all.

"Do you know what I've been doing?" Warrick said suddenly. "Reading a diagnostic medical dictionary. Through your system. I hope you don't mind. A little research, rather too late."

"Into what?"

"Marian told me about you. Or to be precise, about para-investigators. That you were...sick. She said that you—they—were recruited on the basis of their psychological profiles. Personality disorders. The word sociopath cropped up."

He had an urge to ask if she'd mentioned his mother. "So? Listen, everything is going to be fine."

"They don't see people as people. They only interact with their own projections on the world. She said—" In the window he caught a shadow of a frown as Warrick reached for the memory. " 'People like Toreth are dangerous. They charm you and make you think they're something they're not.' You don't care. You can't."

Why the hell hadn't he set it up so that Warrick wouldn't see her die? "You're tired, you didn't like what you saw—fine. But we stick to the plan. We go through the interrogation transcript. You—"

"No." Warrick turned abruptly, and Toreth saw his face clearly for the first time: corpse white, with red-rimmed eyes. "I'm going. Now."

Fear flooded him, with anger right on its heels. If Warrick left in this state, if he was stopped...Jesus, if he was questioned. "Don't be so fucking stupid." Toreth caught Warrick's arm as he started to move. "What the hell are you going to do if you run out now? She's dead, and you can't change that, can you? But she's no

240

deader than she would be after the Administration executed her. And no deader than Kelly, or any of the rest of them. You'll stay right—"

"No!" Carelessly, he lost his grip as Warrick pulled away, and Warrick made it halfway across the room before Toreth caught him, barely managing to grab his sleeve. Experience told him Warrick would fight, which he did, with a ferocity and skill than caught Toreth off-guard.

"Will you—shit!" Toreth twisted, trying to dodge a punch, and Warrick's fist caught him in the ribs instead of the solar plexus. He grabbed for Warrick's free hand and missed, getting a sharp blow to his arm in return. Only ingrained training made Toreth tighten his grip on Warrick rather than release him. The risk of sabotage kidnapping ensured that most corporates were at least trained in how to break a hold and run. With his right hand occupied with Warrick's left arm, Toreth was at a definite disadvantage; it was only a question of time before Warrick broke free. Toreth closed, unbalancing Warrick and bearing him back and away from the door. It took another minute of thankfully quiet struggle before he had Warrick against the wall, holding on to him securely.

"Let go." Warrick's voice rose as he twisted futilely, his face flushed with anger and exertion. "Let me *go.*"

He abandoned approved restraint technique and shifted his grip, getting his hand over Warrick's mouth. If the bastard bit him, he'd break his neck and worry about the explanations later. "Shut the fuck up and *listen,*" Toreth snarled, voice low. "Do you *want* to fuck everything up? Do you want to end up down on level C, where she was, spilling everything for one of the others? You want to commit suicide, go ahead and do it on your own fucking time, but you're not taking me with you. We're sticking to the plan, to the letter. You'll stay in here long enough to make it look good, whatever it takes. I'm not going to risk ending up dead just because you're too fucking gutless to stick it out. It was your fucking idea, so get a fucking grip."

By the time he ran out of steam Warrick had at least stopped fighting, although he was still pale and shaking, his breath hot against Toreth's hand. Breathing quickly, now that Toreth took the time to notice. Almost panting, in fact. Not surprising, Toreth thought, when he considered the position they were in: full body contact, serious restraint, and danger—real danger. Everything the game required. He smiled, unable to help it, feeling himself harden. Relaxing his hold a little, he uncovered Warrick's mouth. Then, before Warrick could say anything, he pulled him close for a deep, bruising kiss.

"No!" Warrick said through the kiss, then jerked his head away. "Stop it."

Toreth pulled him back and did it again, feeling Warrick's lips twist as he struggled to break free. Maybe he'd forgotten the safe word—maybe he thought it wouldn't apply here. Toreth felt no obligation to remind him. Part of Toreth was still calculating, working out how to use this to his advantage. However, the overwhelming idea of having Warrick—here, now—rapidly swept that cold consideration aside.

He held Warrick's shuddering body against his, smothering his protests until he stopped fighting and his mouth opened, hungry. Then Toreth manhandled him towards the desk, keeping his grip tight. Partly because he didn't want to risk him bolting for the door—unlikely as that seemed right now—and partly for the exciting feedback from Warrick's own excitement.

Turning Warrick, Toreth pinned him against the desk, although now there was no need. As he opened the drawer one-handed he felt Warrick struggling again—this time to unfasten his own trousers before reaching back to free Toreth's cock. A brief scrabble in the desk drawer produced hand cream. An even briefer pause before he thrust inside Warrick, honestly trying to take it slowly at first, but losing the fight between his own fierce arousal and Warrick's urgent movements.

The screen on the desk still showed the interrogation room, now empty and silent, but Warrick wasn't looking at it. Or if he was, it had no dampening effect. He braced his hands on the desk, pushing back frantically towards Toreth, making a noise Toreth hadn't heard from him before—harsh, sobbing breaths, pure need and desire.

Shifting his grip, he held Warrick tight, driving into him harder, having trouble controlling the amount of noise he was making himself. A few more deliciously deep strokes, and Warrick bucked under him, but Toreth didn't register the strangled gasp as he came because he was coming, too. He crushed Warrick against the desk, pressing his face into Warrick's shoulder to muffle his own cry, for once the louder of them.

A tiny sound pulled him back to awareness of the room around them. Out of the corner of his eye, he caught sight of the door closing quickly. He'd forgotten Sara and the coffees, although she usually knocked or called through. Ah, well— Warrick hadn't noticed, so no harm done. Made a mess on the desk, though.

Finally Warrick shifted, and Toreth moved back far enough to let him stand up and refasten his clothes. Still sufficiently close, however, that when Warrick turned Toreth could indulge an unexpected and uncharacteristic urge for a kiss. It had an odd sweet-salt flavor, strangely satisfying, that reminded him of their first dinner and the steak. When he finally pulled back, he saw the bright red on Warrick's mouth, like smeared lipstick. Warrick touched the back of his hand to his lower lip, inspected it and licked away blood. "Bit my lip. It seemed preferable to letting the whole office know what we were doing." A deep breath. "Although I didn't think I'd done it quite that hard."

At least he sounded calmer. "Feeling better?" Toreth asked.

"I—" Warrick hesitated, the answer clearly a surprise. "Actually, yes."

"Good." Toreth found a tissue and wiped his own mouth, then the desk. "Now, did the recording work?"

"As far as I could tell." Warrick took another breath, ran his tongue over his lip and winced. "Everything went smoothly, nothing unexpected came up that I couldn't handle. I faked a technical glitch in the system to cover the link between the sim and the genuine recording. The picture synched perfectly with the medical monitors, which was always going to be the hardest part."

"Then we've got one more thing to do, that's all. Go through the files with me, check that everything's solid, and then it's all over."

"All over." Warrick looked at him for a moment, expression closed, then nodded. "Let's get on with it."

Toreth touched the comm. "Sara, I'll have that transcript and the coffees now."

When she brought them in, Toreth was worried that she might say something about what she'd seen. Warrick wouldn't find it funny. To his relief, she gave no sign at all that she'd seen them. "I had a call from Internal Investigations about the prisoner's death," she said as she set the coffees down. Toreth caught a tiny, quickly controlled movement from Warrick beside him.

"And?" Toreth asked.

"They said that, considering the waiver, unless something else comes up or you want to tell them anything, they'll process the inquiry without an interview."

"Tell them that's fine. Transcript?"

"I'm just authorizing it. I'll send it through when it's done."

When she had gone, Warrick said, "Internal Investigations?"

"Int-Sec watchdogs." With big, nasty teeth. "It's a formality. Just paperwork. I told you—they expected her to die."

Warrick shook his head. "Everyone knows, you know."

"Every who knows what?"

"Everyone knows that deaths in custody are often deliberate. Why do we all collude in the pretense that it doesn't happen, do you suppose?" The question seemed to be genuine curiosity. "It isn't as if the Administration doesn't execute people anyway. Criminals and resisters."

Not a good line of conversation. "It keeps things running smoothly. Saves a lot of messy, expensive trials and keeps a lot of nasty secrets. Like this one."

"Doesn't it seem wrong to you?" Warrick didn't wait for an answer before he shook his head again. "No, I suppose it doesn't."

"Not really." Toreth picked up one of the coffees. "Do you want sugar?" When Warrick declined, Toreth passed him the mug and had a sip from his own while he organized his thoughts. "Right, let's get on with it."

It took them an hour to go through every file, every change Warrick had made to the system, until Toreth was convinced there was nothing there that might cause Internal Investigations a moment's doubt. For one thing, he wanted to be sure there would be no need to ask Warrick to come back in. Although, oddly enough, he wasn't that worried—the panic had clearly passed, and Warrick was enough of a control freak not to let things slip again.

Nevertheless, as Warrick was leaving, Toreth stopped him at the door and put his hands on his shoulders, feeling Warrick tense. "Everything's going to be fine. Say goodbye to Sara on the way past, walk out of here, and go home. If anyone asks what's wrong, remember it's fine to tell them that Marian died, as long as you don't say anything more than 'under interrogation.' That's reason enough to be upset. Everything's going to be okay. Okay?"

Warrick nodded.

"Good. Go on."

Then, as Warrick hesitated, hand on the door, Toreth added, "I'll be in touch."

Warrick opened the door without answering, and walked steadily away across the office.

Chapter Thirty

❖

First thing Monday morning, after an unexpectedly restful night, Toreth dropped a note to Tillotson explaining the weekend events and started the paperwork. Sara handled the negotiations with Justice while Toreth tidied up as many loose ends as he could, and prepared the case for submission to the Justice Department's evidence analysis system. At the end of the trial that system would proclaim the final guilt or innocence of the prisoner, although acquittals were rare enough that they counted as a black mark in the file of the para directing the case. Toreth was relieved—and almost surprised—that he found no fatal flaw in the case.

It was half past three when the call from Jenny finally came, summoning him to Tillotson's office. A long time for an important case. Toreth wondered whether Tillotson had spent the day talking to people, and if so, who.

Tillotson kept him waiting outside for almost ten minutes before he called him in. When Toreth walked into the office, the shock almost stopped him dead. Tillotson sat behind his desk, with a pot of coffee and two cups on a tray. Behind him, back to the window, stood a man, his features made indistinct by the bright sunlight behind him. The one clear detail was his hair, a bright ginger. Toreth's stomach knotted. Was it the same man he'd seen coming out of Tillotson's office on the first day of the investigation? Fuck. If Internal Investigations was here...but if they'd been found out, surely he'd have been arrested—or worse—by now? They'd told Sara they were processing the prisoner's death. What the hell had gone wrong since yesterday?

He crossed the room to the section head's desk and stood with his hands behind him, as casual as he could manage to appear. The stranger said nothing, and Tillotson didn't introduce him. In fact, for all the attention Tillotson paid either of them, he might as well have been alone in his office. While Tillotson read something on the screen in front of him, then read it through again, Toreth stood and tried not to fidget. He could glean nothing useful from Tillotson, who seemed absorbed by the screen, frowning slightly. An occasional glance towards the window—not being curious would be more suspicious—revealed nothing either.

Eventually the section head looked up. "Is this transcript accurate?" As an apparent afterthought he added, "Sit down."

Toreth took the indicated seat. "Of course it is—Sara checked it. It's authorized and ready to go to Justice, with your approval. Have a look at the session recording if you want to check."

Tillotson grimaced. "No, thank you."

"Is there a problem, sir?" Toreth glanced at the interloper.

"A problem?" Tillotson shook his head slowly. "Not insofar as it goes, no. But that isn't far enough. The motive is very thin and there are a lot of questions... I'm disappointed with this result, Toreth. The deaths were high profile. A solid result would have been good for the section, as well as for you."

"She did it. I'm absolutely convinced she did; the confession's good and all the evidence backs it. It has to be corporate—someone supplied her with the toxin and the interrogation resistance drugs. If you want my opinion, odds are it's tied into LiveCorp somehow. P-Leisure is the biggest sponsor of SimTech, and Teffera was the biggest corporate target. But it was all arranged through third parties and anonymous messaging, so she didn't know any names. I'd say get Justice to wrap it guilty, corporate sabotage. If it were up to me, that is." Tillotson continued to stare at the screen, flicking his thumbnail against his front teeth. "I can keep the case open, of course," Toreth added. "You never know—something might turn up to show who was behind her."

Finally, the man by the window moved, a single step into the room, which attracted attention although it didn't show much more of his face. "I have some questions, if I may?" he said, in the same voice Toreth had heard in Tillotson's office before. The last thin thread of hope that he might not be in deep shit snapped.

Toreth looked at Tillotson. "Sir?" he asked softly.

"Go ahead."

"Who—"

"Just answer the damn questions, Toreth."

Fuck. He settled back in the seat, crossed his legs, and looked over at the stranger. "What do you want to know?" He knew he must sound wary, but that was hardly grounds for suspicion; anyone would under these circumstances.

As far as he could tell against the light, the man smiled. "This confession is not quite what some people would have expected."

"If you've got some additional information, of course I'd be interested."

"I'm afraid that it isn't quite that simple. We have information, but not evidence. That information makes the details of the confession... surprising."

Now he ought to ask what the surprise was, and the conversation would grow more detailed and trickier until Toreth said something to give the whole game away. Not the way to play. Instead, he sighed. "Okay, who the hell are you?"

246

There was a pause, and the man said, "I beg your pardon?"

"If you're going to stand there and tell me I can't do my job, then I want to know what your job is."

Tillotson started to say something, but the man cut him off. "It's a fair question. My name is Alan Howes. I work in the Research Section of the Psychoprogramming Division." A punch in the face couldn't have stunned him more. The man offered an ID badge, and Toreth took it, seeing nothing beyond the picture. Ginger hair. Once the first shock faded, he wondered how he could have missed it. Ginger hair—the one-line description he'd told Warrick was useless. Marian Tanit's Mindfuck contact.

He wasn't any less fucked, though. If Psychoprogramming had found another way of getting at SimTech and wanted his cooperation, that was almost as bad as being caught. Tanit's murder and the wiping of the files had tied him to Warrick, for good or bad, and Warrick wouldn't go down without a fight. Toreth would go down with him. At least he'd had one piece of luck. He hadn't gone to Tillotson when Tanit had spilled the beans. If he had, he might be dead already. He returned the ID, hoping that whatever reaction had shown on his face could be put down to reasonable surprise. "Mindfuck? What's your interest?"

The nickname was always a reliable irritant, and Howes frowned. "The reason for our involvement isn't relevant, although one part of it is that Marian Tanit trained at the forerunner to the PD."

"I know. Someone had it wiped from her security file." Silence. "I understand why you had it scrubbed." The mindfucker tensed, then relaxed as Toreth continued. "Bit of an embarrassment to the division. But the odd one can always slip through psych screening. If it's a question of that not coming out, I could redo the Justice submissions to—"

"No," Howes interrupted. "Our concern lies in the process of investigation and particularly interrogation."

"I've got IIPs that tell you in long and tedious detail why I arrested Tanit in the first place. Everything that happened in that interrogation room is recorded."

"I'm aware of that."

"So you think I did...what? Tampered with the files somehow?"

The following silence was far too thoughtful for Toreth's liking, and in the end Howes didn't answer the question. "We are satisfied that her guilt is not in question. Only her motives."

"I did everything I could. I even brought Dr. Warrick in to review the transcripts. He couldn't find anything to suggest she knew who the backers were—it's all in the file. She had nothing left to give; I'd stake my career on that."

That drew a brief, cold smile from Howes. "No doubt. But the anomalies remain to be explained and we hoped that you might be able to do so."

"Then you'll have to tell me what those anomalies are, because I can't see them. It's a solid, legit result. If you don't like that, then I'm afraid it's way too late to change it."

Another thoughtful stare. "Yes, indeed it seems to be. From the point of view of discovering the truth, the death of the prisoner is unfortunate."

"She was annexed on a level eight waiver that I didn't even ask for. If that was a fuckup, it was Justice's, not mine." Toreth stood up. "I don't have anything else to tell you that isn't already in a file, except that I'm not carrying the can for someone else's cock-up. If you promised some corporate a nice result, that's not my problem."

"Toreth, sit down and—" Tillotson began.

"I don't object to finding what I'm supposed to find, but *I'm* not a fucking mind reader."

"Toreth, that is *enough*." Tillotson was crimson.

For once Tillotson was probably right, so Toreth sat, muttering, "Well, for Christ's sake."

Howes stood in silence for a moment, arms folded, fingers tapping, and then said, "Now, Senior, I'm going to ask you directly, once more. Do you know anything about Marian Tanit's motives that you haven't included in the investigation report?"

"Everything's in the files."

"And is there anything else about the conduct of the case that might show up unfavorably in an Internal Investigations inquiry?"

Toreth suppressed a snort. Raising the specter of Internal Investigations didn't frighten him. They wouldn't dare bring them in, not when the pair of them had been responsible for Nissim's death. "No. Nothing at all."

"That is you final answer?"

"Yes." Toreth couldn't quite hide a smirk. They had nothing on him. He was home, free and clear.

"A pity. There is one more matter..." Howes took a step back, yielding the field to Tillotson. Playing slimy cop, weasely cop.

Tillotson frowned at his screen. "There has been a suggestion of, ah, professional misconduct. That you have been personally involved with a witness—a suspect—without declaring it."

Ice water drenched his spine. Oh, fuck. Oh *fuck*. After a moment he realized that his mouth was open. Just as he managed to close it, Tillotson looked up. "Do you deny it?"

"Of course I fucking deny it!"

Tillotson shook his head. "I have evidence. A member of your team is willing to give a statement to the effect that he saw you having numerous personal conversations with the suspect in question. And witnessed at least one instance of intimate contact."

Belqola, no doubt, which explained the lack of a knock on his office door yesterday. The devious, spying little fuck. "He's lying," Toreth said, without much hope.

Howes shrugged. "Immaterial. The evidence is sufficient for a charge of gross misconduct, to throw the evidence from the case into doubt, and also sufficient for Internal Investigations to obtain a damage waiver for your interrogation." He smiled for the first time. "After, that is, you have visited 'Mindfuck.'"

Thank God he'd followed Tillotson's order and sat down. Howes was still speaking, but Toreth couldn't hear him, the words lost in a vision of the future. His future. It would be a whitewash. First he'd tell them the truth, give them Warrick and everything else, and then after that he'd say whatever they wanted him to say. Mindfuck could make sure of that. Then, finally, they'd annex him.

Tillotson looked around at Howes, who nodded and said, "Your section head has already asked me to give you one last chance to make a full confession, before you're formally arrested."

Toreth glanced at Tillotson, who coughed. "I don't want to have to do this to you, Toreth. Not just because of the embarrassment to the section and the division. We've worked together for a long time, and—" A tiny gesture from Howes, and he stopped.

"Cooperation from the beginning would be in your best interest," Howes said. "We may be able to arrange a deal with Internal Investigations if you decide to be sensible."

"I don't—"

"Consider carefully, Para-investigator," Howes said softly.

Toreth thought of all the prisoners he'd watched sit and think their way through this exact dilemma. Folding now was so fucking tempting, although the mindfucker was probably lying about any deal. The pair of them had been responsible for the death of a legislator, and Toreth knew that. They'd want him dead, and so would he by the time they'd finished with him.

Toreth looked Howes in the eyes. "I don't have anything to say. I'm sorry, I can't help you. Believe me, I'd love to. But what was in the files is all there is."

The denial would start the long journey through Psychoprogramming and on to an interrogation chair at Internal Investigations. In an odd way, it felt good— knowing that when the crunch came, he'd done it. Fucking hell. He'd really done it. Toreth stayed seated, unable to move, as Tillotson called a security guard in. The man had to help him up from the chair before Toreth regained enough self-control to walk out of the room unaided, without a backwards glance.

As the guard escorted him towards the lift, the numbness lifted a little and he began to struggle for a plan. For some chance, however slim. If fucking a witness was Howes's best card, he couldn't have any hard evidence that they'd faked the confession record, however much he suspected. That would all change with his own inevitable confession, but right now Warrick was still free. However personal it felt, Howes's real target was SimTech—Toreth was just in the field of fire. So look at it from that angle. Warrick was his only realistic hope, and he'd certainly proven resourceful enough in the past. At the very least, if Warrick ran, if he could get away, that would cut the evidence against Toreth dramatically—without Warrick the original recording might never be retrieved. All Toreth needed was to get away from his escort for a minute or two.

At least he knew how to make it look good. Measuring the distance to his target along the corridor, he summoned the images. Water, closing over him. Pouring down his throat. Choking and vomiting. Diaphragm spasming, a buzzing in his ears as his lungs struggled against the flood. He was drowning, and he couldn't force his way to the surface. Gagging in his memory, and now in real life, too. "'Scuse me," he gasped, and pushed past the guard into the toilets as they passed them.

It had worked too well, which proved to be lucky. As he collapsed on his knees in one of the cubicles, retching, he heard the door behind him open and then close again. When he looked around, there was no sign of the guard. Wiping his mouth, he fitted the comm earpiece with shaking hands and called Warrick. "We're blown," Toreth said as soon as Warrick answered, almost surprised to find that he still had the presence of mind to subvocalize. "Get out if you can. I can't—"

"What's happened?"

"Don't argue, just—"

"Toreth, *shut up.*" The sudden authority silenced him. "Now, again, slowly," Warrick said. He sounded far too calm, and for a moment, Toreth wondered if he could somehow be involved. Then he dismissed the idea.

Right. Slowly. "Mindfuck—Psychoprogramming—is here, with Tillotson. They don't buy it. And they've found out we're fucking. Were fucking. That gives them enough leverage to interrogate me."

Silence, then Warrick said, "Will you talk to them?"

"Warrick, I won't have any fucking choice." The truth of that made his stomach lurch again.

"Well, don't tell them anything yet. Do you think they'll intercept this call?"

"I—" Toreth pinched the bridge of his nose, trying to focus. "No. I don't think so. Tillotson wouldn't draw attention yet with a request to monitor my comm."

"Good." Warrick still sounded as calm as though he were running through a sim protocol. "Do you have a name now?"

Toreth frowned. "A what?"

"A name of someone at Psychoprogramming. Someone involved."

"What are you going to do?"

"Do you have a damned *name*?"

It was almost a relief to hear Warrick's poise fracturing. "Yes. It's—" His mind

250

blanked. "Howes. He said Alan Howes. From Research. He had ID, which doesn't really mean much except…" Except it was better than nothing.

"Thank you. I'll do what I can. Try not to panic."

Easy for him to say. Toreth gripped the toilet seat and took a deep breath. "I'm not fucking panicking."

"Then it won't be a problem for you, will it?"

Toreth heard the door open again and he cut the connection, bending over the toilet and coughing while he stuffed the earpiece back into his pocket.

"Sorry, Para," the guard said as he entered. "We've got to go." He sounded genuinely apologetic, and as they started down the corridor Toreth decided not to have the man disciplined for leaving a prisoner alone. In the unlikely event that he ever had the chance.

This was it. After the call finished, Warrick sat back in his chair and stared blindly at the screen. Despite his confidence to Toreth, he'd never honestly given the plan more than a sixty percent chance of success. He'd made contingency plans, and he liked those even less than the original. Run, that was the first option. Wipe the systems as thoroughly as he knew how and run. He had tickets, and a borrowed identity that he hoped would get him outside the Administration. He wasn't confident even of that. This wasn't something he'd ever had to do before.

There were files ready to go to Justice and I&I stating that his fellow directors had no knowledge of what had happened; whether that would do any good, he had no idea. His complete severance from the corporation might help—the founders' clause invoked at last, in circumstances none of them could have envisaged. Other files would go to Asher and Lew, with everything he dared tell them. Enough to give them the best chance possible to defend SimTech, although the odds of their being able to salvage anything from the mess were small. Perhaps they could at least forgive him.

Finally, there was a message for Dillian, so far away on Mars, explaining as best he could. Saying goodbye, and saying sorry, for what little it was worth, because the Administration wasn't kind to the relatives of political criminals. His own crimes should count as corporate, but with Nissim's death to be explained away, anything was possible. Mud would splash and stick, in any case. He had scant hope of ever seeing Dillian again anyway, or anyone else he knew, whether his flight succeeded or not. Contingency plans, which had been too hurriedly laid to be reliable.

How long would Toreth be able to hold out? The question assumed that he would try in the first place, that the seed of hope he'd tried to plant just now would take, and that was a major assumption. Expecting Toreth to trust him over that—

or anything—was optimistic, to put it mildly. He easily could be talking to them right now, spilling everything, in which case sitting here was stupid, bordering on suicidal. Toreth's panicked, mutually incriminating call must have come from I&I, and despite his opinion it might have been monitored. Guards could be on their way to SimTech now. Every minute of delay might count.

He closed the files on the screen slowly, watching them disappear one by one. SimTech work—plans for the commercial production of sim units, which he'd only just begun to hope might again be possible. The future of SimTech. His future—everything he loved.

Run. That was the sensible choice.

Toreth found himself thinking about two things, going back and forth from one to the other as restlessly as he paced across the holding cell. Two memories. Fucking Warrick in his office yesterday, so beautifully hot and desperate. Warrick, jerking back against him as he came, as they both came—maybe the last fuck of their lives. Then Sara's face when he'd come back from killing Marian. She'd guessed something, and that might be enough to doom her along with himself and Warrick. The thought of Sara in an interrogation room hurt more than he would have imagined. Maybe they wouldn't ask him about her. Maybe if they did, he'd be able to hold it back. Questioning interrogators was notoriously difficult. He'd done one himself once, but Internal Investigations took most of them. Soon, they'd have him.

Please, don't let them drag Sara into this.

Warrick had sounded so calm. He had to have a plan, or more probably just a good escape route. No, he'd said that he'd do what he could. It would have to be fast, whatever it was. How long would it be before guards from Mindfuck arrived at I&I to take him? Not long if Howes moved quickly. Once he was in their hands, he couldn't imagine anything Warrick could do. Hell, he couldn't imagine anything he could do now, either. Back to Warrick again, to the feel of him, the smell of him, the taste of blood on his lips, and Sara bringing them coffee. Oh, Christ. Sara.

When the guard returned, it seemed like ten minutes. Normally he had a good sense of time, but checking his watch showed almost an hour had gone by. Exactly the opposite of the SMS, he thought vaguely. The guard escorted him out and down the corridor without a word. No handcuffs yet. The lift took them up again, passing the ground floor, which meant he wasn't being transferred. The overwhelming intensity of the relief shocked him, forcing him to lean against the wall for support.

Back in Tillotson's office again, Tillotson and Howes were waiting for him. Howes had seated himself on the edge of Tillotson's desk, and he gestured for Toreth to sit in the chair before him. Below him. Toreth shook his head in silent refusal, standing beside the chair with his hands behind his back. No one spoke.

Why, Toreth wondered, were they doing this here? Why not down in detention? No point lying to himself by pretending that wouldn't have intimidated him. Tillotson would know that, even if Howes didn't. If they offered the deal again, what would he say? Trust Tillotson, or trust Warrick? Management or corporate—what a fucking choice. At least the men in front of him had the authority to let him go, to try to buy his silence instead of enforce it, which was more than Warrick had.

I'll do what I can. Bizarrely, inexplicably, there was no question who he trusted most.

Toreth watched the bright squares of sunlight creeping infinitesimally across the wall. He paid them more attention than he would have under other circumstances. *If I chose wrong,* he thought morbidly, *it might be the last time I see the sun.*

Finally Howes nodded, apparently to himself, and turned to Tillotson. "The final decision is yours, of course." Tillotson merely grunted agreement. "Thank you for your cooperation," Howes said to Toreth, with only the mildest hint of sarcasm. "Good afternoon." With that, and to Toreth's utter astonishment, he simply walked out.

After the door had closed, Toreth said, "Sir?"

"Close the case." Tillotson looked up, his manner suddenly brisk. "Send it on to Justice, just as you said—corporate sabotage. I don't appreciate Psychoprogramming telling me how to run my section. With the level eight waiver and annex, there's no problem with the death."

Relief swept over him again before boiling into anger. They hadn't even said there'd be no inquiry. The bastards hadn't said *anything.* They'd just dropped the whole fucking thing, as if it had never happened. His hands clenched, nails digging into his palms as he fought the urge to punch Tillotson. An hour in that fucking cell, and then nothing. It must have been a bluff all along—trying to scare him into saying something.

Tillotson's nose twitched. "As for the other matter…there'll be no official reprimand placed in your file, but if I hear about the slightest hint of—of impropriety in any future cases, you'll be out of your office and demoted to junior before you can blink. Understood?"

"Yes, sir," Toreth ground out, through gritted teeth. "Thank you."

As he turned to go, Tillotson added, "Call Dr. Warrick and tell him the damn case is closed. Do it as soon as you get back to your office."

With that, Toreth knew it hadn't been a bluff after all.

The effort of containing his anger all the way back to his office made him feel he might explode. Sara half stood as he crossed the room, then sat down again when she got a better look at him. He slammed his office door with a noise that would set the entire section talking, and then looked for something to throw. Nothing came immediately to hand, so he kicked his chair into the far wall, scattering the pile of the *JAPI* by the window across the floor. Then he sat on the edge of his desk, fuming.

Why he should be so angry, he didn't know. The idea of Tillotson showing any loyalty to him—or anyone else in his section—was something he'd given up on long ago. How big a bribe had Psychoprogramming sent Tillotson's way? Toreth couldn't see him fucking with corporates, even small corporates, for free. Cash, and favors to be repaid, no doubt, and plenty of both. Still, it hadn't been big enough that Tillotson had felt the urge to pass any of it on to *him*.

An hour in that foul fucking cell and all because Tillotson was too fucking tight to share the goodies. He'd let Toreth run the investigation without telling him anything. Perhaps he'd assumed that Toreth would dump the case as a career-busting flop or, at worst, swallow Tanit's story whole if he caught her. Or perhaps Tillotson simply thought Toreth knew the game well enough not to need to be told the desired result. Maybe he ought to feel flattered, but he didn't. He felt used. Used, betrayed, lied to, and sick of the whole thing. Sick of the investigation, sick of fucking Tillotson, sick of Int-Sec and its treacherous rivalries and politics. For a moment, he indulged himself in the old fantasy of handing in his notice. Of walking back into the section head's office without waiting for a summons, telling Tillotson exactly what he thought of him and of the rest of Int-Sec, and then leaving the building forever. Right now, it didn't seem like a bad idea.

With his savings, he could buy out the remains of his training debt to I&I. But after that moment of freedom, where would he go? The only option was selling himself into a corporate contract. Or, much as he disliked the connotations of ownership, taking a personal contract with some rich corporate looking to improve his security. A corporation would be no better than here. The same time-wasting political bullshit, but with less security and more boring work. Toreth rested his forearms on his thighs, letting his hands dangle between them. Resignation was already blunting the hot edge of fury. He knew what he was doing—dusting off the usual justifications and finding them, as always, good enough.

Para-investigation was his job and he was proud of how he did it. More than that, it was his life. I&I was all he had. He belonged here as he would be able to belong nowhere else. With Chevril and the rest of the paras, who were people like him, and with people like Sara who knew what that meant. While he didn't care what it said about him in some psych file somewhere, he recognized the practical consequences. Warrick's outburst after Marian's death hadn't told him anything he didn't already—

Warrick. Shit—he hadn't called Warrick. From the way Tillotson had said it, Warrick had to be behind Mindfuck's abrupt change of heart. What Warrick could possibly have done in such a short time, he had no idea, but it was the only explanation that made sense. This time he fitted the earpiece with a rather steadier hand. If he was careful what he said, there was no reason not to put the call through the I&I comms. He called SimTech, hoping that Warrick would still be there. Warrick took the call on voice only—interesting choice. "Doctor?" Toreth asked.

He had a momentary panic that Warrick might say something stupid. However, his voice was perfectly calm. "What can I do for you, Para-investigator?"

"I'm calling to let you know that the case has been closed. We're submitting everything we have to Justice."

Silence, but he could almost taste the relief flowing over the connection. "Excellent news," Warrick said finally. "May I inquire as to the conclusion?"

"Up to the Justice systems, but I recommended ascribing all the killings to Marian Tanit, motive corporate sabotage. I see no reason why that recommendation won't be accepted."

"I see. Well, deeply regrettable though Dr. Tanit's, ah, involvement is, I'm sure the sponsors will be relieved to hear that the matter is closed. No blame has been attached to the sim?"

Neat touch—just what Warrick ought to be asking. "None at all."

"I'm very glad to hear it. And perhaps, if I could trouble you, some official statement to that respect would be very welcome."

Pushy bastard—back to his usual self, no doubt about that. "No problem. I'll have something written up for you right away."

"Thank you." Warrick hesitated briefly, and then said, "Is that all?"

"Yes." No. How the fucking hell did you *do* it? "Perhaps—" The door opened, and he knew without looking around who it was. Sara, timing as perfect as ever. He closed the connection. "What do you want?" he asked her, more harshly than he'd meant to.

"I brought you a coffee, that's all," she said. She handed it to him, then retrieved his chair. "How was Tillotson?"

Anger surged back at the name. Seriously tempted to throw the mug, or kick the chair again, he sat down heavily, just managing not to spill the coffee. "Tillotson was his usual tossy self."

Her hand rested on his shoulder, her fingers rubbing ineffectually over muscles tensed like stone. "I heard they sent you down to detention. For an hour. What went wrong?"

"He didn't like the result."

"Making trouble over the death?"

"No. Tillotson agreed it's all inside the waiver. Wanker."

She looked at him thoughtfully for a moment, and then glanced at her watch. "It's ten past. Want to leave the coffee, and go get something stronger?"

"Not really."

"Come on." She squeezed his shoulder. "Case closed. You ought to celebrate."

Well, it was probably better than sitting around here until he worked himself into a good enough mood to go back and strangle Tillotson.

When they'd bought drinks and found a secluded seat, they sat in silence for a while. Eventually Sara reached over the table and put her hands over his. In the moment before they tightened, he felt them shaking. He stared at her fingers, the rings concentrating the dim bar lights into points. "All right," Sara said. "What's going on?"

"Sara, I can't—"

"I don't want a transcript. I just want to know if I should arrange for someone to come and feed the cat, that sort of thing."

"You don't have a cat."

"Well, I was thinking about getting one." A quaver sounded in her voice now, before she cleared her throat. "What I mean is...are we expecting Internal Investigations to show up? And if they do, what do you need me to tell them?"

Brave front notwithstanding, she was absolutely fucking terrified. Toreth looked up, suddenly wrenched into an outside perspective on the events of the last few days. "God, no. Nothing like that's going to happen." I hope. "It's—" Taking hold of her hands, he tried to think how much to tell her. "I found something out from Tanit that I shouldn't have done. Division politics—major, serious stuff. Warrick fixed it. Tanit's dead now, so nobody's going to find out. Everything's fine."

From Sara's expression, she didn't believe it any more than he did. "If it's over, what's wrong?"

He shook his head, not sure himself. He didn't usually brood. "I nearly blew it. The whole thing. I was this bloody close. I should've seen it coming. You even asked me, what if it wasn't corporate? It was obvious and I didn't see it. I don't know, maybe I was too fucking focused on a big case. I should know better. If it hadn't been for Warrick...why the hell didn't I let it go?"

She looked at him with the same strange expression she'd worn when he'd asked her what Warrick had to do with anything. "You didn't blow it, though, did you?"

"They could've killed me." Her as well, maybe. Now that it was all over, that felt suddenly, overwhelmingly real.

"But they didn't," she said.

"No, they didn't. And they aren't going to, now. I don't know why I'm so..."

She shrugged, freeing her hands from his and picking up her glass. "Sounds like you had a bloody nightmarish few days. Why the hell shouldn't you be?"

They sat in silence, slowly working their way down their drinks while he thought it over. The problem was...the problem was it didn't feel finished. The bullet had missed, and he had not the faintest idea why, or how, or whether another one would be fired. He couldn't leave it like this—he had to know.

"Toreth?"

"Um?" He focused on Sara to find her looking at him with open concern. What had he said? "I need to make a call."

That didn't seem to surprise her. "I'll get some more drinks."

When she had gone, he pulled out the comm earpiece, hesitating for a moment with it in his hand for some reason he couldn't name. It wasn't as if he didn't have a perfectly good excuse. "Doctor."

"Hello again." Warrick's voice was more guarded this time. "Is there a problem?"

"No, no problem at all. However, there are one or two points I would like to discuss with you, if you could spare me the time for a meeting."

"Points?"

"Yes. About how things were...finally resolved."

"Is there any official compulsion for this request?"

"No, it's completely unofficial. Just to satisfy my personal curiosity, really. It's entirely up to you whether you'd like to meet or not."

The brief silence nicely conveyed the idea that Warrick was thinking about the offer, and Toreth almost hoped someone was listening in so there'd be an audience for the performance. Or maybe he really was considering whether to say no. Finally Warrick spoke again, his voice cool. "In that case, since it's unofficial, perhaps we should meet outside working hours? Perhaps for dinner? Are you free later this evening?"

"That would be fine."

"The Renaissance Center? Two hours?"

"Fine."

"I shall see you then. Goodbye, Para-investigator."

Toreth put the earpiece away, finding unexpectedly that he was smiling. He didn't notice Sara approaching until she set the full glasses down on the table.

"So he said yes, then?" she asked as she sat opposite him.

"What?"

"Never mind. Do you want to make a night of it? Get a meal, go see a film?"

"I'd love to, but—"

She smiled. "Say no more."

Chapter Thirty-one

❖

At the Renaissance Center, he found that Warrick had booked a room—a suite, in fact—and left a message with reception for him. Warrick clearly had no concern about the personal involvement then, and Toreth was willing to concede that a private room was a better place for discussions than a public bar. About to go up, he detoured to the bar to pick up a bottle of something expensive (even though he didn't feel like trying to get this one past Accounts) and two glasses. As the door to the suite closed behind him, and he saw Warrick stand up from one of the deep armchairs, Toreth found himself wondering what to say. How much of the debt should he acknowledge? By the time he'd crossed the room and set the glasses and bottle on a table, he still wasn't sure. In the end, the direct approach seemed best.

"How did you do it?" Toreth asked.

Warrick smiled fleetingly, and Toreth wondered if he'd made a bet with himself over the opening words. And whether he'd won. "I kept hold of Marian's confessions," Warrick said as he sat down again. "The details of Psychoprogramming's plan to destroy SimTech and cheat the investors of their rightful returns. In addition, I took the liberty of borrowing a few other files from the I&I system. A copy of the results of her interrogation resistance screening, a selection of the rest of the investigation files. I hope you don't mind?" Toreth shook his head. He had a horrible sinking feeling as to where this was leading. "Should anything untoward happen to me—or to you—then the information will be released. It will go to the sponsors and a number of other corporates. Automatically and unstoppably. I made quite sure Mr. Howes understood that when I spoke to him."

Exactly what he'd been afraid of. Toreth dropped into a chair, not entirely voluntarily. "Jesus. Warrick, that's insane."

"No, but it is dangerous. Blackmail always is. That's why it was the last resort. It would've been far better for them to think their plan had merely failed for reasons unknown."

"I&I will just show them the faked confessions. Why would the corporates believe you?"

"For one reason, because we—generic corporate we—are always afraid something like this will happen. For another, because the sim-created interrogations have a signature encoded in the recording. An encrypted signature, the key to which is with the rest of the information. If the Administration produces the faked recordings as evidence, the corporates will know."

He hadn't come up with all that in an hour. "You set this up in advance? Right from the beginning?"

Warrick nodded. "Before Marian...before I came to I&I yesterday morning. I finished the details today. I threw in the budget information and the rest of the evidence against Psychoprogramming you'd gathered as well. A statement from Le Tissiet that Psychoprogramming approached him." He smiled. "I think it makes a nice case, all told."

Could be useful if carefully handled. His original assessment of Warrick had been somewhat inadequate. "Why the hell didn't you tell me?"

"I'm sorry." No hint of an apology in his tone. "I didn't think there was any need to bother you with it unnecessarily."

"To bother—fucking *hell.*" An hour in that bloody cell. Was this Warrick's idea of revenge for his own wait in Toreth's office after Marian's death? Except Warrick couldn't have known what Tillotson and Howes had planned. "Get me a drink."

Warrick picked up the bottle and examined the label, eyebrow lifting. "I'm not sure a celebration is really appropriate."

You're the one who booked a suite with a bed the size of my fucking flat. Toreth closed his eyes. "Just open the fucking thing."

The cork popped softly as Warrick worked it off, and after a moment Toreth heard the hiss of pouring champagne. Cool glass touched his hand, and Toreth drained it, the acid bubbles burning his nose and throat. Blinking, he held the glass out for a refill and Warrick complied, wincing very slightly. Toreth downed half of the second glassful. When his eyes had stopped watering, he said, "Mindfuck will never let this go."

"If everything goes right 'Mindfuck' will never find out." Warrick sat down opposite him, leaning forwards with his elbows on his knees. "Howes won't tell anyone what happened."

"But what if he does?"

"Then probably we're both dead." Warrick's tone didn't change. "However, I'm confident he'll keep quiet. Think about it."

"I'm not in the mood for twenty fucking questions."

Warrick lowered his head slightly, looking up at him thoughtfully through his eyelashes, and then nodded. "Very well. Personally, I doubt that the Administration—at the top level—would ever approve a plan involving the frank destruction of a corporation simply to avoid paying technology licenses. However, that isn't relevant. If everything came out, the Administration would start looking for sacrifices to appease the corporations. The upper echelons of Psychoprogramming would direct the blame downwards to whoever came up with the plan, and they in turn—"

"Would swear it was a few rogues, acting without approval. Howes. Tillotson. Fuck—me, even."

Warrick nodded. "Quite so. And once they were tied to Nissim's death no one would be inclined to help them. As the liaison with I&I, Howes's would be the first neck on the block. Very probably he's the only one at the Psychoprogramming Division who knows exactly what happened at I&I today. What do you think the odds are of him passing my threat, and his failure, too far upwards?"

"Pretty fucking small, I suppose." Self-interest was a motive Toreth liked even more than money.

"If I were him, I would inform my superiors that Marian simply refused to cooperate at the last moment. That for whatever reason she changed her mind about destroying SimTech. In fact, that's what I suggested he say," Warrick added.

"Why the hell didn't you do this straight away? No, I'm being stupid. You didn't have a name."

Another nod. "And now I do. A name I made quite sure is all over the documents the corporations would receive, along with Tillotson's. Without the name, I would've had to threaten the whole of Psychoprogramming. Suicidal, to say the least."

The trick to health insurance was knowing who to tell about it. Toreth leaned back in his chair, thinking over the plan and finding no glaring flaws. Unable to keep the admiration out of his voice, he said, "Tanit was right. You're a natural fucking corporate, you know that?"

Warrick paused, then said, "Is that a compliment?"

"Not really." Another mouthful of champagne, and he added, "So it's over."

"Indeed it is. I made quite sure that Howes understood that your safety was as important as mine. We're free to go about our respective lives."

Toreth stared into the glass, watching the bubbles rise and die while he thought about that. He owed Warrick his career and his life... and Warrick owed him SimTech, and possibly his freedom. Not too much of an imbalance there, but a hell of an entanglement, something he always avoided at all costs. A mutual debt like this could never be wiped out. Still, as Warrick had said, there was no reason ever to see him again now that the case was over. Provided, of course, that Warrick's blackmail plan held up, and Mindfuck didn't come after one or both of them, wanting blood. Maybe it would be sensible to keep tabs on Warrick for the time being.

It wouldn't be too much of a hardship—just fucking, in fact, finally cut free of the mess of the investigation. Time in the sim—SMS and whatever other weird and wonderful things Warrick had available. Toreth wouldn't mind the occasional evening in the real world, either. Playing the game with someone else who didn't like to have too many rules. He stole a glance at Warrick, who was slowly twirling the stem of his glass between his fingers, quietly impassive. Fucking control freak, indeed. However, floating on champagne and relief at survival, Toreth found that he didn't mind making an exception to his principle of never openly doing the pursuing.

Perhaps it was because when he asked the question, he was already sure of Warrick's answer. Toreth smiled, and Warrick lifted his eyebrows inquiringly.

"So," Toreth said, "do you want to fuck?"

CPSIA information can be obtained at www.ICGtesting.com
Printed in the USA
BVOW08s2221290116

434811BV00002B/184/P